Love Between Shadows

Savannah Etheridge

One

I stare down at the brown egg in my hand, amazed at how fragile it is. Yet the squawking mother hen never broke it. Just a thin shell is all that would protect the baby chick from the outside world, yet it was enough. How a mother hen could protect her children better than the human species was beyond me. Maybe if my mother collected the eggs instead of me she could learn a thing or two.

My eyes dart back up to the pissed mother hen, who stares at me in betrayal with her beady little eyes. “You act like I don’t do this every single morning,” I tell her, setting the egg in my basket. She shifts in her laying box, making me stick my hand under her again in suspicion. Sure enough, I pull out two more eggs.

“You really need to stop taking everyone else's eggs, thieving ain’t a good trait to have.” I wipe the poop off with my apron and make my way to the next nesting box.

“You talk more to them chickens than you do people,” a voice startles me, making me drop an egg on my shoe. It cracks, the yellow yolk sliding to the dirty coop ground.

“Florence! Look what you made me do!” I snap at my sister, who leans against the coop door. It groans at the pressure being put on it. The wind whips through the coop, making a howling noise that makes my arm hairs stand up. Her plain yellow dress blows in the breeze, making her look effortlessly beautiful, as usual. One of the things I hate most about her.

“He’s already livid. Won’t make much difference. And maybe if you weren’t always in your own little world you would have heard me walking up,” Florence retorts as she pushes her pale blond hair away from her face. She crosses her arms as she watches me gather the rest of the eggs.

“What’s he mad about now?” I don’t know why I bother to ask, it’s not like this isn't how every single day starts. Me taking eggs from underneath thieving Henrietta, and Florence coming out to escape my father’s angry outbursts. Before she can answer I add, “you shouldn’t leave Otis in there alone.” Otis may only be four-years-old, but he’s the only good thing about our family.

“I didn’t, I brought him outside with me. He’s out looking for treasure.” By treasure, she means rocks that will leave dirt behind where he sets them down, causing my mom to quickly come behind him using a wet rag to wipe it up.

I move past her and am followed by a few chickens who make their way out into the grass. They start pecking at the ground looking for bugs while Florence trails after me.

“I’m going into town tomorrow with mama. She’s getting food and you'll never guess what I will be doing...” Florence’s voice is boastful, so I immediately know what she will be doing. It's what she is always doing.

“Let me guess, sucking some boy's face off,” I mutter under my breath, annoyed at the sound of her following footsteps as I make my way towards the house.

Our home looks worse every day, the paint chipping, the window shutters drooping more like they may fall off at any time. I can see a few sticks and rocks sitting in front of the house in a pile, making me smile. Otis must have had a successful treasure hunt.

“You know Hazel, if you would talk to boys instead of chickens maybe you could go on a date, too, one day,” Florence says, but she can’t just leave it at that, so she adds, “and maybe if you did something with that hair of yours.”

My hand reaches up and touches one of the red curls that had fallen in my face.

My hair is my least favorite thing about my looks. Its redness made all the other kids tease me growing up, and the curls made sure I couldn’t wear all the fashionable styles like my sister could. Everyone was always complimenting Florence’s pale blond hair, saying it looked like the sun. Meanwhile, I would be standing next to her like a ghost, like I didn’t even exist.

I ignore her jab as I make my way up the steps to our house, being careful not to step on the middle one that has a hole the size of my head in it. I pause at the commotion inside, my body tensing up immediately. As soon as I hear Otis' cries, my heart sinks to my stomach as I push through the creaking door.

My father is standing above him, his hand raised to strike him. My mother is huddled in the corner of the kitchen by the stove, her arms wrapped around herself and tears coming down her face. Her head is down and looking to the side, staring at the wall. Her eyes never witness what she lets our father do to us.

"Father! Stop!" I run up and grab Otis' shoulders and pull him behind me. My father's face is bright red, sweat running down it, and his dark eyes are bloodshot.

"You need to learn to mind your business and don't be interferin' with things that don't concern you none." His breath reeks of alcohol as he hollers in my face. I squeeze my eyes shut and wait for the slap that surely follows. Except I don't flinch as his hand makes its way across my face.

"Otis, go outside!" I quickly reach behind me where he's gripping my leg and push him back to the front door. I hear his bare feet take off.

"I don't care what your ma says, you ain't my daughter. If you don't mind yourself I will not have you under my roof!" He jerks my arm up, pulling my shoulder out of place and causing a whimper to escape my mouth. He lets me go, makes his way around the kitchen table, and slams the front door on his way outside.

I turn my head to stare at my mother, who is wiping her hands on her apron and turns back to the biscuits she was making at the stove. "That damn hen is a better mother than you!" My heart is pounding as the words come out of my mouth. If there is anyone quieter than me in the family, it's my mother. She offers no reply.

"Letting him hit you is one thing. Even him hitting me. But Otis? He's a child!" I set the basket of eggs on the wooden table. The swirls in the grain are nicked up by the various utensils that have been drug across it during dinner arguments. I pull out a chair and plop down, burying my face in my hands.

"You are his, you know," she says meekly, forming the dough in her hands. I let out an exasperated sigh; that is what she decides to address? I wish I wasn't his, because the fact a part of me comes from him is repulsive.

On my thirteenth birthday, I heard my aunt and uncle talking about how angry my father was when I was born. He immediately wouldn't hold me because of my bright red hair, saying there was no way I was his. My mother denied ever sleeping with anyone else, but he never believed her. They said he was always an angry man, but it drove an even deeper wedge between my parents. Especially since my older sister and little brother look exactly like my father.

It didn't help that I was born a few weeks early, making the timeline blurry on when I was conceived. It put the conception right around when my father left to go hunting for a week with my uncle. I don't know whether to believe my mother or not, because, in all honesty, I wouldn't blame her for finding comfort in another man. I sometimes pretend that

John was not my father and that my real father was a librarian or author who was kind and smart. That I was conceived in love and that maybe one day, a man with red hair would knock on our door and take me away from this place.

"I collected ten eggs today," I offer, hoping to change the subject. Every once in a while I would pity my mother. I watched over the years as he whittled her down to nothing, just a shell of the person she used to be. I remember she would try to shield us from the monster she married. To make our house feel more like a home, she would play music on our record player and sing loudly as she would hold us in her arms and sashay around the living room. That was one of my favorite memories.

But a year ago, we had to sell the record player to help pay for food. At least, that's what we were told. It probably went to my father's booze habit. Ever since the prohibition, things had gotten even worse in our household. Money was tight, my father drank more, my mother stopped smiling, and we didn't go to church anymore.

Florence barges in the door a few minutes later, breaking the silence that hangs in the room. She sits down in one of the living room chairs, which is directly across from our kitchen table. When she does, dust flies up out of the cushions and floats in the air where the sun shines through the windows. I watch as the particles dance in the air, slowly falling down to the wooden floor. She looks like a painting, long legs dangling off of the worn green chair. The faded yellow floral wallpaper behind her almost matches her hair.

"How should I wear my hair tomorrow? I was thinking pinned back or maybe using the rollers?" Florence twirls her chin length hair with her finger. She is obsessed with fashion. Despite being poor, she always manages to look nice. Her hair is styled in a fashionable bob, the newest rage in the hair world. She irons her clothes, and wears the pins and jewelry she's collected from all her boyfriends. She even wears makeup. At first, she looked like a clown, but now that she's figured out how to do it, she looks even more like a model. Some men have even started to stop and stare, not just the teenage boys.

I'm not boy-crazy like my sister, but it would be nice to feel seen every once in a while. But I was always overlooked because I was standing next to her. The older, more outgoing, flirty sister. At school, it was always 'Florence and her sister'. Never 'Florence and Hazel'.

She's even my father's favorite. He's never hit Florence. She was his first child and looks like the female version of him. John was a handsome man. If they weren't bloodshot from drinking, his eyes were the deepest shade of blue. He has the palest blond hair that sets off his skin, tanned from farming. It's no wonder my mother fell in love with him as a young teenager. They had married within a month, and that's when they got pregnant with Florence.

John didn't even try to hide his favoritism as we grew up. One of my earliest memories was of my father coming home one day, opening the door, and crouching down in front of us. His face was coated in dirt and grime from working all day. He grabbed Florence's hands and handed her a piece of candy. "For my girl," he had said. I watched as she bounded off outside, yelling with excitement over the gift. I stood there in anticipation, wondering if my candy would be the same or different. I hoped he would call me his girl as well as I bounced on my feet and stared up at him, waiting. But there was no treat for me. The worst part was the look he gave me, like I was a cockroach in his house and he wanted to step on me with his shoe.

It went on like that for years, until he started to drink so much that even Florence didn't get his affection anymore. By the time Otis was born, he didn't care much about his children at all.

"Are you even listening, Hazel?" Florence sits up from being draped over the chair, her eyes wide and eyebrows high with irritation. I shake my head and grab a rag to start wiping down the eggs.

"Mother and I were discussing tomorrow. I think I am going with my silver barrette and my blue dress," she continues as if any of this matters to me. I simply nod, trying to hurry and finish cleaning the rest of the eggs.

When I finish, I'm planning on going to write under my favorite tree.

"Are you going to come with us?" My mother slides the biscuits into the oven and grabs the eggs I had cleaned. She starts to crack them over the heated pan on the stove.

"I don't think so," I reply. I don't feel like going to the general store with my mother while Florence enjoys a milkshake with her newest victim.

"You should, maybe you can take some eggs into town. If you sell enough, I bet we could get you something special. Maybe a new ribbon?" She gives me a soft smile, which makes me feel guilty. I knew I wouldn't take any eggs with me to sell since we needed every bit of food we could get.

"I don't need anything mama, but I will go with you. I should get out of the house anyway," I finish wiping the last egg and stand up.

"I could use a new ribbon," Florence peers over the edge of her chair at my mother. I roll my eyes so hard I'm afraid they'll get stuck.

Before walking out of the room I look over my shoulder, "actually, I think I'd quite enjoy a ribbon. Thank you." I can feel Florence's glare at the back of my head as I exit the room.

Two

I spend the majority of the morning writing under the tree, scribbling my random thoughts and feelings onto the paper. I miss school, being able to learn and work on my penmanship. I hated the social aspect of it, but everything else I loved. It's been four years since I was taken out of school at the age of thirteen. I had to stay home to care for Otis and help on the farm when my mother had gotten sick. I think my father had worn her down and she spiraled into a deep sadness, but they, of course, wouldn't ever admit that. They simply say she was 'sickly'.

The wind blows, whipping my hair and paper around. I put my hand down on the notebook to keep the fragile paper from tearing. A bird starts singing a song, and I sit very still while I listen. Songbirds were my favorite sound of all.

"Hazel!" I jump at the shrill sound of Otis' voice as he bounds up the hill. I groan a little. He has recently found my spot, and as much as I adore him, I adore the peace and quiet more.

"What is it, bud?" I set my pencil down inside my notebook.

"I'm bored. I cain't look for treasures no more cuz papa got real mad 'bout the dirt my gems got on the table," he flops next to me in the grass. So that was what he was so mad about earlier.

"I bet we can figure out something. Maybe we need to get a bag for you to keep your treasure in. That way it won't get things messy." I reach over and wipe the dirt off his chin. He gives me a big grin, springing up as quickly as he had sat down.

"You're the best sister!" He leans down and gives me a hug before taking off down the hill.

At bedtime, I light the candle next to me and count the money I have stashed under two nightgowns in my drawer. The cost of eggs has risen, and thankfully we have fifteen chickens. Sixteen if you include the rooster. I've saved up $5.12 between the eggs mom would secretly let me sell and the babysitting I do for my aunt and uncle. Not many people in town want to watch their six rowdy children. I count out $1.50 for shopping tomorrow and put the rest back in my stash.

The next morning I sit in front of the mirror, staring at my reflection with frustration. I rake my fingers through my curls, trying to force them to stay down. It's hopeless. I don't bother to put it up, it's so long it gives me a headache to wear it up for more than an hour.

"You should use a little rouge," Florence suggests from her bed. She's been ready for the past hour. She sits criss cross, leaning against the headboard. The sun glares through the window, lighting up the sparkling barrette she wears in her hair and the pin she wears on her blue dress. She woke up at an ungodly hour to start her routine to turn herself into the Florence everyone in town knows. She doesn't wear her ridiculous makeup at home when shucking the stalls.

I often wonder why she turned out the way she did. Mama puts some pride in her appearance, enough to brush her hair every morning and iron her dresses. But not in the way Florence does. No girl in town had been on as many dates with as many different boys as she has. It makes me wonder if maybe boys are a distraction for her, like writing is for me. Maybe she grew up so used to the attention from father that when he stopped giving it, she found it elsewhere.

"I don't think Mrs.Smith is going to mind if my cheeks and lips are rosy or not," I tell her, smoothing out my plain green dress. It matches my eyes, and I had added a strip of fabric that I would tie around my hips to give it shape and resemble the current styles everyone was wearing. It may be boring and nothing to write home about, but it was the nicest dress I owned. The other two were my working dresses, and thanks to the bastard rooster, one had a giant rip in it.

"Mrs.Smith?" Florence scrunches her nose up in confusion. I scoff at her; for someone always accusing me of living in my own world, she doesn't pay anyone attention unless they're undressing her with their eyes.

"The owner of Smith's General Store. You know, the one we have been shopping at our entire life," I tell her.

"Oh," she says flippantly, standing up and making her way next to me. She leans over, sticking her head directly next to mine to get a glimpse of herself in the mirror. Immediately, I feel whatever confidence I had left, vanish. Her sun kissed skin glows, her hair looks like the golden sun, and her eyes look bluer than ever. She is tall and lanky, the figure everyone pines after.

My skin is pale, and even though I spend more time outside than her, the only thing I have to show for it is the freckles splattered across my nose and cheeks. They make me feel like a child, even though I'm seventeen. My unruly curls cascade over my shoulders, making me always look disheveled.

"I wish I looked like you." As soon as the words leave my mouth, I regret them. I don't know why I said it, lord knows she doesn't need more confidence than she already has. Florence rarely looked surprised, but she was clearly taken aback by my comment. Then she does the one thing worse than gloating, she looks at me with pity.

"You know you are beautiful, too. Just in a different way. You look...like a wild lion with a big mane," she smiles, patting my head.

"You know the male lions are the ones with manes," I groan, sliding down in the chair that sat at our vanity.

"Oh Hazel, I mean, honestly. Maybe your looks have nothing to do with why you have never kissed a boy. Maybe it has to do with the fact that you never talk. And when you do, you're correcting someone." Florence throws her hands up in the air.

"Who said I never kissed a boy? I have kissed lots of boys!" I feel my cheeks getting hot.

"And I'm a virgin!" She rolls her eyes and walks out the bedroom door.

"Wait, what?!" I holler after her.

That afternoon we bounce in our car as we make our way into town, the dirt flying up behind us as we drive. The one thing father said we would never sell is our car. He sold and pawned off a lot of things to make ends meet when we had a bad tornado rip through our land, taking half our crops and animals. I think when he sold mama's record player he saw how sad it left her. And he knew how important going into town was to her so he hadn't sold the car...yet.

We all sit up a little in excitement as we enter town. It's a small Texas town, but is growing rapidly. We have a new butcher and even a small fabric store where the seamstress makes all the newest fashionable clothes. My sister will go in for hours and stare at all the shiny fabrics and sequined dresses. She looks at those dresses like the boys look at her, with adoration.

I feel the coins I've brought with me in my small handbag. "I need to stop by the dressmaker and tailor shop," I tell Mother and Florence. They both turn and look at me at the same time. My mom's lips are painted red and her teeth look extra white when she does that.

"Why?" is all she asks.

"A gift for Otis, figure he really deserves it after yesterday," I say, shifting in my seat. She doesn't say anything in reply, just grips the steering wheel tighter. I analyze her face. She has a bruise forming underneath her eye, and I can see the blue tint under her powder. I can see a crack on her lip as well, which explains the red shade she picked for her rouge. It doesn't even jar me anymore. I don't remember the last time I saw my mother without a bruise or mark on her face.

My own arm has a bruise around the wrist from where my father grabbed it a few days ago. Some fathers may leave notes or flowers for the women they care about, my father leaves bruises or burn marks.

I shift my attention from my arm to outside the window as we pull up in front of Smith's General Store.

"You go ahead and run along to do what you like, be back by noon," my mother says as she cuts off the car.

"Gregory is going to drop me off at home," Florence tells her, smoothing her silky hair into place.

"Be smart, and be a lady," my mother warns her. I snort out loud when she says that, causing Florence to stomp on my foot and elbow me. My mother just pretends to not see it and gets out.

"Shut up," Florence hisses in my ear as she scoots next to me to get out.

"Sorry, I didn't know you spread your legs as fast as Moses parted the seas," I say as I get out of the car and shut the door behind her.

"Can you grow up? I have only been with Gregory. We are in love!" She starts to follow me as I make my way to the tailor shop.

"Why are you following me? Don't you have to go choke on Gregory's tongue or something?" I stop walking and cross my arms.

"For your information, I don't have to meet him for another ten minutes and I want to pop in and look at the new dresses that have been made." She walks past me and continues along the sidewalk.

A man exits the barber shop I stopped in front of, slamming into me as he makes his way out of the door. "Pardon me," he apologizes, making his way around me. The smell of tobacco floats in the air as he walks away.

I start after my sister so I don't clog the flow of traffic on the sidewalk. I enter the store behind her, the bell on the door ringing as it closes shut. The store smells faintly of roses and a cleaning chemical I am not familiar with. "Be right with ya!" the seamstress hollers from somewhere in the store, her southern accent thick.

My sister makes her way over to the mannequins that sit in front of the main window, reaching out and touching the sequined dresses with their tassels hanging off the bottom. My eyes trail around the store as I stand in the middle of the shop. Men's hats are displayed on the back wall, a row of women's hats next to them and a gray cat sits on the floor beneath them. His ears are back and his tail flips in different directions, as if he was annoyed. I take a step towards him and a low growl rumbles out of him, causing me to stop in my tracks. Ok, so he does not want to be pet. Understood.

I turn and walk up to the counter that sits in front of the rows of fabric on display. I hum a song quietly while tracing my finger up and down the wooden counter. A cream colored vase with red roses sits next to a little gold bell that has dust accumulating on it, even though the store is relatively new. But the wind blowing in from outside creates dirt and dust something awful. I wipe the bell off as the seamstress makes her way around the counter.

"Sorry to keep you waiting, was tailorin' a suit," she smiles, wiping the perspiration off of her forehead. She is middle aged, with a very plain but kind face.

"I was just looking for a small amount of fabric, not much. Anything with a plain print, nothing floral and girly." I try to not speak so timidly, not wanting to have to repeat myself. Everyone always asks me to speak up because I talk too quietly.

"Got yourself a suiter, hmm? Making something special for your special someone?" She leans forward on the counter, raising an eyebrow. Every woman in this town loves gossip. I let out a short laugh and shake my head.

"Hardly. I'm making a little sack for my brother to keep his rocks in." That obviously was not the answer she was looking for, because she gets a bored expression quickly.

"Is there maybe some scrap fabric that is discounted? I don't need much at all," I add on quickly, suddenly nervous about spending my money I've been saving for so long. One day I was going to buy a train ticket for me and Otis and go somewhere far away from here.

"Sure," she bends under the counter and lifts up a basket with colorful fabric inside. Various textures, colors and sizes of scrap fabric spill out.

I pick out a blue and green striped one, setting it on the counter. "This please, and how much is your ribbon?" I ask.

"They're right over there and vary in price. They have tags," she says as she points to a shelf behind me. I go over and when I do, Florence appears next to me.

"I don't know why you bother to get a ribbon if you don't have someone to impress." She toys one of the ribbons in her hands, flipping satin string around her finger.

"Has it ever occurred to you that there are other things in the world besides men and what they think of how you look?" I snatch it out of her hand and set it back on the shelf.

I see a deep green ribbon and hold it next to my dress. Almost an exact match. I check the price tag and cringe, placing it back. I'd rather get Otis his treasure-holding bag. As I turn to go to the counter, I bump into someone standing behind me. "Hazel, heavens you are clumsy!" Florence accuses as she shoots me a dirty look.

"I am so sorry," I mumble, trying to scoot away, causing my back to hit the shelf full of ribbon.

The man looks at us and smiles, his eyes sweeping us both up and down. My stomach turns queasy and my hands get clammy. A ball feels lodged in my throat as his warm brown eyes study us, his hands tucked into the pockets of his suit pants. An expensive shiny pocket watch catches my attention immediately. His arms are muscular, stretching the fabric of his black suit jacket. My heart flips as his smile broadens, a toothpick hanging out of his mouth. What is wrong with me? Why do my feet suddenly feel ten times heavier?

"My sister is such a clutz, I am so sorry. I'm Florence," my sister steps in front of me, her voice dripping like honey. My eyes cut over to her, what happened to Gregory who she was so in love with 10 minutes ago? I want to disappear at this moment, standing like a shadow behind her, as usual. I imagine how ridiculous I look next to her, with my lion's mane and dull dress with no brooches or pins.

I stare down at my feet, the scuffs on my shoes now seem even more obvious than this morning. My eyes dart to his shoes, and they look freshly shined and polished. I should have worn the rouge Florence offered me earlier.

There's an awkward silence for a moment and I muster every bit of confidence I have, raising my eyes and clearing my voice to introduce myself. "I'm Ha-" before I could get my name out, Florence takes another step closer to him and manages to fully block him from my view.

"And what did you say your name was, sir?" she purrs, sounding like a cat in heat. Like she's trying to sound older than she is, making her words come out slower than normal. Embarrassment and anger rush over me instantly. My cheeks are on fire and I want to grab her short blond hair and slam her face into the ground. She has never been the best sister, but this was a slap in the face. I ball my hands into fists.

Before I have to listen to her make him fall in love with her like every other man, I step around them quickly and set my piece of fabric for Otis on the counter. The seamstress leans around me, her eyes glued to Florence and the handsome man.

"This is all?" she asks, folding the fabric but never taking her eyes off them. She tells me the total, and I count out the money and place it in her hand which was extended out a bit, but not near close enough, forcing me to lean over the counter some. I want to turn and look at the man, just to catch another glimpse of him.

I start to slip out the front door and hear the seamstress dumping the coins into the cash register. I look back and she's still watching my sister and the man, as if it's the most interesting thing that's happened to her all day.

I make my way outside and feel the money in my purse. She was so engrossed in Florence's little scene she hadn't even noticed I jipped her and didn't pay her the full amount. I hadn't originally intended to shortchange her, but as soon as she couldn't even look at me while I was making my purchase I decided it is what she deserved. For poor customer service, not out of jealousy or anything.

I look around the bustling streets and my eyes land on the ice cream parlor. I should go into Smith's General Store to help my mother, but I'm in a sour mood. I knew she was probably just getting started on shopping, having spent the last twenty minutes talking with Mrs. Smith. So I go to buy myself a treat with the money that I didn't give the seamstress. I begin to feel a little guilty and then I remember the man's crooked smile with the toothpick hanging out.

I could have said hi at least, heard what his voice sounded like. But Florence thought for just a second I was going to have a moment of attention, and not her. I deserve a damn ice cream cone.

As I stand at the ice cream counter and pay for my vanilla cone, my thoughts keep drifting to the man. I wonder if he and Florence are currently humping each other behind the seamstress' building? Hell, the seamstress was probably watching it through the window because she can't seem to mind her own business. The thought makes my skin crawl as I make my way outside and my eyes find a little bench sitting in front of the ice cream shop's windows. I sit and watch the people bustle by, their loud conversations drowning out my thoughts. I watch them to distract myself.

A man wearing cowboy boots, jeans and a tucked in stained shirt is loading up feed into the back of his wagon. I recognize him as another local farmer, but I can't recall his name. By the looks of it, he isn't doing too great financially either. The horse and buggy he was using indicate he may have had to sell his farm truck.

"Pa!" a little girl with braided hair runs out to him, holding a homemade ratty doll. He lights up, a smile taking over his weathered face. He picks her up and swings her around. They talk about the things she saw while looking in the shops, and she goes on and on about the spin top she saw with the toys. She begs him to get it for her, and he simply pats her head and gives her an apologetic smile. He turns back to load the rest of the feed, but not before giving her cheek a kiss.

My chest tightens watching them, envy creeping in. I can't imagine a parent loving me that much, especially a father. The little girl bends down and plays with a stick, dragging it through the dirt to draw little pictures. I notice the holes in her dress, and the fact that her shoes look like they were two sizes too small.

I look down at my ice cream cone, untouched because I had been engrossed in the daughter and father's interaction. I stand up and make my way over to her, her eyes getting big as I get closer.

"I bought this ice cream cone, but now I realize how full I am from my lunch, and I don't think I could eat it," I say, crouching down in front of her. "You wouldn't happen to want it, would you?" I hope my stomach doesn't growl and show my lie.

Her head excitedly whips around to her father, waiting for approval. He gives her a nod and she grabs the ice cream cone quickly. I stand up as she begins attacking the ice cream like she hadn't ever had a sweet before. "Thank you. She ain't had one before," the father tells me, a sadness in his eyes.

"Of course," I reply.

I start walking back to the bench when the man hollers, "hey, you're John McCoy's kid, ain't ya?". I stop in the middle of the road, cars honking at me and a few people yelling at me to move out of the way.

I look over my shoulder and decide to lie. “No idea who that is!” I holler back. His expression says he doesn’t believe me but understands why I deny it. Everyone knows John McCoy beats his wife and often his kids. They know he spends more money on booze than food to feed his family.

I collapse back on the bench, feeling emotionally drained. I wish my mother would hurry up her shopping so we could head back home. I watch the little girl and focus on her happiness instead. My eyes couldn’t part from her as she ate the ice cream with her sticky fingers and messy face.

Someone sits down next to me on the bench and I make sure to scoot fully to the side to not take up the whole thing. The little girl is almost finished with the cone already. “Don’t like ice cream?” his voice startles me.

I look over and my mouth hangs open a little before I slam it shut. It’s the man from the seamstress. His voice takes me by surprise, his accent clearly proving he’s not from Texas.

“I, uh I do.” I try to rip my eyes away from him and go back to the little girl, who is now loading up in the buggy to drive off with her father.

“You just thought she would like it more, huh?” The toothpick in his mouth twirls as he waits for my reply.

My spit feels thick as I try to swallow, my hands feeling clammy again and I try to sit up a little straighter. Next time I come into town I am wearing some damn rouge!

“Yes, she looked like she needed it more than I do,” I replied, looking down at my shoes, crossing my ankles to appear more lady-like.

"You shouldn't let her do that, you know," he states, making my eyes snap up towards his.

"She didn't come over and steal the cone from me," I arch my eyebrow. He laughs, the sound filling up the air around me. I don't know what he is laughing at but I can't help but smile.

"I meant your sister," he says, causing the smile to fall off my face.

"Oh."

"You shouldn't let her walk all over you. Does she always do that?" he asks, pulling a brown bag onto his lap.

"You saw her, she could walk all over anyone," I sigh, leaning back onto the wooden bench.

"I did see her, and that's what I don't understand. Why would you let a girl like that cut you off?" He's staring at my face, his expression something I can't decipher. It's not pity, but it's not admiration either. I get a better look at him with his face this close to mine. He has a cut in his eyebrow, making a little scar where the hair didn't grow back.

"A girl like that?" I ask, now curious.

"A girl like everyone else," he chuckles a bit, shaking his head as if he knows something I don't.

"Florence isn't like every other girl, she is gorgeous. She gets everyone she wants, in fact she's currently eating lunch paid for by her newest lover." I wipe off a drop of melted ice cream that had fallen onto my dress.

"I've been to a lot of places and seen a lot of women. She is nothing special. Same haircut, same flirting doe-eyed expression, and same reeking desperation." His voice is serious now, his gaze still studying me. His comment causes me to choke on my spit, I never expected that sentence to come out of someone's mouth regarding my sister. It was possibly the best thing I have ever heard.

"Not to be rude of course," he tacks on.

"Of course," is all I can manage to say. I rack my brain trying to think of something else, but his leg is almost touching mine. My brain feels like mush. I am now shaking my foot out of nervousness, and I can't manage to say anything else. The bench is wobbling with the beat of my foot.

"Here." He places the brown sack on my lap. I stare at it, my hands feeling too heavy to move.

"You're supposed to open it," He elbows my side, making my stomach do flips.

"Here I was thinking I was supposed to eat it," I blurt out nervously. I kick myself at how stupid I sound as I force myself to pick the bag up. I open it, and sitting at the bottom of the bag is the green ribbon. I glance up at him, my eyebrows furrowed.

His expression gets cloudy. "Oh, you didn't like it. I saw you looking at it in the store," he says as he rubs his jaw.

"You were watching us?" I pick up the ribbon, letting it sit in the palm of my hand. My heart is beating fast now.

"No," he says, "just you." I look directly at him now, my eyes meeting his.

"I love it. I don't really know what to say, thank you."

“I thought maybe you didn’t want it, but figured I would take that risk.” He crosses his arms, his watch catching the sun's light and blinding my eyes. Please don’t be noon. I should ask him if he has the time, but I don’t want whatever this is to end.

“I did want it, I just didn’t have enough money with me to get it today,” I tell him, trying to take deep breaths to calm my heart down. I wonder if he can hear it right now, it's pounding in my ears. His head turns to behind us, nodding to the inside of the ice cream shop. His face says he is questioning how I could buy the ice cream then.

I bite my lip and give a sheepish smile, “well, I may not have paid full price for the piece of fabric. So I used the leftover money to get the ice cream.” His eyebrow with the scar raises up to his hairline, a smile tugging at his lips causing the toothpick to twirl again.

“That sounds really bad. I am normally not that kind of person. It’s just that the seamstress couldn’t even bother to look at me, she was just staring at you and Florence. I had to reach across the counter to even give her the money. I could have paid her in rocks and she would have sat them in the register,” I quickly say, cringing as it comes out. I sound like a jealous child. Florence would be sounding a lot more mature right now.

He starts laughing, hard. I try to hide my smile by looking at the ground, and the giggles start to escape my mouth. We both sit there laughing for a good minute until he runs his hand over his mouth.

"You never got to tell me your name." He scoots a little closer on the bench.

"Hazel!" My name didn't come from my mouth, and I want to die as soon as I hear my mother's voice. Could she have worse timing? I have never felt disappointment like I do at this moment. She is standing across the street, putting brown sacks of food in the car. I close my eyes and bite my lip in frustration. Now I really look like a child, with my mother calling out to me.

"Hazel. I like it!" His voice is smooth like butter, and he stands up and reaches his hand out to me. I hesitate before taking it and standing up, I notice his knuckles are bruised and cracked. He lets go sooner than I want. "I'm Theodore."

"It's noon!" my mother hollers across the street. My eyes meet his and I feel a mix of emotions. My heart is pounding, my legs are wobbly and I want to scream at my mother to shut up.

"I have to go," I say regretfully. "Thank you for the ribbon, truly."

I turn to walk away, and as soon as my foot touches the dirt road he grabs my arm. "Can I take you out soon? Tomorrow?" he asks.

"You want to take me out?" I ask in disbelief. Is this a joke? Are Florence and the seamstress hiding behind a tree, watching us while they snicker?

"Tomorrow at four?" he stands in place, his hands in his pockets, his legs standing wide apart. There is something about his presence, he is assertive and confident but somehow non-threatening.

"Ok," I breathe.

"Where do you live? I'll pick you up."

My head turns to where my mother is, now sitting in the car but watching us with a look I cannot make out. She gives me a meak nod; I think she's giving me her approval. I quickly tell him how to find our farm, but not before I tell him not to drive all the way up to our house. "Just stop at the big oak tree, and I'll meet you there."

Before he can change his mind, I walk off quickly to the car. I get in and my mother starts the car, the silence hanging in between us. As we drive off, I look back. I can see him standing in the same place, on the edge of the main road in town, hands in his pockets watching me.

I give a small wave and I can see his smile before the dirt flies up behind the car. I turn around and face straight out the window, opening my hand and looking down at the green ribbon. "You bought a ribbon! I love that color," my mother observes. She rarely speaks, so I know she is trying to make conversation that will lead to Theodore.

Theodore. I don't think I have heard a name I liked more.

"He gave it to me. I was looking at it in the store, and he bought it!" Her head turns to look at me, her eyes raking me up and down.

"Hazel, are you telling the truth?" I can hear the slight excitement in her voice.

"You think you're surprised? He bought it after Florence was trying to dig her claws into him."

She doesn't say anything, but I can tell by her face that she is deep in thought. She looks almost happy, an emotion I haven't seen from her in a long time. We ride the rest of the drive home in complete silence.

For the first time in my life, I feel seen.

After dinner, I write everything that happened in my notebook. I tried to remember every detail I could. The scar in his eyebrow, the caramel color of his eyes and his shiny pocket watch. And the toothpick, I really like that toothpick.

I don't even hear Florence's rambling as I scribble on my paper. The candle flickers in between our beds. The nightstand it sits on was painted white, but the paint started to chip a few years ago. The candle throws light in different directions around the room. The table we use as our makeshift vanity is still cluttered with Florence's makeup and different brooches. Outside, the moon could be seen from our small window, only partially blocked with a tall tree. The room smells faintly of dampness, making me wonder how much mold is in our home.

A pillow lands on my paper, causing my pencil to slide and leave a big mark in the middle of my page. "Florence! Damn it!" I throw the pillow back to her bed.

"You are spacing out again, I was trying to tell you about my date with Gregory," she hisses quietly so we don't wake anyone up.

“I don’t care.” I close my notebook and tuck it under my mattress.

“Oh for heaven’s sake. I’m sorry, ok? I can tell you’ve been in a mood since the tailors. It’s not my fault he was into me. I was trying to save you the embarrassment, I know how shy you are." She sits up more in bed, turning her whole body towards me. My eye twitches. I try to take a deep breath and not let my anger get the best of me. She’s just being Florence. Nothing new here.

“If I wasn’t with Gregory I would be all over that man right now. God, he was dreamy,” she sighs.

“He wasn’t interested in you, Florence. You were just shoving yourself in his face like a floozy looking for attention, as usual” I snap.

“Excuse you?” she takes a deep breath in and looks appalled.

“You heard me. He came out and sat down with me on a bench. He gave me the green ribbon I was looking at. And he said you reeked of desperation and were like every. other. girl.” I speak the last three words slowly, to let them sink in. It wasn’t like me to be this way, but it's like something in me had snapped the moment she stood in front of me. I wasn’t a shadow by nature, she made me that way. Always putting me behind her.

“You’re lying!”

I stand up and yank the paper bag from under my bed. I am standing in between our beds and I shove the neatly folded bag to her chest. I cross my arms and watch as she pulls out the green ribbon. I relish the moment as her mouth opens in disbelief.

"He actually bought this for you? He talked to you?" she fumbles as she puts the gift back in the bag and hands it back to me.

"He asked me out. He's picking me up at four tomorrow." The photo next to the candle catches my eye as the light flickers about.

It was a photograph of our family, before the poverty got really bad. Before the prohibition. When Florence wasn't so obsessed with boys and her appearance. My mother looked like a ghost, ghastly pale and there was a bruise on her neck that was not fully hidden by her hair. My father stood like a statue next to her, arms at his sides with no expression on his face. Florence and I were holding hands.

I sit down on the edge of her bed next to her. "I'm sorry for what I said," I mumble, guilt setting in.

"I'm sorry, too. I didn't think you liked him or anything, you aren't into boys." Florence picks at her bedsheet, pulling off crumbs from bread she snuck in a few nights ago.

"I'm not into boys because they aren't into me."

"They are though, you just never notice. You hide in your own little world and you never talk to anyone. Joshua from school liked you."

"He did not!" I laugh at the thought. Joshua was a bully. He was also much older than I was.

"Hazel, this is exactly what I am talking about. Why do you think he used to tug your hair and call you names? He liked you!" she rolls her eyes, like I shouldn't be surprised that the boy who made my last year at school miserable actually cared for me.

I don't reply. I just sit and think about Theodore. "I am nervous about tomorrow. I am terrified, actually. I haven't ever felt like this," I whisper. My sister unexpectedly gives me a soft smile.

"Just don't clam up too much. You have to talk, ask him questions about his life and where he's from. What he does for fun. Just don't sit there like a quiet little mouse." She tugs a strand of my hair, "And let me help you with your hair and makeup."

"I don't want to look like a prostitute!" I warn. We both smile and I climb back into my bed, scooting under the tattered quilt.

"Hazel, I don't think you could look like a prostitute if you tried." I'm not sure if that was meant as a compliment or insult, but I take it as a compliment.

Three

In the morning, the fog is so thick, I can't see more than 5 feet in front of myself. I walk slowly and carefully to the chicken coop, where the hens cluck in anticipation. I open the coop door, where a handful of chickens are waiting. They take off outside, pecking the ground for food.

I make my way to the nesting boxes, shaking my head as I walk up to the first one. There sits thieving Henrietta, her red feathers fluffing up as I approach. "I need the eggs," I tell her, as if she understands me. She settles down on the eggs even more, shifting her body from left to right. She squawks at me loudly. I sigh and make my way to other nesting boxes, deciding to deal with her later. I count the eggs, only five. She must be sitting on the rest.

"Ok fine, here is the deal. I will let you keep those eggs, sit on them all you want. We could use a few more chicks anyway." She clucks in reply.

I leave the coop door open and head back to the house. When I walk in the door, I set the egg basket on the kitchen table like I do every day. I sit down and start wiping down the handful of eggs.

"Not much today," I tell my mom, who is whisking eggs at the stove. She wears a pale yellow dress and her cream apron. Her hair is pulled back in a simple twist. She doesn't say anything back, which leads me to wonder if I shouldn't have let the broody hen keep the rest of the eggs. That means one less egg every day while she hatches the eggs she is sitting on.

Otis is sitting on the living room floor, playing with the bag I sewed for him yesterday when I got home. He is putting a small toy plane inside it, pretending it was flying into and out of it.

That's when I noticed the tub sitting in the kitchen. "Do I stink that bad?" I tease, smiling at my mom.

"I thought a bath would be nice before your first date," she says softly.

"Date?" my father walks out from their bedroom and I want to crawl and hide under the table.

"Hello, dear!" My mom tries to distract him with a kiss on the cheek.

"Has he seen your hair?" He yanks a chair out from the table and sits down.

"Yes," I glare at him. I look at the pan my mom is making eggs in and dream of slamming it into the back of his head. I wonder if the thud would be loud or not. I try to picture him sober, but I can't even remember the last time he wasn't intoxicated.

My mother said he wasn't always like this. That he didn't even drink until he had tried to enlist in the army to fight alongside his brothers in the war a long time ago. There was some medical reason they wouldn't accept him and it drove him to the bottle. It only got worse when one of his brother's died in battle. I think the guilt ate him alive. I didn't understand how he could want to serve his country so badly, but not be a good husband or father.

"Did he not see your sister?" he chuckles, the smell of liquor assaulting my nose from across the table. My eyes narrowed into slits and I cock my head sideways.

"You ever think one reason you hate me so much is maybe because I am a part of you? And seeing just a little bit of yourself is so repulsive that you can't stand it?" I set the cloth down and push back from the table.

Before I can blink, a hand is across my face with such force I fall out of the chair and onto the hardwood floor. I don't let out a sound as a sob escapes my mom's throat and Otis takes off out the front door with his treasure bag.

I close my eyes and a smile spreads across my face. "There it is," I say.

"What the fuck do you mean there it is? Are you asking for a beatin'?" His boot comes towards me when my mother grabs his shoulder.

"John! John, please. Please honey, come sit down. I made eggs and your favorite bread," she pleads. He turns and shoves her away, she stumbles back to the stove and backs into the pan. It knocks onto the ground, eggs flying everywhere.

He starts a slew of curse words, flipping the kitchen table over. I close my eyes and curl up on the floor, waiting for the next blow. But he stomps out the front door, slamming it shut behind him. I hear the car start and take off quickly. "Hazel, are you ok?" my mother crouches next to me and helps me up.

"Yeah," I mumble, my face throbbing and my elbow bleeding, but that was it.

"You mustn't taunt him like that. What were you thinking?" She pushes my hair gently to the side and holds my face in her hands. My sister enters the front door and her eyes take in the scene.

"What happened?" she asks, out of breath. Her hair is disheveled in the back, but you could tell she had smoothed down the front. Gregory must have paid her a visit early this morning.

"More like who happened," I snap as I pull away from my mother and go out to call for Otis. I hate when he sees our father's outbursts. I holler his name a few times before he appears, crawling out from under the porch. That's where he usually hides when things get bad inside the house.

"I'm sorry, buddy. Hey, did you find any treasure today to put in your treasure bag?" I ask. He slowly shakes his head, his eyes full of tears as he takes in my face.

"He hurted you bad," he says. He grips the bag with both of his hands in front of him.

"I'm ok. Can you go find me some treasure though? That would make me feel so much better," I smile at him. He grins slowly and nods, taking off towards the fields.

I go back inside where Florence and mother are sitting the table and chairs upright. "Oh no, right before your date!" Florence grimaces at my face. I reach up to feel the damage and pull my hand back. My lip is bleeding.

"Shit," I whisper.

"It's fine, it'll all be fine. Just use my red lipstick," my mother speaks up, wiping egg yolk from the floor. Those were the saddest words she ever spoke to me.

After a bath and applying some lavender oil that Florence let me borrow, I feel much better. I brush through my hair, the curls softly bouncing back up each time I rake them through. "You should let me try pin curls," Florence says from her bed. She's sitting watching me like she always does. As if she's supervising and critiquing every move I make.

"I don't think it'll work with my hair."

"Yes it will. It'll make it smoother and the curls looser. It'll tame the mane," she laughs at her joke. I would have normally too, if my stomach wasn't in knots. I felt like I could throw up.

"I don't think I can do this," I put my forehead on the table.

"Oh hush, you'll be fine. I remember my first date. I was so nervous too, especially since I didn't know his expectations, if you know what I mean," Florence says as she makes her way behind me, patting my shoulder. That comment made me sit straight up.

“Expectations?”Oh god. Was he expecting me to sleep with him? Is that why he asked me out? He could tell how inexperienced I was, assuming he could trick me into bed with him on the first date?

She wiggles her eyebrows and starts smoothing my hair into sections, rolling them up and pinning them to my head. “He did seem a lot older,” I say as I chew on my lip.

“If he does try to get fresh, just stop him at kissing. Making them wait is what gets you more dates,” she advises.

“You think he’ll kiss me?” My hands are clammy now.

“Is the kettle black?”.

I don’t want to go anymore. I am too inexperienced to go on a date with someone as handsome and put together as Theodore. I should have started with someone with pimples and body odor. Someone fresh out of puberty. I can’t fully picture exactly what happens between a man and woman, but I know enough.

Farm life teaches you the basics pretty early on in life. That, and I saw Florence and Gregory rolling around in the loft of the barn once. I thought maybe Florence was in pain from the sounds she was making, so I went to inspect. They heard me before things got too serious, but I saw enough kissin’ in places you don’t normally kiss to gather they were probably in need of some privacy.

While my hair was drying, Florence began to apply my makeup. While sitting extremely still, she lectures me on the do’s and don'ts of a first date. Don’t talk too much. But don’t be too quiet. Do flirt. But don't let him get past the kissing stage.

I want to ask how many stages there are between kissing and the actual, you know, finale. But I don't. She applies dark shadow to my eyelids and smudges it underneath. She applies mascara and then mother's red lipstick. You can still see the crack on my lip if you look hard enough, but it isn't horrible. And the bruise forming on my cheek bone is hidden well enough with powder.

"Mom says to bring the lipstick with you, apply it every hour or the cut will be noticeable." She presses the rouge into my hands. I lay out my three dresses on the bed and for the first time, I wish I had more fashionable clothes. Or at least more selection.

I have to wear the green dress he saw me in yesterday, as it's the only one not full of holes or ragged from working in it. Hopefully, he won't notice. I slip it on and let Florence remove the pen curls. My hair falls down to my back and she takes a step back to look at her work.

"Wow. Not half bad," she says. Almost a compliment! I look in the mirror and take a deep breath through my nose. I actually almost look beautiful. My hair isn't in tight frizzy curls, they're smooth and loose. At first, I thought I looked like a bit of a raccoon, but seeing how much older the eye makeup makes me look, I decide I like it. Before getting up, I twist the front of my hair to the back of my head loosely, and tie it with the green ribbon he had given me.

"Thank you," I tell Florence, who just gives me a nod in return.

For the next thirty minutes I sit on the porch and stare out at the large oak tree far down the road. "It's ten till four," my mother says, poking her head out the door. I sit plastered to the rocking chair, feeling sick.

"Just be yourself. That's who he asked to go out, not your sister. Remember that," she says quietly before disappearing back inside.

I stand up and make my way down the road to the tree. She was right. He gave me the ribbon. Quiet, shy Hazel. I could do this. It was this or sit at home scribbling in my notebook for the rest of my life. Watching Florence receive more brooches and fragrance oils.

I am only standing under the tree for a minute or two when I see a car driving down our road. I squint my eyes in the sun to make it out, and I blink a few times. It couldn't be Theodore's car. I don't know much about cars, but I know an expensive one when I see it. This car is white with gold accents, and looks like it costs more than our house.

It slows down as it pulls up, and then comes to a complete stop. Theodore steps out and gives me a smile. My eyes lock in on the toothpick. I wonder if he always has one in his mouth. I wonder if he'd leave it in when he'd try to kiss me, is that even possible?

"What are you thinking about?" He walks around the car, opening the passenger door.

"Your toothpick" I say without thinking, immediately regretting my honest answer. I should have complimented the car. He starts laughing, and I decide song birds are no longer my favorite sound.

"Sorry, your car is very nice," I say politely, feeling suddenly uncomfortable and very out of my depth.

"No need to apologize. In fact, I think I like the fact you were thinking about my toothpick and not my luxurious car." He winks and motions for me to climb in.

I slide in the car and watch as he closes the door and makes his way back to the driver's side. He turns the car around and heads back towards the way he came in. The car has a light smell of leather and his cologne. I start tapping my foot nervously and remember what Florence told me.

"So, where are we going?" I speak up.

"I was thinking we could get dinner at the little restaurant in town and go get that ice cream you gave away?" he glances over at me, causing my heart to do a flip.

"That would be wonderful," I say with sincerity. I hadn't eaten anything but the bread my mother made for breakfast, since we lost all the eggs for the day.

He reaches over and turns the radio on, something our car did not have. I smile and shake my foot with the rhythm of the music. "The ribbon looks nice on you," he compliments me. I feel heat creep up my neck and towards my face.

"Thank you, some odd stranger followed me out of a store and gave it to me," I tease. I hope he has a sense of humor, and to my relief he smirks.

"He must have thought you quite something to do that."

If my cheeks weren't red before, they were now.

"Where are you from?" I ask.

"New York." He keeps his eyes on the road now, so I let my eyes drift over to him. His bruised and cut up knuckles catch my attention as he holds the steering wheel. I want to ask about them, but I don't. He is wearing a gray tweed suit, the jacket open to show the vest underneath. He also wears a matching newsboy hat that covers his dark hair.

"Why did you move to Texas?" I ask, grateful the questions are coming easily to me.

"Oh, I didn't. I traveled to visit a friend here and for some business," he answers. My heart sinks and I feel absolute disappointment wash over me. He doesn't live here. He's going to leave. I'm a temporary distraction while he's in town.

"Oh," I manage to say. I can no longer think of any questions. My chest feels tight and I suddenly feel small in the large car that costs more than my house. What was I doing? Was I really sitting in a car with a complete stranger, letting him use me as a mere fun toy while he was traveling? What was the point of asking someone out one time knowing you were going to hop town?

"Hey," he reaches over and gently touches my knee. As much as I hate it, I want to grab his hand and keep it there when he puts it back on the wheel.

"You know why I bought you that ribbon and asked you out?" he asks.

"Truthfully, I have no idea."

"Your sister was looking at the dresses for herself, as did every other woman who had walked into the store. They all had their hair and makeup done in the current fashion. But you walked in like a breath of fresh air, with your bare face and hair down to your waist. And I heard you ask for the scrap fabric to make your brother a bag, you weren't interested in the dresses like all the other girls," he said.

I was left speechless for a moment, because it was the nicest thing anyone has ever said to me. "Wow." I mutter under my breath, not sure what to say. What do you even say to that? 'Thank you' didn't seem sufficient.

"Then when I went outside to give you the ribbon, I watched you give your ice cream to the little girl who was with her dad. That was when I knew you truly were different, and a ribbon wouldn't be enough. I had to spend time with you," he tells me as we pull into the parking space in front of the restaurant.

He turns off the car and looks at me. "I don't really know what to say to that. You aren't like anyone else I've met either," I admit.

"No one else in town always has a toothpick in their mouth," I add lightheartedly. We both laugh as he exits the car and opens my door, grabbing my hand as I step out.

The town is packed with people from nearby towns, all shopping and eating before dusk sets in. Men tip their hats to ladies, a cluster of them stand together in front of the barber shop smoking thick cigars. I see a middle aged woman wearing a sequined sleeveless dress and a string of pearls around her neck. She is dragging a screaming child behind her, his arm reaching towards Smith's General Store as if he had left behind his most prized possession. My guess was he saw the spin tops and had his heart set on one. We pass them as we make our way down the sidewalk, his shrill screams causing us to walk a little faster.

Theodore doesn't let go of my hand as we enter the diner. The heavy smell of fries and burgers wafts in the air. "I would take you somewhere a lot nicer, but I didn't know what else is nearby" he apologizes.

"Oh, no this is perfect. Just don't order the meatloaf," I warn him as we sit down at a booth. He chuckles and I give him a grave stare.

"Oh, you're serious."

"Quite."

The first few minutes we are quiet, looking at the menu and waiting for the waitress to appear. My eyes scan over the page. "So what's good here if the meatloaf is not?" Theodore breaks the silence with his question.

"Oh, this is actually my first time here," I say, keeping my eyes on the paper in my hand. I see him staring at me, puzzled.

"You haven't been here but you have opinions on what not to order, huh?" he muses.

"Meatloaf is never good," I state as I peer over my menu at him, my lips curling up into a smile.

"Have you lived here your whole life?" he asks. I nod.

“I’m surprised you haven’t been here before then,” he says, making me shift in my booth uncomfortably. I choose not to reply and tell him how we are poorer than dirt and decide to change the subject.

“So how long are you here for?” I inquire.

“Depends,” he sits the menu down as the waitress approaches our table. I recognize her after a minute, it’s Helen from church. She used to sit next to Florence and gossip in her ear the whole service. I hadn’t seen her but a few times in town since we stopped going to church, and it’s been at least a year since I’ve run into her.

She’s wearing a pink striped uniform with a white apron tied around it, showing stains from what I assume was ketchup. That, or she had been out back slaughtering the pigs and cows herself. She pulls out a pen and pad and puts a hand on her hip.

“Is that you, Hazel? My goodness, hardly recognize ya!” she talks way louder than she needs to, her strong accent ringing in my ears. It’s almost painful. I force a smile and tell her it’s good to see her again.

“How is your sister? I miss her so much, golly I miss seein’ y’all every Sunday!” she says, making me wonder if she was ever going to take our order. I don’t want to discuss my sister on my first date.

“She’s fine,” I say, trying to keep my answers short.

“Well, y’all don’t be no strangers. Come pop in for a preachin’ sometime. Now, what can I get y’all to drink?” she puts her pen to the paper, her smile showing her stained teeth.

"Just water please," I say, shifting my eyes to Theodore.

"Coke, thank you," he tells her, keeping his gaze on me the entire time. I start to feel flustered and nervous again. She walks off and shortly returns with our drinks, the whole time his eyes never leave me as I try to pretend to keep reading the menu.

She takes our food orders and disappears.

"Don't believe in God anymore?" he asks, taking me by surprise. I choke on my water and put a hand up to my mouth.

"That is a deep question," I say, playing with the napkin on my lap. Florence had said to keep the conversations light. This was certainly not a light topic.

"Well, I just want to get to know you. Not just what your favorite color is or what you do for fun," Theodore says, crossing his hands on the table and leaning in.

"So, you want to know if I get to dance in heaven or burn in hell?" I raise an eyebrow, my response makes him tilt his head back and chuckle.

"I don't know if I ever believed in God," I say honestly. I figure if he is going to be passing through town, I might as well just be blunt and fully authentic. No need to fuss about manners or keeping topics light since there probably won't even be a second date.

Before he can ask me another religious question I ask him one. "You said it depends on how long you're going to stay. Depends on what?"

"Depends on you," he says.

My stomach turns in knots and the ball in my throat is back. I feel like there are a million bees buzzing in my head and my hands start to shake as I grab my water to take a sip. I let out a nervous giggle as Helen makes her way to the table.

"Two burgers and fries," she announces, setting down the food in front of us. I see her eye Theodore and then look me up and down. She obviously was just as confused as me.

I remember Theodore's words, 'you were like a breath of fresh air'. Maybe I'll have a chance of a second date after all.

"So what do you do for a living?" I ask, remembering to ask him lots of questions about himself like Florence had said.

"This and that." He takes a bite of his burger and then a drink of his coke. This and that?

I want to ask him what that meant, but by his response I guess he wasn't in the mood to talk about work. "Have you traveled much?" he asks me.

"Not at all. I haven't ever left Texas," I say after eating a bite. I try to not make it obvious how hungry I am and how delicious the food is. I can't remember the last time I had a proper meal or when I had last been out to eat. No wonder Florence was always in a good mood, one could get used to this.

"Do you want to?"

"Every day," I mumble.

He laughs as if what I had said was funny, but I was being dead serious.

"So, tell me about yourself." I smile as I continue to eat.

"What do you want to know?" he leans back in the booth, raising his chin slightly so he's looking down his nose at me. I swallow and ponder how a man can be so confident without coming across as cocky.

"Everything," I answer breathlessly.

"Well, I'm 26 years old. My brother lives here in Texas, that's who I'm visiting while I'm here for business. My mother lives back in New York, my father passed away when I was young. I enjoy a good whiskey and frequent horse races," he says.

I take in his words. 26 years old. That is nine years my senior. No wonder he was so confident, he has been around a lot longer than me. I am a little disappointed he didn't describe what he does for work, or what business he was here for exactly.

"Now, I want to hear all about Hazel McCoy."

I realize he is far more interesting than me, and I feel my answers will be far too dull. He has traveled all over and seen so many things. Meanwhile, I'm just an inexperienced teenager who is too blunt with her answers.

"Uh, let's see. I like to write, nothing important or interesting-," before I can finish he raises his hand up and waves it to stop me.

"Don't do that, don't sell yourself short! I bet your work is compelling," he assumes. "I would love to read it."

“Oh, no. It’s not meant for anyone to read,” I quickly reply.

“What’s the point of writing if no one gets to read it?” he questions.

I don’t have an answer for that so I continue, “I spend a lot of my days taking care of my little brother, Otis. And I probably spend too much time with our chickens.”

He chuckles and cocks his head to the side as he finishes his food. “Chickens, huh?”

We sit in comfortable silence as I finish my food. His caramel eyes have a sparkle as he looks at me and reaches into his suit. He pulls out a toothpick and pops it into his mouth. We both smile as he does this, as if we both know I’ll be thinking about it the rest of the day.

“How does an ice cream cone sound? One not paid with money that was supposed to be in the seamstress' cash register?” he asks, pulling out a wad of cash that I quickly avert my eyes from to not be impolite. I laugh at his question, but can’t help my eyes from flickering back to the bills he lays on the table. It was double what the food had cost and I could imagine Helen’s joy when she saw the tip he left. It was more money than I had seen in a very long time.

As we walk out of the restaurant, my arm looped through his, I have a hard time believing that any of this is real. Things like this, men like this don’t happen to a girl like me. There must be some glitch in the universe. If God was real, why was he suddenly caring about me?

He holds open the ice cream parlor's door and we make our way inside. It’s a tiny shop, owned by an elderly man and his wife that had moved to the town not too long ago. The old man was standing behind the counter, his wife sat in a chair not too far from him, knitting something. “Howdy!” he greets us, tipping his head towards us and wiping his hands on his apron.

“What can I get ya?” he asks us as we stand in front of the counter. Theodore motions for me to order first. He looks out of place in the parlor, his suit stated he had money. Something most of us did not have. There were a few people sitting at the table and chairs enjoying their ice cream. Their eyes watch us curiously, focused on Theodore and his presence, which commands attention.

I clear my throat and ask for a vanilla scoop. “Make it two scoops,” Theodore tells the old man, who looks up at him and then back at me. He simply gives a nod and scoops up two heaping balls onto the cone. He extends it over the counter and I grab it, looking up at Theodore as he orders a double chocolate scoop.

“That’ll be thirty cents," the old man says as he places the scoop back into the chocolate ice cream container.

“Keep the change," Theodore tells him as he drops the coins into his hand. The man smiles graciously as I loop my arm back into Theodore’s.

“I know this special bench we can sit on,” Theodore winks at me as he guides us back outside. The sun is starting to beat down on us- it’s only spring, but the temperature is already beginning to rise. I wasn’t used to being so full, causing me to be a little nervous on how I was going to eat both scoops of ice cream.

“Thank you very much for lunch and the ice cream,” I say as we sit down on the same bench we found ourselves sharing the day before.

“Of course, it’s my pleasure.”

“So what happened there?” he asks as he motions towards my face. My hand shoots up to my lip as panic fills my body. I had forgotten to reapply the lipstick. I was so dumb, I couldn’t remember to do anything right. I fumble for my bag and pull out the rouge my mother had given me. I giggle nervously as I turn my head to the side and blindly apply the lipstick as quickly as I can.

“Oh, goodness. I must look silly,” I blurt out as I slide the rouge back into my bag.

“So what happened?” he asks again. He watches me as he pulls out the toothpick and puts it in the ashtray next to the bench.

“Bully rooster,” I lie to him as I start to eat the ice cream.

He seems to buy this answer and licks his chocolate ice cream. “Strong rooster to give you a black eye,” he says. Ok, maybe he didn’t buy it.

“We feed him a special diet,” I tease. He doesn’t press the issue anymore and scoots a little closer to me on the bench.

The closer he gets, the more details of his face I can take in. His eyebrow isn’t the only place with a scar, he has a very light one that is under his eye resting on his cheekbone. It was jagged and almost shimmered from the sun beating down on it.

"How did you get those scars?" I ask, my question comes out a whisper because he is so close to my face now.

"A mean rooster," he answers, making me roll my eyes. I guess neither of us were big fans of the truth.

His right hand holds the ice cream cone and his left hand is resting on the bench next to my leg. I hate how aware I am of his every move, my body tingling when his hand moves even the slightest bit.

The air is filled with various smells floating from the stores and the street is loud with chatter as we sit here. Many people start to load into their cars and buggies, heading home before sunset. "Where are you staying?" I ask him, breaking the silence that hangs between us.

"A hotel in Dallas," Theodore answers after a bite of ice cream. A melted drop runs down his bottom lip and onto his chin, coating the stubble that grows there. He wipes his mouth as I process his reply.

"Dallas is almost two hours from here!" I say, shocked that he isn't staying in a closer town. Theodore nods and finishes his ice cream. I look down and realize I was eating at a much slower pace than he was. Was I talking more than him? 'Don't talk too much,' Florence's words rang in my head.

"Did you really drive all the way back to Dallas yesterday just to come back today for our date?" I ponder.

"Of course," he states, "and I'd do it again."

“Are you asking me out for a second date?” I hesitate, unsure if he meant he wants to see me again or he simply didn’t regret this one.

“I am, if you would entertain the idea, of course.” He casually puts another toothpick to his lips.

I never would have thought I’d want to be a toothpick, but here I am.

“I suppose I will entertain it,” I say soberly, before finishing the vanilla cone. He walks me to his car and opens the door. As I sit down I notice the people stopping on the sidewalk to gawk at his car, talking amongst themselves and pointing. I feel too plain and out of place to be sitting in such a nice vehicle and wish Theodore would get in faster so we could leave.

Once in the car, he turns towards me, and to my dismay, doesn’t start the car. “How about this Saturday?” he proposes. Four whole days away! It seems like an eternity, but I nod and give him a smile.

“What time?” I ask.

“Noon,” he states as he starts the car and looks over his shoulder to back up.

As we drive out of town, we pass the new houses that are built closer together with sidewalks in front of their gates. My eyes follow them out of the window. I wonder what it was like to live inside one of them. I imagine the homes are filled with laughter and fathers who love all of their children. Mothers who smile and read books to toddlers. I turn my head forward and watch the houses turn from new to old, becoming more spaced apart from each other. I imagine the families going from joyful to miserable the closer we get to my house.

We ride in silence, but it's not the bad kind that hangs in the air from tension. It's the comfortable kind, like when you see a sunrise and bask in its beauty, not needing to say unnecessary words.

It's almost dark as we start to near our land and I feel dread wash over me. I don't want to go home. I don't want to be in this desolate place. My face must have shown my thoughts because Theodore reaches over and sets his hand on my knee as he pulls in front of the large oak tree. His hand radiates heat as he leaves it there.

I look over at him and watch the tooth pick twirl around. Is he going to kiss me? Do I want him to kiss me? Do I let him kiss me?

"I had a nice time" he mutters, his eyes taking in my face.

"I did too," I whisper. To my disappointment, he clears his throat and adjusts his suit. He opens his car door and walks around the front, the headlights bouncing off his watch that sits on his wrist. He opens my door and reaches out for my hand to help me out.

I stand in front of him and over his shoulder I can make out our front porch, and there's someone standing on it. "Just meet me here again on Saturday," I tell him, wanting to rush our goodbye in case whoever is on the porch decides to come this way. Our front door swings open and I see a tiny figure flying down the steps. Otis.

"Are you sure you don't want me to drop you off closer to your house? You don't need to be walking all this way in the dark." Theodore turns to gesture to my home and I interject quickly.

"No, no. It's fine, truly! I should go now, thank you," I awkwardly pat his shoulder. He bites his lip and his cheeks rise as he stifles a laugh.That is not how you tell a handsome man wearing a suit goodbye on your first date. I feel my cheeks heat up with mortification and I rush around him and start walking home. Florence would have hit me over the head with a bag of flour had she seen what I just did.

"Goodbye!" I hear him holler from far away as I put more distance between us. I turn to wave but he is already in his car now and turning around. Did I just mess that up? Will there still be a second date?

Otis is almost to me now, running with his treasure bag in hand. "You're back!" he exclaims when reaching me. He throws his dirty arms around me and hangs on.

"I am! Did you miss me terribly?" I ask. He bobs his head up and down in response as he takes my hand and walks next to me. As we approach the house, I notice our car is gone and I let out a sigh of relief that I won't be seeing my father.

"Did you kiss that man?" Otis wrinkles his nose.

"That is not an appropriate question to ask, Otis." I tisk at him, "but no, I didn't." I walk up the porch steps, they creak underneath me.

"I'm goin' to shut the chickens in the coop!" Otis shouts as he takes off in the other direction.

My mother is sitting in one of the old rocking chairs father had bought her when they first got married. She places the knitting needles down in her lap and glances up at me in anticipation. I walk past her when the door is thrown open and Florence bounds out almost out of breath. "So?" she demands as the screen thuds shut behind her.

My mother's head leans in and her lips are pursed as she waits to hear my answer. "My goodness, you would think you were waiting to hear if the doctor had told me I was dyin' or not!" I jest as I cross my arms.

"Oh come on Hazel, we have been sitting and waiting for hours," Florence says exasperatedly. My mother quietly taps the rocking chair next to hers and, since I am not a terrible person, I sit down.

When I do, I see her rare smile, the slight dimple in her cheek showing in the moonlight. Florence sits on the porch floor across from us and leans her back on the rails.

"It went really well, I think," I admit.

"Ok, we need more than that. We need details!" Florence claps her hands together in a demanding way. I suck in a deep breath and let it out as I try to think of what all I should tell them.

"For one thing, he is incredibly handsome. He drives the nicest car I have ever seen, people in town even stopped and stared," I tell them, Florence's eyes look as if they are going to bulge out of her head.

"You think he has money?" she whispers.

"I know it. He tipped Helen, who is a waitress by the way, more than the bill was," I say. My mother's face looks cloudy as she chews on her lip. "What is it?" I ask.

"Why do you think he asked you on a date?" she questions. My mouth hangs open at her rude comment. "I don't mean it to offend you dear, I just wonder why a rich man like that is interested in a teenage girl," mother hurriedly explains.

"He told me I was like a breath of fresh air and different from most girls he had met," I answer. Her expression softens a little and she looks less worried.

I continue to tell them about some of our conversations and how he took me to get ice cream after dinner. When they find out there is a second date, they both grin from ear to ear. I feel like I told them enough, but Florence throws up both her hands. "And?" she demands.

"And what?" I mumble.

"Did you kiss?"

My body tingles with embarrassment and I drag my hands from my forehead down to my neck as I look up. "What? Why are you making that face?" Florence gasps, "did you kiss terribly? Oh, I knew it. I could just see you giving a slobbery pursed lipped kiss like Otis does!"

I extend my pale leg in an attempt to kick her but can't reach. "I didn't kiss terribly, there just was no kiss," I retort.

"He didn't try to kiss you?" my mother finally speaks up.

"He probably would have. However, I chose to pat his shoulder instead," I groan. At that moment, they both burst into laughter, my sister holding her stomach and leaning over.

My mother's eyes wrinkle as she giggles, her hands wiping tears from her face.

I try to act irritated as I stand up from the rocking chair, shaking my head at them. But I can't help but crack a smile from the sight of my mother, laughing for the first time in what felt like years. I enter our house, the door shutting softly behind me.

The house has a gentle hum when no one's in it. The kitchen's painted white, which has become slightly dingy over time, the yellow wallpaper reflecting off of it in the living room, making it look warmer than it is. A black stove sits in the corner of the kitchen with a silver teapot on it that has started to rust. The same damp smell that's in our bedroom hangs in the air everywhere in the house.

Later that night, I lay in bed until the house becomes still, the only sound is the crickets chirping outside. White curtains blow in front of the cracked window, dancing with the wind. Once it was silent for a stretch of time, I pull the quilt back slowly and touch my feet to the floor.

I tiptoe into the living room with my journal and pencil in hand. I sit down at the kitchen table and light the candle that sits in the center. My pencil scribbles across the pages as I write about a mysterious man who wore a tweed suit and twirled a toothpick in his mouth. I lightly sketch a photo of Theodore's side profile underneath the words. My pencil flies across the page as I become engrossed in the words I use to describe the man with bruised knuckles and a slit in his eyebrow. I am unaware of the hours passing as I hunch over the journal, the candle wick burning close to the bottom as my time runs out.

A quiet thud interrupts my thoughts and I sit up straight. I squint to try to see past the candle and into the living area. My father stands by the couch only wearing muslin pajama pants cinched with a drawstring. He has a bottle of hooch in his hands and stares at me with a look I cannot make out. I slowly close my journal, as if to not startle him. "It's late," he states. I nod and stand up, causing the chair to scrape against the floor.

"Went out, did you?" He takes a few steps closer and the candle lights up his face.

"Yes," I answer quietly. My heart thumps inside my chest as my eyes dart to my bedroom door.

"You think you're somethin' now? Like you're special?"

I shake my head. "You ain't ever going to amount to nothin'. You're going to sit here in this house for the rest of your life, wipin' chicken shit off eggs while your sister marries and moves out," he snarls. My chest tightens and I feel a pang strike my heart.

"T-That's not true!" I stutter and take a step around the table, looking between him and my door.

"You think a man is gonna want you? He may spread your legs but that don't mean nothin'. You're gonna be a McCoy your whole damned life." He slaps his hand on the couch. I flinch and take off towards my room. Once inside, I slam the door shut. I lean against it as my chest rises and falls with every heavy breath I take.

The commotion makes Florence gasp and sit up in bed. "Goodness gracious, what's happened? I heard his yellin', what did you say to him?" she whispers. Tears roll down my cheeks as I swipe at them angrily.

"Nothing. Just go back to bed," I say as I climb into bed holding the leather journal to my chest.

"Are you crying?"

I turn my back to her and squeeze my eyes shut to try to stop the tears from stinging my eyes. I stiffen as I feel my mattress sink with new pressure being put on it. I feel Florence's body push against my back as she pulls the quilt to our shoulders. Her arm drapes over mine and we lay there, with her holding me like a fragile doll. I feel like something inside me breaks, like the thread that was keeping my heart together came loose. Sobs escape with such force that my body heaves with each breath.

We lay there like when we were young children, before we were separated by our differences and Father's love for Florence and hatred for me. She would hold me as I cried each day after school, when the boys would tug my hair and the girls would call me names. Then, as we aged, she would hold me after father would tell me I was unlovable, she held me after the first time his hand made its way across my face. Then, one day, it was the last time she held me. I'm not sure what day that was or why it was the last time. But there was one day years ago that I laid there and cried myself to sleep, alone, for the first time.

Four

My eyes flutter open, light blinding me and causing my head to throb. I rub my face and look around. Florence is sitting at our makeshift vanity, brushing her hair. She makes eye contact with me in the mirror and tells me good morning.

"What time is it?" I ask, noticing the full stream of light coming in from our window.

"Little past nine," she replies.

I hurry out of bed and slip off my nightgown and grab my torn dress from the cherry wood dresser. "I overslept," I groan.

"Don't worry, Otis collected the eggs for you. I told them you weren't feeling well and that you wanted to rest," Florence tells me, as if she does favors for me frequently. I try to hide my surprise and I thank her.

I step over to the window and push the curtain to the side to look out. Flowers bloom on the edge of the woods. Dead things become new under the spring sun. Otis flies out of the outhouse that sits in front of the rows of trees. He shuts the door before he leans over and grabs one of the barn cats that saunters by. I can see its ears go back in annoyance, but it hangs there like a ragdoll as he drags it around with him. The chickens walk around, pecking and foraging for food. My father always said they were like pigs and only existed to eat. That it was all their brains could remember to do.

"I'm going out with Gregory today, he got the day off," Florence interrupts my thoughts.

"Have fun," I say nonchalantly. She opens her mouth to say something else, but then closes it as she takes her sparkly barrette and slides it into her hair. The little crystals that form small flowers shimmer in the sunlight. It was a gift from Gregory for their one year anniversary. It had only been a few months, but she wore it almost every day and I was tired of seeing it.

"Say, how about we go on a double date one day?" Florence asks on her way out of the bedroom.

"Sounds delightful," I lie through my teeth. I would rather kick rocks.

That evening as I help mother make dinner, Otis sits on the kitchen table with his legs dangling off the edge. His scraped knees show under his filthy trousers." And I got this stone, it's a magic one!" He keeps the rock hidden in his fist after he pulls it from his treasure bag.

"I can't see it when you have your hand around it," I tell him as I put the pulled rabbit meat into the stew. My father had gone hunting when I was with Theodore and had been successful, to all of our relief. Biscuits and eggs were becoming old and weren't very filling.

"That's cuz it's my magic rock! It's gonna make me super strong and it ain't gonna work if I lose it. So I ain't gonna set it down," Otis remarks as his knuckles turn white from the grip he has on it. My mother and I exchange smiles. Father sits in the living room, reading a newspaper with his feet up and shakes his head at Otis.

Florence has returned from her date and helps set the table, careful not to break the glass dishes mother received when father and she married. The white and blue dishes were chipped but still beautiful. My mother always cleaned them carefully, and I would often catch her staring down at them with a far away look. I imagine she can see memories reflecting back at her, back when father danced with her in the kitchen.

I look over at him from the corner of my eye. I hated him more each day. I heard about men coming back from the war angry and different, but never heard of a man doing it because he couldn't go. Mother had told me he had lost one of his dearest friends to the war, and that he felt guilty, which I didn't understand. Wouldn't you be glad it wasn't you?

"Suppertime, dear!" my mother calls out to my father. He sits the paper down and stumbles over to the table and takes a seat. The bottle of hooch gets placed in front of his seat like it does every evening. My eyes turn into slits as I scoop the rabbit stew into the bowl in front of him. I hate serving him.

There were many times I dreamt of dumping a hot dish over his head.

Everyone is quiet at dinner tonight, one of the only sounds is Otis' loud chewing and slurping. He eats with one hand, the other still grasping his magic rock. After dinner, I help mother wash dishes while Florence plays with Otis on the living room floor, something she rarely does.

The next few days pass slowly, with the same boring routine. I collect the eggs, wipe the eggs, write under the tree on the hill and rush Otis out of the house when Father becomes engulfed in his rage. At night I sit in bed next to the flickering candle, scribbling words and sketches about the man with a toothpick.

It's Friday night, and as I lay in bed, my mind swims with thoughts of Theodore and of our date the next day.

"Florence?" I whisper in the dark.

"What?"

"Can I borrow one of your dresses tomorrow? I don't want to keep wearing the same one."

"It may be a little tight." Was she calling me heavy?

"The flowy yellow one will work," I say, staring up at the ceiling.

She lets out a heavy sigh, "fine."

I stand in front of the mirror, smoothing out Florence's dress. It did fit looser on her, but I don't think Theodore will notice nor mind it clinging more to my body. It has a sweetheart neckline, flowy sleeves that reach my elbows, and ruffles from the waist down. I have Florence show me how to do my makeup this time, and I apply it softer with no red lips. I pull my curls back behind my head and twist them up before pinning them. I don't want to try too hard, like my sister.

"Fifteen minutes," I say to myself.

To pass time, I go into the living room to play with Otis. I sit next to him while he flies his small metal airplane in the air. I smile at the magic rock he keeps in between his crossed legs. I'm impressed he hasn't lost it yet. "My, that's a fast airplane," I observe.

"I hope it doesn't crash!" he gives me a toothy grin before diving the plane into my arm. I feign excruciating pain, holding my arm and rocking back and forth. His head leans back with laughter and he stands up, holding the toy above his head and running in circles around the sofa. He continues to crash his plane into me, as I continue to fall over and make exploding noises.

My father is in the kitchen slicing a piece of bread when he turns his body to yell at us to quiet down, his arm swinging and knocking one of the white and blue bowls to the ground. Otis and I quickly fall silent when the glass shatters on the floor, shards flying in every direction. My mother lets out a loud gasp as she stops chopping potatoes at the table.

As quickly as the bowl shattered, my mother is standing up and yelling. I had not seen her yell before. She is waving the knife she had cut potatoes with in her hand, screaming at my father for always drinking and breaking the only item she had kept from when they first married.

My father's hand grips the wrist of the hand that is holding the knife, and he strikes her face, sending the knife flying across the kitchen. "Otis, go outside," I whisper, getting onto my knees and pulling him up from the floor where he sits. He stares at our parents, body frozen in place. "Now!" I snap, as I try to yank him up with me. He pulls away from me and starts to cry.

"Go to your room, please Otis!" I beg as I push him away. My mother is now on her hands and knees on the floor. My father grabs another bowl off the shelf and hurls it at the floor next to her, and it breaks next to her face.

"I'll break every damn bowl if I please!" he slurs, crouching down next to her.

I rush to the kitchen and push my father as hard as I can with both of my hands, causing him to stumble back and fall onto the floor. His hand grabs my ankle and pulls my foot from under me. I land in between him and my mother, glass crunching beneath me. He grabs a piece of glass and points it towards me. "Tell me one reason I shouldn't kill her now!" He yells to my mother, who is screaming for him to stop.

Florence is now in the living room, Otis clinging to her leg. Her eyes are wide and she doesn't move, as if her feet are glued to the floor.

Suddenly, the front door swings open and Theodore barges in, his head swinging around in different directions. He puts both of his hands up and slowly takes a step towards the kitchen.

"Who the hell are you?!" My father grabs the kitchen table and pulls himself up, still holding the piece of glass.

"Calm down. Don't make things worse than they are," Theodore says slowly. My father pants, out of breath and his eyes frantically looking around the room. He looks like an animal backed into a corner.

"Why don't you go outside, go for a drive?" Theodore isn't suggesting, he is commanding. His voice doesn't leave room for argument. My father drops the glass and staggers to the door, before pausing and pushing his body against Theodore's side. He leans in and breathes heavily in his ear, waiting for him to react. Theodore doesn't move, his face stone cold.

"Hmph, that's what I thought," my father says as he exits the house, slamming the door behind him.

Theodore runs over to me, pulling me off the floor and wrapping his arms around me. I realize I'm crying. My mother is off the floor now. She takes a rag off the sink and wipes the blood that drips down her arm. "Are you ok?" he asks us both, pulling me back away from him to look at me.

"Yes," I mumble as my mother nods her head.

"Good, stay here," he orders as he storms out the front door. I stand still for a moment, trying to take in what had just happened. My chest is rising and falling with every heavy breath.

"I'm so sorry, I don't know what I was thinkin'." My mother is staring at the shattered glass on the floor.

"You finally stood up to him!" Florence exclaims as she makes her way over to us. She grabs my mother's hands that are now cut and bleeding. The three of us stand in silence for a minute. "Let's get you cleaned up," Florence says gently as she pulls my mother to the basin of water sitting on the counter.

I slowly walk to the front window and pull back the white curtain to peer outside. Theodore has my father's shirt in his fist, pulling it up towards him. He's saying something to him that I can't make out, and my father's face looks ghastly pale. I see him nod over and over, leaning back to get away from him. Theodore lets go suddenly and my father falls back into the dirt.

Theodore straightens out his vest that he wore over a crisp white shirt and dusts it off as if being near my father had gotten him dirty. He looks up at me and makes his way up the porch steps. I rush out to meet him so he doesn't have to go inside our home again. I see my father taking off in the car, leaving nothing but dust flying up and a crying wife behind him.

"Let me see," Theodore says as he grabs my arm and examines it.

"Why did you come in?" I ask.

"I sat in front of the oak tree for ten minutes. I thought maybe you had forgotten, so I came to check. Then I heard shouting."

"You shouldn't have."

"I'm glad I did. So that was the bully rooster." His hands cup my face as his eyes take in the bruises. I let out a small laugh and shrug. He looks like he wants to say something but no words leave his lips.

"Is your mother alright?" He asks. I nod and try to keep the tears from my eyes. "Then let's get you out of here."

I want to tell him I need to stay with my family, but this is just a part of our normal life at this point. "Let me say goodbye to Otis first," I tell him as I pull away.

Inside, I find Otis sitting on my mother's lap and talking about his magic rock. She gives me a weak smile and keeps her hand on his head, running her fingers through his hair. "I'm going to leave with Theodore for a while."

"Can I come?" Otis looks up at me.

"Sorry, not this time." I walk over and kiss his forehead. I turn on my heels and go to walk out the door, but before I close it behind me, I turn to my mother and say, "I'm proud of you." I close it before she can respond and before I can see her expression.

Theodore is standing by his white and gold car, and I finally take in how he looks today. He didn't wear a suit today, but a more casual outfit. He wore a gray vest over a white long sleeve dress shirt with gold cufflinks, his pants match the vest and his black tie pulls it all together. But the best part of it all was the toothpick that twirled in his mouth as he watched me walk up to him.

"You look handsome," I say shyly, my cheeks warming up.

"Thank you," he tips his black hat at me and opens my door.

I smooth out my dress as he gets in on his side and starts the car. I try to think of something to say but can't. "I had planned a picnic, I'm not sure how good the food will be by now," he tells me. I look over at him, stunned. A picnic? Isn't that too romantic for a second date? It is impressive and rather sweet that he packed food for us. When I don't respond immediately, he raises an eyebrow and asks, "Don't care for picnics?"

"No, no I do. I am just flabbergasted you thought of that," I admit.

The edges of his mouth raise and he chuckles. "I always love your choice of words."

"What do you mean?"

"You just speak differently than where I'm from is all. For instance, you say 'ain't'," he says as he puts the car into a faster speed. I furrow my eyebrows and cross my arms.

"Y'all don't say ain't in New York?"

"Nor do we say 'y'all'." Theodore looks over with a grin. I don't know whether to be embarrassed or not, but with the way he's looking at me I really don't care.

"Maybe you should bring it over there, I bet they'd quite like it," I respond with a smile.

"Or maybe you should."

His words catch me off guard and I suck in air. "I think most of the food should still be alright, if you feel up to eating," he says before I can think of a way to reply. I am grateful for the change in conversation and nod my head.

We drive for a little while before he pulls off onto a curvy road and stops at the bottom of a large hill. "Say, how about way up there?" He squints and points to the top.

“Making me really work for this picnic, aren’t you?” I eye the size of the hill and back at him.

He pulls a basket out of the back seat and grabs a folded red and white checkered blanket. I hear clanking sounds rattling from inside the wicker basket as he treks up the hill, looking behind him to make sure I am coming.

By the time we reach the top, I lean over, out of breath. Theodore acts as if he’s just taken a leisurely stroll and lays the blanket out under one of the trees. “Look at that view!” He stands with his hands on his hips and looks over the land, lush with flowers and tall green grass. “And here I thought Texas was all flat dusty land!”

We sit down next to each other and he pulls out a bottle of wine and two crystal glasses. My stomach turns in nervousness as I eye the alcohol. “It’s not illegal to consume it,” he reminds me.

“I know, just to sell it. But I haven’t had wine before.”

“Well, it won’t burn like whiskey or moonshine.” He pops the cork open and pours the red liquid into a glass.

“I haven’t had that either. I haven’t drank before,” I say softly as I lift the glass and stare down at it.

“Oh, I forgot how young you are. Nevermind.” He reaches to take it back and I pull my hand away. I swiftly put the glass to my mouth and lean my head back, emptying the entire thing into my mouth.

He puts his hands behind his back on the blanket and observes me. “I’m not that young.”

"Well, you were supposed to sip that," he pulls the toothpick out of his mouth and takes a small drink of his wine.

"Oh."

He leans over and refills my drink before pulling food out of the basket. He sets out two plates, silverware, some kind of bread that was in twists, ham sandwiches, deviled eggs, grapes and two small slices of cake.

"Wow, where did you get all of this?" I stare at the cake, not able to remember the last time I had any.

"Various places next to my hotel." He unfolds a napkin on his lap and hands one to me.

We eat the sandwiches first, looking around and taking in the scenery. "How long has your father been like that?" he questions as he pulls apart the bread and sits a piece on my plate.

"Since I can remember."

"Hooch can do that to a man."

"Don't make it right."

"No, I suppose it doesn't."

"Let's talk about something else."

Theodore stretches his long legs in front of him and pops a grape in his mouth. His stubble had turned into a very short beard in the few days it's been since I've seen him. I liked it. It made him seem even older and more distinguished, far from the boys that ran around town.

"Tell me about your writing." His eyes are looking down at my feet and they make their way up to my knees. I tug my dress down to cover them, feeling self conscious and silly. I had worn my stockings and garter to try to appear older and more fashionable, but I still feel like a child playing dress up.

"I don't know what to tell you."

"Well, what do you write?"

"Just all sorts of things, random thoughts I have, things I've done."

"Do you write about me?"

I grab the wine and take a few big gulps, my mouth suddenly dry. I grab the bottle and fill it to the rim again, taking a few more generous sips. His mouth curls and opens slightly in amusement.

My head starts to tingle and my body feels light, like I could jump off the hill and float away. "That's your fourth glass," he observes.

"I 'spose it is," I giggle and cover my mouth after how loud it came out. What was wrong with me? I lean back on the picnic blanket as my head spins like a top.

"You never answered my question, doll." He scoots to lay next to me and folds his hands under his head as he looks up to the sky.

"I write about things I think about," I answer as I turn to look at him.

"I think about you," his voice sounds deeper as he speaks. Like someone put gravel down his throat. His eyes flicker down to my lips and I feel my heart start pounding out of my chest. All of my nerves are gone, my body just gently humming and buzzing.

"What do you think about?" I mutter, my face an inch from his.

"This." He puts his hand behind my head, my hair weaving in between his fingers. He shifts his body to where he hovers half over me, one knee in between my legs and the other on the outside of my leg. His other hand braces himself as he leans down and touches his lips to mine. I close my eyes and open my lips a little as I breathe him in.

He smells like cigars and tastes like grapes, and his body heat makes me want to raise my chest to touch his. The kiss deepens as his hand releases the back of my head and makes its way to my collar bone. His palm slides up to my neck and his hand gently wraps around it, making me moan softly into his lips.

It trails down to my dress and he slides a hand in and touches my chest. I tense up in surprise and he pulls off of me, taking his warmth and scent with him. I lean up in exasperation, not wanting whatever was happening to end. When I sit up my vision blurs and the trees spin.

"I apologize," he clears his throat as he sits up on his knees. He adjusts his tie and then his pants. I feel my face heat up and I avert my eyes.

"Don't be sorry," I mumble. If he was sorry, that must mean he regretted kissing me. Did I kiss like Otis? I sure didn't feel like a four year old boy at that moment, I felt like a grown woman who came alive for the first time. He starts to grab the food and put it into the picnic basket. I watch as he sets the cake that we had not yet eaten up and closes the basket.

“Well, you acted as if I did something wrong.” His voice sounds irked and I start to panic.

Thoughts race through my head and I sit up and my head spins, “no, no I am sorry. I don’t know what’s wrong with me.”

“Perhaps you shouldn’t have drunk half the bottle of wine,” Theodore accuses. I feel my heart squeeze and a lump forming in my throat. I was ruining our second date. I shouldn’t have gotten stiff when he was only doing what a grown man does. I was acting like a child.

“I’m sorry, Theodore. It’s my fault, I truly am sorry,” I mutter, “I’m having a grand time.”

He lets out a sigh and rakes his hand through his thick hair. “It’s fine,” he mumbles, sitting back down next to me. I chew on my lip as I look back over at him.

“We can continue,” I offer, but it comes out like a pitiful plea.

“It’s kind of ruined now,” he responds.

I try to not let him see the tears swell up in my eyes, embarrassment washing over me. Ruined. I ruined it. “Sorry, it’s fine,” he finally offers, and gives me a tight smile. I smile back and swipe a tear off my cheek.

We sit in silence for a while, and he reaches over and softly touches my hand on the blanket. Relief fills me when he does it, he wasn’t terribly angry with me after all. “I should probably get you home soon.”

I want to beg him to not take me back. But instead, I simply smile and help him fold up the blanket. We make our way down the hill and I replay the kiss over and over in my head. How he tasted, the soft inhale he took as his lips touched mine.

We drive back to my house and this time he doesn't stop at the oak tree. I figure if he saw the darkness that hid behind the door of my home, he could drop me off at the porch.

"Thank you for the picnic. And for...well, for coming in when you did," I tell him as he shuts the passenger door after I get out. I want to ask him exactly what he had said to my father when they were alone, but I don't.

"Of course." He leans in and kisses my cheek quickly. I try to hide my disappointment that it was only on the cheek. I stand there for a moment before turning to walk up the steps.

"Come to Dallas with me next Friday? For the weekend?" he asks as my foot touches the first step. I turn around in shock. My head is still humming from the wine and I stutter trying to find an answer.

"I-I don't think it would be proper," I say slowly.

"In separate rooms, of course. Your own private room," he offers.

"I'm not sure, I mean I would love to but..." I breathe, my thoughts racing. Was that appropriate? Isn't it way too soon for weekend getaways?

"Pardon me, forget I asked," he says respectfully, tipping his hat and making his way around his car.

He opens it to slide in and I call out, "Wait!" He looks over at me and waits.

"I'd love to spend the weekend with you," I add, "in separate rooms."

A smile spreads across his face. "I'll pick you up around four."

I make my way up to the porch and wave goodbye as he drives away. Once in my bedroom, I collapse on the bed and little stars appear when I close my eyes. I try to count them, but a new one sparks as one disappears.

I hear footsteps and the squeaking of Florence's bed. "I'm waiting!" she exclaims.

"He took me on a picnic. I drank over half a bottle of wine. We kissed, it was amazing. I felt like I was flying," I confess. I hear her gasp.

"But I ruined it."

"What do you mean ruined it?"

"He reached inside the top of my dress, and I made a big deal out of it by getting flustered."

I hear her groan and I open my eyes to see her shaking her head. "You can't act like a timid deer, Hazel." She clicked her tongue in disapproval.

"I just wasn't expecting it...I don't think I'm ready for that," I softly admit. The words come out like a whisper.

"Then maybe you aren't ready for dating a man like that. Grown men have needs. You can't tease them!" She sounds exasperated. I sigh and run my hands over my face. I am in over my head. I'm a seventeen-year-old from a tiny town and he is a twenty-six-year-old from New York. My mind wanders, thinking about all the women he probably runs into from big cities. Grown women, with sultry voices and experience. Women who would let him do far more than put a hand in their brassiere.

"I won't mess it up next time," I say, more to myself than to Florence.

"I sure wouldn't. If I let a man like that slip through my fingers, I would never forgive myself!" She sounds as if she has been daydreaming about him all day. I cut my eyes over to her and give her a look. She shrugs her dainty shoulders and lays back in her bed on top of the quilt.

That night I toss and turn, unable to sleep. I feel torn on my commitment to going to Dallas. It felt sudden. But I felt like I had known Theodore for my whole life, and I wanted to spend every minute with him before he went back to New York. I replay the kiss in my head over and over until I finally succumb to sleep.

Five

The next few days pass swiftly. We were all on edge the day after my father had his huge outburst that was stopped by Theodore. But to our shock, John simply brooded in his chair with his drink and newspaper. He didn't hit any of us, not even once. He continued to berate us and yell, but that didn't hold in comparison to the violence he usually inflicted. His hand raised once to my mother, but something flickered across his face and he slammed it down on the table instead.

I remember the look he had on his face when Theodore was speaking to him. He hadn't come back home till the next morning. I wonder what Theodore had told him.

"We haven't been getting as many eggs as usual, did we lose a chicken?" my mother asks on a sunny Thursday morning. I sit at the table wiping down the last egg and I gnaw on my lip.

"I let one of the hens keep a few eggs to hatch," I admit.

She looks over her shoulder at me. "Did you now? It would be useful to have more chickens," she reckons. I sigh in relief and stand up to help her at the stove. I whisk the eggs as she makes the dough for biscuits.

"So, I have somethin' I need to tell you," I begin. I feel the mood in the air shift and she looks over at me, her hands still moving the dough. She nods for me to continue. "Theodore asked me to go to Dallas this weekend, he's stayin' at a hotel there. He said I'd have my own room." I gulp.

I realize how ridiculous it sounds. What young lady travels to stay in a hotel for the third date? It was too soon. But Theodore didn't seem like the type to waste time. And I was the type that shouldn't even get this chance to begin with. I couldn't waste it.

She is quiet for a moment and then her hands stop working. "You are old enough to start making your own choices, Hazel. I can't stop you. I don't think it's a good idea. Please be careful. I don't know about him-" before she can finish I cut her off.

"He's the reason you haven't had a split lip this week," I remind her, trying to sound gentle and not harsh. She ponders for a minute before replying.

"I think it's time we had a certain talk."

"Mama! I am seventeen, it's too late for that."

"Are you positive? Because you need to be aware of what men try to swindle you into," she starts to warn.

"Please!" I hold my hand up and groan.

"Just be a lady." She sounds as if she's begging me, not just asking. I wonder if she would think I was a lady if she knew I drank half a bottle of wine and wanted to drown in his kisses.

"I like him a lot." I pour the eggs into the cast iron skillet and watch them sizzle.

"I know you do," is the only response I get. I feel frustration creep up and I want to tell her she doesn't get an opinion on my choice of men. Theodore was more of a man than John could ever be.

I sit under the tree after breakfast, writing in my journal. I stare down at my sloppy handwriting. I am pretty sure I have misspelled half the words. I write about the man who tasted like grapes, the man who made my stomach do flips when he touched me. I write how next time I will not ruin it with my immaturity.

What I don't write is how the look he gave me after he sat up made me want to crawl under a rock and hide. How embarrassed I was that I drank too much by accident. I don't write about the chocolate cake that I didn't get to eat because I ruined the moment.

That night before bed, Florence sits up with me talking. "So, separate rooms? Are you sure he isn't just saying that and it's only the one?" She raises an eyebrow.

My hands get clammy at the thought. "No, I don't think he would do that." I try to convince myself as well as her.

"If you say so. Even if you have separate rooms, you know if you go into his at any point what is bound to happen," she smirks.

"I am not discussing that with you!" I fluster.

"Just remember, if it's not you, it's someone else," she says under her breath. My head snaps over to look at her and I rub the back of my neck. I wonder if she's right, or if she's just had horrible taste in the boys she dates. But at this point she has way more wisdom on the subject than I do.

Later, I lay in the dark with my stomach in knots. I pull the quilt off so I will stop sweating and can finally drift off.

The next day I walk through the living room with a bag packed for the weekend, my mother's eyes fixed on it as she knits on the sofa. "Hazel...," her voice trails off.

"Be a lady," I recite with an annoyed undertone. She takes a deep inhale and closes her eyes before exhaling.

I walk out the front door and close it behind me. Otis greets me from the steps where he sits. "I'm waiting," he states. I sit next to him and set my bag in my lap.

"Waiting for what?" I push his hair out of his eyes.

"That man to come over. I like him."

I blink a few times and respond, "I like him too."

"Can I go with you?" He glances at my bag.

"No bud, you can't. But maybe one day." He puts his chin in his hand and looks toward the large oak tree. His magic rock is cradled in his other hand as he waits.

Just a few minutes later, Theodore pulls up in his shiny car and Otis jumps up and races to him. "Hey mister, I sure like this!" Otis exclaims as his hands drag across the bumper of the vehicle.

"Otis, don't touch!" I scold.

"It's fine," Theodore holds up his hand and makes his way over to me. He grabs my bag and kisses my forehead, causing me to blush. "You look pretty," he compliments me. I thank him as Otis comes up and tugs my green dress.

"Can you ask him if I can come?" he begs. I hush him and Theodore bites his lip to hide a smile.

"I'll tell you what, I hear you have a treasure bag. Why don't I give you something to put in it?" Theodore proposes.

Otis' eyes get as wide as saucers and his head nods up and down quickly. Theodore holds up a finger, signaling for him to wait as he turns back to his car. He returns with three peppermints in his hand, and a quarter. He places it in Otis' hand, causing Otis' mouth to hang open. "Gee, thanks!" he exclaims and takes off towards the house.

"You didn't have to give him that much, he doesn't know the difference between a penny and a quarter," I smile at Theodore.

"But *you* do." He winks at me and carries my bag to the car. He sets it in the back seat and opens the passenger door.

As I sit down, I try to take a calming breath to settle my nerves. Theodore climbs in next to me and I take in his appearance. He has worn something different each time I have seen him, making me squirm in my green dress. I had brought Florence's yellow dress for tomorrow, so at least I didn't have to wear the same thing two days in a row.

He wore all black today, his jacket just slightly darker than the vest underneath. Even his tie and shoes were black. The only hint of color was the golden gleam of the pocket watch that peaked under his suit. I liked him in black, it was what he was wearing the day I bumped into him at the seamstress' shop.

"Tell me, have you ever been to a theater?" Theodore asks as his hands lightly hold the wheel, gently turning it to avoid dips in the dirt road.

"No, I haven't."

"Well, after tonight you can say that you have. I have two tickets to the Majestic Theater, apparently it's quite something."

I sit up in my seat and take a panicked look at my dress and my scuffed shoes. The Majestic Theater? I can't fathom how much the tickets had cost, and how elegant all the women who would be attending would look. The Majestic Theater had been in the newspaper headlines for months when it opened, rumored to have cost 30 million dollars to build. My head couldn't even grasp that amount of money when Florence had told me.

"That's not necessary, truly. I left my fancier dress at home," I lie to him.

"Nonsense." He waves his hand in the air, "I already got you something to wear."

My stomach turns when the words leave his mouth and my mouth hangs open. He bought me something? "No, no that's too much," I protest, feeling uncomfortable and starting to wish I had stayed at home. A man shouldn't buy someone a dress on their third date, should he? I need Florence here, she would know.

"It's nothing, I swung by the seamstress that you swindled. Figured I would make her cash register right by buying one of those sequined dresses she had on display." A smirk took over his face as his toothpick rolled to the other side of his mouth. I turn red and put my hand over my mouth to hide my smile.

I find myself at a loss for words once again. It seems this is a common occurrence when I am around him. "Well, if there was any kind of drama happening in the shop while you paid, she probably didn't even count it," is all I can think of to say after a moment of silence. He shakes his head and the car picks up speed.

"Figured we would go to the hotel, put your bags up and let you get dressed. Then dinner prior to the theater?"

I nod in response, my mind racing. Did he really mean for me to get dressed? Or did he have other intentions? I chew on my lip and gaze out the window. "Deep in thought?" he asks.

I look over at him and give a smile. "Just a little nervous," I answer as honestly as I can. He gives me a look that helps settle my upset stomach and his hand reaches over for mine. I slip my hand in his, amazed at the difference in their sizes. His hands are slightly rough, with little knicks and scars scattered about.

"No need to be nervous," he assures me. I try to believe him, because being next to him feels so right, but something I can't pinpoint feels slightly wrong. Maybe it was my mother's disapproving scowl when I walked out the door after mocking her. I feel a stab of guilt and try to shake it off. She didn't have the right to suddenly parent me after sitting idly by while my father beat us.

"What is your favorite memory from childhood?" Theodore questions after ten minutes of silence. I look over in surprise.

"That is quite random," I say, unsure of what my answer is.

"Mine was when I must have been around ten or so, and my father took me to a horse race. He always had a bag of peanuts in his pocket. We sat there and ate peanuts while we watched. He won a lot of money that day," Theodore muses. "I remember the look on his face when he found out how much money he had won. He put me on his shoulders when we left. That was one of the best days I had as a kid."

I smile as he shares his memory with me, feeling grateful that I get to hear it. I wonder how many other women he had told this story to. I tell myself maybe I am the only one who knows it.

I think for a minute, memories of my childhood flicking through my mind. Most of them were bad. My parents yelling, items being thrown at walls, Florence getting asked to the town's dance and not me, us going to bed with our stomachs hurting from hunger. Finally, I smile and land on one.

"The day my brother was born," I answer. "My mother had such a fast labor. She had sent Florence to get the closest neighbor, but it took her too long to run down there and mother had Otis in the living room. I was there, absolutely horrified the whole time because I thought she was going to die. But then Otis was born and I was the first one who got to hold him."

"That must have been something to experience, especially so young." Theodore shakes his head like he can't imagine having to see what I had seen.

"It was horrible and beautiful." I look out the window and smile as I remember Otis' cries and the way his tiny hand held onto my finger. In that moment, I had felt such a strong urge to protect him, even at that young age.

The two hour drive to Dallas flies by quickly as we tease each other and ask questions to get to know one another better. Theodore's favorite color is black, he has two brothers, his father died from a gunshot wound, his favorite kind of food is pasta and he hates cats. He doesn't elaborate much on how his father passed and it felt too invasive to ask any questions.

My eyes take in the tall buildings and crowded streets as we enter Dallas. I haven't seen so many vehicles in my life! People of all colors and sizes bustle through the doors of the shops, muttering what I assume are apologies to each other as they bump shoulders. We pull to a stop as people walk with urgency in front of us to cross the road. Men from different directions nod towards Theodore's car, eyes wide and faces full of envy. I could see what they were thinking, it was what I thought, too, when I first saw it...how could anyone afford such a car?

"Here we are!" Theodore clears his throat as he turns the wheel to pull in front of a large hotel.

"The Adolphus," I whisper, reading the words out loud. A man in a suit steps out into the street and opens my door.

"Mr. Greenwood," the man nods to Theodore as he motions for me to step out. I realize I didn't even know his last name until now. Theodore Greenwood.

I step onto the brick sidewalk in front of the towering hotel. Theodore exits the car as the man gets into the driver seat, grabbing my bag and stepping next to me. He looks up at the building with me, glancing at me from the corner of his eye.

The building was made up of small red bricks, with cream trim and large windows and details etched everywhere. Men carried luggage through the large swinging doors that glistened from a fresh cleaning.

"You're staying here?" I ask, marveling at the building's beauty.

"For now." Theodore puts a hand on the small of my back and guides me through the doors. For now. I remind myself that he lives in New York as we make our way to the front desk.

The hotel is filled with people, multiple accents and voices drifting through the lobby. I notice the lighting everywhere, electricity is something we can't afford and something we always dreamed of. "Mr. Greenwood, is this your friend who is occupying the suite this evening?" A tall man with a gray beard stands behind the counter. Theodore nods and takes a key with a piece of paper tied to it from the man's hand. Mr. Greenwood, that's two people who knew his name without asking it first.

Theodore grabs my hand with my bag in his other and we make our way to a black wall covered in golden detailing. A large screen sits in front of what looks to be a giant door. Theodore presses a button that was mounted on the wall next to it and it lights up red. I stand in silence, slightly confused as other people make their way next to us. We stand there waiting until Thedore pulls the screen to the side and pushes open the door.

It's a tiny room with no other opening. "An elevator," he chuckles at my bewildered expression, guiding me inside it. I feel slightly panicked as the rest of the people enter in front of us. I can no longer see the door because of the tall men in front of me. Someone closes the door and the screen, and I feel a jolt as the elevator starts to move up. I clutch Theodore's arm and take a deep breath. "First time riding one?" he whispers close to my ear, his toothpick brushing my neck. The hair on my arm stands up at his close proximity.

"Yes, I have heard of them, of course. But I never used one," I answer, inching towards him to avoid touching the other riders.

Just as quickly as we had gotten on, we are no longer moving and begin making our way out of the elevator. "Fourth floor," Theodore says as he takes a left once we exit the elevator, pulling me behind him. The carpet has a golden hexagon pattern that goes as long as my eyes can see, causing my vision to almost blur. Rows of doors line the walls on both sides of the hall.

We make our way down the hall for a few minutes before he stops at a door and reads off the number displayed on it. "Three twelve," he announces, unlocking the door and pushing it open. As we step inside, I freeze in place. The room is bigger than half our house, and ten times fancier. A big light fixture hangs above the large white sofa, a round table sits in the middle of the room with the biggest bouquet of flowers I have ever seen.

"This is too much," I say as I start to back out the door. Theodore's hand firmly plants itself on my back and inches me forward as he shuts the door behind us.

"You don't realize what you are worth, Hazel." Theodore smiles and walks in front of me, opening one of the doors that was behind the sofa. He disappears into the room and quickly comes back without my bag.

"I ain't ever seen a room like this," I remark as I sit down slowly on the sofa, sinking back onto the decorative pillows.

"I've never seen a *girl* like you," Theodore says as he stands behind the couch and puts his hands on my shoulders. My breathing hitches and I feel my stomach turn.

"I'll let you get dressed. I put everything on your bed, is thirty minutes enough time?" he asks, walking back to the door.

"Plenty," I answer. He smiles, nods and shuts the door behind him.

Six

I sit in the giant room, feeling as small as ever. If Florence could only see this. I grab a flower out of the vase and carry it with me as I make my way into the room Theodore had gone into.

My bag sits on a wooden bed that was four times the size of mine at home, the walls covered in a modern wallpaper with paintings hung on them. I sit the rose down on the bed as I stare at the large box that's next to my bags. I pull the lid off and lift up the red dress. The tassels feel almost like feathers in my hands, the top shimmering with tiny sequins. It's the most beautiful thing I have ever held and I feel too dirty to hold it. I get up and quickly find the bathroom, washing my hands in the golden sink. Running water in the house, another thing we don't have.

I return to the dress and shimmy off my green one, folding it up on the bed. I stand there in my slip and stockings, admiring the dress. I pull it over my head and let it fall down past my knees. It feels like what I always thought luxury would feel like, soft against my skin.

I go into the bathroom and stand in front of the mirror. I stare at my reflection, barely recognizing myself. I look like someone of importance, someone who matters in the world. I hurry back to my bag and get the rouge mother had sent with me. I make my way over to the mirror and carefully dab it on my lips.

I pace back and forth for what feels like hours, planning my every word and movement for when we go to dinner. I remind myself to cross my legs and to sit straight. "Don't talk too much, don't talk too little," I mutter to myself and jump at the knock on the door.

I pause before opening it, and as soon as my eyes fall on Theodore my nerves disappear. "My God," he breathes, "you are the most astounding thing I have ever seen!"

I blush and step out, grabbing his hand. "Thank you, I haven't owned such a beautiful thing before," I say as I look down at the red dress.

"Well, I plan to get you quite used to fine things." He grins and tugs my hand down the hall, "let's go to dinner."

As we make our way onto the sidewalk and head towards the restaurant, I walk with pride for the first time in my life. I feel like I am floating on clouds and don't shy away from the glances we both get. "Say, that dress really is something with your hair." Theodore's eyes glance down at me as we walk.

"Well, keep talking like that and my cheeks will match it." I smile and look at my moving feet.

"They say this place is new, have you ever been here?" he asks me as he holds the large door open to the restaurant. I know he is asking out of formality rather than truly wondering, as it was apparent how poor I was by now.

"I have not," I answer.

The restaurant is large and crowded, people occupying all of the tables that were adorned with lace tablecloths and tall candles. A woman with a low bun stood at the entrance, holding a pen and a large notepad. "How many dining today?" she asks, blinking her eyes up at him in a flirty way.

"I have reservations, Theodore Greenwood," he informs her. A big smile crosses her face and she turns her eyes to me. They flick up and down to take in my frame. I stand up a little taller, trying to appear older and more sure of myself.

"This way," she finally says, and sharply turns and walks off, her heels clacking on the tile. We follow her to a table in the corner.

Once we sit, I look around and shake my head. "This must be the nicest restaurant in all of Texas," I tell him, counting how many tables there are. I stop at thirty-eight and look back at Theodore. He sits silently, his eyes watching me intently.

A waiter wearing a suit appears and holds his arm behind his back as he greets us. "May I take your order?" he asks. I open my mouth to say I haven't looked at the menu yet, but Theodore starts to speak.

"We will both have the filet, red in the middle and potatoes on the side."

The waiter gives a curt nod and walks off stiffly. Theodore's gaze never leaves me, even when he ordered, which makes me shift in my chair. "You deserve all of this, to experience this all the time." Theodore uses his hand to motion to the restaurant.

"Hardly," I mumble and pick at the lace on the tablecloth. I look down at it and pull a loose thread out and set it on my lap.

"Look at me," Theodore says. "This dinner is nothing in comparison to what you should have." No words come out of my mouth as I try to speak, my brain is empty and I feel jittery. I manage to smile a little and nod. "Plus, I think I may have to fight off all of the men with you wearing that dress. They have been staring," he tsks with a smirk.

"They have not!" I protest.

"Hazel, you are blind." He laughs and pulls the toothpick out of his mouth and sets it in his suit pocket.

The waiter arrives and sets a bucket full of ice and a tall jar of water on the table. "I love ice," I comment. Theodore starts to laugh and raises an eyebrow. "Summers here are so hot you truly couldn't believe it. Most of us folks don't ever get to have ice, and boy you would kill for it in August," I explain, watching water drip down the bowl.

"I haven't experienced a summer here, don't think I would enjoy it much. Our winters in New York get rather cold, I bet you don't get snow like we do. You think you like ice until it's hanging off everything outside." He pours the water into my crystal glass.

"I've never seen snow," I say.

"It's never snowed here?"

"No, I would love to see it one day."

"I would love for you to see it as well," he says with a certain undertone, like he means he hopes I see it *with* him.

Our food arrives quickly and I am shocked at the portions. Heaps of red potatoes sit next to the steak that's smothered in butter. Meat was rationed at home. Other than the occasional chicken, most of our meals went without it. I take a bite and put a napkin over my mouth as my eyes widen. "This is the best thing I think I have ever tasted," I tell him, nodding my head in approval. He smiles and takes a drink of his water.

We make small talk as we eat, he talks more about New York and the weather they get there. He tells me there's a pond by his home that freezes over in the winter and you can slide across it if you are brave enough. "Just don't do it as it nears spring. A friend of mine fell in a few years back," he chuckles.

I laugh with him and sit my fork down on the plate. "I hate to be wasteful, but I don't think I can eat another bite," I admit, hoping it wasn't terrible etiquette to not finish my food. My stomach feels stretched to capacity and I am afraid I will burst if I eat more. Theodore has already finished his plate and sticks a toothpick in his mouth.

"Of course, let's head to the theater." He stands up, grabs a few bills out of his money roll and tosses it onto the table. I cough on my spit when I see the amount, my eyes bugging out of my head. He couldn't have spent that much on *food*! Food for one night? That much could feed our family for a month. "Don't even worry about it," he warns me, my thoughts obvious.

I press my lips together and take his hand as I stand. We make our way to the front door of the restaurant. "Have a swell evening, Mr. Greenwood!" the hostess exclaims as we exit. I feel a little jealous at her blatant attraction to Theodore and I wonder if he thinks she is pretty.

"It's right here on Elm street," he tells me and pulls me close to him as we stroll. The sun is setting and the sky projects an orange hue over everything. I see a few men stumbling around on the street. They are loud and obviously drunk. Cars honk at them and they kick their bumpers as they pass.

I see the red flashing sign of The Majestic Theater as soon as we turn onto Elm street. You didn't even notice the buildings that sat next to it because it was so large and grand, like it was the only building on the entire street. It reminded me of Theodore, expensive and lavish looking, commanding everyone's attention.

People file through the doors, a few standing outside to smoke and talk. Laughter and conversation fill the air as we make our way closer. Theodore ushers me in front of him as a man holds the large golden door open. I feel excitement rush over my body as my eyes dart everywhere, overwhelmed by what I see. The floor is marbled, a grand staircase with white columns on both sides sits in front of us, the ceiling even has designs and intricate details on the edges where it meets the walls.

"I take it you're impressed?" Theodore whispers in my ear, causing my arm hair to stand up. "I never imagined it to be so…" I trail off, unable to find the right word.

"It's supposed to be quite the show tonight. A magician and acrobats." He smiles, guiding me to the stairs. I'm not sure what an acrobat is, but I don't want to sound dumb so I don't ask.

"This whole evening feels like a dream," I tell him, looking at the stair railing as we make our way up. It shines as if someone's only job was to sit and buff it every morning. I drag my hand across it as we continue up the stairs. Once we reach the top we take a left, and Theodore shows our tickets to a man standing in front of an open door. He moves to the side to let us pass and I gasp at the rows and rows of seats. People are shuffling everywhere to get seated, scooting past each other to get to their spot.

We walk down a few aisles and squeeze past the people sitting on the end until we get to where Theodore stops. We both sit down on cushioned chairs and I look down at the stage below. Even more people sit below us and I don't think I have ever seen so many people in one building. A large red curtain hangs on the stage, fluttering from movement behind it.

We both sit in anticipation when the curtain opens slightly and a small pudgy man steps out. The whole theater quiets and I see everyone's backs straighten in excitement.

"Welcome to the Majestic Theater! Tonight, you won't believe your eyes when you see one of the best magicians there has ever been...Alberto Ewig! And you surely will be on the edge of your seats when you lay eyes on the daring and brave Viola Sisters, who will be performing their acrobatic act for you fine ladies and gentlemen!" He bellows as loudly as possible, his voice echoing in the theater.

Everyone claps and nods their heads to each other, eager for the show to begin. "Without further ado, Alberto Ewig..." he announces, exiting to the right of the stage behind more curtains. Clapping rings in my ears and the main curtains pull to the side as a tall man wearing a jet black suit stands in the middle of the stage.

A skinny blonde stands next to him in a rather short, shiny dress. The woman walks slowly up to him, twirling her hair and blinking her eyes furiously. Everyone laughs at the obnoxious display of flirting. *This would be the perfect job for Florence.* She stands in front of him and puts her finger to her mouth and blinks her eyes again. The man shivers dramatically and pats his pockets with a bewildered expression. Out of thin air a wand appears in his hand and we all gasp. I squint, trying to figure out where the wand came from. The woman stomps her foot and huffs, unimpressed. He turns and looks at the crowd and rolls his eyes, causing everyone to laugh. Suddenly he swirls his hand in the air and a rose appears in it. The woman claps and snatches it, twirling happily as applause fills the room again.

I finally pull my eyes from the scene to look at Theodore, and to my surprise he is staring at me, instead of the performers, with a smile on his face. “Did you see that? He pulled a rose out of nowhere!” I whisper excitedly.

“Did he?” he grins, still not looking at the stage.

A loud noise comes from the stage and I return my focus back to it as a large wooden box is being wheeled out. They open the box to show that the inside is empty and they knock on all the walls to prove they are intact. The magician pulls handcuffs out of a bag and holds them in the air for all to see. He then puts them on the blonde’s hands, cuffing them tightly. She holds them up and pulls to show they are secure. My eyebrows furrow in confusion as she gets into the wooden box. She stands there as the magician then takes a chain and wraps it around her feet many times.

He slams the door shut and locks it. People start to murmur to each other, all slightly confused. He takes a few steps away from the large box and loudly claps his hands together once. A loud explosion causes everyone to jump and smoke floats in the air in front of the box, making it impossible to see. Just as quickly as it happened, it was over. The box still sat in the same place, locked and sturdy as the smoke in front of it fades away. It’s dead silent as the magician unlocks the box and swings the door open. Gasps and rounds of applause fill the silence as everyone leans forward to see the empty box. The woman simply gone.

“How did he do that? That black curtain behind them didn’t open, she couldn't have slipped out of the back using a secret door!” I exclaim to Theodore, not taking my eyes off of the show.

“Magic!” he says teasingly, but I can’t think of another explanation at that moment.

The show passes too quickly, people gasp and laugh through the magician’s impressive act. I wish it would never end, but the man and woman hold hands and take a bow before exiting to the left of the stage.

The main red curtain closes for a few minutes before opening again. There are two women wearing tight silver outfits, with a piece of fabric made of out tassels hanging from their hips. There are a handful of other men and women behind them, but they all wear black. I assume the women in silver are the sisters. I scoot forward eagerly, waiting to find out what “acrobatics” mean.

My eyebrows shoot up to my hairline as both women do backflips at the same time, four right in a row without stopping. Their bare legs show as they do, and I can imagine my mother disapproving at the brazen act. Two muscular men stand as still as statues as each sister climbs onto one and stands on their shoulders, with hands held up high to the ceiling. I watch with my mouth hanging open as the women start slowly making their way into another position.

The crowd gasps and women shriek when the sisters start to balance on the men’s heads with just one hand, it being the only thing holding their bodies up in the air. I want to cover my eyes because I am sure they will fall and break their necks. Their entire legs show now, sticking straight up in the air. The men holler and women gasp at the act. Theodore is watching and clapping now.

Seven

The evening passes quickly, the crowd not wanting to blink and miss a second of the show. The men and women in the act do all sorts of climbing, spinning, body arching and flipping that I didn't know was possible before tonight. I forget all about my life at home, my father's screaming, my mother's tears and Otis always hiding under the front porch.

As the acrobats bow and the red curtains close, I turn to Theodore and smile so hard my cheeks hurt. "I can't believe my eyes. That was the most spectacular thing I have ever seen!" I grab his hands and squeeze them. He looks at me fondly and squeezes them back.

"It was very entertaining, I was unaware people could bend like that," he laughs.

"Thought they would just snap in half!" I exclaim as we stand and follow the lines of people out the door and down the grand stairs.

We stop talking because the chatter is so loud we can't hear each other anymore. People's expressions are the same as mine, eyes big as if they will never be the same after seeing such things. When we exit the building, cool air hits us in the face and sends a shiver down my body. Theodore immediately shrugs off his suit jacket and drapes it around my shoulders.

"Let's head back to the hotel, I could use a drink after that." He smiles and I feel my stomach turn. Did he mean to have a drink together? In a hotel room? I brush off my nervousness and remind myself that if women can hold themselves up with one hand on a man's head, I can sit in a hotel room with one.

We make our way back to the hotel and enter the elevator. I feel less nervous this time, but still uneasy about the contraption. We make our way off the elevator and to room 312. My room. I stand there and watch him pull the key out of his pocket. He opens the door and holds it open, motioning for me to go first. I step inside and he follows me. The door shuts quietly behind us and I stand there in silence, unsure of what to do.

"I had a wonderful evening," he starts, "and it can end now. I would love to sit and have a drink with you, but I understand if you are too tired."

I look back at the sofa and the bouquet of flowers that sit in front of it. A drink won't hurt. "I don't think I can sleep again after the excitement of the show," I answer and walk over to the sofa and sit. Theodore picks up a glass off the cart that is pushed against the wall and pours a dark drink into it.

"I brought this from home. Want a glass?" he offers. I nod and don't bother asking what it is. It looks different than wine, but I don't want to sound like a young girl if I ask.

I sit as lady-like as possible, back straight and ankles crossed. He sits next to me and hands me the glass. He leans back onto the pillows and tilts his glass towards mine. "To a wonderful night together," he offers. We clink our glasses and both take a drink. As it passes my lips it burns my mouth and throat, causing me to sputter and cough. I put my hand to my mouth to try and recover. Theodore laughs and pats my back.

"I'm sorry, I wasn't expecting...that." I wrinkle up my nose and look down into the glass.

"Whiskey is a bit stronger than wine," he admits.

"A bit," I mutter and take a tiny sip again, trying to choke it down.

I don't understand why people drink this for fun, it feels like you're guzzling fire. I let out a loud sigh and start to relax after a few more sips, sinking back into the sofa. "I wish everyday was like this," I say.

"So do I." He sounds sincere as he tucks a piece of my hair behind my ear.

We sit there and discuss the show, laughing at the magician's act. Theodore puts a flower in his sleeve from the table and tries to pull it out without making it noticeable, trying to make it appear out of nowhere. I cough on my drink as I chortle at his ridiculous act, putting my thumb down and booing. He puts his hand to his chest and acts offended.

"I am hurt," he chastises.

"Not as hurt as I am from having to witness that terrible magic trick!" I tease. Our laughter dies down and we sit in silence for a few moments.

"I dread going home tomorrow," I whisper after I finish my drink. He takes it from my hand and walks over to the cart. I watch as he fills my glass and then his own. When he comes back, he sits closer than he did before. He puts the crystal glass to my mouth and tilts it as my hand covers his. I take the glass from him as I swallow, the whiskey barely burning now, the warmth slowly making its way down my body.

"Come to New York with me. I leave Monday," Theodore says as he puts his hand on my knee. I look down at his hand and back at his face, stunned.

"Are you serious?" I gawk. Before he answers, I take three big gulps of the whiskey.

"Very," he answers, his eyes telling me he is.

"I-I can't go with you. It wouldn't be proper. It's scandalous!" I stutter.

"Then marry me."

I start to giggle loudly, unable to stop the laughter from escaping my lips. I cover my mouth and look at him, his expression making me quiet immediately. I expect him to laugh with me but his face is grave with seriousness.

"Hazel," he says sternly. I feel my body buzz and my head tingles again like it did the day of the picnic when I had too much wine.

"Yes?" I quietly ask.

"I am serious. Marry me. I have never met a girl like you, you know you don't want to go back home. They don't deserve you. I'll treat you right, every evening can be like this. Just like this." He sets his whiskey down on the glass table and takes mine and does the same with it.

I stay silent as he takes my hands and shifts closer to me, our legs now touching. "Why wait? We can marry in New York in my church. It'll be grand," he continues, "you don't want to stay with your parents forever, do you? Come with me Monday, I don't want to leave you."

I swallow and stare at him, my mind racing. I think about the moment I laid eyes on him and how my world instantly stopped. How I spent every second since then thinking about him, writing about him or talking about him. And he was right, I don't want to go home.

"But Otis. I can't leave him," I whisper.

"Your father won't lay a hand on him again. I made sure of that," Theodore reassures me.

"How can you be sure?" I chew on my lip.

"You can't always take care of everyone, doll. At some point you have to put yourself and *your* happiness first."

No. This is ridiculous. I can't marry him this soon.

I don't even notice my foot tapping the floor in nervousness and I try to slow down my thoughts. Otis would be ok, he had mother and Florence. My mother. What would she say?

"What if one day we come back for him, if your mother approves?" Theodore asks. "After we get settled," he adds on. I look up at him and smile a little.

"You would be ok with him living with us?"

"Maybe, is that a yes?" He grins.

"I think so." I let out a nervous laugh and shake my head, unable to process everything.

"We leave Monday. Tomorrow, once you're home, pack all of your things. I will call home tonight and have some people start planning the wedding," Theodore proclaims.

My mind is racing. He's talking so quickly.

"When will we get married? Where will I stay until then?" I ask, rubbing my temples and trying to calm my nerves.

"Two weeks. New York is a long drive and it'll give you enough time to settle once we are there. You can stay in the guest house," he assures me, rubbing his hand on my knee. Guest house? People have a separate house for strangers?

"But wait, who will plan the wedding?" I inquire.

"Friends. And I have many people who work for me, it'll get done. You don't need to worry about a thing."

"But-" I start, but before I can get out the rest of my sentence his lips meet mine. My body relaxes and I put a hand on his chest, feeling his heartbeat under my fingers. I close my eyes and part my lips to let him deepen the kiss, and his hand reaches behind my neck and pulls me closer.

His other hand leaves my knee and slides up my leg, leaving my skin tingling. We get lost in each other, our lips colliding and hands running over each other's bodies. Theodore moans softly into my lips, his hands circle my waist and pull me into his lap. My legs straddle his hips and my lips never leave his.

His body hardens under me and I let my hands run from the top of his shirt to his belt.

"I want your dress on the floor," he mutters against my mouth, his hand tugging at the fabric. My stomach flutters and I feel my nerves rise up again, but I shove them down as I sit up and pull the red dress over my head. I blush and want to hide, feeling vulnerable in just my slip. Theodore leans up and pushes my hair behind my shoulders to show more of my body. His hand trails down to my chest and he cups my breast before pulling my head back down to him.

Our lips connect again and his hands run down my back, the roughness of them catching on the silk fabric. He squeezes my hips and we both gasp into each other's mouths. "I love you," I blurt out, my head pounding from the whiskey. His hands still and he pulls back from me, looking at me intensely.

"I love you, too." He grabs my face with both hands and doesn't let go. I smile slowly, tears filling my eyes, and I'm not sure why. I'm not sad. I realize that I have been looked at more in the last few weeks than I ever had been in my life.

"You make me feel seen," I whisper.

He pushes me back onto the couch and hovers over me, staring down at me intently. He unbuttons his shirt and I help him slide it off and toss it onto the floor with my dress. I grab the back of his neck and pull him close to me. "See me," I whisper in his ear.

His mouth crashes down onto mine, and we inhale each other. It doesn't go slow like I always pictured it, but almost frantic and panicked. Like we can't get to each other fast enough, kiss hard enough or undress quickly enough. His pants and my slip get thrown down next to my dress and his shirt.

His hand reaches down, slipping under my panties and between my legs, touching a part of me that has never been touched. I gasp and put my hand on his shoulder as he kisses me deeper.

He continues to touch and kiss me, loving me deeper than I thought possible. My back arches and I feel my whole body explode, my eyes see stars as I lay my head back on the sofa. I breathe heavily and open my eyes to look at Theodore. He grins as he begins to pull my panties down, pausing as if to ask permission. I nod, and he pulls them off, then spreads my legs apart as he slowly kisses his way up my ribs, across my breasts, skimming my collarbone and neck, and finally to my mouth. He reaches one hand between us as he prepares to take me completely.

Our souls intertwine in that moment, and I know I will never be the same. We kiss urgently and his hands grab a fistful of my hair, pulling it as he kisses me deeper. I'm unaware of the time passing as we roll off the couch and onto the pile of clothes on the floor. His hands run all over my body, little stars covering the back of my eyelids when I close my eyes. He huffs loudly and falls onto me just a few moments later and becomes still. "What's wrong?" I breathe, confused and stiff.

He starts to chuckle and shakes his head, pushing himself up with one arm to look at me. "Nothing is wrong, I just sealed the deal" he grins down at me.

I turn red and my mouth opens slightly, "*oh*". We both start to laugh and I feel a little embarrassed but relieved it was over.

"That was amazing, future Mrs. Greenwood!" He rolls off me and lays next to me on the floor. We lay on our backs and stare at the chandelier hanging above us.

Mrs. Hazel Greenwood.

"Do you really want to marry me?" I question, keeping my eyes closed. I prepare myself for him to tell me no, that it was all just a joke.

"Now more than ever." He sounds like he's smirking, so I peak over at him and smile because he is.

"I don't know what my parents are going to say," I mumble.

"It doesn't matter what they say," Theodore states with an annoyed tone. Theodore pushes himself up and stands, smiling down at me. "I suppose I better go back to my room, it's late."

I look up in confusion. "We can save the first night in bed together for our wedding night." He winks, and I laugh because he's right, the bed hasn't been touched. I nod and watch him get dressed, not remotely shy about being stark naked in front of me. I wonder how many women he has been naked in front of.

"Goodnight," he tells me as he turns to leave.

I lay there for a while before sitting up and looking around. Did all of that just happen? My stomach starts to turn and I feel like I may be sick. *I'm not a virgin anymore.* I cover my mouth with my hand. *I'm engaged!*

I stumble into the bedroom and climb into the bed, pulling the covers up to my chin. I can't just go to New York, Otis needs me. He will be heartbroken if I leave him. My thoughts drift away as darkness washes over me, sleep pulling me in.

Eight

A loud banging jolts me awake. I sit up in bed and look around. At first, I'm confused about where I am and what's happening. Then everything comes back to me, and I realize I'm in the hotel room and someone is knocking at the door. I look around for something and grab a decorative blanket and wrap it around myself as I stand up. I make my way to the door and unlock it, cracking it open to peer out of it.

Theodore stands there with a brown sack in his hand and I open it more to let him in. He slips in and closes the door behind him. "Good morning, I brought breakfast!" He holds up the bag and walks into the main area, taking a seat on the sofa. I pull the blanket around me and look over at the bathroom.

"I just woke up, I didn't get ready yet." I touch a hand to my hair, feeling its unruliness. Theodore pulls out a few muffins from the bag and looks over at me with a smile.

"You look beautiful, come eat."

"Just let me get dressed." I disappear back into the room and pull Florence's yellow dress over my head. I try to smooth my hair down with my hands and I go back to the sofa. I sit down next to him and take the blueberry muffin he hands me.

"Do you remember everything from last night?" he asks, crossing his arms and leaning back.

"Yes," I say with a mouth full of muffin, putting my hand in front of my mouth.

"Just making sure, you had a lot of whiskey." He raises an eyebrow.

"I don't know if I can leave Otis. And I haven't ever left Texas..." I trail off, looking away from him.

"I'm not going to force you into anything. But I have to leave on Monday, and I don't want to leave without you."

"Can't you stay a little longer?"

"No, I've already been here a week longer than I was supposed to. I have business back home I have to return to."

I take a deep breath and lean my head back on the sofa. I think of my father's voice, 'you'll always be a McCoy'. I didn't want to spend every day of my life cleaning poop off of eggs and having to watch my mother cower next to the stove. I was tired of going to bed hungry and watching Florence bounce in the door with gifts from her boyfriends.

"What kind of wedding will it be?" I ask Theodore, turning my head to look at him. A smile takes over his face.

"A grand one," he answers.

"Why don't we get married here, before we leave? Then my family can be there!" I grab his hands, but he pulls them away from me and shakes his head.

"I must marry in New York, at my church. It'll be everywhere if I show back up married to some girl no one knows."

I gulp and my face darkens with a frown, hurt by his words. *Some girl no one knows*. "But my family..." I start, before he grabs my hand and interrupts.

"Your family? The family that hits you, berates you, makes you feel invisible?" He sounds irritated. I bite my bottom lip because maybe he's right, why would I want them there anyway?

"Ok. You're right," I agree. He grins and leans over to kiss me.

"If there is anything specific you want, just tell me. Otherwise, I'll have it all taken care of," he promises. I feel butterflies in my stomach and I finish the muffin, looking down and cringing at the crumbs covering my lap. He could have picked something a little less messy.

We pack up and as we exit the lobby, one of the men working for the hotel pulls up front in Theodore's car. Theodore hands him some money and opens my door, closing it behind me after I get seated.

As we drive back home I ask him questions about New York. "How long a drive will it be?"

"We'll take a train, it's much faster," he answers.

"What about your car?" I furrow my eyebrows.

“My brother is coming up to New York next month, he’ll bring it then,” Theodore replies.

“But then you won’t have a car for a month?”

“I have other cars,” he chuckles. I sit in silence and reflect on his answer. He has other cars? Are they as nice as this one? I can’t wrap my head around it, so I shake it off.

“So you have a guest house? Will I stay in it, alone?” I ask.

“Well, yes. But the servants will make sure everything is taken care of, you won't have to do any cleaning or anything like that.” he answers. I look over to see if he was making a joke, but he isn’t laughing.

“You have *servants*?” I scrunch up my nose, feeling like nothing was making sense.

“Yes, it’s common where I’m from,” he answers, keeping his eyes on the road ahead of us.

“What do they do?” I ask.

“Whatever I need, really. I have a chauffeur, butler, maid, and cook. If I need someone to run an errand, I have someone for that, too. I have staff to care for the horses,” he rattles on for a minute, listing all the hired help.

“So,” I pause, “what will I do?”. I try to picture my mother with maids and butlers. She would just sit all day. I can’t just sit.

“You’ll enjoy life!” He looks over and smiles at me. I don’t reply because I don’t know what to say, or what I think. I figure at some point we’ll have babies and then that will be my responsibility.

When we pull up to my house, I stiffen when I see my father's car sitting out front. I'm going to have to tell them I'm leaving. "I'll pick you up around eight in the morning." Theodore reaches over and grabs my hand. I nod and stare out the window as Otis flies out the front door and onto the porch. My heart seizes at the sight of him, knowing I'm going to leave him.

"I don't want to tell him, Theodore," I whisper.

"You can tell him he can come visit soon, I can send someone for him and he can stay the summer with us. Tell him he can come ride the horses." Theodore reassures me, patting my hand. I nod and open my door before he can get out and do it for me. "I love you!" he calls out as I close the door and walk to the porch. I smile and turn to wave goodbye.

"Hazel!" Otis yells, bounding down the porch steps. He flings his arms around me and hugs my legs. "Ma's makin' potatoes for supper," he informs me as we make our way up the steps and into the house. It smells like rosemary and potatoes and the air is warm and heavy from the stove. My mother is standing by the stove, stirring a pot and staring blankly at the wall in front of her.

"Hello, mama," I greet her, standing by the kitchen table. She turns and gives me a weak smile, her face making my stomach sink.

"He hit you!" I groan. Her eyebrow has a large knot above it.

"He didn't mean to, it was an accident." She hushes me with her hand and continues to stir the potatoes.

"Do you hear yourself? An accident? How many times has he done this! I can't even count." I say exasperatedly as I sit down.

"It's my fault, I wasn't payin' no attention to where I was walking and I knocked his drink over. His whole bottle went all over the floor, and he stood up so fast that he made me fall over." I put my face in my hands and let out a sigh. "You needn't worry about me, Hazel." My mother says. I look up at her with frustration.

"Yes, I do! Because I am leaving tomorrow mama, I am going to New York. I am marrying Theodore and *you* are all that Otis will have. *You* are going to have to protect him from the monster you call a husband!" I try to keep my voice down but it starts to rise.

"What!" Otis and my mother exclaim at the same time.

I look over and cringe when I see Otis sitting on the couch, peering over the edge at me. "You're leavin'?" Otis' voice trembles like he's going to cry and I shoot my mother a look to tell her to not press the issue while he's here.

"Yes, but Theodore has a surprise for you! You can come stay with us in the summer and ride the horses he has." I try to sound excited when all I really want to do is cry with him.

"I don't want you to go!" He swipes tears from his cheek with his hand that's holding his magic rock.

"I know buddy, I want to stay here with you. But I am a grown up now and grown ups get married. Theodore says there's a special magic horse, just for you," I lie. He perks up, giving me a guarded look. I nod, "it's true, it's a special horse. You'll have to come see it this summer."

He finally smiles and stands up from the couch. "I'm going to show it my magic stone!" he exclaims, holding the rock in the air.

"That's a swell idea! Why don't you go hunt for more magic things?" I suggest, glancing back at my mother, who is no longer stirring her pot.

After Otis takes off outside, I turn to face her and prepare myself for an argument. "You're marrying him?" she asks.

"Yes, he asked me last night. We went to a nice restaurant and then to the Majestic Theater. He already sent word back to his friends in New York. We'll marry in two weeks. He has a guest house I'll stay in until the wedding, so it will all be done properly." I talk quickly, trying to get it out before she can interrupt.

She puts one hand on her stomach and the other on the side of the stove. "It's too soon. Are you sure, Hazel? Marriage is forever," she warns with her face dark and gloomy.

"He treats me right. Like a man should treat a woman. He's the opposite of father," I boast as I cross my arms. Her expression looks hurt and I regret my words.

"Mama. He loves me. He has wealth you wouldn't believe, and can take care of me. It'll mean one less mouth to feed for you, that's more potatoes on Otis' plate," I say gently. She looks back at the pot, surely wishing there was more in it besides potatoes, carrots, water, and rosemary. "But mama," I plead, "you have to care for Otis. I won't be here to do it."

“I’m his mother, Hazel. Of course I will.”

“No. It can’t be like how it’s been. You can’t let father hit him. He can’t see all the things I saw when I was his age. Please.”

“Ok.” Her words are so soft I have to strain to hear them.

“Swear to me. Swear to me on your grave,” I demand. She looks at me aghast, her mouth parted open and eyes wide.

“I swear,” she finally promises, and I slouch in my chair with relief.

“If it ever gets bad you have to write to me. Before I leave tomorrow I’ll have Theodore write down the address. He has a telephone, too, if you can ever use one in town to call,” I instruct her. She nods.

I stand up to go to my room, but as I look at her a memory floats in my head. I was ten years old and dancing around the kitchen with a kitten in my arms. It flopped around and meowed while I skipped around my mother who was cutting potatoes at the table. “Hazel Mccoy, that poor cat is going to have a broken neck!” she had laughed at me, shaking her head.

“We are dancing partners!” I exclaimed. My mother smiled, sat the knife down and stood up. She scooped the kitten from my arms and cradled it to her chest as she danced with me, humming a tune. We did that for what had felt like hours, dancing with the kitten and singing different songs.

I look at my mother now and wonder what happened to that woman. I walk up to her and wrap my arms around her. She stands there stiff with her arms at her side. She finally loosens her body and puts her arms around me. "I'm going to miss you," she whispers. I pull away, staring into her eyes that are filling with tears.

"I will miss you too. But I will write often," I promise her. She nods and quickly turns back to the stove and resumes stirring.

When I open my bedroom door, Florence looks up from the vanity. She stops brushing her shiny hair and stands up quickly. I ignore her and set my bag on my bed, sitting down next to it.

"How did it go?" She demands.

"We went to a really nice restaurant and you wouldn't believe where else." I speak slowly, letting her fidget in anticipation. "The Majestic Theater," I finally tell her. Her mouth hangs open and she gasps.

"You are yanking my leg!" she says, shaking her head in disbelief.

"It was amazing! He bought me this dress from the seamstress to wear there. You wouldn't believe the magician's tricks. Oh! And these people called acrobats. They climbed on each other and did all sorts of flips and bent their bodies in weird ways." I pull out the red dress and hold it up in front of me.

"No way," she remarks, reaching out and touching the dress.

"Did you really have two rooms?" she asks. I turn red immediately and tell her yes. "Why are you blushing so hard then?" she squints her eyes at me accusingly.

“I’m not!”

“Yes you are. Tell me. What is it? Did he make advances?”

“It’s none of your business.”

I start to fold the red dress carefully and place it back in my bag. I open up the drawers next to the bed and pull out my other two dresses and pack them. “What are you doing?” Florence’s face bunches up in confusion. I inhale deeply and sit back down on the bed.

“Sit,” I instruct her.

She lays across from me on her back and raises an eyebrow. “He asked me to marry him,” I explain. She gasps loudly and holds a hand up to her chest.

“Oh my god! Is that really true? How did he do it? What exactly did he say? What did you say?” she starts to rattle off questions faster than I can process, so I stop her.

“Florence!” I snap.

She is out of breath now, her chest heaving up while her eyes bulge out at me. “We, uh, we were spending time together,” I turn red as I continue, “and after, he told me he is leaving for New York tomorrow. And he wanted me to go with him. He asked me to marry him, the wedding will be in two weeks at his church.”

“You’re truly going?” her voice is quieter now and I start to fiddle with her yellow dress I’m wearing.

“You know nothing like this will ever happen to me again. He is too good for me. I can’t stay behind.” I am now speaking quieter, too. We both sit in silence, staring at each other and realizing what this means.

"When will I see you again?" she asks.

"Theodore said Otis can come stay for the summer, surely you can too," I reassure her. She smiles a little and bites her lip with a grin.

"Maybe he has some rich friends he could introduce me to!"

I roll my eyes and stand up from the bed. "What happened to dear Gregory?" I say his name mockingly. She tsks and leans back on her bed, watching me pack.

"You can't take my yellow dress, I need it!" she remarks.

I pull it over my head and toss it at her, and she catches it and shakes it out. I pull my torn working dress on and put my journal and pencils in the bag. I add the drawings Otis made to the bag, along with my other few possessions.

Later in the evening, we sit at the kitchen table and eat the watery potato soup. I add an extra scoop to Otis' because I had the muffins earlier that day. Otis shovels the food in his mouth like he's starving, and slams the spoon down on the table. "I'm done! Can I go play now?" he asks.

"You *may* go play now," my mother answers.

We all watch him push back in his chair and climb up his ladder to his small loft. I hear him making airplane noises and smile. "John, dear, we have some exciting news," my mother clears her throat. Dread fills my body and I want to tell her to not tell him and let me just disappear tomorrow. My father looks at her with a dull expression, his eyes red. I shoot my mother a look.

"Hazel is going to New York, to marry Theodore." She tries to keep her voice happy and light, but I can hear it shaking with nervousness. My father's eyes turn to me and I feel myself shrink in my chair. I feel like a small child, waiting for him to stand and yell at the dinner table. To tell me I can't finish my food and to go to my room hungry.

"Is that so?" He directs this question to me. I nod meekly and fumble with my spoon as I try to take a bite of the watery soup. My stomach is queasy and I try to steady my breathing.

"You knocked up or somethin'?" he sneers. My mother coughs on her food and Florence looks down at her lap.

"No," I whisper, keeping my eyes on my spoon.

"Why the hell would a man like that want trash like you?"

I stay silent as he puts his bottle to his mouth and tilts his head back. I look up at my mother who looks like she's trying to figure out a way to lighten the mood. "I made a cake. For Hazel's last night at home," she offers, trying to grab my father's hand. He yanks it away and looks at her with a twisted expression.

"Where in tarnation did you get money to make a damn cake? And you go wastin' it on *her*?" He flings his hand towards me, making me flinch even though he was across the table.

"I already had all the ingredients." She trembles as she stands up and goes over to the kitchen counter.

She lifts a flour sack towel off the plate and reveals a yellow cake with chocolate frosting. She takes a knife and starts slicing it with her shaking hand. My father stands from the table, the chair scraping under him. "I hope he knows he can't bring you back, I ain't havin' you under my roof again." He glares at me as he leans over the table. I press my back against my chair to create more distance between us and I nod my head.

I don't know why I feel so disappointed when he turns and leaves, slamming the front door behind him. I should know he wouldn't suddenly decide he loves me and would be sad by my leaving, but I sit here with a rush of emotions that confuse me. Tears fill my eyes and I realize that was probably the last time I would ever see my father. There would be no hug, no apology for the last seventeen years. Just one last insult and slam of the door.

My mother sets a piece of cake in front of me and Florence before going to the living room and yelling for Otis. I smile as he climbs down from the loft and gasps at the dessert. We never have cake, even for our birthdays. "Cake!" he exclaims as he pulls out his chair and plops down.

We all sit together and slowly take bites, making sure to savor it. I glance around and realize maybe I will miss being here. Because even though there were so many bad moments, there were a few good ones, too. Like a little crack of light that shines through a dark and dreary room. "Thank you," I softly say to my mother, who looks up from her cake with tears falling down her face.

"I should have made you cake more often."

"You did what you could," I try to comfort her, not fully believing the words as they leave my mouth. She nods and looks over to Florence.

"You have to step up, you have to help with your brother," she tells her. Florence looks flustered and glances over at Otis and then back to mother.

"Fine," she says around a mouthful of cake.

After dinner, I help with the dishes one last time, drying them and setting them in the cupboard after my mother washes them. Otis tugs my dress and holds up his airplane with a sad smile. "Will you play with me?"

We play all night on the living room floor, him using me as a pretend mountain to crash into and giggling together when I fall over. I chase him around the sofa pretending to be a wild animal that's going to catch him. I look at the clock and its past nine. I know Otis is getting tired because he keeps stopping to rub his eyes. "Let's get you into bed. I'll tuck you in tonight." I force a smile and lift him up, his lanky arms wrapping around my neck as I grab a candle and carry him to the ladder.

I climb up behind him and bend over in order to not hit my head on the ceiling. I sit the candle on his table that's next to his mattress on the floor and help him pull on clean underpants and his bed shirt.

The back of his hair sticks up from his unruly cowlick and I smooth it down with my hand as he gets into bed. My chest tightens as I watch him lay his head on the pillow and close his eyes. "I love you," he whispers.

"I love you more." I kiss his forehead and watch him drift to sleep.

I feel guilty as I blow out the candle and climb down from the loft, knowing that was the last time I will tuck him in bed for a while. *He can come in the summer, I can't live here forever.*

Mother is sitting on the sofa knitting when I reach the bottom of the ladder. She can tell by my expression what I'm thinking. "It'll be okay, I'll watch over him like you do," she promises. I don't say anything as I walk to my room and pause when she speaks again. "Your father does better when you're gone. I don't know how else to say it, but he does. He's always had a hard time with you."

I turn and look at her, trying to read her face.

"He always knew you weren't his." She hesitates, staring down at the scarf she's making.

I become still and feel like I can't move my feet. She sits the needles down on her lap and finally looks up at me. "You were conceived out of love, Hazel, and he knew that," she whispers. I blink as I try to process what she's saying.

"John isn't my father?" I finally speak.

"Your father was gone all the time. Leaving me with Florence for weeks at a time, with barely enough money," she explains, sounding as if she is pleading for me not to judge her. "I grew up with this little boy who had red hair and always liked me as a teenager. But I paid him no mind and married your father instead. That boy was just too shy for my liking. He was timid and sweet. Then I ran into him when Florence was just a baby and your father was gone hunting for who knew how long."

I feel myself barely breathing, not wanting to miss a word as she rambles, fussing with the yarn in her lap. I stand still and nod for her to continue. "He could tell we were poor and that Florence was hungry, she was so tiny. He said he would bring some food to us, and that he had plenty at home. He did, he brought enough food to feed us for over a week. He was still that same kind soul," she whispers, tears flowing down her face.

"You mustn't judge me, Hazel. I just wanted to feel loved, even for a night. I always wanted to tell you, but I couldn't. I couldn't risk you letting it slip in front of your father.." she pauses and adds, "I mean John."

"What's his name? Where is he? I need to meet him!" I demand, feeling my heart beat out of my chest. Her eyes become cloudy and she puts her hands on her face, trying to collect her emotions.

"His name was Henry."

"Was?"

"I found out a few years later he had died in a coal mining accident. That's what he did, worked in a coal mining factory in Ohio. He had come back to visit his mother because she was dying. I never told him about you, I couldn't risk what your father may do." She starts to cry, tears falling onto her lap.

I take a few steps back and shake my head. John wasn't my father. A man named Henry was, but he was dead. "Why are you telling me this?" I snap.

"I want you to know that it's not your fault, how your father treats you. It's mine."

"It's not your fault," I apologize, "I just don't know how to feel. Truthfully, I think I'm glad he's not my father, I detest him."

"I'm so sorry," she whispers, glancing at the front door as the doorknob rattles. It swings open and John saunters in with a bottle in his hand. He glares over at me and I feel relief wash over me when I realize that no part of him created me. The room becomes quiet as he walks over to the sofa and falls down onto it next to my mother.

"Goodnight, I love you." I look at my mother and tell her with my eyes that I forgive her and I won't ever bring up our conversation again.

"I love you," she smiles and tries to hide her tears.

I go into my room and close the door behind me, leaning against it. Florence is already in bed and shushes me. I pull off my dress and stockings before I climb in bed wearing just my slip. I lay there awake for what feels like an eternity.

That night I dream about the man with red hair named Henry, and what my life would have been like if he would have whisked me away. He gives me candy and reads me stories on his lap and my mother is always laughing and dancing.

I dream about being fully loved.

Nine

"Hazel!" Florence shakes my shoulders and causes me to startle awake.

"What? What!" I snap, looking around the room in confusion.

"You slept late and Theodore is here, he's waiting in the living room," she whispers, tilting her head to the bedroom door.

I sit up straight and panic. "Shit," I mutter as I stand up and put on the green dress I had laid out the night before. Florence quickly braids my hair and ties it with the green ribbon while I sit and apply makeup at the vanity. "Hurry!" I panic as she finishes tying the ribbon.

I fling the bedroom door open and see Theodore sitting on the sofa with Otis, who is showing him his treasure bag. Theodore looks up and grins. "I am so sorry I overslept!" I say exasperatedly.

"It's alright, we have a long few days ahead of us, so I'm glad you got some rest." Theodore stands up and adjusts his gray tweed suit.

"Let me grab my bag." I go back to my room and return with it.

"Is that all?" he asks, eyebrows furrowing. I nod and he takes the bag from me. "We better get going so we don't miss the train," he says.

"I need you to write your address down so mother can write to me," I tell him quickly, going to the kitchen to grab a piece of paper and pencil. I hand it to him and he scribbles it down, folding the paper and handing it to my mother who stands behind the sofa. Everyone walks out to the porch and Theodore puts my bag in the car, then waits by the door.

I turn to my mother, Florence and Otis. My stomach turns and excitement and sadness fight inside me. "Goodbye," Florence steps forward and gives me a quick hug. I pat her back and she steps away, letting our mother stand in front of me. Her eyes are filled with sadness and she looks over my shoulder at Theodore.

"Are you sure this is what you want, Hazel? You can stay. I can deal with your father. You don't know this man that well," she says quietly so Theodore can't hear.

"Mama," I warn, "I love you, but I am going." She hugs me tightly and I feel empty as she pulls away from me.

Otis stands there and stares up at me, not moving. "Can I get a hug from my favorite person?" I try to smile through the tears welling up in my eyes.

"Please don't leave," he begs, as he runs up to me, throwing his arms around me as I crouch down. I hold him and kiss the top of his head.

"I'll see you soon, I promise, just a month or two when it's summer."

He wipes his runny nose and opens my hand up. He sits something in my palm and closes my hand around it before I can look at what it is. "My magic stone, to make you super strong." He beams up at me, smiling through his tears. I feel a sob escape me as I take him back into my arms and squeeze him one more time.

"I love you," I tell him before letting him go and walking down the steps with his rock in my hand.

"I love you, too. I can't wait to see my magic horse!" he yells after me. Theodore gives me a reassuring smile and opens the car door for me to get in. I turn to look at my family one more time, and they're standing close together, Florence holding Otis' hand.

"Remember, you swore!" I yell to my mother. She nods and gives me a serious and understanding look.

"Write to me!" Florence hollers, waving goodbye.

"Bye! I love y'all!" I wave back and Theodore closes the door. I turn my head and watch them from the back window as we drive off, tears running down my cheeks. Otis' tiny body is hunched over like he's crying. I try to remember what Theodore had told me. *He can stay with us this summer.*

"You're supposed to be happy," Theodore finally speaks.

I turn to look at him, angry at myself when I see his frown. "I'm sorry, I am happy. I'm just sad to leave them," I explain. He still looks displeased, so I scoot closer to him and run my finger down his arm. "I'm sorry, *you* make me happy. I am so lucky to have you," I promise.

He smiles a little and twirls his toothpick in his mouth. "It'll take us about four days to arrive in New York," he tells me.

"I haven't ever been on a train," I admit, feeling excited to experience one.

"You will have your own small suite, it's a room you sleep in at night. They have about fourteen small rooms. The rest of the passengers sleep in their seats or pull down beds," he explains.

"I get my own suite? Where will you be?" I ask.

"I have one as well. I figured you wouldn't want to share one." He raises an eyebrow. "Unless I'm wrong?"

I turn red and avert my eyes from him. "You are correct. Just two weeks until the wedding."

"Speaking of, I called back to New York again today and made sure everything is going well. We booked the church for April 12th." He looks over at me and I smile.

"I can't believe it. Should I wear my green dress or my red one?" I think out loud.

"Neither. You have to wear a real wedding dress, they're already working on it," he answers.

"Wait, they're making me an actual wedding gown?" I question.

"Of course. Hazel, I don't think you understand," Theodore starts, "I am a very wealthy man. Most people in New York know of me. The church will be full of important people. This has to be done right."

I am floored by his response and I start to fidget in my seat. "I don't understand..." I mutter.

"Don't fret about it," he cuts me off, his watch shining in the sun as he turns the wheel. "The dress will already be started on when we arrive, but they will get your exact measurements and you can finalize some of the things once we get there."

We continue to drive for a while and I see the train station from far away, the steam floating in the air. "Will you just leave the car here?" I ask.

"Yes, I paid someone who will take it back to my brother," he replies, pulling the car in a space not far from the train.

He holds our bags as we walk to the large building. "The train doesn't leave for another twenty minutes, but we should probably board now," he tells me, setting the bags on the wooden platform and pulling out two tickets from his suit pocket.

"I can hold them," I say, as I pull them from his hand.

I follow closely behind him as he walks to the train. People yell from the platform to those already on the train, who lean their heads out the windows and holler back. A small child leans out one of the windows and reaches out to a woman standing on the platform. She smiles and waves at him, trying to appear happy. I pull my eyes from the little boy, squeezing Otis' magic rock in my hand.

I hand the tickets to the man who guards the entrance of the train. He takes a device and punches a few holes in them, then gives them back. I follow Theodore up the steps and take in the train. It's fancier than I expected, with gold carpet and red seats.

We squeeze past people who are pushing their luggage into the overhead storage and keep walking until we get to a hall with mini rooms. He stops and opens one of the waist level swinging doors and we enter the small private room. It has two small booth seats that face each other, with a table in between them. "The suites are just a few doors down the hall," Theodore informs me as he sits the luggage on the floor next to the seats.

I sit down and look around. The wall has a small lamp attached to it that flickers slightly, and there are four glasses on a small tray that sits in front of me. I turn the blinds on the large window and let the sun light up the small room.

Theodore sits across from me and crosses his leg over his knee. "I can't wait to see New York!" I clasp my hands together and look out the window.

"I can't wait for New York to have you in it," Theodore smiles.

"I'm nervous to not know anyone."

"I'll introduce you to plenty of people. My friends will become yours."

The train whistle blows and I hear loud shouting. The train starts to move, lunging me forward slightly at first. I grab the table and watch outside the window as we start to move.

I watch the people wave goodbye to loved ones and I swallow, wishing my family was there for one last farewell. They disappear quickly as the train picks up pace and starts to chug along. We ride in silence for a while before a woman wearing a black and white modern outfit stops in front of our room. "May I offer you a refreshment?" she asks.

Theodore looks at me and I clear my throat, "water, please". Theodore asks for tea and she walks off.

"What exactly do you do for work, Theodore?" I force myself to finally ask when the woman is gone. He blinks a few times and takes off his newsboy hat and sets it next to him. He runs his hand through his dark hair and thinks for a moment.

"A lot of different things. I own some race horses and have a good bit of money in the races themselves. And a speakeasy among some other businesses," he finally answers.

"A speak what?" I ask, perplexed. He chuckles and drops his hand from his hair.

"A speakeasy. It's an establishment that sells liquor and often has gambling," he explains.

"But selling liquor is illegal," I say slowly.

"That's correct, which is why most of them are underground, so to speak. I own a restaurant that used to be a bar, the speakeasy's in the basement," he says, making it sound simple. I feel my stomach turn at the thought of him doing something illegal.

"But what if you get caught?" I whisper, looking around the door to make sure the woman wasn't nearby.

"That's why you keep certain people on your payroll. There's plenty of fuzz who frequently occupy our joint," Theodore says matter-of-factly. I try to think before I speak, but my head is swimming with questions.

"So you're a criminal?" I blurt out.

I hear thumping coming from down the hall and I see the woman from earlier pushing a small cart. She pulls out a tall clear glass full of water and sets it on the table along with a small cup of tea and a bowl of sugar cubes. "Enjoy!" She smiles and pushes the cart back down the hall.

I steady my breath as I open the tall narrow glass and pour it into the small crystal cup on the table. I take a sip and peer over it at Theodore. "Hazel, you must understand not to speak about this to most people. And don't ask too many questions. I promise you have nothing to worry about," he says before taking a drink of tea. I nod slowly and slump back into my seat.

I look at his expensive tweed suit, his shiny watch and fancy haircut. I glance down at my plain scuffed shoes and wonder why he picked me. What was wrong with him that made him pick *me* instead of a rich girl from New York?

"What's wrong?" he asks.

"I don't understand why you would pick me," I answer honestly.

"There's no girl like you in New York. You'll see. All they care about is money, partying and sleeping around. The amount of women that throw themselves at me like Florence did is unbelievable. I knew when I watched you give that ice cream away and not go buy another one that you weren't self obsessed and money hungry like the rest. You weren't born into money," he smiles. I believe him so I don't ask any more questions, just sit back and watch the trees fly by the window.

Night approaches quickly, our room darkening as the sun goes down. The woman had appeared with a cart and handed us turkey sandwiches and grapes for lunch. But that was hours ago, and my stomach growls, making Theodore look up from his newspaper and glance down at his watch. "Say, how do you feel about some dinner and stretching our legs?" He sits the newspaper down on the table.

"I feel like that's the best thing I've heard all day!" I laugh and stand up, stretching my arms to the ceiling.

"Let's head to the dining car." He loops my arm through his and we walk down the hall. We pass other passengers exiting their private booths and pass the main seating area when we reach a large door. Theodore pushes it open and I am surprised by what looks to be a very small restaurant.

We follow a waiter to our table, where he hands us two menus and walks off. We both sit and look over the menu. It has two different meal options and a few different drinks. Theodore glances at the menu and raises his hand to catch the attention of the waiter again. The man walks back to the table and smiles, his white teeth shimmering against his chocolate complexion.

I find myself smiling back when he looks at me to take my order. "Italian meatballs and water, please," I say, handing the menu back to him. Theodore orders the same.

"I can't believe what they can fit on a train," I say, looking up at the hanging light fixtures.

"It's quite impressive," Theodore says, before thanking the waiter who returns with our drinks.

Our food arrives quickly and I try to eat slowly and remember my manners. "My mother is excited to meet you," Theodore tells me before taking a bite of his food. My head snaps up and I set my fork down. I forgot about his mother.

"Oh goodness, I didn't even prepare to meet her. Please tell me about her."

"Her name is Mary. She's hard to describe, you'll just have to see when you meet her." Theodore wipes his mouth with his white napkin and I frown.

"That's not enough information. Just her name? What if she hates me!" I panic.

"She doesn't like most people," Theodore says, as if he's just thinking out loud.

"Oh God," I groan.

"Just don't ask too many questions around her," he warns.

"Does she not know about the *speakeasy*?" I whisper the last word to make sure no one else hears.

Theodore laughs, almost choking on his meatball. I cross my arms and wait. "She owns a part of it, she doesn't like nosey people," he finally replies. My mouth hangs open and I try to picture an old lady who owns a liquor establishment.

"She gets a certain way about family and family business is all," Theodore says.

“But won’t I be family?” I ask. He thinks for a moment before speaking, like he is choosing his words carefully.

“You will be after a while.”

We eat the rest of the dinner in silence. I picture my mother and her knitting needles, and I feel like this Mary will be nothing like her. After dinner, Theodore shows me to the suites, finding my door and opening it. I note that it’s across from the ladies room, which I am grateful for. He puts my bag on the bed and tells me he will be in suite seven if I need anything.

I close the door when he leaves and examine the room. The walls are cherry wood and it smells faintly of cigars, like the previous occupant had smoked. It’s a very small room but functional, with a small sink, narrow bed, a chair and a table. A beautiful lamp with a multi-colored glass lamp shade sits on the table.

I change into my nightgown and pull out my journal. I sit on the chair and start to write, appreciating the green and orange hues from the lamp that shine on my paper. I write about the last few days, the Majestic Theater, losing my virginity, how Theodore asked me to marry him. Then I write about today. I scribble down how Theodore sat across from me and told me about his race horses and how he owned a speakeasy, and about his mother who, apparently, was in on it as well.

The words stare back at me, as if they’re mocking me and how little I know about my fiance. I slam the journal shut and shove it at the bottom of my bag under the clothes. Before I get into bed, I put Otis' magic rock under my pillow. I close my eyes to drift off to sleep, picturing his face, so I'll dream of him.

Ten

The next two days pass quickly. I wake up and freshen up in the bedroom sink, meet Theodore for breakfast in our seating area, and he reads his newspaper while I write or look out the window, then we have dinner in the dining cart.

It's the third day, and I sit staring out the window, wishing the train would go faster. "Deep in thought," Theodore observes, his newspaper folded on his lap as he watches me.

"I'm just feeling a bit...trapped." I look around the small room and then back out the window.

"Tomorrow night we'll arrive. Then just an hour car ride to the house," he reassures me.

"Tell me about your house, and about New York," I request, leaning my head back and staring at the ceiling.

"It's *our* house now."

"Then tell me about our house."

"It has a big fountain in front of it, with a driveway that wraps around it, like a big circle. I had a custom gate made a few years back for the entrance, and I think it's rather grand," he muses. I nod for him to tell me more, and his toothpick moves to the other side of his mouth as he thinks. My eyes focus on it, wishing he would take it out and kiss me.

"The house sits on a substantial amount of land. The barn is a few acres away and we have a lake on one side of the house; you can see it from our bedroom." He winks at me when he says 'our', making my heart flip.

I write in my journal until it's time for dinner. We eat a beef stew with a side of bread and Theodore walks me back to my suite. I am so used to the train's movement that I forget we are on one as he opens the door and leans against the frame.

"Goodnight," he says. before grabbing my chin and tipping my head up to look at him. My heart beats faster and I look down at his lips.

"Goodnight," I mutter.

He leans down and kisses me softly. I put my hand on his chest and he grabs the back of my head, beginning to deepen the kiss when someone walking past in the hall clears their throat loudly. I hear giggles and I turn red and pull away. Theodore looks back over his shoulder and gives me a pained look. "I should have shut the door," he smirks.

"You should leave, I think I know what would happen if you shut the door," I tease, pushing his chest so he's standing in the hallway. I unbutton the top two buttons on the front of my dress and watch his mouth part and his hand grab the door frame.

"Goodnight, Theodore," I say and shut the door in his face. I hear him groan and laugh before walking off. I grin as I undress, thinking Florence would be proud. I was learning how to flirt, after all.

I lay in my bed with the lamp casting its colorful light on the walls as I sketch a photo of Theodore looking out of the train window. I make sure to include the toothpick that usually hangs out of his mouth. I smile down at my journal and trace my finger over his face lightly, taking care not to smudge it.

I hide the journal in my bag before closing my eyes and trying to sleep. But I toss and turn, thinking about arriving in New York tomorrow evening.

The next morning, I open my eyes and pull the blankets back over my face. I let out a groan and turn my head to try and relieve my stiff neck. I had barely slept and when I did, I had nightmares of meeting Theodore's mother and her immediately hating me. I lay in bed for a while until someone knocks on my door.

"Hazel? Are you alright?" Theodore's voice comes from the other side.

"Yes, I just didn't sleep well," I answer, wondering if I should get up and open the door.

"Do you want to just meet me for lunch?" he asks, sounding like he's moving closer to the door.

"Yes, please," I reply loudly. I hear his footsteps as he leaves and I close my eyes.

I shiver slightly and wish I had another blanket. The further we had gotten from Texas the colder it became. I had brought my only jacket but it was light and I worry New York will be far colder than I thought it would be during Spring.

I try to go back to sleep and can't, so I sit up in bed and daydream instead. I imagine it's four years from now and Theodore and I have a child, a little girl with his dark hair. We go on picnics and she rides the horses every day. I imagine that we end up having four or five children together, and that we love each other more every day. I smile when I think of Theodore with graying hair, I know he will look handsome as he ages.

A few hours pass and I put my journal down and look at the clock that hangs on the wall above the door. Twenty till noon. I shove the journal at the bottom of my bag and pull on my red dress. I want to be wearing the nicest thing I own when I go to Theodore's home that evening. I stand in front of the small mirror that hangs above the small sink and wet a few strands of my hair that are frizzy, twirling them around my finger to reshape them.

I pull out the few makeup items I had stolen from Florence and apply them carefully. Well, not stolen. More like *borrowed.* I figured she had so many things she wouldn't notice if three items were missing. I blink slowly when applying the mascara, cursing under my breath when it smears on my eyelid. I try to wipe it off with my index finger and it spreads across my eyelid more.

After perfecting my appearance as much as possible, I take a step back for one final look. Good enough. I turn and quickly pack everything up in my bag so I am ready later that evening. It took five minutes to put all my belongings back in the bag. I carefully tuck Otis' magic rock in my small purse that I place on top of my clothes.

As I open the door I see Theodore standing there, leaning against the wall. "There she is." I smile at him and close the door behind me.

"I thought I would meet you in the dining car," I state, looping my arm through his elbow. His eyes look down at me and he raises an eyebrow.

"Who are you trying to impress by wearing the dress I bought you?" he asks, taking me by surprise.

I give him a small laugh, unable to tell if he's being serious or not. "Just you, of course. Well, and the ticket master if I am being honest," I whisper as if I am telling him the most serious gossip. The ticket master was an eighty-year-old man with long gray hairs that poked out of his nose. To my relief, Theodore starts to chuckle and shake his head.

We enter the dining car and sit at the same table we have been using for the past few days. When we look at the menu we both start to laugh. "Meatloaf!" Theodore exclaims.

"You should never eat meatloaf," I say, remembering our first date at the diner.

"We must order it," he insists. I roll my eyes and ignore him, looking at the other option. *Tuna.* I wrinkle my nose when I read it, looking back up at Theodore's smirking face.

"Fine," I groan.

When the food arrives, he looks at me in triumph, waiting for me to take a bite. I poke at it with my fork before raising a small bite to my mouth. After I swallow I look up at him and shake my head at his face. "Ok, it's not that bad. It's actually almost good," I admit, shrugging my shoulders. He grins and takes a few bites.

"No, this is actually disgusting," he says quietly, looking around to make sure no one heard. I start to laugh and remind him that he is the one who insisted on ordering it.

"I can't believe how cold it is," I say as I pull my black jacket tighter around my body.

"Tomorrow, first thing in the morning, I am having a friend take you to get some clothes and other necessities," Theodore says after taking a bite of mashed potatoes. I look at him blankly for a moment before speaking.

"A friend?"

"Yes, her name is Nellie," he replies, dabbing his mouth with the napkin. I look down at the silverware and realize he's been using a different fork than I was. *Why are there two different forks?*

"What's she like?" I try to sound curious and unbothered but really I am worried about this 'friend'. Is she truly just a friend? Has he slept with her before? Did she love Theodore?

"Hazel," Theodore sounds amused. I look up and watch him put a toothpick in his mouth. "She's someone I grew up with. Nellie and Peter have been by my side since I was probably Otis' age," he says.

"Who's Peter?"

"Sorry, a friend who works for me."

"At the *restaurant*?" I put emphasis on the last word to let him know what I mean. One side of his lip raises in a small smile and he nods, "that would be correct."

"Are you sure she won't mind? Nellie, I mean. She doesn't know me and I don't want to impose on her day." I pull at the tassel on my dress, feeling uneasy about meeting his friend so soon. I didn't have many friends growing up, so other women make me nervous. What if I say the wrong thing? What if she doesn't like me and tells Theodore to call off the wedding?

"Trust me, if there's one thing Nellie likes more than partying, it's shopping. Especially if she gets to help spend my money," Theodore mutters.

"I have some money with me, you don't need to pay for anything," I tell him, mentally counting how much money I had in my purse. It would be enough for a warmer jacket.

"You're going to be my wife, my money is yours. And I want you to have everything you need, doll. Things in New York are different than in Texas, you'll have a wardrobe full of clothes."

I smile when he calls me doll and nod, but I feel uncomfortable thinking about spending his money. I remind myself that even though it's not a good comparison, my mother always spent whatever money John had. Granted it was usually on flour and potatoes, not multiple dresses and jackets.

We finish up our lunch and make our way back to our sitting area. I tuck my dress under my leg to remain modest as

I sit and look out the window. "We're in New York," Theodore tells me, looking outside with me. It's prettier than I imagined, with plenty of trees and flowers.

"Just wait until you see the city," he says.

"Do you live in the city?" I ask. He shakes his head and crosses his leg.

"No, but about thirty minutes outside of it. The restaurant is in Manhattan," he informs me. I had heard of Manhattan before, John had always said it was a city crammed full of people who would pickpocket. Florence had argued with him and said it was just a modern place. I remember him yelling at her and threatening to hit her for the first time for talking back.

Theodore interrupts my thoughts by shaking the newspaper open to read it. I glance at the headlines, something about stocks and I wonder how someone could read something so boring so often.

We drink tea and watch the sun start to set as the train pulls to a stop. I set the teacup down on the tiny platter and look up at Theodore. "Ready?" He stands and grabs our bags he had set next to our seats.

"I suppose so." I take in a deep breath and stand up, following him into the hallway. Other passengers are already making their way out of the train and down the steps when we exit the hallway.

Theodore says something to me but I can't hear him over everyone's voice and the sound of the train's whistle. He goes down the train's steps first, holding my hand as I step down. I start to shiver when the cold wind whips through the train station, hitting my skin. "Here, this way," Theodore yells, holding onto my hand and pushing his way through the crowd. We find a spot by the station's entrance and he pulls a suit jacket out of his bag. He drapes it over my shoulders, the bottom of it hitting my knees. I never realized how much taller he was until that moment. I look up and thank him when he looks over my shoulder like he recognizes someone.

"Frank!" Theodore yells, his voice ringing in my ears. I wince and pull away, turning to see a man dressed in all black standing in front of a nice car. I take note of his gloves and hat as he walks towards us.

"Mr. Greenwood." He tips his hat towards us, keeping his eyes on me.

"Frank, this is my fiance, Hazel." Theodore hands him two of the bags. Frank tips his head to me, his gray mustache rising when he smiles.

"Good evening ma'am, it's nice to meet you." His voice sounds raspy and old, but friendly.

"Nice to meet you, as well," I say shyly.

I follow Frank and Theodore to the car, where our bags get put in the trunk and Frank gets in the driver's seat. Theodore opens the back door and I slide in, scooting to the next seat so Theodore can sit next to me. We start to drive and I look at the back of Frank's head. His gray hair is thinning but he keeps it short as if to hide the fact that he's aging.

"Mrs.Greenwood wanted me to inform you that she is visiting this evening. She should be there by the time we arrive," Frank finally speaks after a few minutes of silence. I look over at Theodore and he gives me a frustrated look.

"Looks like you'll be meeting my mother tonight," he gripes. I feel panic fill my chest and I want to lift my arm to smell myself, I know I probably have an unpleasant odor. It had been nothing but sponge baths on the train.

"Oh," is all I can manage to say.

"I'm sorry, I had planned to give you a day or two to settle in. Seems my mother has other plans."

I chew my lip and am thankful I had at least put on my red dress this morning. Things could be worse. "Is there anything I need to know before meeting her?" I ask. He makes a face I can't quite distinguish and pats my knee.

"Just don't mention how you stayed at the hotel."

I nod and fold my hands in my lap, staring out the window the rest of the drive. I plan what I am going to say in my mind. *Hello, nice to meet you*. Did that sound too much like a teenager? *Hello, I am glad to finally meet you. Theodore has told me so much about you*. Well, that was just a lie.

I get distracted from my thoughts as we enter what I can only assume is Manhattan. Buildings and shops were everywhere, people crammed on the sidewalks and even the road. I'm shocked that so many people are out as night approaches. "Is it always this busy?" I ask as I lean my face closer to the window.

"Always," Theodore answers.

The women all wear fashionable dresses with long jackets, most of them wearing cloche hats. I touch my head and realize I don't even own a hat. Maybe I can get one when we go shopping tomorrow.

We drive out of the busy city and start to pass land and large houses. My eyes widen when I see the size of them, easily five times the ones we had in my little town. We start to pass a large lake and I feel dread mixed with excitement as we near Theodore's house. I'm not ready to meet his mother.

We pull up to a large opened brick gate that has 'Greenwood' made out of metal at the top. Frank slows the car down as we enter and turn a curve. Shrubs and different plants line the long driveway, and I try to look around them to catch a glimpse of the house.

When I see it my mouth drops.

There's a round driveway with a fountain spewing water in the center, outlined with trimmed shrubs. The house is made out of white brick and is enormous, with beige shutters and trim. Flowers and greenery overflow from the front garden beds, a man hunching over to prune them. It didn't seem real.

"It's beautiful!" I exclaim, looking over at Theodore. His eyes are fixed on my face, and I turn red wondering how long he has been watching me. "I've never seen such a large house," I add.

He smiles as we pull to a stop in front of the house. My heart starts to beat fast as Frank walks around the car and opens my door. I take his hand and step out. He goes to get the bags and Theodore comes over and takes my hand in his.

"Ready?" he asks. I shake my head and he chuckles. "Well, too bad," he teases. We make our way up the stairs to the front door. It opens before we reach it, a short middle aged woman wearing a maid uniform standing on the other side.

"Mr. Greenwood! And you must be the future Mrs.Greenwood," she greets us excitedly.

"Hazel, this is Margaret. She is the head housekeeper. If you need anything at all you can ask her." Theodore guides me inside the home, Margaret stepping to the side to let us in.

"It's nice to meet you." I smile, my eyes dart around the foyer looking for Theodore's mother. The foyer is large and has a red rug lining it. A table sits in the middle of the room with a big bouquet of flowers with different crystal decorations around it.

"Your mother is in the main living area. I will put on some tea." Margaret has a pinched smile as she speaks before turning and walking out. Theodore takes a deep breath before smoothing out his suit and pushing his hair back. I haven't ever seen Theodore stressed before, it makes him appear even older.

"This way." He extends his arm to me and we walk down the foyer.

Eleven

We enter a large room and in the middle are two large staircases that meet at the top of the second floor. A large chandelier hangs in between them, casting little shimmers of light on the walls and the tile floor. I look around at the different paintings as we walk through one of the multiple open doors.

A fireplace catches my eye immediately, a flame flickering inside it. The brick goes all the way to the top of the high ceiling. A large cream sofa with gold trim and detailing sits in front of it, and a woman is seated there with her back to us. Her hair is dark with gray streaks running through it and she wears a fashionable hat. I swallow and realize this must be Mrs. Greenwood.

"Mother," Theodore announces as we come to the front of the sofa. The woman stands and holds her hands in front of her. I notice the mole near her mouth right away, Theodore has one in the exact same spot. She has a hardened expression and her red lips are in a straight line. Her skin has makeup caked on it, showing the wrinkles around her eyes and mouth.

"This must be the girl then," she says, looking straight at me. Her golden eyes look me up and down slowly, pausing at my scuffed shoes. I shift my feet uncomfortably and glance at Theodore.

"This is Hazel. Hazel, this is Mary Greenwood, my mother," he says.

"Hi," I mumble quickly, feeling my heart pounding in my chest. I cringe at my greeting and I watch as one of Mary's eyebrows shoot up in judgment. "It's very nice to meet you," I try to recover as swiftly as possible.

"And you," she quips, sitting back down on the sofa. Theodore motions for me to sit down on one of the matching chairs that is next to the fireplace. I sit down slowly, making sure to tuck my dress and cross my legs. He goes over to the sofa and takes a seat next to his mother.

I shift uneasily in the chair, feeling awkward and vulnerable. "So Hazel, tell me about yourself," Mary says, making it sound like a challenge.

"Uh- I am from Texas. I was raised there," is all I can think to say, trying to not stutter as I speak.

"And your parents? New or old money?" Her eyebrow raises again, her eyes looking at my shoes. I didn't expect her to be so blunt.

"No money," I joke, giggling nervously.

"I see."

"Mother," Theodore clears his throat, "Hazel grew up on a ranch. Her parents had quite a bit of land."

I look at him in confusion, because we only had roughly ten acres. And my parents were farmers at best. Why is he lying?

"Mm," is all his mother says.

I shoot a panicked look at Theodore. This isn't going well. "Everyone at book club is talking about the wedding," she says after we are all silent.

"I figured word would travel fast," Theodore chuckles. I feel relief as the tension starts to leave the room.

"I invited them all, and the ladies from church, of course." She holds up her hand and examines her fingernails.

"Mother," Theodore warns.

"You're the first son of mine to get married! Don't deny your mother after all I do for you," she says as she pouts. Theodore sighs and holds up his hands.

"Perfect, because I also invited the butcher and his wife. Everyone has been begging for an invitation! Your cousins are coming from the west side as well. Oh, and I made sure the seamstress knows the gown needs to be a soft white and not a bright white," she rattles off.

She stands up abruptly and looks over to me. "You do like lillies don't you? I am having the florist make the most splendid bouquet with them."

"Oh, that sounds wonderful," I smile, standing up to say goodbye.

"Good, it sounds like there won't be any problems. Theodore, you need to come into The Crystal tomorrow morning. And you need to make a few phone calls tonight." She pulls a folded piece of paper and hands it to Theodore. He opens it quickly, glancing down at it and then nodding. He puts it inside his suit and stands up.

He kisses his mother on the cheek and she turns to look at me. "Welcome to New York," is all she says before walking out of the room.

"She doesn't like me," I mutter as soon as I am sure she is far enough away.

"She just needs to get to know you," Theodore reassures me, avoiding eye contact.

"It's getting late, how about you get settled in the guest house? I have some work I need to take care of. When you wake up, come over for breakfast," he suggests.

"That sounds good, I'm exhausted," I admit.

"Margaret!" Theodore calls suddenly, causing me to jump. She appears quickly.

"Yes, sir?"

"Would you show Hazel to the guest house?" he asks. I look over at him, disappointed that he won't be taking me there himself.

"Of course, this way." She gestures for me to follow her.

"Goodnight." Theodore leans down and kisses my forehead. I mumble a goodnight back before following the housekeeper. Her posture is perfect as her heels click beneath her feet as I follow her outside. We walk down a narrow path made out of small rocks and I see the guest house. It's like a miniature version of the main house. It was about the size of my old home, but made out of the beautiful white brick and cream trim. It looks to be one story and has flower boxes under the windows.

"Here we are!" Margaret announces, turning the golden door knob. She pushes the door open and walks inside. I step in behind her and glance back at her.

"Thank you, Mrs. Margaret."

"It's just Margaret. If you need anything, please don't hesitate to ask. Breakfast is served at seven." She smiles, her kind eyes bringing me some comfort. She is half way out of the door when I clear my throat.

"Margaret?" I ask.

She stops and looks back at me. "Does Mrs. Greenwood hate everyone?"

Her hand grabs the doorway to steady herself as she starts to chortle. I look down at my feet to hide my smile, relief washing over me. "Listen," her voice is soft as she looks around, "Mrs.Greenwood doesn't like many people besides Theodore. I have worked for them since Theodore was born, and she has smiled at me only a handful of times."

"Thank you," I sigh, pushing one of my curls out of my face.

"It must have been a long journey, I'll have someone bring over dinner with your luggage." She gently pats my arm and turns to leave.

I close the door behind her and scan where I'll be staying until the wedding. There's a decent sized living room with a small fireplace that's already lit, an emerald green sofa with a high back and a wooden side table.

There's a door on the right side of the living room and I push it open. A large bed with a tall headboard sits in the middle of a wall with a matching wooden nightstand next to it.

I look out the window that the desk sits in front of and can see the lights coming from the main house's windows. It's pitch black outside, so I pull the dark red curtains closed. I make my way out of the room and open another door. It's a bathroom with white tile floor and a large white bathtub. Excitement rushes over me as I touch the golden faucet and knobs.

"Miss?" I hear a muffled voice and a loud knock. I go open the front door and see a slender man holding a tray. I step aside and he makes his way into the living room and sets the food down on the oval table. I grab my bag off of the porch and set it inside.

"My name is Edward, I am the head butler if you need anything at all," he introduces himself. I notice his mustache curled up towards his blue eyes. I hadn't seen a mustache so styled before.

"Is that wax on your mustache?" I ask, squinting and leaning towards him.

"Erm, yes ma'am." He awkwardly takes a step back and turns red. Was that rude to ask?

"It looks nice," I say quickly, rubbing my arm with my hand. "Thank you for bringing my bags, and the food," I add.

"You're welcome." He nods and walks at a fast pace to the front door, tipping his hat before leaving. I scared poor Edward. I never saw a man turn red so quickly. Maybe we're related.

I turn on my heels and plop down on the sofa. I pull the bowl of soup off of the tray and stir in the crackers. I glance at the cup of tea and decide to not drink it. I hadn't had hot tea much back home and it wasn't my favorite thing. People here seemed to drink it like it was water.

I eat the soup quickly, my mind on the bathtub. I look around and try to think where to put the tray. I decide to leave it on the table and bring it back to the house when I go for breakfast.

I shut the door to the bathroom and reach for the knobs. I turn one of them and water shoots out of the faucet, causing me to jump. I watch the water start to fill the tub and I shrug off my clothes, folding the red dress with care.

I touch the water that is pooling in the bottom of the tub and gasp, yanking my hand back. It was flaming hot. I turn the other knob and stick my hand under the running water, finding it cold, and it starts to cool down the burning hot water.

I sink deep in the tub, letting the water stay on until it reaches my armpits. I lay in the tub for what feels like hours before the water starts to get cold. I grab the bar of soap and scrub my body, washing my hair with coconut hair rinse that came in a glass bottle. I am shocked by the amount of bubbles that suds up in my hair as I rub the liquid in. We just used a single bar of soap at home for both our body and our hair.

Once out of the bath, I stand on the small rug, water dripping from my body. I squeeze the water out of my hair and wrap the towel around my chest. Back in the bedroom, I dress in my nightgown and pull my brush out of my bag. I prepare for a headache as I run the brush through my hair, but to my surprise, there are minimal tangles. "I'll be damned, that glass bottle wash really is somethin'," I mutter to myself.

I yawn and glance at my journal that I had pulled out of my bag, but my eyes beg me for rest. I remember I have to meet Theodore's friend tomorrow morning, so I pull out the rollers I had permanently borrowed from Florence. I roll my hair up in a few sections as fast as I can, then turn the light off and climb into bed, falling asleep as soon as I hit the pillow.

Twelve

The next morning I stand in front of the bathroom mirror and apply my makeup before pulling out the hair rollers. My hair bounces and I rake my fingers through each curl to loosen them. I wear my green dress, frowning at my reflection. It was a plain dress back in Texas, here it must be terrible. I let out a frustrated sigh and walk into the living room, glancing at the clock. 6:52 AM.

I walk outside and shut the front door behind me, my eyes trying to find the birds that are singing. Songbirds. It reminds me of home and I smile. I follow the rock path to the front door of the house, knocking lightly and trying not to laugh when Edward opens it and stands there stiffly.

"Good morning, this way." He hesitates before turning and marching off, and I hide my smile as I follow him past the grand staircase and into a dining room. Theodore sits at the head of a long wooden table with a bouquet of flowers in the center. He stands up and gives me a hug. He smooths my hair away from my face and smiles.

"Good morning, doll. Your hair looks great, and smells good, too."

"Thank you, I haven't ever used products that were so nice," I smile.

"That's all Nellie. She came a few days ago and dropped off a few things," he informs me, pulling out a chair for me and sitting back down. After I sit down, a wide set woman shuffles in holding a tray. Her hair is disheveled and she is breathing heavily.

"Here we are!" she announces as she sets the tray down on the table.

"Coffee, dear?" she directs the question to me, wiping her hands on her apron. Before I can answer she claps her hands together, startling me and Theodore.

"Oh my, I forgot I had made orange juice! I'll go grab that and your coffee," she pipes, turning and hurrying out of the room.

I blink a few times, staring down at the tray of food. I don't drink coffee. "That's the cook. She is always like that." Theodore shakes his head in amusement and pulls the toothpick out of his mouth.

"She seems...flustered." I watch as Theodore scoops a pile of eggs onto my plate.

"Toast?" He asks. I nod and he spreads jam on the piece of bread before setting it down in front of me. I want to tell him I am capable of making my own plate, but I figure he is trying to be kind.

"Fresh juice from an orange!" a loud voice giggles behind me. I turn to see the cook again, this time holding a tray with coffee and a glass of orange juice. "I didn't know how you took your coffee so I put a splash of milk and a little sugar." She smiles at me, placing the tray down next to me.

"Hazel, this is Cora," Theodore finally introduces us. Cora freezes and puts her hands on her cheeks in horror.

"Oh heavens! Dear, please forgive me. I have been in such a tizzy I forgot my manners!" She sticks her hand out to me and I shake it.

"It's nice to meet you. This all looks wonderful," I nod to the food. Her round rosy cheeks rise as she smiles. I hear a loud crash and what sounds like pans banging together and she stands up straighter and lets out an exasperated sigh.

"They can't be trusted to do anything," she mutters under her breath as she quickly walks off.

I take a bite of egg and wonder how I am going to remember everyone's names. Frank the driver, Edward the butler, Cora the cook. Cora should be easy to remember.

"Frank will be taking you and Nellie into Manhattan once we finish breakfast. Knowing Nellie, she will arrive late," Theodore says after taking a drink of coffee.

"Okay, I was thinking of a jacket and maybe another dress that will blend in with what everyone else seems to wear here?" I ask, feeling uncomfortable.

Theodore raises an eyebrow and shakes his head. "You need a whole new wardrobe. I've already told Nellie what I want you to get."

"I don't need much."

"Just do what Nellie says, she knows about these kinds of things. She's always reading those women's magazines."

I push the eggs around on my plate and nod in agreement. "What will you be doing today? Can we spend time together when I get back?" I ask.

"I need to take care of some business today, I'll be back around three. Meet me by the lake and we'll go for a walk." He smiles.

We finish our breakfast and he stands up. "I'd like to give you a quick tour of the house before Nellie gets here."

"I would love that!"

I follow Theodore to the kitchen where Cora is scrubbing a pan and a lanky teenage girl stands awkwardly next to her. "You must scrub like *this,*" Cora tells her. The young girl's head bobs up and down in understanding.

A large island sits in the middle of the room, surrounded by oak cabinets and hexagon tiled countertops. The air smells of eggs and something sweet. I see the pastries sitting on a plate on the island and watch Theodore grab one. He offers one to me and I take it with a smile.

"This is the kitchen," Theodore states the obvious. Cora spins and faces us, some kind of flour scattered across her large bosom. I turn red and avert my eyes when I realize I'm staring. I hadn't seen someone's chest so big and her tight apron only accentuated it.

"It's not normally such a mess in here," Cora apologizes, trying to wipe up a splattered egg on the counter, knocking over a glass of orange juice as she does. She mutters under her breath and scrubs vigorously.

"It *is* always a mess in here," Theodore whispers in my ear

We make our way out of the kitchen and he guides me up one of the staircases. He shows me three guest rooms and two bathrooms. He pauses at one of the doors and unlocks it before opening it a little, but doesn't step inside.

"This is my office. I prefer to not be bothered when I'm in here. Only because I am usually on the telephone," he says. I peek around him a little and see a large wooden desk with a gold telephone and papers scattered on it. A leather sofa sits in front of the bookshelves lined with an array of different sized books.

He closes the door before I can see anything else and we walk down another hall. "I'm afraid I will get lost if I'm alone," I laugh, feeling like we had already been down this hall before.

"You'll get used to it." He smiles as we approach another door.

"This is *our* room," he winks. I smile shyly and follow him inside. I gasp when I see the inside. Four large windows take up one wall, the sheer white curtains blowing in the wind. I can see the large lake from the room, the water glistening where the sun touches it.

A large gold and white bed catches my eye. It has more pillows on it than I have ever seen. There's a lamp on the wall on each side of the bed, along with matching nightstands. A painting of a baby, a man and a woman hangs up on one of the walls. I walk over to it and touch it softly. "Who's this?" I ask.

"Me and my parents, before my brothers were born." Theodore sounds like he doesn't want to talk about the painting, so I move on. "The bathroom is right here." He opens up a door and gestures for me to walk in.

How many bathrooms could one house need?

The bathroom is as big as my old bedroom, with a large clawfoot bathtub and what Theodore said was a shower. He turns it on and I watch as the water falls from the top, like it was raining. "Instead of a bath," he explains.

"Oh, yes," I say, like I had seen one before.

There were two counters with a sink and different products on them. "This is your side of the bathroom. Nellie insisted a woman needs all of *this,*" he points to the different jars and glasses. I pick up a jar and read it. Some kind of thick cream for your face, it specified it was to be used at night. I sit the jar back and look at Theodore.

"This is exquisite," I say.

"Just wait until you see the closets. I was using both of them until now. I had Margaret move all of my clothes to just one of them so you can have the other."

He goes back into the bedroom and opens one of the doors. "You don't use an armoire?" I ask, looking past the door he had opened.

"No, they are much too small," he answers.

My jaw drops when I see the rows of open shelves and bars with hangers on them. "How can you need this much room!" I exclaim.

"You just wait and see, I bet you will fill it up in no time," Theodore chuckles. I don't see how I could possibly need so many shelves, you would have to wear a different dress every day for an entire year.

"I have arrived!" I hear a woman's voice shout.

"Be right there!" Theodore hollers back.

Thirteen

We make our way back down the staircase and I see a tall slender woman standing at the bottom. Her black shiny hair is in a fashionable short cut and she's wearing a beautiful flapper dress. She throws her arms up in the air and lets out a shrill shriek.

I glance at Theodore and he laughs loudly, their sounds echoing in the room. "This must be her!" She claps her hands and looks me up and down as we reach the bottom step. "I'm Nellie!" She grabs my arm and gives me another once over.

"Nice to meet you, I'm Hazel," I smile cautiously.

"Say, your hair is the bee's knees! I've never seen such a pretty color!" she exclaims as she grabs a curl and examines it. Her accent is strong, she doesn't pronounce her 'R's at all.

"Oh, thank you," I reply, wondering if she was being genuine. Everyone usually mocked my hair.

"I'm stealing her away now," Nellie tells Theodore, grabbing my arm and pulling me to the front door.

"You ladies have a nice time." Theodore leans over and kisses me softly on the lips. I turn red when Nellie makes an *'ooh'* sound.

I pull away from him and follow Nellie out the front door. Frank is standing with the back door open on a red car, just as nice as the one he had picked us up in from the train. How many vehicles could one person own?

Nellie slides in and pats the seat next to her. I sit down in the car and the smell of leather and some kind of cleaner hits my nose. Frank starts to drive and Nellie crosses her legs and turns to me.

"So, how did you meet Theodore? I need to know everything!"

I smile because she reminds me of Florence, wanting all the gossip. "Uh, we met at a shop. He was getting a suit tailored and I was there shopping with my sister. I ran into him," I say, "literally. I actually ran into him."

"And then what?"

"Uh, then he followed me outside and we talked for about ten minutes. And he asked me on a date. We went to eat and got ice cream." I smile at the memory.

"I just can't believe it. Theodore finally settling down. And to someone he only just met!" Nellie says as she's thinking out loud. "Oh! I don't mean that in a rude way, of course. He just hasn't ever shown serious interest in a woman before. And if he asked you to marry him that quickly, I knew you must be something else," she quickly tells me. Her head bobs and moves a lot when she speaks, causing her long earrings to swing. I smile and nod.

"You think *you're* surprised. I never had anyone show interest in me before," I admit. She scoffs and flicks her wrist.

"Oh, horsefeathers! I don't believe that for a second!"

I can't help but grin at the way she speaks, no one in Texas said the things she did.

"Well, I am ecstatic to have a new friend. Truth be told, Peter and Theodore can be so dull sometimes. Always drinking their whiskey, smoking cigars and talking business. I need someone who wants to have some fun! The women who were born here can be so full of themselves, they're all old money," Nellie whispers, her eyes flickering to Frank as if he cared about her gossip.

"Not that I can talk, of course, my daddy has his fair share of wealth." She shrugs her shoulders and pulls out a cigarette from her purse. "Want one?"

I shake my head and watch her light it and take a slow drag. She cracks the window and blows the smoke out. "Where are we going?" I ask.

"A few different places. There's this swanky store that sells the *best* dresses."

"I don't need much, I have four dresses already."

Nellie bursts into laughter, coughing up cigarette smoke and putting her hand to her chest. I stare at her as I chew my lip. "Oh, *oh* you're serious!" she gasps. I nod and tuck my hair behind my ears, looking out of the window to hide my awkwardness.

"Well, that just won't do. You'll be attending different parties and social gatherings, so you'll need a full wardrobe. And you're lucky it's warmer today, but it gets frigid here, so you'll want an array of jackets."

"Parties?" I ask, furrowing my eyebrows.

"You don't like parties?" she sounds horrified at the thought.

"I just haven't been to many. I mean, I went to a few parties my town would throw at the neighbor's barn near Christmas. But I liked them alright," I recall.

"No, not parties like *that*," Nellie giggles. I wait for her to explain and she takes a deep breath. "Parties here in New York have different meanings. Some are just big displays of money and a reason to have fun, those are my favorite. But then there's the parties you will have to go to with Theodore for business and such."

I nod my head so I don't appear dumb, but I'm confused. "Speaking of parties, we need to sit down soon and go over your wedding. I figure Theodore will want the reception at the house after the church ceremony," Nellie says as she flips open a small round travel mirror, checking her eyeliner and rouge.

"We haven't discussed the wedding much, actually. I don't know what he wants," I admit.

"Ah! We are here!" she exclaims suddenly. I look out the window and realize I haven't been paying much attention as we drove through the city. “Stay here, will you?” She asks Frank. He gives a curt nod and we climb out of the car and onto the sidewalk

I look up at the tall building and watch as Nellie shimmies, letting her dress fall into place. I glance at her bare knees. Mother would have had a fit if I wore a dress so short. “Let’s go, I have Theodore’s money right here.” She pats her purse, her thin eyebrows wiggling.

The first store we go to is filled with various women’s clothing and accessories. Risky flapper dresses and even lingerie was on display, something we never saw in our town. I turn red when I look at the lace undergarments. “You need something special for the wedding night,” Nellie says as she holds up a light pink silk chemise with white lace detailing.

“I couldn’t possibly be seen buying that!” I whisper, my cheeks burning as I look around the store.

“This is New York. We’re modern!” she holds up the chemise in front of me, eyeing my size. She seems satisfied with the one she has picked out and lays it over her arm. She grabs another in baby blue as well, adding it to her arm.

I watch her go over to the counter and tell the lady working that we will be making a large purchase, and to hold our items as we shop. The gray haired woman looks over at me, her eyes judging me. I know what she’s thinking. I don’t belong in this store.

Nellie drags me over to where the dresses are, rambling about the different fashions and what would compliment my skin tone. “You need something modest enough for church and charity events. But you also need dresses for the parties," she tells me, holding up a cream dress covered in black lace and sequins, complete with black tassels hanging from the bottom. It had sleeves and a high enough neckline, and I nod in approval. She holds up a dress with thin straps and I shake my head.

"It's too short!" I exclaim. She scoffs and lays it over her arm anyway.

"Theodore told me what to get, so I am listening to him," she boasts as she walks off, plucking multiple other dresses up as she goes.

"I don't need that many dresses. Most of them look the same!" I start after her.

"You don't want to be seen wearing the same dress at multiple parties in a row!" Nellie sounds distraught as she looks over her shoulder at me. I notice a mole near her mouth, similar to Theodore's. I get closer to her and realize it's drawn on with makeup. How bizarre.

"Now the stockings." She grabs a few different kinds and brings them to the counter. She lays down the stack of clothes and the lady behind the counter looks at us in shock.

"*All* of this?" she confirms, eyeing me up and down again. Nellie puts her hand on the counter and leans forward slowly.

"Are you not able to count that much money? Is it too much math?" Nellie retorts.

I put my hand over my mouth as the woman's mouth purses together and she blinks a few times. I can't believe she just said that. "Of course not, is there anything else you need? We have a wonderful sale on our hats." Her voice is forcefully polite now. Nellie looks pleased with herself as she shakes her head and starts pulling out cash. My eyes widen when I see the roll of bills.

After we pay, I help Nellie carry the bags, my arms hurting as soon as we exit the store. "That cost a fortune!" I exclaim, shaking my head in disbelief.

"Welcome to New York! And we still have to get shoes, pajamas and a few accessories." Nellie laughs as we walk to the car that is parked in front of the sidewalk.

Frank is reading a newspaper in the front seat and jumps when Nellie taps the window. He quickly exits and makes his way over to us. "Do you mind putting these in the trunk? You can stay right here, we will be back soon." She hands over the ridiculous amount of bags to him and he carries them to the trunk. I follow him and unload the bags I have in my arms into the trunk after he does.

I follow Nellie down the sidewalk as we hit shoulders with other people, muttering an apology every ten seconds it seems. "You don't need to apologize! This is just how it is!" she hollers over her shoulder at me. I watch as a man looks at Nellie's legs and winks at her. She maintains direct eye contact with him as she turns and waves her fingers at him when he passes by.

And I thought Florence was bad.

We walk for a few minutes before she comes to a halt in front of another store. "This is it!" She tells me as she pushes open the door. The inside smells strongly of leather and shoe polish. It was a smaller store than the place with the dresses, but was just as nice. There were rows of shoes on display along with different hats on the walls. The white floors shined as if they had just been cleaned and a large gold and red rug sat in the center of the store.

"Good morning, how can I help you?" A small framed man with a black mustache appears and greets us.

"Hazel, what size shoe do you wear?" Nellie turns and asks me.

"I think a six." I shift uncomfortably, not remembering the last time I bought shoes.

"We need a variety of shoes for every occasion in a size six," she tells the man. His eyebrows raise but he doesn't say anything, he just walks off and starts looking at the shoe boxes. "Do you like any of these hats?" Nellie asks me as she walks over to one of the walls.

I look at all of them, overwhelmed by all of the different styles and colors. "That one is nice," I point to a simple black bucket hat with a bow.

"It's rather plain, but if you like it. What else? Oh, that straw one!" She points to a floppy straw hat.

We each pick out three hats and go over to where the employee had stacked up about ten pairs of shoes. "These are our most popular shoes. The white tennis shoes and the velvet slippers have been all the rage." He opens one of the boxes to show a red slipper with black fur lining the opening.

"Oh yes. Those are a must!" Nellie remarks. I pick out a pair of shiny black pumps and a pair of brown leather oxfords with a small heel. Nellie adds another five pairs that she insists I need, and the small man carries them to the counter. The stack of boxes is almost as tall as he is as he rings us up.

We carry the bags and boxes out of the door and I walk extremely slowly to not drop anything. Two men stop and insist on helping us, and Nellie bats her eyes in appreciation when they do. I awkwardly follow them to the car where Frank helps them unload them into the trunk.

Nellie puts her hand on the taller one's arm and asks if he has a pen and paper. I watch in astonishment as she writes her name and phone number down and places the paper in his hand, her fingers lingering longer than they need to.

We climb in the car and giggle as we watch the man's friend slap him on the back and teasingly try to pull the paper from his hands. "Successful trip, I assume?" Frank looks at us in the rearview mirror.

We stifle our laughter and I nod, "very!".

I lean back in the seat, wondering how one could be so tired from shopping. "You have a way with men, don't you?" I look at Nellie as she adjusts her hat. She smirks at me and stretches out her lanky legs.

"It's entertaining really, to see how many men you can get to fancy you. They're so easy," she chuckles, leaning her head back.

"Theodore was my first kiss. I am terrible at flirting," I groan.

"I'll have to teach you. Oh it'll be fun! Like classes." She claps her hands together as I scoff and shake my head. "I could teach you a thing or two to do in the sheets as well," she whispers as she leans close to me.

"Nellie!" I gasp and feel my neck and face turning red.

"I'm just saying. A man like Theodore is bound to need to be impressed."

"What do you mean?"

"Nothing, it's just he's really experienced is all."

"Experienced with what?"

"Women," she says simply.

I frown and begin chewing on my lip.

On the ride home, she talks about the different ways I should style my hair to compliment each dress, and what shoes to wear with what. I try to listen, but my mind keeps floating back to her comment about Theodore. How many women had he been with? She said he hadn't been that serious about anyone else before.

We pull in the large gate and park in front of the water fountain. Frank tells us he will bring the clothes to the guest house and Nellie walks with me inside Theodore's house. "I had a grand time. How about I come back in two days and we can chat over tea?" she asks.

"That sounds nice, thank you for today." I look at the clock on the wall and am disappointed to find it's only one o'clock.

Nellie blows a kiss and waves goodbye as she walks out the door and Edward closes it behind her. "Lunch is ready, miss," he tells me, standing stiffly by the front door.

Fourteen

I sit alone at the large dining table, feeling awkward eating by myself as Cora brings out roast chicken and a small salad. "Cora?" I ask as she starts to walk off.

"Yes dear?" She turns and smiles.

"Is there somewhere else I could eat? This is just too much for me to eat alone here." I gesture to the long table and big room.

Her expression softens and she nods. "How about a nice lunch in the garden? There's a few tables and chairs scattered about in the yard."

"That's perfect. Have you eaten?"

"No ma'am, I eat once lunch is finished and cleaned up."

"Would you mind eating a little early with me? I'm not used to eating alone," I admit, feeling slightly embarrassed for asking. She blinks a few times and then wipes her hands on her apron.

"I think I could do that."

We sit at a small metal table outside in the garden in front of the lake, surrounded by trimmed hedges and rose bushes. We make small talk about the weather that New York gets and talk about her favorite dishes to make. I like Cora's presence, she was like a scatterbrained, yet comforting mother. I breathe in the fresh spring air and let the sun shine down on my face as I finish the last bite of salad.

"So, are you excited for the wedding?" Cora asks, folding her napkin and setting it on her empty plate.

"Yes, it doesn't seem real though. I don't believe that I actually get a happily ever after."

Cora is quiet and leans back in her chair, looking up at the clouds. "I wouldn't count on happily ever after. Marriage isn't like that," she advises.

"I know it won't be perfect, but Theodore's pretty close to it."

"Just be careful," she says as she stands and collects the dishes.

"What do you mean?" I ask, shaking my foot in anxiousness and peering up at her.

"You're so young. I know how it feels to be so in love, just be careful." She pats my hand and walks off with the dishes stacked in her arms.

I stare after her, watching her wide figure disappear around a corner. I feel slightly irritated at her comment. *So young.* I roll my eyes as I stand up and make my way to the guest house.

I sit on the sofa and write about my day. I close my eyes and replay everything in my head, trying to remember all of the little details I want to include. I write about the wall of hats and the light pink lingerie.

'Fragile and light, soft and smooth. Made to be hidden from the world, but all the real nonetheless. Shameful, yet acquired. Maybe I am a pink chemise and not a seventeen year old.'

I read over what I wrote and scratch out parts and rewrite them. I chew on my lip as my pencil scribbles and I turn page after page. I write about Nellie's fake mole and her forward comments to men.

I start to laugh at a sentence I begin to write when a loud banging makes me drop my pencil. I look up and realize it's the door so I jump to open it. As soon as I do, Theodore pushes inside and turns towards me.

"Are you ill?" he asks, looking me up and down with his eyebrows furrowed.

"What?" I look at him in confusion.

"You were supposed to meet me nearly twenty minutes ago! I stood by the lake waiting."

"Oh, I am so sorry, I forgot. I got so caught up in my writing. I was actually just writing about how Nellie-" I start to giggle when he cuts me off by raising his hand.

"I don't know why you think my time isn't important, but I will not stand for nearly half an hour waiting on you again. Next time look at the clock, you have one right there!" He points to the golden clock ticking above the fireplace. My chest squeezes as I take a step closer to him and take his hand, panic filling my body.

"I am *so* sorry. I should have kept track of the time, I'm horrible. It won't happen again," I promise. He sighs and takes his other hand and rakes it through his hair. "Please forgive me," I beg, a small part of me worried he will want to call off the wedding because of my foolishness.

"It's fine. I just had a stressful day." He chews on the toothpick that hangs from his mouth and pulls his hand away to sit on the sofa. He picks up my journal and glances down at it before setting it on the table. I take a seat next to him and cross my legs as he lets out a loud sigh and runs his hand over his face.

"Why was your day stressful?" I ask.

"I had a lot to take care of from being gone so long- that extra week really put me behind on some things," he says. I feel guilt wash over me instantly. He had a horrible day because he stayed an extra week in Texas for *me* and then I forgot to meet him by the lake and left him waiting. *Get it together before you make him realize you aren't good enough for him.*

"Well, I bet I can make your day better!" I try to say as seductively as possible, feeling silly when the words leave my mouth. His mood lightens as his lip curls up in a smirk.

"Is that so?"

I pull the toothpick out of his mouth and lean in closer to him. He kisses me gently and wraps his hand around my neck softly. I open my mouth and let him deepen the kiss as his hand moves from my neck to the top of my dress. I pull away and smile, shaking my head. "I want to wait until the wedding night," I say quietly.

"Isn't it a little too late for that?"

"I just figure it's not even two weeks. It'll make it more special." I shrug, feeling embarrassed and unsure if I should have just kept my thoughts to myself.

"If that's what you want," he says, sounding less than thrilled. He gives me a smile and raises an eyebrow. "Kissing is still on the table though, correct?"

I nod and he grins before going back to kissing me. His kisses start to drift from my lips to my neck and I start to laugh as I pull away. "You didn't specify *where*," Theodore smirks. I push his shoulder and shake my head at him.

"Can we talk about the wedding? Nellie said you wanted to have the reception here?" I ask.

"Yes, I have the caterer already lined up, lobster will be the main course. The florist and rental suppliers will be here that morning to get everything set up. Margaret has a list of everything and knows every little detail." He tucks a curl behind my ear and his gaze flickers down to my lips.

"So there's nothing for me to help plan?" I try to hide my disappointment.

"I didn't want you to have to stress about anything. And things need to be just so, and I know you come from a different background than people here," he says. I frown and sit up a little straighter.

"What does that mean?"

“You aren’t old money or even new money, doll. Things are just done differently. Are you unhappy?” He rubs my leg over my dress. *He’s right. If I planned a wedding I would surely mess it up. I would embarrass him.*

“No, you’re right. I’m sure it will all be wonderful. If you have anything to do with it, it will be perfect.” I smile and lean my head on his shoulder.

We sit at the large table that night and eat dinner together, pork chops with red potatoes. “My mother wants to come over tomorrow. To discuss the wedding,” he tells me. I look over at him and try not to frown. His mother seems rather involved.

“I thought Margaret had every detail already. So it seems like it’s all planned.”

Theodore sets his fork down and looks at me. “Every detail that has already been made, yes. My mother has been the one creating a lot of those details.”

“Oh.”

“Is there something wrong, Hazel?” I can’t tell if his tone is sincere or challenging, so I shake my head. “Good. I think she plans to stop by after lunch.” Theodore wipes his mouth with his napkin and stands. “I have some things I need to catch up on in my office, it’ll probably be a late night. I will see you tomorrow.” He kisses the top of my head before leaving.

That night in bed I toss and turn, fretting about being in the same room as his mother again. There was something about her presence that unnerved me. Like she was peering into my soul and knew all my secrets, yet wouldn’t ever bring them up, just simply wait for a confession. Like I was a pot and she was fine with sitting and watching the water come to a boil.

I'm a good person. I don't have any secrets.

Images of the seamstress' outstretched hand and me handing over just a little more than half of the coins needed flashes in my mind. *Ok fine, maybe I have one or two shortcomings.*

Fifteen

The next day I sit and have breakfast with Theodore, Cora bustling in and out as she forgets multiple dishes. I wear one of the new beaded dresses, and I can tell Theodore approves by his lingering gaze. "Do you like it?" I ask, as we finish eating and make our way outside for a walk.

"I like anything that's on you. I would like it more if it wasn't on you though," he smirks, causing me to look away in embarrassment. I could tell he likes it when I turn red and he catches me off guard. Like it's a game to him. I can't say I mind it either.

We walk along the lake before Theodore sits on the ground and watches me skip rocks across the water.

"Do you want children?" I ask him after a few minutes of silence. I look over my shoulder at his stunned face and wonder if I shouldn't have asked. *We are to be married, shouldn't we discuss these things?*

“Maybe someday,” he says slowly.

“Maybe?” I echo.

“It’s just a big responsibility and I’m not sure if my life lines up with having children.”

I try to hide the disappointment on my face. *It’s fine, he said maybe. Not no. And Theodore can be enough for me.* “But, if there was anyone who could convince me, it would be you.” He stands up and walks next to me, putting his arm around my waist.

I smile up at him and then look out across the lake, squinting to see the large homes on the other side. We spent the next hour sitting and watching the water, me sitting in between his legs and his arms wrapped around my shoulders.

Before I know it, we are sitting in the main living area having a light lunch and waiting for his mother to arrive. Theodore glances at the clock and clears his throat. “I have to go to The Crystal and do some work. My mother should be here soon to keep you company.” I gather that The Crystal is the speakeasy.

“Uh, you’re leaving? I was hoping you’d stay.”

“I wish I could, doll.”

I watch as he exits the room and I’m left sitting there, alone. I feel panic fill my chest as I pick at my nail cuticles. I hear Edward greet Theodore’s mother and I sit up as straight as possible when her footsteps approach. The slow click of her heels against the tile proves she is in no rush to get to me.

“Mrs. Greenwood.” I stand up and say hello when she enters the room. She wears a black quarter length sleeve dress that falls below her knees. Her hair is bobbed and curled under towards her face. I notice how heavy the rouge is applied on her cheeks as she sits down in the chair by the fireplace.

"Margaret!" she yells, instead of greeting me. I flinch at the sudden noise and Margaret quickly appears. "Bring me some tea, and Hazel too. Two cubes of sugar."

I don't care much for tea. But I don't like Mary's beady eyes staring at me in scrutiny even more, so I accept the cup when Margaret returns with a smile. Theodore must have inherited ordering other people's food for them from his mother.

"So tell me, what exactly is your plan here? Who sent you?" Mary finally speaks. I look up in surprise and scrunch my eyebrows together in confusion.

"I'm sorry?"

"Don't play daft with me, honey. Some little town girl doesn't just run into a man like my son and convince him to marry her in a few weeks without some ill intentions. So, who sent you?" Mary takes a sip of her tea and her eyes never leave me.

I shift uncomfortably and wish Margaret would come back. My brain is swimming with thoughts and I stare at her in confusion. "I'm sorry, I truly don't know what you're talking about. Who would send me? And why?"

Mary observes my face and turns her nose up slightly. "I'm not sure I believe you. But I suppose we will see." I feel frustration building up inside of me and replacing the nervousness.

"Who would send me, Mrs. Greenwood?" I ask.

She waves her hand in the air to dismiss my question. "I assume there will still be a wedding? If so, we have a few things to discuss."

I let out a small sigh and nod.

We spend the next fifteen minutes discussing the schedule and itinerary for the big day. Some aunt of Theodore's will arrive in the early hours of the morning to start on my hair and makeup, I will have a light breakfast and then get dressed. Frank will drive me to the church and the ceremony will begin, and she warns me it will be long.

"The cathedral is large and it will be filled with guests," she tells me. Cathedral?

"Theodore is Catholic?"

Her mouth opens in shock and she shakes her head in a panic. "Oh, oh no. You *are* Catholic, aren't you? You're not a..." she trails off before croaking out, "Protestant?"

I want to tell her I don't know *what* I am. But I don't think saying 'oh, don't worry, I am not protestant. I actually don't believe in God!' would be the best thing according to her current expression.

"No, I'm not protestant. I just wasn't aware Theodore was catholic." I force a smile and reassure her. She sighs and leans back in her chair in relief. So now she thinks I am Catholic. Great.

"If you're going to be a part of this family there are some things you will need to learn."

I swallow and nod, ready to listen.

"Don't talk about The Crystal with just anyone. Don't ever discuss the things you may hear when business is being discussed. And learn how to shoot a pistol."

"A pistol?" I ask cautiously.

"You are from Texas, aren't you? I assume they have guns there?" She stares at me pointedly.

"We do, but I haven't ever had to use one." I mutter.

"Theodore will teach you. I must be going now. Tomorrow I will send the dressmaker over to get your final measurements." Mary stands and looks me up and down, "I thought you would be smaller framed."

I don't know what to say to that, so I sit in silence and watch as she exits the room. Once she's gone I let out a loud sigh and sink down into the sofa. *A pistol? Why would I need a pistol? Is New York really that dangerous?*

I spend the rest of the evening writing and wandering around the large house, looking around to make sure I am alone as I peek in drawers and linen closets. I find myself in front of Theodore's office and I chew on my bottom lip as I stare at the door knob. I hesitantly reach for it and as I turn it, I find myself disappointed. Locked.

"That's Mr. Greenwood's office. No one is allowed to enter it."

I jump at Edward's voice. I turn to him and look around quickly. Where did he appear from? "Oh, I just got so turned around in here. I was trying to find the bathroom," I explain. His expression remains cold and unchanged as he points down the hall.

"The bathroom would be that way."

I smile and thank him before briskly walking down the hall. I shut the bathroom door behind me and put my hands on the counter, staring at my reflection. *Today has been one of the strangest days of my life.*

Theodore arrives late and misses dinner. I stand next to one of the large columns outside the house when I see his car drive up. I smile and wave as he exits the car.

"Good evening, doll."

"I didn't know you would be so late."

"Well, that wasn't the greeting I was hoping for. I wasn't aware I had to report everything to you."

I take a deep inhale at his response and watch as his face softens and he begins to laugh. "I was just teasing." He puts his hands on my waist and leans in for a kiss. I find myself melting as soon as his lips touch mine. He pulls away and pushes my hair back from my face. "Let's go inside, it's cold out here."

I follow him into one of the smaller sitting rooms that has a large cart full of alcohol. He pours two glasses and hands one to me. "Oh, I wasn't going to drink any," I mumble. He stares at me and I decide to take a sip anyway. He smiles and sits down on one of the chairs.

He lets out a loud sigh and stretches his legs. "So, how was your day?" I ask.

"It was fine. Productive."

"What did you do?"

"Work," he teases with a small smirk.

"Your mother told me I needed to carry a pistol. Why would she say that, Theodore?"

His mouth twists and his head cocks to the side. "My mother says all kinds of things."

"Theodore." I try to sound as serious as possible.

"Hazel, listen. I have a lot of enemies in my line of work. You have to realize that."

"I don't understand. People hate you because you own a speakeasy?"

"They hate me for a lot of things."

I suck in a deep breath and try to calm myself. I can feel my temper flaring up and my foot shakes in frustration.

"I deserve more than that. I am going to marry you. I haven't pressed and asked many questions. But I *need* to know some things. I can't be told I need to carry a gun and then be given these vague answers!" I exclaim, my voice rising the more I talk.

Theodore throws his head back to finish his drink and he stands up to make another. My frustration grows as he stays silent and stands by the cart, sipping his whiskey.

I stand and throw my hands in the air. "Do I have to go walk around New York asking, 'who hates Theodore Greenwood and why?' Maybe I should go into the Crystal myself and start asking around!"

"Hazel..." Theodore warns.

"Your damn mother seems to tell me more than you!" the words come out louder than I intend.

"Damn it, Hazel! Sit down!" Theodore shouts as his hand raises and the glass crashes on the floor. A vein I hadn't noticed before throbs on his forehead as he yells. My butt hits the seat immediately and I stare at the broken whiskey glass he threw on the ground. My body becomes stiff and my eyes avoid his as he lets out a loud sigh.

Images of my father throwing his and mother's wedding dishes flashes in my mind.

"Shit," he mumbles, "I'm sorry."

He picks up a few of the pieces and sets them on the cart and clears his throat. "Hazel. Look at me."

I glance up and relax a bit when I see him. His face looks worried and he's raking his hand through his hair. He's nothing like John. And I am nothing like my mother. "It's ok," I whisper.

"You can't ask too much about certain things, alright doll?" He walks over and cups my face in his hands. I nod and bite my lip, my heart still hammering inside my chest.

"Ok, I'm sorry," I say.

"My work is something we are better off just not discussing much. It's better that way."

I try to smile but my face feels heavy. *I pushed him too far. Look what I made him do. He obviously didn't want to talk about it.*

"Let me walk you back to the guest house, it's late." Theodore pulls me up.

Once we're at the front door of the guest house, he twirls one of my curls around his finger. "I love you, you know that right?" He talks quietly, his voice almost guilty.

"I know."

He leans down and kisses me, putting his hand around my jaw gently. I open my mouth to deepen the kiss and the broken whiskey glass disappears from my mind. "I want you so bad," he groans against my mouth.

"Just a little over a week," I tease, as I pull back and open the door. He gives me a pleading look and I slowly shut the door on him, giving him a small smile as it closes.

The next day at noon, Nellie and I are sitting in the sunroom, the large windows all open and letting in a gentle breeze. I shift my lunch around my plate with my fork as I find myself lost in thought.

"Hazel? Is vanilla cake not what you want?" Nellie interjects.

"Oh, sorry." I look up and lean back in my chair. "Vanilla cake is fine."

She nods and writes something down on the paper she had brought with her. She pops a grape in her mouth and watches me intently. "What's wrong?" she asks as her red lips frown.

"Theodore and I kind of had a fight last night."

Nellie pauses and takes in my face before speaking. "What do you mean a fight? There's still a wedding to be planned, is there not?"

"Yes, there is still a wedding. We just, I don't know. It was my fault. I started pressing him about something his mother had said to me. I made him mad and he threw a whiskey glass on the ground."

"Oh, I see."

There's an awkward silence and Cora comes bustling in with a small tray. Her big smile fades as she takes in our faces. "I made pie!" she announces with a forcefully cheerful voice.

"Thank you, Cora." I smile and take one of the small plates off of the tray. Nellie does the same and we watch her quickly turn and leave.

"Theodore's mother told me to carry a gun," I whisper, after looking over my shoulder to make sure no one was around. Nellie doesn't react the way I thought she would. In fact, she doesn't react at all. She takes a bite of her pie and nods.

"I think that would be wise."

I scoff and my eyes widen. "Do you hear yourself! *Me,* carry a gun? Do you have one?"

"No, but I'm not marrying Theodore."

"I don't understand. No one will tell me anything. Many people own speakeasies. I know it's illegal, but is it bad enough that people want to hurt your wife?"

"Look, you're better off just being like other wives. Just don't ask many questions, buy your pretty dresses and enjoy your nice house." Nellie waves her hand around the sunroom.

"I'm not going to be like other wives. Theodore says he picked me because I am not like other women. That's his fault, not mine. So you either tell me or I am going to find someone who will."

She takes a big inhale and lets out a sigh as she peers over my shoulder to make sure we're still alone. "You swear you have to keep your mouth shut, do you understand me?"

My head bobs up and down.

"You know alcohol isn't illegal to consume, but it *is* illegal to make and distribute?"

I nod my head again.

"Well, there are certain people who make that alcohol and distribute it. And above them is the man who tells those people who make and distribute it what to do. They may have a bunch of men in a certain, um, group, let's say, that work for them."

"Are you saying that Theodore is in like a...gang?" I whisper. My heart starts to pound in my ears and I feel my palms get sweaty.

"No. I am not saying anything at all. But, whatever it is that he does, Theodore is always on top. The boss, if you will," Nellie slowly chooses her words.

My mind is cloudy as I try to take in what she's saying. No he isn't in a gang? Or is he? Or does he run the gang? Or does he just tell people how to make alcohol?

Nellie gives me a reassuring smile and grabs my hand across the table. "I grew up with Theodore and I am telling you, he will protect you. You have nothing to worry about."

I swallow and try to nod. "I-I don't know..." I stutter. I start to realize that maybe I don't know Theodore like I thought I did. I have been on this earth seventeen years and I have known this man a month out of all that time?

"Listen, you better shake off whatever silly thought you're having or I won't ever be honest with you again. I thought you could handle it, you seem strong," Nellie demands. I look up at her and nod again.

"I can handle it. I am strong," I say quickly. I start to eat my pie to end the conversation.

I am strong. I left home. And I am never going back to that place.

"Good. Now, back to the wedding. Vanilla cake with a nice buttercream frosting. They are going to make a tiered cake, it'll be exquisite!"

"Pardon me, the seamstress is here. She's in the living room," Edward speaks behind me. I look over at him and back at Nellie. My stomach turns in excitement and nervousness. I had forgotten about the wedding dress fitting.

Nellie lets out a squeal and stands up. "Let's go make sure Theodore can't keep his eyes off of you." She grins and pulls me after her. I follow her into the main living room where a short woman near my mother's age stands. She's adjusting a full length mirror that's on wheels.

"Good afternoon," she says, extending her hand. We each shake it and introduce ourselves.

"I went ahead and had the windows shut so we could start." She motions to the pulled curtains and starts to pull her items out of her large bag. I look at the large dress bag on the sofa with eagerness. "If you don't mind undressing to your undergarments," the seamstress finally says after standing in silence for a few moments.

"Oh, yes, sorry. That would probably be helpful," I laugh and look over at Nellie who has now taken a seat on the sofa.

"I've seen it all before. I have the same parts, you know," Nellie muses. I turn red and start to shrug my dress off. I hand it to Nellie and she folds it neatly. I stand there in my old slip and Nellie clicks her tongue. "We need to get you some more slips."

I ignore her and watch as the seamstress pulls the dress out of the bag. Nellie and I gasp at the same time as the woman holds it up with pride. It's made out of a white satin, covered in shining silver beads and crystals. The neckline was a deep V, but had a see through fabric going over the chest, covered in tiny crystals. "That is the most ritzy thing I have ever seen!" Nellie exclaims. I don't know what ritzy means, but I know it's good.

"I had your rough size, but not exact measurements. So it will be a tad big, but I can easily take it in," the seamstress tells me as she helps me into the dress. I look in the mirror as she moves away from me and I let out a small laugh when I see my reflection.

"Is something wrong?"

"No, no, not at all. I just never thought I would be in something so elegant as this. I don't feel like I'm good enough to wear it," I mutter. The seamstress blinks at my honesty and then gives me a big smile.

"Well, I think that attitude is refreshing," she says. She starts to pull at the dress in certain areas and measures as she goes.

I keep my eyes on the mirror and a small smile takes over my face. I look like royalty, the dress is a little loose but feels like it's made for me. The deep neckline shows just enough cleavage, but the thin fabric that goes across it makes it just modest enough. The light bounces off every little crystal and bead when I move slightly, making me think of Florence's flower barrette. *She would die if she saw this.*

"Do you like it? Is there anything you want me to change?" the seamstress asks as she pins a few more places on the dress to take in.

"It's perfect."

She helps me out of the gown and puts it back in the bag. "Have you decided if you're wearing a veil, a head piece or a hat?" Nellie asks.

"Oh, I hadn't even thought about it."

"I think your hair is something unique about you, I wouldn't cover it with a hat," she suggests. "If I may," the seamstress injects, "I think a long veil for the ceremony and a nice diamond hair piece for the reception."

"Oh, yes! And finger waves for your hair. You have to wear it down," Nellie nods in approval.

"Ok, whatever you think," I say. I don't care much about little things like veils or hair pieces. I just want Theodore to think I'm beautiful.

I walk the seamstress to the door and wave goodbye as she leaves. Edward closes the door and I realize this house will be *my* home. I will walk guests to the door and the hired help will also be working for me, not just Theodore. I look around at the maid carrying a stack of towels as she bustles by and feel uncomfortable at the thought. *I don't want to be in charge of people.*

"Edward?" I ask. He looks at me with a hint of dread, like he's scared of what is going to come out of my mouth. I try to hide my amusement. "Can you ask Frank to bring the car around?" I try to sound confident in my request, but I'm secretly nervous to be asking for anything.

He nods and disappears. A few minutes later a red car is out front and Frank opens the back door. I slide in and swallow my nerves. "Where to?" he asks as he sits down in the driver's seat.

"The Crystal Room," I instruct. It comes out unsure and I watch as his eyebrows raise. He opens his mouth to say something but then closes it and starts to drive.

Sixteen

I look outside the window as we enter the large city, the tall buildings and crowds of people overwhelming me. We pull in front of a nice brick building with windows in front. I look at the large red and black sign that reads 'The Crystal'. I feel regret as soon as I step out of the car. *What am I thinking? Showing up unannounced?*

I stand up as straight as possible and hold my head high as I open the door and step inside. *I am his fiance. I should be able to come see him whenever I want.*

The inside has rows of tables, a bar that looks to only be sitting people to eat now, and mirrors lining the walls. The restaurant wasn't empty but there were only a few couples sitting and eating. A waiter looks over at me and makes his way over. "Just one?" he asks.

"Actually, I'm here to see Theodore," I say.

"Oh, I'm sorry Mr. Greenwood isn't here."

I raise an eyebrow and cock my head to the side. I muster up every bit of confidence and try to look him up and down like I am studying him. Like Theodore's mother does. "I am his fiance."

I watch as his whole demeanor changes and he apologizes. "Pardon me, I will recognize you from now on," he says as he leads me into a hall. The lights are dim and I hesitate as he knocks on the door at the end. It has a cut out that slides open from the other side and a pair of eyes peer back at us. It opens quickly and the waiter motions for me to go ahead. I take a step into the door and freeze.

I am standing on top of a staircase and below me is a large basement that feels like another world. A large chandelier hangs from the ceiling and two long bars are on both sides of the room. A man wearing a suit stands behind one of them and is drying off glasses. On the center wall, there is a large stage where a few flapper girls wearing almost nothing are sitting and chatting with each other as they put on their shoes.

There are many tables with white tablecloths and candles, but they are all empty. Except for one. I see the back of Theodore's head and two other men who are sitting with him. They are focused on a piece of paper, all reading and pointing at it. They glance over at me and Theodore's expression is shocked. He sets his whiskey glass down and quickly stands up. I give a nervous smile as he almost runs to the stairs and climbs his way up to me.

"Hazel, what are you doing here?"

Once at the top of the stairs I can see he isn't as excited to see me as I am him. "I just wanted to see you. Thought it would be nice to surprise you," I say, feeling uncomfortable as the intimidating men wearing all black stare at me from the table. Theodore's face softens a little and he grabs my hands.

"I am glad to see you, but you can't just show up here unannounced. I'm in a meeting."

"So, I can't be here but the half-naked women can?"

His grip tightens around my wrists. "Hazel, they work here. It's different," his voice comes out lower and more hushed.

"Ah, I see. So how do I apply?" I ask, pulling my hands away and crossing my arms.

"I am doing this to protect you."

"I didn't ask to be put in a situation to need protection. And I certainly didn't ask to be protected," I keep my back straight and my head level.

"Look, you can wait at another table until I am finished, alright? Have a drink while I finish my meeting," he says slowly, giving me a look that tells me to not cause any trouble. I nod and give him a sweet smile as I lean in for a quick kiss. I want to deepen it to give the flapper girls a message, but I don't.

I follow him down the stairs and he introduces me to the man behind the bar. "Whatever she wants," Theodore instructs before he kisses the top of my head and walks back over to the table. I sit on one of the bar stools as the bartender pours me a glass of wine.

As I take a sip, one of the flapper girls saunters over and slides onto the stool next to me. She has heavy blue eyeshadow and her hair is styled like Florence's. Her large chest hangs out of the strappy black dress. I look down at her fishnet tights as her dress rides up when she crosses her legs.

"You must be the new Mrs. Greenwood," she says as she extends her hand, "I'm Ruby."

"I'm Hazel," I shake her hand and try to smile, but I feel jealousy fill my chest. So this is who Theodore is around all day?

Just one of her breasts was bigger than my whole head. We grew cantaloupes on the farm smaller than them. I resist the urge to look down at my own chest and compare.

"We couldn't wait to see what woman had finally snatched Theodore up," Ruby motions back to the other dancers who sit on the stage watching us and whispering.

"Well, uh, here I am," I say awkwardly and reach for my drink. To my horror, my hand knocks the glass over and wine spills everywhere. "Shit!" I exclaim, jumping off the bar stool as the liquid drips down the bar.

"I am so sorry," I apologize to the bartender who grabs a rag and quickly starts to wipe it up. I hear a few snickers and I look over to the stage and see the flapper girls covering their mouths.

"Don't pay them any mind," Ruby scoots over to another barstool and pats to the one next to her. I peel my eyes from the women mocking me and I sit down again.

The bartender sits a new glass in front of me and I watch him pull a new rag from under the bar and casually stuff it in his back pocket when he thinks I'm not looking. *Great, he's already preparing for round two.*

"I sure made a great first impression," I mutter and I stare down into the new glass.

"It shows you're human and not some stuffy rich snob. Which is what we were all picturing when we heard Theodore was finally going to settle down. Some girl so beautiful and rich that he couldn't refuse." Ruby shrugs her shoulders and crosses her thin legs.

"Not that you aren't beautiful," she quickly adds. I laugh and shake my head.

"No, you're fine. I'm not anything special to look at and I come from nothing. I don't get it either."

"The girls are just jealous. Half of them have been stuck on Theodore since they started working here."

I look over at them and try to keep my jealousy from showing. I want to ask if any of them had been with him before, but I'm not sure I want to know the answer.

"So, what exactly do you do? I've never been to a speakeasy before," I admit sheepishly. Her eyebrows raise in surprise.

"I dance and sing. I entertain the customers while they drink or gamble."

"Gamble?"

"That's what those tables are for," she says as she points to a section of felted tables.

"Oh."

Theodore gets up and walks over after shaking hands with the men. I see one of them glance at me before going up the stairs to leave. I feel uneasy as I make eye contact with him.

"What are you two ladies talking about?" Theodore asks as he sits on the barstool next to me.

"You," I answer. He laughs as if I was joking and I smile to let him believe it.

"We open in thirty minutes, tell the girls to get ready," he tells Ruby. She nods and gets up.

"It was nice meeting you," she tells me before heading back to the stage and motioning for the girls to get up.

"She's...nice," I say as I pull my eyes away from her and glance to see if Theodore is watching her. His gaze stays on me and he smirks.

"Is she?"

"If you can peel your eyes off her two giant assets and listen to the words coming out of her mouth, yes." I shake my head with a smile and Theodore bursts into laughter. I let out a huff and cross my arms, trying to be frustrated, but I can't when I hear my favorite sound.

"I love you more and more every day." He pulls me in for a kiss and I close my eyes and forget where I am for a moment.

Theodore puts his hand behind my head and grabs a fistful of my hair and pulls slightly. I hear the bartender clear his throat and I pull back quickly. I turn red as I jerk my body away from Theodore's and my elbow hits the wine glass. I let out a groan as I hear the clink of the glass hitting the bar top.

The bartender pulls the rag out of his pocket and starts to clean it up, for the second time. "I think you should be a fortune teller, not a bartender," I tell him, apologizing with my face. He tries to hide a smile and keep a stoic face.

"Let's get you home," Theodore stands and starts to pull me up.

"I want to stay! You said it opens in an hour," I protest.

"I want you to see it on a Friday night, when we are our busiest. I want everyone to see you."

I feel my cheeks warm up and I smile. "Ok, fine. Will you come home with me?" I ask.

"I really should stay. But I will be home for dinner tonight, I promise."

I pout as I follow him up the stairs. He walks me out to the front door where Frank sits, still waiting. "I'll see you tonight, doll," Theodore leans in and kisses me on the forehead.

"I'll be waiting."

I slide in the car and watch as Theodore turns and goes back into The Crystal. I sigh and slump back in my seat, disappointed I didn't get to stay. My mind drifts back to the dancers and their short dresses. *What if they try to sleep with him?* I shake off the thoughts and decide Theodore wouldn't ever do that. I didn't want to be that insecure person anymore.

Once we arrive back at the house, I sit in the smaller front room and drink some bitter tea Cora had brought. I asked for sugar, but I assume she forgot and I don't want to bother her when I hear pans clashing and her frantically yelling at the poor girl who helps her. "Where are the yams? Dinner is in two hours!" I hear her exclaim.

I sit in silence with my tea and the room feels much bigger when you are alone in it. *I need a hobby.* I think of my mother and her knitting, but shake my head at the thought. I'm not an old lady. I could sew, but I don't know how.

When Theodore's car pulls into the driveway, I find myself giddy as I run to his door. I smile as he opens it and steps out. I kiss his cheek and grab his hand to walk with him into the house. "I could get used to this every time I get home," he chuckles and follows me into the house as Edward opens the door.

"Smells like dinner is ready," I observe, sniffing the air. We make our way into the dining room and sit down.

"Here we are!" Cora enters the room as we get seated. She huffs from being out of breath and sets our plates in front of us. Some kind of silver fish stares back at me. Like really, it *stares* at me. I try not to grimace as I look at its open eyes. Mother never left the head on the fish.

"What's the matter, dear?" Cora twists her hands in worry.

"Oh, nothing at all," I lie.

"Doll, if something isn't as you want it, you just need to say the word," Theodore tells me, cutting into his fish and taking a bite.

"I'm just not used to...the eyes."

"Oh! Well here, let me just take this and I will give you some of the leftover brisket," Cora grabs the plate and starts to walk off.

"No, that's ok! Truly, I'm sure I'll like it!" I protest, feeling embarrassed.

"It's no bother, dear! I'm just learning what you like. From now on, no eyeballs," she waves her hand in the air and winks at me before exiting. Theodore is smiling as he takes another bite of the fish.

"I didn't mean to have her do that," I say quietly.

"She works for us, doll. It's fine."

She works for *us*. I smile at his choice of words. "I can't wait to see The Crystal this Friday night."

Theodore looks up at me.

"Well, we aren't going this Friday, that's tomorrow. And next weekend is the wedding. It'll have to be after."

My stomach flips when I realize we are getting married in a little over a week. "Why not tomorrow?"

"I have too much to do tomorrow. I'm taking a week off work for the honeymoon, and I have some loose ends I need to tie before that."

"A whole week? Just us?" I grin. He nods and crosses his arms as he leans back in his chair.

"I wanted to plan some exotic honeymoon where we travel, but Nellie insisted we stay home instead since you just got here," he tells me.

"That train ride was enough for me, I would rather stay here and just see New York. This is traveling to me."

Cora ambles in with my plate and sits it down in front of me. "Thank you, Cora, truly." She smiles and pats my hand before walking away.

After dinner, we sit in the living room with the fireplace going while I write and Theodore smokes a cigar. He leans back in the chair and watches me as I lay on the sofa and scribble on the paper. I flip the page and start to draw a sketch of Ruby with her large chest holding the fish with the eyeballs. I try to stifle a giggle as I draw her breasts even larger than they really were, making them take up half of her body. I know it's immature and something a child would do, but I have to deal with my emotions somehow.

"What's so amusing over there?"

I look up from my journal and watch as Theodore exhales smoke. "Oh, nothing."

"Oh come on, you're always intently scribbling away. Do share!" Theodore stands up and walks over. I hold the journal to my chest and try to hide my laughter.

"No, it's private. It's silly and for no one to see."

"Don't make me beg."

"Fine, just this one time. But I have to warn you, you won't look at me the same after you see it."

I open it to the page of Ruby and the fish and hold it up for him to see. Laughter erupts from him, and he laughs the hardest I have ever seen. He swipes tears from his eyes and holds his stomach. He tries to say something but more laughter comes out instead. Finally, he gathers his breath. "Please, rip that out and let me have it," he pleads.

"Absolutely not! What if someone saw it?" I exclaim, shutting the journal closed.

He walks back to his chair in defeat and tries to take a puff from his cigar but can't because of the chuckles that escape him. "I warned you," I shrug.

"I don't know what I expected, but it definitely wasn't that! Her tits aren't that big are they?" he laughs. I shoot him a look when he mentions her chest and he puts his hands up.

We sit together for another hour before I yawn and stretch my arms. "Let me walk you to the guest house," Theodore says as he stands. He carries his whiskey glass with him as we walk outside. The gravel crunches beneath our feet as we make our way down the path.

"I can't believe we're getting married in a week," I say as we stand in front of the door.

"I can't believe I am lucky enough to have you marry me," he smiles and grabs my chin. He tilts my face up to his as he kisses me. "Goodnight," he says as he pulls away and lets me go inside.

I shut the door behind me and toss the journal on the sofa. I take a bath before climbing into bed in just my underwear. As I pull the satin sheets to my chin, I fall asleep thinking about the fish with the open eyes.

The next couple of days pass slowly as I try to occupy myself. Nellie comes over for dinner one evening when Theodore works late. I take multiple walks around the garden and write until my hand is sore.

On Wednesday morning, I look at the eggs we are eating for breakfast and let out an excited gasp. "That's it! I know what I need."

Theodore looks up from his plate and takes a bite of toast. "What do you need?" he asks.

"Chickens! I want chickens," I say. He looks confused and shakes his head.

"Why would you want to deal with all the mess when we can get eggs from the store?"

"Because it reminds me of home. And I loved my chickens, as silly as it sounds." I think about thieving Henrietta and wonder how many chicks have hatched.

"If you want chickens, I will get you some chickens, just tell me how many and where you want the coop."

I grin and take a bite of the eggs. "Six would be nice," I say.

"Six it is," Theodore smiles and folds up his napkin as he finishes his breakfast. He gets up and stands above me. "I have to go to work, don't forget my mother is coming today."

How could I forget?

I kiss him goodbye and finish my breakfast alone. I wait in the living area for Mary to arrive. I drink the tea that Cora brought me, pleased that she remembered to put the sugar in it. The room is quiet except for the peaceful rain that hits the windows.

I hear the doorbell ring and footsteps approaching. The clack of heels grows louder and then she stands there at the doorway, holding her clutch and a notepad tightly in front of her with both hands as she walks in.

"Good morning," I greet her. "I wouldn't say good. This weather is so dull and dreadful," she says gruffly as she sits down in the chair across from me.

"Rain brings new life," I offer. She lets out a scoff and places her notepad in her lap.

"The wedding is just a few days away. We have just a few things to go over," she talks to me as if I am a ten-year-old.

I wait for her to continue as I take a drink of the lukewarm tea. "Everyone will be at the wedding, it's been the talk of all of New York the last few weeks. Everything is to be perfect, including you. No mentioning Theodore's work. Only drink a glass of wine, nothing more."

I blink and stare at her. Is she telling me I can't drink more than a glass of wine at my own wedding? "Alcohol loosens the tongue. We don't need anyone knowing things they should not," she looks at me with her nose turned up slightly. I nod slowly and hold the teacup to my mouth.

"Are you pregnant?"

I choke on my tea and place my hand over my mouth in shock. "Pardon?" I cough.

"Is that why this wedding is happening?" she asks. I narrow my eyes and set the teacup down as I lean forward.

"I am only going to say this one time. I ain't going to be bullied by you," I start before the anger wears off and I become timid again, "I can tell you are used to pushing people around and gettin' your way. You don't have to like me. But you do have to respect me. Like it or not, your son picked me."

My stomach turns and my palms become sweaty. I prepare for her to throw the notepad at my face. But instead, a dark smile slowly takes over her face. A smile so sinister it almost was a snarl.

“Maybe I will like you after all,” she chuckles.

I lean back against the sofa and let out a deep breath I didn’t know I was holding in. “There is one thing,” she says. I look at her and raise my eyebrows. “Respect is earned, not given. So I will be watching closely.” Mary stands up and walks to the side of the sofa, dragging her hands across the arm of it.

“Understood,” is all I can manage to say. She doesn’t say goodbye as she walks off, the sound of her heels clicking echoes in the hall.

The next morning I am sitting outside writing when one of Theodore’s workers from the stables comes up and greets me. His skin is tan from working outside and he looks near my age. I forget his name as soon as he says it, and I hope I don’t need to remember it at a later time. *There are too many people here.*

“Mr. Greenwood asked me to take you down near the stables to show you something,” he awkwardly shifts on his feet. I hold my journal in my arms as I follow him down the path to the bottom of the hill where the stables sit.

I let out an excited gasp when I see a wooden chicken coop sitting 20 feet away from the stables.

“He already got the coop?” I ask.

“He requested one yesterday, and it was delivered this morning. The chickens as well,” the teenage boy tells me.

“There are chickens in it?” I start to walk faster down the hill and stop in front of the coop. It’s smaller than the one at home, but much nicer. I open the small door and jump back as six squawking hens run out of it. I grin as I watch them immediately peck at the ground and my shoes. Two of them are white and three are a red shade.

"We will change the bedding every few days and do their feed and water daily," the young man tells me. I look over at him and smile.

"Thank you, if you don't mind, I would prefer to feed them though. And gather the eggs. If that's ok," I say.

"Oh, if that's what you want. The feed is this way."

I follow him into the large barn and realize I haven't seen the stables yet. There are rows of paddocks and horses lean their heads out of them, watching me intently. One jerks its head up and down greeting me. The worker shows me the room where all of the hay and feed are kept, then opens a bin full of chicken feed. At home we just fed them whatever scraps we had left over, which usually wasn't much.

"Am I allowed to pet the horses?" I ask.

"Yes, but don't go into the stalls unless you have someone with you. Some of them kick," he warns. I nod in understanding and walk up to the brown horse who had greeted me. I smile and run my fingers between its eyes.

I think back to the horse I had as a young child. We had named her Lily, the name my mother had suggested the day we bought her. Florence and I would ride her almost every day. Then money got so tight we could no longer afford to feed Lily and my father sold her. We cried so hard that day, which made my father livid.

I shake off the memory and go back out to see the chickens. They run from me when I try to pick them up and I huff and cross my arms as I watch them. I decide I will have to win them over slowly with treats.

And that's what I do for the next two days. After every meal I sneak into the kitchen and grab the leftovers when Cora turns her back, and I slip out the side door. I find they like bread and apples the best.

Seventeen

On Friday morning, I walk to the stable after breakfast with leftover toast and an apple in my hands. The chickens squawk in excitement when they see me and waddle as fast as possible to get to me. I pull the toast apart and lean my hand down to feed them out of my hand. They scoot away from me at first and then slowly start to peck the toast. I watch as they each grab a piece and take off to eat it near their coop.

I walk into the stable and smile as the brown horse neighs and throws its head up and down. "Good morning, Dancer," I say to her as I hold out the apple. I watch her large teeth chomp down on the fruit and eat it in a few bites. The boy who worked in the stables told me her name and that she was one of Theodore's best racehorses.

Over the last two days, I have started to bring her treats every time I come to see the chickens. I want to ask if I can ride her but I already know that I don't have enough experience to be riding such an expensive and important horse.

I spend the rest of the day sitting outside with the chickens. The house was filled with people frantically cleaning and Margaret shouting orders. Everyone was preparing the house for the wedding reception. The man who kept up the garden was obsessively cutting at shrubs and pulling tiny weeds from the flower beds.

I finally convince Cora to eat lunch with me outside so I don't have to eat in the hectic house. We sit and eat in the garden like we did the first time she visited. She made sandwiches with orange slices.

"Will you be at the wedding? Or will you be here, cooking?" I ask.

"I will be there. They are having a caterer for the reception," she smiles.

"I'm so nervous," I admit.

"Nervous about what?"

"All of it I guess. I am going to be a wife. I have never been a wife."

"When I started working for the Greenwoods I had never been a cook. And here I am, I like to think I am doing well," Cora leans over and pats my hand like she always does.

"How long have you worked for him?"

"Let's see, goodness, it's been seven years already."

"And you didn't know how to cook?"

She laughs and takes a bite of her orange. "I could cook, that's something my mother had drilled into me at a young age. How to cook and how to bake. But I had never been a cook for someone else. Never been paid for it," she says. I smile and nod for her to continue talking.

"I had just lost my husband. I was a widow and my son was only fourteen years old. I didn't know how I was going to survive. Mrs. Greenwood went to a ladies club with my sister, and I had baked a pie for their event. She mentioned how good it was and my sister told her my story. A few days later I received a letter offering me a position as a cook for Mr. Greenwood. I moved into the servant's quarters with my son, Anthony. He started to work in the stables and has been there ever since."

That was the boy's name I couldn't remember. Anthony. "I wasn't aware he was your son! He looks quite a bit younger than he is," I say.

"He gets that a lot, don't tell him that," Cora chuckles and finishes her sandwich.

I was thankful to hear a good story about Theodore and how kind his heart is. Especially after my conversation with Nellie. *Someone in a gang wouldn't hire a poor widow and give her a job*. Sure, maybe he sold some alcohol. But many people do that.

"Well, I better get to cleaning up the kitchen," Cora says as she stands and starts to gather the plates.

"Let me help you!" I exclaim, standing up as well.

"Oh no, I am sorry but I cannot let you do that, it isn't proper."

I furrow my eyebrows and cross my arms. "I want to though!"

She pats my shoulder and gives me a small smile, "sorry, dear."

I watch her walk off with the plates stacked on a tray and sigh. My mind drifts to tomorrow and I feel nerves fill my chest when I remember tomorrow is April 12th. The day I get married. I look up when I hear footsteps and smile when I see Nellie.

"What are you doing here?" I ask.

"I have been sent to make sure everything is ready for tomorrow. I'm staying the night here, so I'll be here early in the morning. I'm the maid of honor after all," Nellie smiles and sits down next to me. I try to hide my surprise and she snorts at my face.

"Yes, I forgot to mention that, I suppose. I am your maid of honor and Theodore has two cousins as the bridesmaids. Since you had to move far from your friends, it only seemed right," she explains.

"Well, to be frank, I didn't have any friends, so it works out."

She extends her long bare legs and crosses them at the ankles. She wore blue eyeshadow again and the little fake beauty mark was there as well. "Everyone will be here early in the morning, so I would bathe before everyone arrives," she instructs.

"I believe Theodore's aunts will be coming to do my hair."

“Yes, then the seamstress will arrive with the dress. And of course, all of the caterers and florists and such will be here starting to get everything ready,” she waves her hand back towards the house. “The reception dinner will be outside, but don’t worry, it is going to be grand. Then the inside will open up for entertaining guests as well,” Nellie informs me.

I don’t tell her that I couldn’t care less about all the little details. I just want to get married. Before Theodore realizes he could do so much better and changes his mind.

“Now, for the important part,” Nellie says in a hushed tone as she leans in towards me. I wait for what I assume is going to be rules on what to do and say during the wedding ceremony. “The tips and tricks for the wedding night.”

“Nellie!” I sputter, looking around to make sure no one was nearby to hear her.

“What? It’s important! And no offense, but you don’t seem too experienced,” she looks me up and down. I scoff and shake my head. “How many men have you been with? Two maybe?” She raises an eyebrow.

I feel my cheeks warming up and I stammer, trying to get a sentence out. “You aren’t a virgin are you?” she gasps.

“No! I have done it once before,” I exclaim, crossing my arms and looking away.

“Once?” she echoes.

“Yes, I told Theodore I wanted to wait and not do it again until after we are married,” I say.

“And he waited? He’s actually waiting?” She sounds shocked. I furrow my eyebrows and glance back at her.

"Yes, it was only two weeks after all."

"Wow," she mutters, "well, nonetheless, you need to know some of these things."

I groan and wave my hand for her to continue. I try to not let on how eager I am to hear what she has to say. I quickly regret my willingness to listen as soon as she starts to describe in vivid detail the ways to 'make a man's toes curl' as she put it. My eyes widen with terror as she starts to use her hands to describe and motion on what to do.

"I am *not* doing that with my mouth!" I exclaim in horror.

"Listen, the way to a man's heart is through his pants," she lectures. I grimace and nod, letting her continue.

She rattles on for another ten minutes before taking a final deep breath. "And then grab the pillow under your head and grip it like your life depends on it. Make sure you exclaim loudly when you do it, they love that. If you can, make your legs shake a little bit too. It's a great final touch."

I blink at her, my face no longer red after listening to her go on and on. "That sounds like a lot of work," I finally say. She shrugs and pulls out a cigarette and lights it.

"Just make sure to spice it up sometimes. Most married men get bored after a while and that's when they start to wander off," she lets out a puff of smoke.

My mind drifts to Ruby and her chest that's bigger than my head. *Ok fine, I can grip a pillow and do my mouth like that if I need to.* Lord knows how many women throw themselves at him daily.

"Theodore will be staying at his best man, Peter's house tonight, so he doesn't see you tomorrow before the ceremony," Nellie says. I look over at her.

"He won't be home tonight?" I frown.

"No, but tomorrow you will get to see him plenty," she smirks. I blush and smile as I stand up and motion for her to follow me.

We walk around the garden and the birds chirp loudly around us. "I hope his mother likes me someday," I mutter.

"Don't plan on it," Nellie rolls her eyes. I stop walking and look over at her.

"She hates everyone. She's always been a bitch, but it got worse when her husband died," she says this quietly as she looks around the garden. Not too far away the gardener is hunched over a rose bush, clipping away. We walk farther away from him and continue talking.

"What happened to Theodore's father?"

"It's not really my place to say," she looks over at me and shrugs her thin shoulders.

"Please," I beg.

"He was shot over a bad business deal. I don't know too much about it," she answers.

"A bad business deal? What do you mean?"

"What Theodore does has always been a family business."

I open my mouth to implore her to explain more but Margaret appears in the garden and waves her hand at us. "Mr. Greenwood telephoned and has asked for your things to be brought over to the house. We wanted to let you know they're moving your things over!" she hollers.

"My journal!" I mutter to myself and start walking as quickly as I can past Margaret and to the guest house. I race past some of the staff and squeeze past one of them and into the door.

"Wait up!" I hear Nellie yell from outside. My eyes dart around the living room and around the staff carrying some of my clothes out of the door.

I see the journal sitting on the sofa and let out a sigh of relief. I snatch it up and hold it to my chest. Nellie shoves past the men carrying a box of my things and raises an eyebrow when she sees me. "Say, you run quite fast," she pants and leans against the wall.

"I didn't know they'd be moving all of my stuff!"

"When Theodore gives an order they jump on it."

"I can see that."

We go back to the house and watch as everyone carries my items up the stairs. "So, I sleep in Theodore's room tonight?" I ask Margaret who is instructing everyone on what to do.

"Yes, but it is your room, too," she answers. I look up the giant staircase and swallow. *It's my room too.*

Nellie and I spend the rest of the day hanging up my clothes and organizing my few possessions. We had to argue with Margaret for a good twenty minutes to let us do it instead of the staff.

I sit on the bed and watch Nellie hang up the last dress. She takes a step back and admires our hard work. "Can you believe a closet could be so big?" I ask. She shrugs like it's not anything special and walks out of the closet, sliding the door closed behind her.

"So is any of your family coming tomorrow?" she asks as she sits on the velvet chair across from the bed.

"Shit, I keep forgetting to write them. I'm terrible!" I groan. What kind of older sister am I? I look over at Otis' magic rock that sits on my new nightstand and feel tears fill my eyes.

"Sorry, sensitive subject?" Nellie asks.

"I just miss them. Well, not my father. But everyone else." *He's not your father. Stop calling him that.*

"Well, look where you are now. Sitting on this giant bed with a closet full of dresses!" she exclaims. I force a smile and nod, but all I can think about is Otis running up to me and my mother making eggs in the morning.

Nellie and I eat dinner together, a light soup. Cora made sure to let me know it was so I look thin for the wedding. After dinner I tell Nellie I would like to get some rest and go to bed early. She takes one of the guest rooms and I turn on the lamp next to the large bed.

I take one of the pieces of paper out from my drawer that I got from Margaret earlier in the day and start to write back home. I tell Otis all about Dancer and the new chickens. I tell him I can't wait for him to come visit in a few months. And I write a section to Florence and my mother describing the mansion I now call home. I smile when I write about the shopping spree, imagining Florence's mouth hanging open with jealousy. I sign the letter and draw a little heart next to my name, then fold it up and set it on the nightstand. I turn the lamp off and crawl under the fancy blanket that feels like it's stuffed with feathers.

I lay awake for hours, butterflies in my stomach, as I think about the wedding and the fact I will be married tomorrow. Theodore's face floats in my mind and I can't believe how lucky I was to have bumped into him in that seamstress' shop.

Eighteen

"It's the big day! Call the press, tell them the most dazzling couple ties the knot today!" Nellie's loud voice jerks me out of a deep sleep. I wipe the drool off of my cheek and blink rapidly, trying to adjust my eyes to the bright light. Nellie stands at the end of the bed wearing a satin robe. I groan and rub my eyes.

Margaret walks in and pulls the curtains open, revealing the low sunrise. "Get up! Theodore's aunts will be here in twenty minutes and you need to get in the bath," Nellie barks her orders while pulling the sheets off of me.

A few minutes later I am soaking in the steaming hot bath that was waiting for me in Theodore's giant marble bathroom. I scrub every inch of my body with the floral smelling soap that sat on the edge of the tub.

Once out of the bath, with my skin as red as my hair, I dry off quickly when I hear Nellie yelling at me from the other side of the door. His aunts had arrived. *Please don't let them be as horrid as his mother*. I suck in a deep breath of air when I open the door with the towel around my body.

To my horror, Nellie is standing right in front of the door with two women next to her. "Oh!" I exclaim, tightening the towel around me even more.

"Ah! Here she is!" one of them yells, grabbing my cheeks and squeezing. She wore a scarf with sequins around her head, her gray and brown hair peeking out underneath it.

"I'm not dressed," I hesitate, unable to move around them because they're blocking the door. Nellie stands between them and thrusts a white robe forward.

"Put that on, darling. We have much to do!" the aunt with the head scarf says. I shut the bathroom door and slip the robe on, trying to cover up as much of my chest as possible.

I open the door and clear my throat. "Can I at least have some undergarments?" I ask. The two aunts are setting up their tools and makeup on a table that must have been brought in when I was showering. Nellie is sitting on the bed and tosses a pair of white satin and lace underwear at me. I blush and hurry to the bathroom to pull them on.

"I'm Queenie, you call me Aunty Queenie," the aunt with the head scarf pats the chair for me to take a seat. I do as she motions, wondering what kind of name Queenie is.

I glance over at her sister, who looks almost the exact same. "I'm Nancy," she introduces herself. I notice the biggest difference between them is that Nancy's hair has a thick stripe of gray through it, almost like a skunk.

They immediately start to pull hair brushes through my hair while adding drops of oils to it. Nellie continues to sit on the bed as she rattles off all of the things to remember. She mentions communion and I pause and look over at her. "What?" I ask.

"Communion, you know, Jesus' blood and all that."

"Oh, yes."

I chew on my lip as I see the glance that the aunts exchange with each other. Margaret pops her head in the room and wears a stressed expression. "Mrs. Greenwood will be here soon," she says. I hold back a groan and to my surprise, Queenie rolls her eyes.

"Get ready for the queen to arrive," Nancy mutters under her breath.

"Not a fan of your sister?" I ask. I feel their hands pause on my head.

"Mary is not our sister. Our brother married her," Queenie explains.

"We warned him," Nancy adds on.

"Now just let your hair dry while we do your face." They lay out all the makeup on the table. The bedroom door opens and Mary saunters in. She wears a floor length shimmering dress that screams wealth. She nods her head to acknowledge the aunts as they stop doing my hair and walk over to her.

"Mary, it is just so good to finally see you again!" Aunt Queenie's voice is higher pitched as she leans in and kisses her cheek. My eyebrows furrow as I watch them all but kiss her feet. *Well, they sure took to liking her quickly.*

Nellie looks over at me and rolls her eyes to the back of her head and makes a gagging expression. I bite my lip to hide my laughter as the aunts turn back to me and start applying my makeup.

"Theodore is downstairs, so make sure to stay on the top floor," Mary tells me.

"Theodore is here?" I smile.

"He was supposed to be at Peter's!" Nellie huffs, throwing her arms in the air.

"You know how Theodore is, he had to come to make sure everything was just right. He is currently instructing the florist on how the table arrangements are supposed to be," Mary pulls out a cigarette and lights it.

"Oh, I can't wait any longer!" Nellie exclaims, standing up from the bed and pulling a box out from under the bed.

"What is that?" I ask.

"It's from Theodore, he told me to give it to you when you are all dressed and ready. But I can't wait!" she giggles and hands me the box. I can feel everyone's eyes on me as I pull the ribbon and pull the lid off.

My mouth parts when I see the glistening jewelry. The necklace was made out of large diamonds and came to a point where a blue crystal hung. A pair of matching earrings sat above it. "Something blue," Nellie smiles.

"It's beautiful," I whisper, tracing my finger over the crystals.

"A sapphire," Aunt Queenie examines it above me.

"I want to tell him thank you," I say as I try to stand. They all exclaim 'no!' at the same time and Nellie shoves me back down.

"He can't see you!" Aunt Nancy chastises.

"I can yell down the stairs!" I beg.

"You will do no such thing," Mary says as she pulls the box out of my hand and sets it down on the bed. I think about stabbing her in the hand with the sapphire earrings.

"I am going to get dressed and ready," Nellie tells me. I nod and she leaves the room, closing the door behind her.

My eyelids get patted with a glittery loose powder and my lips painted with a red rouge. After what feels like hours, they finish and stand back to admire their work.

As they do, Nellie walks in wearing a long cream and gold dress. The neckline is deep, showing her bony chest. Her short shiny hair had a feathered clip to pull back one side and a string of pearls hung around her neck. Her mole was painted on and her lips were a shiny red.

"You look amazing," I say honestly.

"And you look like a different person!" Nellie gasps as she walks over.

"Beautiful!" Aunt Queenie nods.

When I stand in front of the bathroom mirror, I have to convince myself that the person in the mirror is me. My eyes look larger, my lips fuller and my complexion perfect. I look like a woman, not a girl.

"Breakfast!" I hear Cora announce from the bedroom. I make sure my robe is tight as I exit the bathroom and smile when I see Cora's sweaty face. She wears an apron like she always does and is holding a tray full of food. She smiles at me before leaving.

"Eat!" Nellie says as she scoops eggs onto the plates. I sit next to her on the bed and eat while Mary watches me with her beady judgmental eyes. After we eat, Aunt Nancy goes downstairs and forces Theodore to leave.

After everyone is sure he's gone, we go downstairs and I hold my long robe to my body as we pass some of the men carrying furniture out of the largest entertaining room.

Men and women holding giant vases of flowers walk past us and into the big room. "The seamstress is waiting in here," Mary tells me over her shoulder as she leads us into the smaller front room. When we enter the room I smile as I see the white gown draped over the small sofa.

"Jesus, Mary and Joseph! Look at that dress!" Aunt Queenie exclaims. Mary shoots her a disapproving glance.

"Let's get you ready," the seamstress smiles at me. I look around at everyone and awkwardly rub my arm.

"It's nothing we haven't seen before," Aunt Nancy sits down on one of the chairs.

"I just ain't used to being naked in front of people," I clear my throat.

"Well, get used to it before tonight," Nellie smirks.

"Nellie!" I fluster, shooting her a glare. I avoid looking at Theodore's mother.

"You need to put this on first," Nellie hands me a bag. I look into it and shake my head.

"I can't put this on in front of you all!"

"Let us see!" Aunt Queenie insists. I hand her the bag while my cheeks burn. She pulls out the see through brassiere with white lace detailing and then the high waisted drawers that matched.

I avert my eyes from them and catch Mary's expression. She is staring at me with a small smirk. "Theodore doesn't usually go for shy women, this is quite the change," she muses. I narrow my eyes. *She enjoys watching people be uncomfortable. This is like a fun game to her.* She raises an eyebrow like she is almost challenging me.

I decide I have to pick whether I cower beneath her for the rest of my life or show her that she isn't going to be the queen like Aunt Queenie calls her. I stand up straight and pull off my robe completely, letting it fall to the floor.

Nellie chokes on her spit and starts to laugh. I hold still for a moment, staring down at Mary. Her eyes stay on my face and her smirk disappears. I raise both of my eyebrows, waiting for her to say something. She remains silent so I turn and snatch the lingerie set from Aunt Queenie. They all look down at the floor as I pull them on and toss the underwear I had on before to the ground.

The room is quiet other than Nellie's giggles. I look in the mirror that the Seamstress had leaned against the wall and admire my reflection. I had never owned see through undergarments. They left little to the imagination.

“Well, let’s get this on.” The seamstress pulls the dress over my head carefully. She steps back so she is out of the reflection and a smile takes over my face.

“Wow,” Aunt Nancy mutters.

“You look like royalty,” Nellie compliments.

“You did a superb job on the dress,” Mary tells the seamstress. *Of course she can’t say anything nice to me.* I run my hands over the fabric, the sequins tickling my fingers. It fit a little snugger than the time before, showing my hourglass figure that I usually hid with my baggy dresses.

“Let’s get your hair finished.” Aunt Queenie stands and starts to take the pin curls down. My hair falls over my shoulders and Aunt Nancy runs her fingers with oils through each curl to soften them. Nellie stands and pulls the jewelry from the box she had been holding. She gently puts it around my neck and clasps it behind me. I put on the earrings and hold still as the aunts add the veil to the crown of my head.

I gasp when I see myself in the mirror, touching my hand to the necklace and then the veil. I have never felt more beautiful in my life. “Go get the photographer,” Mary tells Nellie.

“The what?” I ask.

“We hired one for today, for portraits. Theodore wants one of you before the ceremony.”

A man with a large black camera and stand walks in. “Where would you like to take this?” he asks after pausing and staring at me.

“In front of the staircase would be best,” Mary quickly says.

I grab the front of my dress and lift it while Nellie holds the train and we make our way to the double staircase. Every servant we pass stops and gasps. They whisper to each other and a few compliment me with a smile. "Right here," Mary instructs as she positions me in between the two grand staircases.

I feel like I am floating and in a dream as the photographer tells me to smile and the flash blinds me. "Beautiful! Magnificent!" he boasts. I thank him as two young women wearing the same dress as Nellie walk in.

"It's about time!" Aunt Queenie looks irked at them and shakes her head.

"I'm sorry, we lost track of time when doing our hair," one of them says as she pats her styled bob. They introduce themselves to me and explain they are Queenie's daughters.

"It's time to leave," Mary announces, clapping her hands to command attention. My stomach turns and my palms become sweaty as I lift the front of my dress and follow her out the front door. Frank stands in front of a white car I haven't seen before.

"You must be the most beautiful bride there has ever been," he greets me.

"Thank you, Frank," I smile and carefully get in the backseat. Nellie gets in next to me and helps adjust the train of the dress. Margaret appears at the open car door and hands us two bouquets. My bouquet is so large it is heavy to hold, so I set it on my lap. To my disappointment, Mary gets in the front seat and looks at me out of the corner of her eyes.

She explains how the ceremony will go and what to expect. "The bridesmaids will enter first. Then they will open the doors and you will walk down by yourself. Don't walk too fast, like you are in a hurry. Keep a steady, slow pace," Mary tells me. I nod, feeling nauseous from the nerves. She tells me Nellie has Theodore's ring and will give it to me when it's time to put it on.

"Theodore is going to faint when he sees you," Nellie reaches over and squeezes my knee through my dress. I smile at her and wonder what his face will look like. *Please let him like my dress.*

I panic as we pull up to the church. It was made out of gray bricks with crosses at the top and large windows everywhere. I notice the cars lining the street, going down for as long as I can see. I feel a lump in my throat as Nellie helps me out of the car. Mary holds the bouquets and Nellie holds my train as we walk to the bottom of the steps in front of the church.

Mary and the aunts take a side door of the church to be seated near the front. "Stay here until we go up and when they close the door after we enter, you go wait at the top of the steps. When they open up the doors, walk in," Nellie smiles at me and hands me my bouquet. I swallow and nod.

I watch as she and the cousins stand in front of the closed doors. Two men wearing suits push the doors open towards them and I hear music pour outside as they walk in a line into the church. The doors close and I take a deep breath and walk up the steps carefully, holding my dress to not trip. I feel my stomach turn and my palms become sweaty as I hear the music continue.

Am I really doing this? A month ago I was in Texas wiping poop off of eggs every day. What am I doing? Is this actually happening?

The music stops and changes to a louder and slower song. It sounds like a harp and a piano. I let out a shaky breath as the doors start to push open. Rows of people stand from the pews and turn to stare at me. I can't see Theodore but I start to walk forward. I can feel my heart beating in my ears so hard I could barely hear anything.

The church is beautiful, with chandeliers and rows of stained glass windows. I focus on my breathing as hundreds of strangers' faces smile at me and whisper to each other. *How many people can fit in one church?*

Candles and flower petals line the aisle.

When I get halfway to the altar I see Theodore and my breath catches. He wears a dark gray suit with a lily on the jacket pocket. A smile spreads across his face and he rubs his jaw when he sees me. I grin so hard my cheeks hurt and my foot catches inside my dress and I stumble forward. I hear a few gasps and I feel my heart drop as I brace myself to fall. I straighten my back as fast as possible and stop myself from falling. My fingers hurt from gripping the bouquet so hard. Bile rises in my throat.

I keep walking and try to pretend that I didn't trip but heat spreads from my neck to my ears. *Shit. Could I be any clumsier?* Theodore doesn't bother to hide the amusement from his face as I stand at the bottom of the altar. He walks down the steps and takes my hand. The musicians stop. He turns to face the priest at the top and helps me walk to the top. *Don't trip. Don't trip.*

We reach the top of the steps and onto the altar. Theodore lets go of my hand and clasps his hands in front of him. Nellie steps closer to me and takes my bouquet. I hold my hands in front of me like Theodore does and look at him from the corner of my eyes. The priest starts his long speech. He reads from the Bible and we take a bite of a dry cracker and a sip of wine from a golden cup. *That must be communion.*

"You look beautiful," Theodore whispers, keeping his eyes forward. I smile and look over at him. He shaved his stubble that had started to grow and his hair was cut a little differently.

"You look handsome." I am so nervous I don't look around and notice the groomsmen that stand on the side of the altar.

The priest instructs us to face each other and take hands. Theodore's hands are warm and cover mine completely. I never felt petite until I was with him. We smile at each other and I can't pull my eyes from his as I repeat the vows the Priest recites. Theodore clears his throat and does the same.

To love and protect. In sickness and in health. Till death do us part.

"Do you, Hazel McCoy, take Theodore to be your wedded husband?"

"I do," my voice comes out barely above a whisper.

"Do you, Theodore Greenwood, take Hazel to be your wife?"

A smirk takes over Theodore's face and he squeezes my hands. "I do," he says.

"Theodore, kiss your bride," the priest says as he takes a step back. I feel my stomach lurch as Theodore's hand comes behind my neck and he leans down. His mouth meets mine and he kisses me hard. The church is filled with loud clapping and the guests let out loud cheers. I turn red as I pull away from him and giggle, pushing his chest. He breaks the kiss and grabs my hand again.

"Mr. and Mrs. Greenwood!" the priest announces. The musicians start to play a fun jazz song and Nellie hands me my bouquet. I hold it with one hand as Theodore and I walk hand in hand down the aisle. My ears ring from all of the applause and congratulations coming from the guests. I try to smile at them all as we exit the church.

Once outside, I take in a deep breath of the fresh air and turn to Theodore. "Kiss me again, Mrs. Greenwood," he says as he grabs my face with both of his hands. He kisses me passionately before Nellie interrupts from behind us.

"There will be plenty of time for that tonight, but you two have a reception to get to," she shoos us with her hands.

Frank opens the door to the white car and we both get in. "I knew you would look beautiful, but my God," Theodore turns and rakes his eyes up and down my body. I blush and smooth out my dress.

"I can't believe we're married," I whisper.

"I can," he smirks and rubs his hand up and down my leg.

“Of course that’s what you are thinking about,” I giggle and push his hand away.

“What else would I be thinking about? I have half a mind to tell them the reception is called off so we can get right to it,” he grins.

I shake my head and laugh as we start to drive to the house. “We are supposed to wait in the house while the guests get seated for the dinner,” Theodore says.

“Okay,” I smile.

“That gives us time.”

“Theodore!” I whisper, glancing at Frank's reflection in the rearview mirror. He remains focused on the road and I figure if he heard us, he had a good poker face. “You can wait a few hours,” I whisper and roll my eyes. I fidget with my bouquet, thinking about what is going to happen later that night. *Don’t be nervous. You have done it once before.* I wonder if I could have a few drinks before it happens.

Theodore stares at me with his deep brown eyes and pulls a toothpick out of his suit and puts it in his mouth. I can’t help but smile when I see it and my nerves start to fade away. We laugh about how I tripped and talk about the music as we drive back to the house.

Once we pull through the gate and make it in front of the house, half of the staff is standing out front waiting for us. Frank goes around the car and opens the door. Theodore gets out first and helps me out. All of the staff starts to clap and congratulate us as we walk up the steps and into the front door. We both thank them and go into the front room.

The photographer is waiting with his camera set up and a ridiculous amount of flowers covering the room. I gasp when I see the hundreds of flowers and tall vases. "I want to capture this moment and have it forever," Theodore smiles.

"Stand right there," the photographer motions towards the array of bouquets.

Theodore stands next to me and puts his hand around my waist. I hold my bouquet loosely in front of me and try to hold a smile until the flash appears. "One more with you kissing."

I turn my body to him and he puts his hand behind my head and the other on my waist. I put a hand on his shoulder and let the bouquet fall next to my body with the other. He kisses me and keeps his lips on mine so long waiting for the photo to be taken that I start to giggle. I try to remain serious but I am belly laughing by the time the flash explodes.

"Wonderful!" the photographer exclaims. Theodore pulls away and thanks him. We are alone in the room when he pours me a glass of wine from a bottle that had been chilling in a bucket on the table next to the sofa. We sit and drink together for a few minutes before Margaret tells us they're ready for us.

We walk past the giant entertaining room and I stop to gawk. "Wow," I breathe as I take it all in. Candles and flowers are everywhere, a piano has been brought in and tables with chairs surround an open area for dancing. Each table had little crystals in the middle with a tall candle.

"Let's go outside," Theodore whispers in my ear.

We walk hand in hand to the back door where Margaret waits. She opens the door and the warm air hits us. Round tables with white lace linen draped over them sat all the guests. A group of musicians sat on the side of the lawn and played their harp and violins. The guests look up at us and start to clap. We wave and make our way to the main table where the wedding party sits.

Nellie winks at me and I sit next to her. Theodore takes the seat on the other side of me and the large doors on the back of the house open again. The food gets brought out and a fancy plate with lobster gets sat in front of each guest.

While the catering company bustles as quickly as possible to bring the food out, the man who sits next to Theodore stands up. He clears his throat and taps on his whiskey glass with a spoon. The guests go quiet and all eyes turn to him.

His hair is short and curly, he was more broad and muscular than Theodore but much shorter. He looks as if he may not even be taller than I am. "My name is Peter, and I am the best man. I was told I had to give a speech or Theodore would fire me," he says loudly. The crowd laughs and Theodore grins up at him. "I have known Theodore since we were young boys. I remember one time we were fishing in a pond that had frozen over. We were probably ten years old. We walked out on the ice and I fell through. Theodore has always been brave and never one to second guess himself. He stuck his whole upper body down in that icy water and pulled me out. He saved my life. If you are chosen to enter his family, he will protect you until the end of times. Hazel, I don't know you, but I know if Theodore married you, you must be something really special. I wish you both the very best," Peter raises his glass in the air. "To Theodore and Hazel!" he toasts.

"To Theodore and Hazel!" the guests all say at once, clinking glasses fill the air. Theodore and I smile at each other and clink our glasses.

I take a sip of the wine as our plates are sat in front of us. Peter sits down and leans in front of Theodore. "I'm Peter, by the way," he smiles shyly.

"I gathered that. It's nice to meet you," I laugh. We start to eat and chatter fills the air.

"I almost face planted walking down the aisle," I mutter to Nellie. She laughs and covers her mouth to keep her food in her mouth.

"I saw that," she giggles.

"It's not funny! No one knows me and here I come, tripping down the aisle," I groan.

"It wasn't very noticeable," one of the cousins leans forward and talks around Nellie.

"I mean, half the crowd gasped," Nellie mutters. I scoff at her and we both start to laugh. After dinner is finished Theodore and I dance slowly in the middle of the entertaining room. My heart thumps inside of my chest as he pulls me closer to him.

"You deserve all of this, Doll," he whispers in my ear. I smile and lean my head on his chest as we sway to the music with everyone watching us.

The evening flies by, people dancing to the jazz music, men drinking whiskey and women drinking wine. I get introduced to so many people I start to forget their names as soon as I am told them. Nellie and I dance with the crowd of people, throwing our heads back laughing and holding each other's hands.

As the sun sets, Theodore and I stand outside watching the guests mingle and take bites of the wedding cake that had been served. He stands behind me and wraps his arms around my shoulders. We sway slightly to the music that floats in the air. "You know how I said the day we went to the theater was the best day ever? I lied. This is," I remark.

Theodore brushes my hair to the side and kisses the back of my neck softly, causing the hairs on my arms to stand. "I agree," he whispers.

Once the sun fully sets, the guests start to trickle out and we tell everyone goodbye. I let out a yawn as we go inside and close the door. Servants walk quickly around us, picking up empty bottles and trash off of the floor. "That's enough for tonight, you may leave. This can be picked up tomorrow!" Theodore announces loudly, causing all of us to jump.

I look over at him in confusion. "I want some time alone with my new wife," he yells, pulling me behind him and to the staircase. I turn red as I see a servant bite her lip to hide her smile.

Nineteen

When we get into the bedroom I turn to Theodore in surprise. "I had them do it earlier," he says. I look around at the flower petals covering the bed and the candles lit all over the room casting flickering shadows everywhere. I see his smirk in the dim light. He closes the door and takes a step closer to me. My heart hammers inside my chest and my skin tingles under his touch as he runs his hand over my shoulder and down my arm.

"I love this dress, but I really want it off of you," he says, his voice deep and scratchy. I nod at him and take it off. I step out of it carefully and look at the expensive gown now on the floor. I keep my eyes down as I feel his eyes taking me in. "Damn," he mutters.

"Do you like it? I've never worn lingerie before," I ask, feeling my cheeks warm up.

He grabs my waist and pulls me closer to him. His hand trails from my back down to my butt and I let out a small laugh when he grabs it. “As much as I like it, I want to see you wearing *only* that necklace,” he grins. He pulls the veil out of my hair and tosses it next to the gown.

Theodore pushes me back onto the bed, causing the flower petals to fly into the air. His mouth meets mine as he pulls the lingerie off with two quick movements. *So much money spent on something to only be worn for two minutes.*

“Let me see you,” he pins my arms above my head and leans back away from me. I squirm and let out a nervous giggle.

“Theodore, come on,” I say shyly.

“I want to see my wife wearing the gift I got her, that’s all.”

He pulls his suit jacket off and starts to hurriedly unbutton his shirt. He fumbles with them so I lean up to help him. Once it’s off, he shimmies out of his pants and I avert my eyes.

This time is different from the first time, because he skips the kissing and touching stage entirely. Within seconds he’s on top of me and breathing in my ear. “I love you,” he groans next to my head.

“I love you, too,” I whisper, feeling slightly breathless from his weight on top of me.

He keeps a steady rhythm as he pulls back and looks into my eyes, causing me to blush and want to look away. I turn my head slightly and his hand grabs my jaw and gently turns it back to him. He holds my jaw in his hand as he stares into my eyes with a look I can’t quite describe. A mix of lust and something else. “Every bit of you is mine now,” he moans.

I furrow my eyebrows a little and become more still. His hand lets go of my jaw and softly cups the side of my face and he slows down his pace. "You are the most beautiful bride," he says. I smile and wrap my legs around his waist, causing him to groan. *Grab the pillow.*

I reach behind me and grab the sides of the satin pillowcase. I try to copy the sounds he makes, but softer. Which must have been the right thing to do, because he collapses on top of me and rolls off to the side. His chest is glistening with sweat as he turns his head and kisses me on the cheek.

"What was, holy shit, that was good!" he pants, out of breath. He removes something from himself and I turn red when I see it.

"What is that for?" I ask.

"So you don't get pregnant," he says as he stands up and tosses it in a trash bin next to the bed. I stand up and grab a light blanket off the edge of the bed and wrap it around myself. I go to the bathroom and sit on the toilet, trying to process the day.

I'm officially married. The wedding night wasn't like I thought it would be. *Should have had more wine.* I look down at the necklace resting on my chest and smile. *Be thankful he married you. Look where you are right now.* I look around the bathroom and wonder how much money just the tub alone costs. The golden faucet and knobs glistening from a recent cleaning.

"Are you alright?" Theodore hollers from the room.

"Yes!" I say and hurriedly finish. I pop my head out of the bathroom. He's laying sprawled out on top of the bed with his hands behind his head. His pants are on but they're unbuttoned. "I just need to wash my face, so say goodbye to the beautiful bride you married," I tease.

"You're beautiful without all that crap on."

I close the door and scrub my face with hot water and some kind of soap in the sink. I pat my face dry and stare at my face in the mirror. My freckles show now and I look like a teenager again. I notice the toothbrush laying next to the sink, obviously put out for me. I pick it up and brush my teeth, not used to using a toothbrush, but a rough washcloth back home. I smooth down my hair before going back into the bedroom.

I pick out a pair of light pink pajamas and pull them on in the closet.

I walk over to the bed as Theodore blows out all the candles. I climb under the covers next to Theodore as he pulls off his pants and climbs into bed fully nude.

He scoots closer to me and wraps his arms around me. "We're married," I whisper in the darkness.

"To think I was just going to Texas for a business trip," he laughs.

"Thank you, for everything. For today, for all of it," I let out a yawn and close my eyes.

"Any time, doll."

We fall asleep with his arms around me and his stomach pressed to my back.

The next morning the light streams in the room and Theodore stretches his arms above his head. "Good morning," he leans over and kisses my forehead.

"Morning," I reply.

"I'm starving," he climbs over me and grins.

"Ok, let's go eat," I say as I try to wiggle out from under him, my stomach growling.

"I'm not hungry for food."

I let out an embarrassed giggle as his hand trails down my body and in between my legs. I let him, even though I really want to tell him all I want is toast and eggs.

Twenty minutes later, I'm smoothing down my messy hair and standing in the closet trying to choose what to wear. I pick out a more simple linen dress with stripes that hugs my hips. It reminds me of something a movie star would wear to the beach.

As we eat breakfast I giggle at the jokes Theodore makes about Cora and her scattered mind. She forgets the orange juice again, blaming it on the incompetent teenager she has helping her in the kitchen. "So, what are we going to do this week?" I ask excitedly before taking a bite of toast.

"I'd like to take you around New York. There's an opera, superb restaurants and on Friday night I'll take you to The Crystal."

"I can't wait. What are we doing today?"

"I have to spend a few hours making some phone calls in my office, then we can go into the city and check out the zoo?"

“The zoo? I haven’t ever been!” I smile but it fades quickly. “Wait, I thought you said you weren’t going to be working for the whole week?”

“Doll, I have to do some work. I just won’t be going traveling or going into the Crystal is all.”

“But you said-” I start to protest when he pushes his chair back and stands up. He looks down at me with a disapproving face and puts a toothpick in his mouth. I watch it twirl from one side of his mouth to the other as his face scowls.

“I don’t want to hear any nagging from you, Hazel. Me working is what pays for that dress you’re wearing.”

I glance down at the dress Nellie had picked out when we went into the city and I nod slowly. “Ok,” I whisper.

“Grand, now give me just a little bit and I will take you to see a lion,” he leans down and kisses the top of my head. I smile up at him as he leaves, but it slides off my face as soon as he’s gone.

Cora is standing at the other doorway with an empty tray and walks in like she hadn’t been eavesdropping.

“If you’re finished, I’ll just take these dishes out of the way,” she gives me a big smile and collects Theodore’s plate. I let her take mine as well and sit at the table for some amount of time, alone.

The clock ticking is the only sound as I stare down at the wooden table in front of me. *Stop complaining about your husband having to work. You probably sounded like a brat.*

I sit in the front room and write until Theodore comes down and tells me he’s ready. He tells Frank he wants to drive himself this time, which makes me happy because I want as much alone time as we can get.

With the windows rolled down and the sun beaming on our skin, we drive to the zoo. I reach my arm out the window and let the wind hit my hand as the radio plays jazz music. "Is there really a lion?" I ask, speaking loudly over the music. Theodore turns and grins, the toothpick moving when he does.

"Yes, bigger than both you and I put together."

"I've never seen a lion. Oh, do you think they have monkeys?"

"I know they do."

I clasp my hands in anticipation and bite my lip with a smile. When we finally arrive at the zoo, I'm in awe of all of the cars in the parking area. I adjust my wide brim hat as Theodore opens the door for me and helps me out. We stand in line and Theodore purchases the two tickets.

We hold hands as we walk through the entrance that's decorated with beautiful flowers and shrubs. Small children's excited squeals and laughter surround us and we make our way to one of the animal enclosures. I gasp when I see the alligators through the metal bars, lurking in a shallow pool of water.

"Those have to be the ugliest things I have ever seen," I tell Theodore who doesn't let go of my hand.

"But look at those pearly white teeth!"

I giggle as he tugs me to the next exhibit. A large black bear sits on the concrete in the enclosure, staring straight at us with a blank stare. My chest tightens when I see it and I feel a mix of emotions.

“It’s beautiful, but...” I trail off and frown.

“But what?”

“It looks sad. It’s lonely and it probably misses nature,” I say as I shrug and give the bear a sympathetic look.

“You’re too sensitive, doll. It’s just an animal,” Theodore chuckles and squeezes my hand.

“I’m not sensitive,” I say defensively.

“Hazel, you’re a woman. Of course you’re sensitive.”

I don’t reply and resist the urge to argue as we walk over to the monkeys. I start to laugh when I see them swing around on the few trees they have inside the exhibit. The children around us grasp the metal bars and wave at them, trying to get them to come closer. I smile at one of the little boys whose wild cowlick reminds me of Otis.

“When can Otis come? He would love this,” I ask Theodore whose eyes are on the monkeys.

“I’m not sure, let’s talk about it later.” I let out a sigh and let go of his hand. He looks over at me with a questioning face and I wipe my hand on my dress with a smile.

“My hand was getting sweaty,” I apologize.

He reaches back for it and grips it tighter this time. I try to move my hand so his fingers will loosen but he doesn’t seem to notice as he pulls me farther into the zoo.

“They have ice cream! Want a sweet, my sweet?” he winks and pulls my hand up to kiss it. I snort at his corny joke and nod. We sit on a bench and eat the vanilla ice cream while watching the people walk by. "It's like our first date," Theodore says as he licks his cone. I notice some of the women eyeing him as they pass us, then glancing at me.

"I think it would be fun to go back and visit my family one day. We could recreate our first date!"

"I don't want to ever go back to that dusty town. It's too much of a trip anyway."

"Yeah, you're probably right," I sigh and watch the ice cream drip down the cone.

"But, maybe they can come here soon," he pats my leg gently.

"Can we talk about it now? Otis coming?" I ask.

"Maybe later. Let's just enjoy our day."

We spend the rest of the day strolling around the zoo and looking at the different animals. We stood the longest at the lion exhibit. I couldn't believe the size of it and its mane made me think of Florence's comment about my hair. I started to miss her just a little bit, so I decided to think about something else instead.

After dinner we both sit in the bathtub facing each other. The bubbles were to the brim of the tub and there were so many you couldn't see under the water at all. All the lights are off, the only light coming from the flickering candles Theodore had lit. We sit in the quiet while we stare at each other.

"What's your favorite animal?" I break the silence.

He cocks his head and thinks for a moment. "Probably horses, but maybe that's because they bring in money for me."

"But if money wasn't involved?"

"But it is."

I roll my eyes and sink farther in the tub, letting the bubbles reach my chin. "What about you?" he asks.

"Chickens or a lion." He starts to laugh and I smile at the sound bouncing off the large bathroom walls. He sits up a little, revealing his muscular chest and wide biceps.

"Those are two very different animals," he muses.

"I don't think they would do well together, but they are my favorite."

I notice the stubble on his jaw and I wiggle my eyebrows. "I think I like the stubble," I compliment. He reaches up and runs his hand over his chin.

"I forgot to shave this morning."

"Maybe you should grow it out," I suggest.

"Would you like that?" He raises his scarred eyebrow. Before I can answer he leans forward and smirks. "Do you think you'd like the feel of a beard against your thighs?"

"Theodore!" I exclaim, splashing water towards him. He chuckles and leans back against the tub, wiping the bubbles off his face. "I swear you like to embarrass me," I say as I give him a stern look.

"I do, I very much enjoy it."

We stay in the bath until the skin on my fingers becomes shriveled and sensitive. He eagerly helps me dry off, patting every inch of my body with the fluffy white towel. We fall asleep in the bed with his arm flung over me and my foot touching his leg.

Twenty

The next few days pass quickly and effortlessly. We go to an amazing Italian restaurant in the city where the owners know Theodore and refuse to let him pay. We go to an opera and I wear a gown that touches the floor. My hair is pinned in an updo that I attempted to do myself. Before we are seated a few women stop me and compliment my dress. I smile and blush as I thank them, not used to getting compliments.

During the opera I try to remain interested, but after the first song, I become bored. I find myself relieved when it's over and we start the ride home. "Peter and Nellie are coming over tomorrow evening for dinner and drinks," Theodore tells me as he drives.

"Oh, that will be fun! I haven't been able to get to know Peter at all. I really enjoy Nellie."

"He's a great fellow. Much quieter than Nellie, that's for sure."

I laugh at that, because I imagine most people are more reserved than Nellie. I have never met a woman quite as intense as her. Once we get back home, Theodore goes into his office to do some work and I write another letter to my family to pass the time.

We eat dinner together, and even though I want to ask about Otis coming in the summer, I don't. I poke at the steamed carrots and push them around my plate. The only noise in the room is the clock and Cora's shouts from the kitchen. "And dessert for the newlyweds!" Cora exclaims as she sets a plate of cookies down in front of us. I smile as I thank her and reach for a cookie. I eat one and pick up another as Theodore cocks his eyebrow and makes a 'hmph' sound.

"What?" I ask.

"You already had ice cream today and now you're having two cookies? Make sure you can still fit in all of those new dresses I bought you."

I pause and look over at him. He takes a sip of his whiskey and laughs. I sit the cookie back down on the plate and wipe my mouth. "I think I will go to bed," I clear my throat and stand up from the table.

"I'll be up shortly."

After I wash my face and change into pajamas, I slide into bed and turn the lamp on. I pull my journal from the drawer of the nightstand and start to sketch the bear from the zoo. Its sad and empty face stares back at me as the door to the bedroom creaks open and Theodore walks in. He starts to undress and tosses his clothes on the floor for one of the maids to pick up.

I realize it irks me when he does, because it only takes a minute to put them on the chair and not throw them across the floor. But Theodore has people who do everything for him and he's not concerned about making their job any easier.

A sigh escapes my lips as he pulls the bedding on his side back. I close my journal and put it back in the drawer and turn off the lamp. The room is black as I turn on my side away from him and try to sleep. He kisses the back of my head and a small smile takes over my face as I drift to sleep.

The next day I check my appearance in the hall mirror one more time before I hear the doorbell ring. The top half of my hair is pulled back in two braids and tied behind my head. As I walk down the stairs, the satin emerald green dress clings to my legs. I smile when I hear Nellie's loud accent ringing down the halls.

When I enter the main living room she is standing next to Peter and her arms go up in the air. "My my, look at that babe!" she whistles and looks at my dress.

"Stop it," I laugh and give her a quick hug. She plants a big kiss on my cheek and turns to Theodore.

"Now, tell me you have been just in bliss on your little stay-at-home honeymoon."

"I am always in bliss when I am with her," he replies and takes my hand.

"Good to see you again," Peter nods towards me.

"And you," I say. We stand in silence for a moment before Theodore clasps his hands together.

"Drinks! That is what we need!"

He pours everyone whiskey and I have to force myself to take sips, not a fan of the strong burn it leaves behind. We sit around the table near the large windows and Theodore shuffles some cards. He deals them out and they walk me through how to play a card game I have never heard of. I find myself confused and finally tell them to just start playing and I will learn as I go.

Peter leans over within the first five minutes and gives me advice when I start to lay down a card that I apparently shouldn't. Nellie gossips about people I don't know for the entire game. Some man with the last name of Princeton. Theodore and Peter exchange annoyed looks as she continues to babble.

I look at her above my cards and wonder if she realizes they aren't paying her any attention. "Older men sleep with younger women all the time," Theodore finally acknowledges her gossip and shrugs.

"He is *married*! And not only that, but he's fat, too." Nellie scrunches up her nose in disgust. I let out a small laugh and try to look serious when they all turn to look at me.

"Well, their life is not our concern," Peter says, his voice so quiet you almost had to strain to hear him. The complete opposite of Nellie, who was on her third glass of whiskey already. I look down at mine and realize I need to catch up so I finish it and Theodore reaches over and pours more in.

We laugh and continue to talk as we near the end of the game, I finally catch on, thanks to Peter leaning over and correcting me every few minutes. Nellie somehow manages to win and she hollers and does a little shimmy with her chest to rub it in.

"We need music!" Nellie exclaims and stands up from the table. She saunters over to the record player, her hips swinging as she walks. She plays upbeat jazz music and turns it up loud. She holds her drink high in the air as she sways to the sound. I throw my head back to drink half of the whiskey as quickly as I can and as I set the glass back down, Theodore fills it up.

"Come, dance with me!" Nellie begs me. I shake my head before she comes over and grabs my hand, yanking me up. I spill a little bit of whiskey on the table as she does but manage to keep a grip on the glass. My skin is warm and my head tingles slightly as I dance with her, my feet clumsy and my body awkward.

I hold the glass up to my lips and drink as my body sways with Nellies. She's humming loudly with her eyes closed and her head bent backwards. Theodore and Peter sit on the sofa, watching us amusedly and smoking cigars.

I'm not sure how much time passes but my glass is empty and my head is buzzing. I continue to dance with my eyes closed. When I open them, I see Nellie sitting on Peter's lap, her legs on both sides of his. She is facing him and looks to be kissing him, so I turn red and avert my eyes.

Theodore nods at me from the cart where the whiskey and glasses sit. I stumble across the room to him and glance back at Nellie and Peter, who have seemed to have forgotten there are other people in the room. Theodore hands me a new glass and I accept it, letting the liquid slide down my throat. It feels warm and no longer burns. *How could I have ever not liked whiskey? This is wonderful!*

I hiccup and giggle loudly, slapping my hand over my mouth. I somehow miss and hit my chin instead, sending me into further fits of laughter. Theodore shakes his head and tries to take the glass from me, but I wrap my fingers around it tightly. "How dare you, sir!" I gasp.

"Hazel, you're going to get sick," he laughs and warns.

"I am sick, sick in *love*," I slur. He runs his hand over his chin and down his throat slightly, looking amused but concerned.

I watch the toothpick twirl in between his lips and I down the rest of the whiskey before tripping over my feet slightly. Theodore catches me and pries the glass from my hand. "It's time for bed," he says.

"Boo!" I exclaim.

"We are departing for bed, you two enjoy yourselves. But not too much, not on my sofa." Theodore warns Nellie and Peter. Nellie giggles and waves at us, not even breaking the kiss. Peter pulls back and clears his throat and begins to say something, but Theodore is already dragging me out of the room. I stumble around, feeling like my legs are made of noodles.

"Careful!" Theodore says as I hit the wall and almost knock over one of the mirrors. "Let me carry you," he insists as he throws me over his shoulders. I giggle loudly as his hand cups under my butt and gives it a squeeze. My head spins and I watch the stairs underneath us as he climbs up them. His shoulders feel like rocks as I lean over them, hiccuping and laughing.

He tosses me on the bed in our room and helps take my shoes off. He starts to pull my dress off when I slap at his hand. "I can do it!" I attempt to sit up and yank it off but it doesn't budge and my fingers feel like they are made out of butter. The room spins around me as he pulls it over my head.

He turns the lights off and I hear him undressing. The light from the bathroom comes through as he opens it and goes to take a shower. I lay my head on my pillow and start to doze off.

I can't tell what is a dream and what is real life when I feel hands touch me. My head buzzes and my heart pounds as I feel skin pressed against mine. I open my eyes but can't see anything and my whole body feels like it's floating. *Am I dreaming or is it the drinks? Where am I?*

I realize I am naked and I feel breath against my neck as a hand gropes my breast. "What?" I manage to mumble into the darkness. I try to sit up but my body feels heavy and tired. I move my leg to try to place it on the ground but the hand grabs it and pushes it back. I smell cigar smoke and I realize it's Theodore's hand and that I'm in our bed. "Stop," I mutter, trying to speak as loudly as possible.

He doesn't seem to hear me as he rolls me over and, in what feels like just a blink of an eye, I'm on my stomach and the pillow is squished against my face. "Theodore," I try to say around the pillow. I stiffen up my body and try to roll on my back to tell him I don't want to do anything, but his hand is planted firmly on my lower back.

"I want to sleep," I slur into the pillow that is now becoming damp from the spit that I can't keep from escaping the corner of my mouth. *What are you doing? Look at you, drooling like a dog. You should be ashamed of yourself.*

I let out a startled sound when he pushes forward and inside me. My stomach turns and I feel a ball in my throat. He continues and my head throbs and the room seems to keep spinning even when I squeeze my eyes shut.

I try to push myself up but his hand still remains on my back, bracing himself as he thrusts. Suddenly I turn my head off the side of the bed and empty the contents of my stomach onto the floor. My body heaves as I puke and the liquid burns my throat as it comes up.

"Shit, shit!" Theodore yells and jumps out of bed. A light turns on and my eyes slam shut when the light causes my head to feel like it will burst. "Damn it! Oh, that is disgusting, hold on. Don't move. "

I keep my eyes shut and feel a tear slide down my cheek as I lay there on my stomach and wait. I try to open my eyes but the light is so bright I close them again. I hear Theodore drop what sounds like towels on the ground over the mess and he curses under his breath.

My heart is pounding in my chest, my palms are sweaty and I feel shaky. "God. I'll get someone to clean this up in the morning," Theodore mutters. The bright light is turned off and he turns on the dim lamp on his side of the bed.

Twenty One

I open my eyes and blink, trying to get them adjusted to the sudden darkness. There's a pile of towels on the floor covering where my vomit is. I look over at Theodore who is pulling on his pajama bottoms.

"You drank way too much," he says accusingly. I find myself sobering up quickly with a pounding in my head.

"You kept refilling my glass!" I blurt back. He furrows his eyebrows and crosses his arms, his biceps protruding when he does.

"I was sleeping. I ain't wanna, I mean didn't wanna-" I stammer and try to keep my thoughts together. My head continues to throb and my stomach hurts badly now. I feel more tears start to fall from my eyes and I swat at them.

"You ain't what?" he asks mockingly.

I stare at him, hurt. My heart twists and I find myself breathing heavily. *What is going on?* "Hazel, don't try to make me be the bad guy here," Theodore says. "You drank so much you could barely walk. The first time we ever get together with my friends and you get fried! You started to embarrass me."

My heart sinks down to my stomach. I feel my face heat up and shame wash over me. "I'm sorry," I whisper.

"Well, now you are trying to make me feel bad. I was just trying to make tonight a good night and not let it be ruined from you drinking half the liquor cabinet," he says exasperatedly and sits on the edge of the bed with his back to me.

I sit up and crawl over to him. *Think. Think. Don't ruin this, this is all your fault. Make him forgive you.* "I'm sorry, truly sorry. Let me make it up to you," I offer, trying to put my hand around him and towards his pants. He shoves my hand away.

"It's too late. I can't after watching you vomit all over the floor."

I sniff and blink my eyes rapidly, trying to see through my tears. I feel stupid and like an immature child as I go back to my side of the bed and pull the covers over me.

How did this evening go downhill so fast? I need to get myself under control. I feel confused and embarrassed as I close my eyes. I cry silently for hours before falling asleep listening to Theodore's light snores.

The next morning Theodore wakes me up by carrying a tray into the bedroom and sitting it on the bed. A small crystal vase sits in the middle of the tray with lilies inside of it.

"Good morning, doll," he smiles and sits next to me. I give him a small smile as he hands me my plate. My head feels dull and I still feel nauseated.

"The eggs are from our very own chickens," he says, "and the flowers are lilies. Those are the kind we had for our wedding, right?" I give him a real smile and take a bite of the eggs.

"That's correct. This is really sweet, thank you." My brain feels foggy as I try to remember everything from the night before.

Silence hangs between us as we eat. I butter the toast while Theodore keeps glancing over at me. We continue to eat the rest of the meal quietly before he clears his throat.

"I'll have someone clean that up in a bit, I wanted to give you a chance to sleep in," he motions to the side of the bed.

I look over confused and see the pile of towels. The night comes back to me in pieces and my stomach feels unsettled. "Oh," I finally say.

"You feel alright? You seem like you don't feel good. Do you remember anything from last night?" he asks cautiously.

I focus on my breathing and my head is filled with thoughts pulling me in different directions. "My head hurts. I don't remember much," I lie, feeling conflicted on what to say.

I feel more sick when I see a slight relief flash over his face before he chuckles. "You drank quite a bit. But everyone had a great time. You and Nellie danced the night away before we finally went to bed. You fell asleep as soon as your head hit the bed," he pulls out a toothpick and puts it in his mouth. I wait for him to mention whatever had happened last night before I threw up. But he doesn't.

I swallow and start to wonder if what had happened was just a weird dream that I was getting tangled up with real life. *He would mention it.* I look over at him and he pulls his toothpick out to give me a kiss on the forehead. *What man brings you breakfast in bed? And remembers the kind of flower you had at your wedding? He's perfect.*

"I love you," I say.

"I love you more, doll."

We spend the morning walking around the property. I hold his hand as we walk in the stable and I grin when I see Dancer throwing her head up and down. "She thinks I'm bringing her an apple," I explain to him.

"Oh, are we making friends?"

I laugh as I reach over and pet her in between her eyes. To my surprise, Theodore tells Anthony to saddle up one of the older horses. "You want to ride a horse, Texas girl?" Theodore asks me with a smirk.

"I haven't ridden in so long, I would love to!"

He helps me up onto the black horse and I grip the horn of the saddle. I lurch forward when he guides the horse out of the stable. He holds the reins as he walks us around the beautiful property. My cheeks hurt from smiling so much as my body bounces on the saddle.

That afternoon we play a card game with just the two of us in front of the fireplace in the living area. We laugh as we eat the dinner we had Cora bring to us instead of going to the dinner table. I like eating at places other than the large dining table that feels empty and lonely.

The next day I watch the clock, waiting for the afternoon when we go to The Crystal. While I sit in the garden, Margaret appears with a letter in her hand. "You received some mail," she smiles when she sees my excited expression.

"Thank you!" I exclaim and take the letter from her.

I tear it open as quickly as possible and grin when I see three pieces of paper folded up. The first two pages are from my mother. I scan the page and read it a second time to take in a few of the sentences.

'Dear Hazel,

I am so happy you are doing well in New York. It sounds wonderful. Everything is good here. Your father is gone most days and nights. He is drinking a lot more. Otis asks every day if it is the day he is going to see you. He wants to know if you have gotten any super strength from the magic stone.'

My heart clenches when I read about Otis and tears fill my eyes. I can't tell if they're happy or sad tears, but I know I have to bring it up to Theodore soon. I need to see him.

'We are lower on food than usual, with your father's drinking increasing. But your chicken did hatch out six chicks, so we are grateful to have more eggs soon. Otis collects them every morning and walks into the house holding the chicks all the time.'

They're hungry. That's what she's telling me, but with different words. John is letting his family go to bed with their stomachs growling because of his own selfish wants.

I take a deep breath and pull out the third piece of paper, which I can tell is from Florence by the handwriting.

Hazel,

I cannot believe you have a whole new wardrobe. How many dresses would you say you have now? Feel free to mail some to me, I bet Theodore won't even notice.

You are living my dream. I can't say I'm not jealous. Gregory and I broke up. I told him I wanted to get married soon and I wouldn't keep giving him the goods with no ring on my hand. You know what they say, 'why buy the cow when the milk is free'.

Well, he decided he would rather go get free milk from some scrawny goat instead. You remember Helen? The little waitress from church? He's with her now. That bitch knew we were together for over a year and she scooped him right up.

I am fine though. Better off without him. I am going to find an older man like you did. Write to me more about the dresses and accessories you have, I just need to know.

Your sister,

Florence

I scoff at the letter and shake my head. I feel bad for my sister because I know she is pretending she doesn't care, but she must be distraught over her and Gregory's ending.

I let out a loud sigh and lean my head back to let the sun hit my face. I chew on my lip as I think about Otis being hungry. I stand up and walk quickly into the house and up to our bedroom. I shut the door softly and my stomach flips as I set the letter in the drawer and close it.

No, you can't do this. I try to shake off the thoughts. *Just ask Theodore. He surely won't mind. But what if he does?* I look over at his nightstand and pick at my cuticles.

He has so much money. He won't notice. I walk slowly over to his table and open the drawer as quietly as I can. I glance back at the door. Inside the drawer is a little black pistol and a giant wad of cash. I take out a few bills from the middle and place it carefully back how it was.

I write a letter back to my family. I tell them that Otis will be able to come very soon and I would write back within the week with the dates. I tell them to hide the money from father and to use it to buy food. I hastily describe the dresses and hats to Florence before tucking the money in the folded letters and sealing the envelope.

I write the address and name on it before walking downstairs to hand it to Margaret. I bump into Theodore in the hall and my heart starts to beat so loud I can hear it in my head. I feel guilt wash over me when he smiles down at me. "Writing to your family?" he asks.

"Yes. They finally wrote back," I reply quickly.

"What did they say? Are they doing well?"

"I guess. Florence broke up with her boyfriend."

"Oh, that's a shame."

"It is."

"We leave for The Crystal in thirty minutes."

"Ok, I'll get ready."

After giving the letter to Margaret, I bound up the stairs and put on one of the nicer dresses I have. It's black with gold designs and beading. I add a glittery clip that reminds me of Florence and her barrette Gregory gave her. *I bet she hates that thing now.*

Frank drives us into the city and Theodore compliments me a handful of times. I start to bring up Otis coming to visit when we pull up in front of The Crystal. "We will discuss it later," Theodore assures me. He scoots out of the car and I see people filling in a line to get into The Crystal. Theodore helps me out of the car and I try to focus on walking in the shoes with a heel higher than I am used to.

"Theodore, good evening!" a man from the line calls out. People murmur greetings towards us as Theodore tips his hat and guides me past the line of people and straight in the door. People part out of our way quickly, it's obvious everyone knows who Theodore is.

He knocks at the door in the dark hall that leads to the basement, and it opens right away. The room is loud with music and people talking and laughing. Lights point towards the stage where the flappers dance and kick their legs high in the air, showing almost every inch of their skin.

“Let me introduce you to some people,” Theodore hollers over the music, holding my hand as I step down the stairs. I feel everyone’s eyes on us as we walk down into the basement.

Theodore introduces me to multiple people. I shake their hands and a few of them kiss the top of my hand. One of the wives of a man wearing an expensive gray suit kisses my cheeks and goes on and on about how beautiful our wedding was.

We make our way over to the bar and Theodore hands me a pink drink with a red cherry floating in it. To my relief, it tastes much better than plain whiskey. He ushers me to a table right in front of the stage that has a paper that says ‘reserved’ on it. We have to squeeze past the full tables to get to it.

Ruby stands in the center of the line of flapper girls, her giant chest on full display as she sings and shimmies. Theodore and I exchange glances and must be thinking the same thing because we both start to laugh. “I truly wish you would have given me that drawing,” he tells me.

“Shh!” I hush him while giggling.

“But, I could frame it and hang it on the door to the basement. It would be perfect!”

I roll my eyes before people start to come up to the table and introduce themselves to me. One woman asks when we are taking the next step and having a mini Theodore. “One day,” Theodore assures her and avoids looking at me when I try to give him a questioning look.

The dancers are entertaining and, to my surprise, Ruby can actually sing. Maybe the boulders on her chest give her vocal cords an extra oomph somehow. The dancers take a break and loud chatter fills the rooms. Ruby comes over to the table and whispers something in Theodore's ear. I feel jealousy creep up as she leans down to speak to him.

I mean, could she put them any closer to his face without suffocating him in between them?

Theodore doesn't seem to notice and his face looks frustrated when she finishes speaking. "Damn it," he mutters.

"It's good to see you again," she finally greets me. I plaster a smile on my face and give her a nod.

She goes back onto the stage after getting a drink from the bar and I pull my eyes away from her. "What did she say?" I ask.

"One of the dancers didn't show up this morning. She quit apparently."

"Oh, that's not good. Well, you can just hire someone else."

"Not that simple. You have to be very careful about who you hire in a speakeasy. My girls have been working here for years. One wrong person can destroy your whole business," he says as he takes a drink of his bourbon. I resist pointing out that he said 'my girls'. I don't care much for that.

"I didn't even think of that. Not like you could just go hire some woman off the street," I think out loud.

"But, I don't need to worry about it tonight. Tonight is all about you," he raises his glass and clinks it against mine. I smile and finish my drink.

The rest of the evening we spent drinking, mingling with people and even playing a round of poker. I, of course, lost and Theodore won. He insisted on splitting the money he won across the table, which caused everyone to raise their glasses and cheers to him.

My feet start to get sore from the high heels, so we end up leaving around eleven. It's dark outside when we drive home and I lean my head on Theodore's shoulder. "What are you thinking about?" I ask, noticing his stressed face.

"I just don't know what I'm going to do about the dancer that quit." I rub his leg and assure him he'll figure it out.

The weekend passes too quickly and before I know it, it's Monday and Theodore has returned to work. Anthony lets me ride the older horse a few times during the week, and Cora obliges in joining me every day for lunch. I find myself growing very fond of her.

On Friday afternoon Nellie comes over for a late lunch. "It feels like ages since I've seen you, even though it was just a little over a week ago!" She flops down on the sofa in the small front room. I find myself preferring the smaller rooms over the large ones. It feels less empty when you're in a cozier space.

"Did you and Peter, you know?" I clear my throat. She looks up at me with her round doe eyed expression she does often, like she's trying to swindle you into falling in love with her. She laughs and shrugs her thin shoulders.

"Maybe," she winks.

"I didn't know y'all were together."

"Oh, we're not. I grew up with Peter. He's a dear friend."

"But you sleep together?" I ask, confused.

"Yes, it's just like scratching an itch. We both know it means nothing. And if either one of us are dating someone, we stop," she answers. I nod like I understand, but really I can't imagine sleeping with someone so casually.

"So, can I ask you something, kind of embarrassing?" I ask.

"Go for it," she says without hesitation. I fumble with the pillow I hold on my lap and I bite my lip.

"The other night, when y'all were over, I drank. Like, a lot. And I fell asleep on the bed and I don't think it was a dream, but maybe it was, but Theodore kind of..." I trail off and try to think of the right words. I let out a sigh and shrug my shoulders.

"He kind of what?" she asks.

"I don't know. He started to, you know, initiate. And I thought I was saying no. But then again, I could barely speak or think correctly. He didn't hear me I guess. And then we ended up doing it and I threw up. It just felt...I don't know."

"Ah, I see. So what are you asking exactly?" she asks after thinking for a moment.

"I don't really know. If you have ever had anything happen like that I guess. The next day he pretended like it didn't happen," I reply.

"Well, I guess I have. I mean, I have drank so much I have passed out and I wake up in bed with someone. It's a risk you take when you drink giggle water," she laughs and leans back against the sofa. I don't say anything so she leans forward closer to me and studies my face.

"When we were drinking, you really flirted with him and kept telling him how much you loved him. And you were on your honeymoon after all, he probably thought you wanted to. It probably felt embarrassing for him that it wasn't great for you and he felt inadequate, so he didn't mention it," she assures me. I nod and realize she's right.

"That's true, I'm just so new to all of this. I feel silly," I admit.

"Don't feel silly. Have you had sex since then?" I turn red at her bluntness.

"Yes, a few times. I know it makes him happy," I say.

"I'm sure it does. That *is* the way to a man's heart after all," Nellie laughs.

I think about the time we did it after the night I had drank too much, and remember how I felt nervous and almost uncomfortable when he touched me. Like my skin wanted to run away from his touch. *I need to stop acting like a teenager and grow up.*

"I know what we need to do," she grins.

"What?"

"You have to come with me to a party, it's tonight! I wasn't going to go because I felt like staying in. But I think it would be grand if you came along!" She bobs her head up and down like the decision was already made.

"Oh, I don't know..." I shake my head.

"You said yourself earlier that Theodore would be working really late tonight. Why should you spend the evening all alone? Cooped up in the big house by yourself!"

"Ok, let me try to call him," I offer. I go over to the telephone and try to remember how to use it. I call his phone at his work and wait but no one answers. I sigh and try again. Nothing.

"Just leave him a note and tell Margey or whatever her name is to tell him where you went. You will be with me after all," Nellie waves her hand in the air to dismiss my worries.

"It does sound nice to get out," I smile.

"Just dandy! I'll need to borrow a dress, this frumpy thing won't do," She looks down at her dress.

"Let's go get ready now!" She pulls me off the sofa.

"But, we haven't eaten dinner," I argue.

"There will be food served there, silly. We need to get ready now. And lucky for us, I drove myself today, so no one will be in our business!"

I follow her up the stairs and into my closet, where she takes an eternity picking out what we should wear. She holds up countless dresses in front of me and clicks her tongue at each one. "This one!" she gasps, pulling the dark red dress off the hanger.

"Theodore bought me that when we went to the theater in Dallas," I smile, fondly remembering that day. It felt like yesterday, but so distant at the same time. I somehow felt like a different person than I was just a month ago.

"You wear this one, get dressed. I will find something that works for me," she says as she tosses the dress in my direction. I catch it and undress in front of her, not bothering to shield myself. I pull on the dress and watch as she puts on one of the shorter dresses I had not been brave enough to wear yet. On her tall lanky legs, it looked even shorter.

"Let me do your hair and makeup," she pleads.

"No, no. I'm just going to go like this," I explain.

"No offense, hon, but wearing a dress like that with hair and makeup how you have it should be a criminal offense," she says lightly, giving me a grimacing smile.

I scoff and laugh. "You are terrible! Fine, whatever. Have it your way," I roll my eyes and sit on the vanity Theodore had moved into the bedroom for me. She twirls my hair into an updo and places a glittering comb behind my head to help secure it.

"I have never seen someone with so much hair," she groans as she puts the twentieth pin in it.

She does my makeup rather heavy handed and reapplies her beauty mark before we head out. Before we leave, I scribble on a piece of paper, explaining to Theodore how Nellie wanted to go to a party and how I tried to call. I hand the note to Margaret, whose lips are in a tight line. "A party?" she asks.

"I tried to call Theodore, twice," I explain. She tightens her lips even more and gives a curt nod, then finally takes the note from my hand.

I sit next to Nellie in her expensive looking car and she starts to drive. I clutch the side of the seat when she takes the corners sharp and rather fast. "I'd like to get there in one piece, Nellie!" I holler.

"Oh, have some fun!" She rolls her eyes and presses her foot harder on the gas. My heart hammers inside my chest and my back pushes against the seat as she flies through the city.

"Where do you live? Alone?" I ask.

"No, of course not. I live with my father, he and my mother divorced years ago."

"Oh, I'm sorry to hear that. Do you see her often?" I ask.

"No, never," she replies, not offering any more of an explanation, so I don't ask any other questions.

"I was dating a man I really thought was the one, but he was too old school. He told me he wanted me to have an army of children and stay at home with them. He didn't want me going out and wanted me to not drink!" Nellie shakes her head and scoffs at the thought.

"So what did you do?"

"I left him, of course! It was rather dramatic really. We got into this big fight. So I took it out on his car. He had this absolute obsession with the stupid thing, it wasn't even that nice!"

"You did what to his car?" I ask, intrigued and my eyes wide.

"I took one of his golfing trophies to it. Beat the snot out of it," she giggles and looks over at me. My mouth hangs open and I don't believe her. "I'm serious, it was amazing!"

I laugh in disbelief and fold my arms. "And what did he do?" I ask as she turns around a corner fast, causing me to grab the handlebar on the side.

"He begged me to come back!" she spurted out with laughter.

"You must really be something in the bedroom," I muse. She looks over and winks.

We drive for another forty minutes before we pull up to a house almost as big as Theodore's. Cars are lined up in front of it and I can hear the music from inside the car. My eyes widen when I see a couple making out on the front lawn, for all to see.

"Perfect, we arrived late. You never want to be the first to arrive at a party, makes you look desperate," Nellie lectures me as she cuts off the car. I get out and follow her up the tall steps to the entrance of the house.

I feel my nerves rise and I want to go back home. *I am not a party girl, what was I thinking?* The door opens before we get inside and Peter stands on the other side of the door. He looks at me in surprise and then back at Nellie. "What is she doing here?" He yells over the music.

"I wanted to bring her! Theodore is working late!"

"I know that, I work for him," Peter reminds her and waves for us to come inside. I follow Nellie and squeeze past the people going out at the same time. It looks like hundreds of people are inside the house, dancing and throwing confetti into the air.

I look around in amazement at the little pieces of paper falling from the upstairs banister where people toss it over the edge. "Is this your house?" I yell to Peter.

"No, a friend of mine. What can I get you two to drink?" He asks.

"Get me a French 57!" Nellie instructs.

"Uh, that sounds fine," I say when Peter looks over at me. He disappears into another room and Nellie drags me to a room where people are dancing in the center. A woman is standing on the piano and shaking her chest when we walk in. "What kind of party is this?" I ask close to Nellie's ear.

"A liberated one! For young, liberated people!" She announces loudly.

I turn red when some people turn and look at us, but to my relief, they cheer and raise their glasses. "But what are they celebrating?" I ask.

"Life!" Peter answers loudly as he shows up next to me and hands us the drinks. It's yellow and fizzy and in a glass I haven't seen before.

"It's gin and champagne," Nellie explains to me, sensing the confusion on my face.

"Oh, I knew that," I say as I take a sip. I look around the room and take in all of the different types of people. People of all colors, shapes and sizes dance in the room. Something you never saw back home in Texas.

"My friend has no family and no other way to spend his money, so this is what he does." Peter hollers over the music, waving his drink to the middle of the room.

“I think I should marry him!” Nellie professes. I laugh and Peter rolls his eyes.

“So why aren’t you working with Theodore?” I ask Peter.

“He does a lot of things on his own, or with a different group of people,” he says.

“Like what kind of group of people?”

“Different employees,” Peter remarks.

“How are they different? Why not you?” I press. He looks around and then glances back at me. We are at eye level and I notice the flecks of green scattered in his mostly brown eyes.

“I don’t like some sides of the business is all. Theodore and I are different that way. So he lets me stay out of some things.” He finally speaks, barely loud enough for me to hear what he is saying.

I suck in a breath and don’t ask what things he likes to stay out of, because I can imagine what they are. I nod and take another drink of the fizzy beverage. “Come dance!” Nellie pleads with me, tugging my arm.

“Maybe later, you go ahead,” I tell her, feeling uneasy when I look at all the people dancing. There seems to be little regard for personal space and some of the couples are making out as they dance.

She sighs and gives me a pouty face but shimmies backwards away from me into the crowd. I laugh at her ridiculous moves and turn my head back to Peter. He is watching me with a serious look and I take another sip nervously. “What is it?” I ask.

“Just trying to figure out who you are, I guess,” he shrugs.

"What do you mean? I'm Hazel McCoy, that's who I am."

"Hazel Greenwood," Peter corrects.

I look away from him and search for Nellie in the sea of dancing bodies, "Yes. Hazel Greenwood."

"Does Theodore know you're here?"

"No, I tried calling him at The Crystal but he didn't answer."

"You should have stayed home then."

I cut my eyes at him and cross my arms, careful to not spill my glass. "I left a note. I am not one of his servants," I snap.

"I know that," he says gently. I feel bad for being short so I finish my drink and ask for a refill to change the subject. He nods and takes the glass from me and shoves past people to get out of the room.

I stand watching the woman on the piano when someone bumps into me. "Pardon me," a man says and then stops to look at me. I smile and nod to tell him it's fine but he continues to stare at me. I avert my eyes and glue them on the lady on the piano.

"You're Theodore's girl," he finally says. I look back at him and feel uneasy as he nods. "That's where I know you from!" He exclaims.

"Where is he?" the man asks as his eyes scan the room.

"He's not here," I say. That seems to be the wrong answer because his eyes light up and he takes a step closer.

"Then you're all alone?" a crooked grin takes over his face.

"No," I shake my head and try to back up but there's people behind me.

"I wouldn't think Theodore would let his beautiful wife go to a party alone, especially a party like this."

I open my mouth but Peter steps next to me and hands me my drink. "She isn't alone," Peter says gruffly. It's the loudest I've heard him speak so far. The man with the crooked grin glares at him and sulks off.

"Who was that?" I ask.

"Probably one of Theodore's countless enemies, who knows," Peter shakes his head and takes a drink of what looks to be water.

"Do you not drink?"

"I do sometimes, but not much." He looks around the room.

"I wonder if Nellie is even still in here," I stand on my toes to try to look around with him.

"She's probably already met some poor chap," he remarks.

"That fast?" I ask.

"That fast." He echoes.

After an hour my shoulders slump and I let out an annoyed sigh. "Do you want to go somewhere to sit that's more off to the side? Maybe she'll see us," He yells over the loud noises. I nod and we make our way to the front open area where the confetti was being thrown earlier, and sit in two of the chairs that are open. Confetti covers the floor and people walk slowly on it to keep from tripping.

Twenty Two

“This isn’t my type of thing,” I decide out loud. Peter looks over at me and raises his eyebrows before nodding.

“Me neither, I don’t know why I came, to be honest. Trying to be a good friend I guess,” he says thoughtfully.

“I’d rather be at home with my chickens. Or writing,” I tip the glass back into my mouth.

“You write?” Peter asks. I still have to strain to hear him, and I wonder if it would be rude to ask him to speak louder.

“Just for fun. For myself. I like to draw as well,” I smile.

“So do I, but I don’t tell anyone that. I know they would try to get me to show them. And I can’t imagine any being worse,” he says.

“I can understand that, I don’t want anyone seeing my journal either.”

We sit in silence for a while and I keep my eyes open for Nellie. Peter gets me another drink when I finish my second and my stomach growls. A man wearing a tux and holding a tray up high passes us. I stop him and take a few sandwiches and olives that he is serving to guests. Peter declines when I offer him one.

After the fourth drink, I stand up and look around annoyedly. “She has to be around here somewhere, I’m going to find her,” I announce. I feel a bit unsteady as I walk and the buzzing has taken over in my head.

“I’ll go with you,” Peter nods and follows me as we check around the house. Finally I see her coming out of a bedroom and I call out to her. She turns to me and grins, smoothing down her messed up hair.

The door she just left opens again and a man tucking his shirt into his pants comes out. He looks at us, then back at Nellie and dips his head down and walks the other way. I turn to Peter and his expression is stone cold, no emotions showing. *That has to sting a little.*

“There you are!” Nellie says as she approaches us.

“Here *we* are? We have been looking for you!” I scoff.

“I was just gone for maybe ten minutes,” she says out of breath. I roll my eyes and grab a drink from a man walking by with a tray. I don’t know what it is but I pour it down my throat anyway.

“Are you ready to go?” she asks me, looping her arm through mine. “

“Yes, it’s getting late and I want to go home to Theodore,” I sigh. She nods and kisses Peter goodbye on the cheek. He nods his head to me before turning and walking away.

When we get in the car I realize Nellie is tipsy and I ask if she's ok to drive. She insists she is. "Who was that man?" I ask, clinging to the sidebar again as she tears out of the driveway.

"Just some lounge lizard," she shrugs.

"A what?" I laugh, unable to stop the giggling once it starts.

"A ladies man," she explains.

"Was it good?" I ask bluntly, then put my hand over my mouth. "I didn't mean to be so forward, I just drank a lot," I apologize.

"Oh, I couldn't care less! It was amazing, rocked my world. I could tell when I saw him, he had that sex appeal." Nellie looks as if she's daydreaming and recalling all the details.

"Huh," I say in amusement. We giggle like school girls at the most ridiculous things the whole drive home. I curse under my breath and grip whatever is closest to me when she swerves the car around the roads.

We pull up to the house and I see Theodore standing on the porch, leaning against one of the columns. He is smoking a cigar and tosses it to the floor and puts it out with his foot as we approach. He makes his way down the steps as I get out and I go to hug him but stop when I see his expression.

"Where the fuck did you go?" he asks loudly. I stop walking closer to him and glance back at the car. Nellie was getting out of the car but she has stopped now and sits back down in the driver's seat.

"I left a note with-" I start to explain and he cuts me off.

“I saw the damn note. You just took off to some party?” his voice raises. I swallow and try to keep my balance as I stand on the gravel.

“I-I just thought it would be nice since you were working late,” I stammer.

“You thought you could sneak in before I got home and noticed?”

“No, that doesn’t even make sense. Theodore, why would I have left the note if-" I try to speak again when he stops me by raising his hand.

“Have you been drinking?” he demands. I look back at Nellie who’s now looking down at her lap and avoiding eye contact.

“Nellie and I both just had a few drinks.”

“I didn’t ask about Nellie, did I?” he sounds exasperated. I shake my head and see Cora peeking through one of the windows. I feel awkward and rub my arm as I shift my weight from one foot to the other. “Were you trying to get some attention? Is that it? Need to go to a party to be told you’re pretty by other men?” He crosses his arms and waits for my reply.

“Theodore..” I trail off, looking around. “Can we not do this right here?” I ask.

“This is my fucking house. I can talk anywhere I want!” He is yelling now, swinging his arms around to gesture to the property.

“I know,” I mutter.

"Get inside," he finally says. I nod and don't look back at Nellie as I hurry up the steps, tripping over one of them and scraping my knee through my dress. Theodore stays behind me as I push myself up and go through the front door.

He throws his hand to the two staircases and I walk to our room, my heart slamming against my chest. I breathe heavily and my blood feels cold as I open the bedroom door and walk inside. He shuts the door behind him and locks it.

"What the hell are you doing?" he shakes his head and drags his hands over his face.

"I was just trying to go out to a party, I tried to call you!"

"You are a married woman, Hazel! You don't just go to these parties filled with loose people and do it behind your husband's back."

"I won't do it again," I promise.

"I know you fucking won't!" he laughs, stepping closer to me. I can smell the alcohol on his breath and I notice the redness in his eyes.

"You're drunk," I say.

"Don't you accuse me of anything! I have been sitting here, drinking and waiting for my wife to get back home. Looking like an idiot while the staff thinks my wife is out fucking someone else!" His voice begins to raise again and the vein shows on his forehead when he yells.

"I was doing no such thing! Peter was there, the whole time. He can tell you!" my voice starts to quiver and tears fill my eyes.

“You even wore the dress I got you in Texas. Look at your face, you look like a clown!” he reaches over and swipes his finger across my lips, smearing the red rouge and holding his thumb in my face for me to see. I swallow and try to take a few deep breaths.

“You wouldn’t even have this dress if it wasn’t for me, and you wear it out to parade yourself around with Nellie!”

“I went out with a friend and just tried to have a good time!” I exclaim, my voice coming out louder than I intended.

“You wouldn’t even be noticeable if it wasn’t for me. The only friend you have is because of *me*!” he chastises.

“Theodore, you’re being ridiculous! You sound crazy. Like a damn lunatic!” I yell, shoving my pointer finger hard against his chest. I hear muffled voices from the other side of our bedroom door and Theodore’s eyes widen when we both realize there’s staff on the other side listening.

His head whips around back to me and before I can blink, the back of hand is across my face.

Twenty Three

I let out a sharp cry and the sting radiates across my cheek. A sob escapes my mouth and Theodore looks at me with shock. I slap my hand over my mouth. Horror takes over his face and he steps closer to me urgently. I back up as the tears stream down my face and I hit the bed.

"Hazel, I am so sorry!" he whispers. My chest is falling and rising with each shaky breath I take in. "You made me so angry, you can't speak to me that way. The staff won't respect me," he whispers, his words come out quickly, in a panic. He reaches out and caresses my face.

"I had too much to drink, I am sorry. I will never do that again," Theodore pleads when I remain silent.

I finally nod and bite my lip hard to stop the sobs from escaping. My body doesn't move, I just stand frozen with the back of my legs touching our bed. Theodore twists his hands in front of him, his face showing worry and regret. "I love you, I am so sorry," he says again.

"I'm going to draw you a bath, you've had a long night and you deserve to relax." He disappears into the bathroom and I hear the water turn on. I sit down shakily on the edge of the bed. *He hit me.*

Theodore comes back and pulls me gently into the bathroom, where he lit a candle and turned the lights off. He helps me out of my clothes and he softly takes my hair out of the pins. He kisses the back of my neck before letting my hair fall.

I step into the bath and sink down until just my head is above the water. I welcome the scalding heat against my skin. I let the night wash off of me as I scrub my body with the bar of soap.

Theodore doesn't leave the bathroom. He leans on the edge of the bathroom counter watching me. After a few minutes, I glance towards him. To my surprise, a tear is running down his cheek. He swipes at it and gives me an apologetic look.

"Theodore..." I start, my voice breaking.

"I'm so sorry," he whispers. We look at each other, with the candle flickering light on our faces.

"Come get in with me," I offer. A small smile curves his lips up and he undresses.

I pull my legs up and he sits across from me, causing the water to rise to the top of the tub. Water sloshes over the side and neither of us care. We keep eye contact as his eyes are misty with tears.

"I sometimes get in these moods. I've had them since I was little, after my dad died," his voice is deep and quiet. I wait for him to continue and he exhales loudly. "I saw him get shot, right in front of me. We were at a horse race. We were in the bathroom, about to walk out. I lifted his head off the ground because I didn't want his head to be on the hard floor and screamed for help when he died."

I let out a small gasp and my heart hurts thinking about the younger version of Theodore having to go through something so horrific. "Theodore, I am so sorry," I whisper.

"Ever since then, I see red sometimes. Like something inside me snaps," he confesses.

"I shouldn't have gone to the party. I shouldn't have yelled at you. You aren't crazy, I didn't mean it," I apologize quickly, the words spilling out of my mouth.

We wash each other's bodies and when we get into bed, we make love. Not like previous times. But this time actually loving each other with our bodies. Like if we love each other hard enough, everything that is wrong will be washed away and made alright. Theodore kisses every inch of my body, gently caressing every curve and dip.

Twenty Four

The next few days are perfect. Before Theodore goes to work, he wakes me up with breakfast in bed. When he gets off work we ride horses or take walks in the garden. He teaches me how to drive a car, which is a near death experience for the both of us. One evening he even helps gather the chicken eggs with me.

One afternoon I finally get a letter back from my family and I open it on our bed. My mother thanks me several times for the money and says she was able to get some necessities they were out of. Florence goes on and on about the dresses. She lectures me on how to wear my hair with them and what shoes I should absolutely never wear with a flapper style dress.

I smile as I write back to them. I draw a sketch of the older black horse for Otis and write 'your magic horse' above it. I look over to Theodore's nightstand and crawl across the bed. I open it slowly and grab twice as many bills as I did the last time. I carefully close it and fold up the money. I chew on my lip and make a new letter, writing 'mom only' on the front of the paper.

'Mother,

I am startin' to send money for you to stash away. Don't let anyone else see this. Save it until you have enough to get away from John. It should be enough one day for you to leave for good.

It's going to be okay. I am going to get you out of there. Take care of Otis. Remember your promise.

With love,

Hazel'

I fold it up around the money and put it in the envelope. I seal it and write on it before taking it down to Margaret. When I hand it to her she smiles and walks off, never speaking a word to me.

I noticed the shift in the mood and how everyone treated me after the incident with Theodore that one night. I wonder what servants were listening and what gossip they had spread. Most of the staff tiptoes around me, almost like they are avoiding me. *Do they think I was actually sleeping with someone else?*

The only one who acted unbothered is Cora. She finally lets me in the kitchen one afternoon after days of begging.

I stand in front of the big kitchen island and help her knead the bread. She shows me the right pressure to apply and how to not overwork the dough. "Cora?" I ask. She glances over at me, her brow wet with sweat. "Did you, you know, hear about the other night?"

"I keep my nose in my own business," she answers.

"I saw you watching from the window when I got back though."

She pauses and looks at me from across the island. "I was making sure you got home safely. I was worried to be honest, that you went out late with just that Nellie girl," she admits.

"I guess I made a bad decision," I say quietly. She reaches over and pats my hand.

"Dear girl, life is all about making decisions. And we are bound to make some that are not the greatest."

I smile and she shows me how to put the dough into the bread pan. I ignore her protests and insist on helping her clean the kitchen and the mess we made as we wait for the bread to rise.

The next afternoon when Theodore gets home, he wants to eat dinner in the dining room. So we sit at the large table and eat the roast Cora made. "I had an idea today," he says.

"Oh?" I look up from my plate.

"I can't find someone trustworthy to take the empty spot for the dancer that left," he explains. "And I was thinking you should write to Florence and offer her the position. She fits what we're looking for, and she is family, so we can trust her to keep her mouth shut."

I look up and set my fork down. "What do you mean, she fits the position? She doesn't know how to dance like a flapper," I say with an annoyed tone.

"She fits the look," he answers.

"Oh, so you think she's pretty? Has a good chest like Ruby?" I narrow my eyes and sit back in my seat.

"Hazel. You sound like a jealous school girl." Theodore finishes his last bite of food and crosses his arms.

"She can't live here with us!"

"Of course not. Two of the dancers rent an apartment and have an extra room. I've already spoken to them and they're fine with her moving in with them."

"Oh, it seems like you have this all planned out," I mutter.

"I thought you would be pleased. Sometimes I feel like you're impossible. You miss your family, don't you? She could ride on the train with Otis so he could visit."

"Otis can come?" I ask, my mood changing.

"For a week or so, yes."

"Yes! I will write them tonight," I say excitedly and shovel the last few bites of green beans into my mouth before standing up.

That night I write to Florence and my mother. I explain the job vaguely to Florence and tell her to find a phone and call us for more details. I tell my mother Otis can ride with Florence on the train to come visit. I don't include any money because Theodore reads the newspaper in bed.

I go to bed with a smile on my face and an excitement I hadn't had in weeks.

Twenty Five

The next few days pass slowly as I wait for a response. The telephone rings a few times a day and I eagerly run to it, waiting for Margaret to tell me it's Florence. But she doesn't.

Theodore and I argue a few times over stupid things. One day he wanted to sit in the dining room for breakfast and I wanted to sit outside. He wanted to spend Friday evening at home and I wanted to go to The Crystal because I had been cooped up in the house all week. Nellie stops by finally, after over a week of not hearing from her, and avoids talking about the night of the party. She gossips about people I know nothing about instead.

One weekend we finally go to The Crystal and I find myself thrilled to be out of the house and getting attention from people. I realized I liked having people be interested in talking to me. I feel seen when the men's gaze lingers on me just a little too long. I feel important when the women all clammer around to talk to me and ask me questions about my dress. I get invited to tea at one of the women's houses for the following week.

On a Tuesday evening, I'm writing when Theodore comes home in a bad mood. He walks over to the whiskey cart in the front room and drinks straight from the bottle. I glance up at him from the sofa, but return my eyes back to the journal.

He lets out a huff and takes another drink. "Are you just going to ignore me?" he asks. I don't take my eyes from the journal.

"You seem to be in a mood so I thought I would let you have a drink first," I say with little emotion to my voice.

"You're my wife. You're supposed to greet me with a smile," Theodore says exasperatedly.

"I must have missed that part in the 'how to be a perfect wife' book," I say sarcastically.

"You need to drop that attitude," he warns. I look up at him finally with a challenging expression.

"Maybe you aren't the only one who gets to have bad moods."

"I run a stressful, dangerous business all day that pays for you to sit in this giant house. Eating food made by a cook, wearing the dress I got you and sitting on the sofa that I paid for! I get to have a fucking mood if I want, you do not," his voice raises and he pours a glass of whiskey and paces back and forth.

I scoff and feel my skin burn with anger. "This house feels like a prison! I can barely leave without wondering if it's going to set you off. You act like I am another one of your possessions!" I shout.

"You are, you are my wife!" he throws the drink down his throat. My mouth hangs open and I stare back at him, wondering how this is the same person I married just a month ago.

My anger turns to rage when I try to ignore him and focus on my writing. My hand shakes as I try to scribble down the words. I reach over for my glass of champagne I had poured earlier and take a sip. Theodore walks over and rips the journal out of my hand and tosses it down on the table. I jerk my head up to look at him and stand up.

"We should have stayed strangers," I say as calmly and slowly as I can. I watch as hurt flashes across his face, and then gets replaced with fury. He stands so close to me that I can smell the alcohol and faint cigar smoke.

"I could have married anyone. And you think you can talk to me like that," he tries to keep his voice quiet but it raises as he speaks. I roll my eyes and cross my arms.

"If you wanted some perfect housewife you should have married someone else then," I snap, gripping the glass in my hand tighter.

I storm out of the room and his loud footsteps follow me. I pass Margaret who gives us a nervous glance. A maid continues to dust a shelf as her eyes follow us as we stomp up the stairs. I reach halfway up the stair banister when I turn to him and glare down at him.

He stands two steps under me, with his whiskey glass in hand. "Leave me alone," I whisper and glare.

"Go up to the bedroom where we can talk about this away from everyone," he grumbles under his breath.

"You can't tell me what to do."

"I am right now. Go...to...our...room," he says each word slowly and deliberately, trying to keep his anger in check. Without thinking, I narrow my eyes and toss the rest of the champagne from my glass onto his face. The maid dusting gasps.

Just as quickly as I tossed my drink at him, his hand is around my arm and yanking me down to him. He jerks me so hard that I trip down one of the steps, he loses his grip on my arm when my body falls down the step under him.

My champagne glass shatters when it falls out of my hands and I try to brace myself. I lose my balance completely and fall down multiple steps, my rib cage taking most of the force. Screams escape Margaret and the maid.

I land at the bottom of the steps on my side as tears start to fall from my face. I try to push myself up but someone is already helping me. I look up to see Edward's concerned face. His gloved hand takes mine and lifts me to my feet.

He looks up at Theodore who is rushing down the steps. "Hazel! Are you ok?" he sounds truly worried as he reaches for me. I pull my arm away from him and wipe the tears from my eyes. His expression falters for a moment when he sees the servant's gazes on us.

"You really have to be more careful drinking and walking up the stairs, doll." He gives a nervous laugh and puts his hand at the bottom of my back. He helps me go up the stairs and instructs one of the servants standing around to go clean up the broken glass.

Once in our room he shuts the door and turns to me, quickly grabbing my hands. "I am so sorry, doll. I didn't mean for you to fall. You must have tripped."

"I didn't trip, Theodore. You *pulled* me down!" I cry out.

"I just meant to grab your arm to stop you, that's all!" he swears. I shake his hands off mine and go over to the bed and pull my clothes off. I wince as I move, my body throbbing all over.

"Oh god," I hear him mutter from behind me. I turn and see him staring at me with a slack jaw.

"What?" I ask.

"Your back..." he trails off. I limp into the bathroom and look in the mirror. My ribs and back are already bruising. I gasp and reach back to touch them, wincing when I do.

"Do I need to go to the doctor?" I ask myself.

"No, no you're fine. You just need to rest." Theodore assures me, leaning against the bathroom door and frowning as he watches me. Remorse plastered on his face. I walk past him, making sure to not touch him.

I climb in the bed and pull the sheets over my head. "Please talk to me, doll." I ignore him the rest of the night and pull away from his touch when he tries to cuddle me to fall asleep like we always do.

The next morning I wake up to the sound of the telephone ringing. I sit up in bed excitedly, but groan when the pain radiates all over my body. I carefully stand up out of bed and notice the bruises trailing up my legs.

I pull on the white robe from the wedding and the slippers that sit next to the bed. I walk down the hall and find Theodore in the living area hanging up the phone.

"Good morning, beautiful." He smiles and kisses my forehead. I don't pull away but I can't force myself to smile. "That was Florence," he nods to the phone.

"What! I wanted to talk to her! What did she say?" I ask excitedly, but frustrated I didn't get to speak to her.

"I didn't want to wake you up. She's thrilled about working as a dancer. She understands the importance of keeping information to herself. I'm having her get on the first train available."

"And Otis too? We need to get the room ready for him! Oh, do you think we could take him to the zoo?" I clap my hands with joy.

"He won't be able to come, actually."

I stop and stare at him. "What do you mean?" I ask.

"Your mother apparently found out about the speakeasy, she read your letter to Florence. And apparently Otis is sick and has been fighting something off for a few days," Theodore says.

"But, wait, no! I can talk to her!" I protest.

"Hazel, you already ruined your chance. You shouldn't have mentioned anything about the speakeasy in the letter. You should have just told her to call," his voice is full of pity.

Tears well in my eyes and I shake my head. "No, no this isn't fair. I am going to write to her!" I spin on my heels and run up the stairs, ignoring the pain that throbs all over my body.

I write hastily on the paper, explaining to my mother that he will be safe and will just stay in the house with me. That we won't even leave if she doesn't approve. I beg her to let him come see me once he feels better. I ask what is wrong with him and if she has taken him to see a doctor. I grab a generous amount of money from Theodore's drawer and add it to the letter, telling her to use it to pay for any medicine he may need.

The next two days I barely leave the bed. I can't force myself to leave the room. I barely eat. On the third day Nellie storms in the room and throws the curtains open, letting the light fill the room.

"Enough of all of this! We are going out!" Nellie chastises as she pulls the sheets off of my head. She lets out a small gasp when she sees the fading bruises on my body.

"Hazel..." she whispers. I avoid looking at her as I force myself out of bed. "I don't want to go out," I say.

"Did Theodore do that?"

"I fell down the stairs when we were arguing."

"Did he push you?"

"No."

I pull the sheets up to make the bed as best as I can and fluff the fancy pillows into place. “We have been invited to tea at the Brown’s home. Dorothy Brown invited us specifically. You know who she is don't you? Wife of the famous golfer?” Nellie rattles off as she goes into my closet and starts sifting through my dresses.

“No, I don’t know who that is.”

“Well, we have to go. You’ve been home too much. People will start to talk,” Nellie pulls out a long sleeve yellow dress that reaches mid calf. “This will do, it will cover up all of that,” she motions to my legs.

I let out a sigh and shrug. “Come on,” she assures me. I finally give in and get dressed, brush my teeth and let her apply a little makeup. I wear my hair down and slightly unruly, it’s the one thing I won’t compromise on with Nellie.

“It gives me a headache when I wear it up,” I tell her as I run some oil through it to tame the frizz.

“Fine, fine.”

Theodore seems happy that I am leaving the house and kisses me goodbye with a smile. Nellie’s driver takes us to a giant home not far from ours. I feel nervous as we approach the front door. I can hear female voices and laughter from inside as the butler opens the door.

“Nellie! Oh, and Hazel, too! I am so glad you could make it,” Dorothy Brown comes out of the room where all the laughter is coming from.

"Thank you so much for having us," I smile. She leads us into the room where six other women sit, all sipping tea and giggling.

To my relief, no one asks me too many questions or expects me to speak much. I just sit and listen, laughing at their jokes and agreeing with their boring opinions on fashion and what kind of flowers are best to plant in the summer.

We promise to attend again after Drorthy tells us they have tea time every other weekend and that we must be there. During the drive back home, Nellie asks if she and Peter can come for another game night. "Sure, how is tomorrow night?" I ask.

"Splendid!" She smiles.

When I get home Theodore is waiting for me on the porch. "Did you enjoy yourself?" he asks.

"I did. Peter and Nellie are coming tomorrow for a game night."

"That sounds great. Your sister is arriving tomorrow actually," he says. I pause and look up at him.

"Already?" I ask, surprised.

"Yes, I was thinking she could stay the night here when she arrives? Then Monday I will take her with me to work and introduce her to the girls. Then she can start work and start staying in the apartment."

"Yes, that seems like a good idea."

Twenty Six

The next day I put on one of my nicer dresses and wait eagerly by the front door until I see Frank drive up. I run outside and down the steps as Florence steps out of the car. She looks the same as when I left. Her shiny blond hair glows in the sun and I want to roll my eyes when I notice the flower barrette sparkling on her head. “Look at you, Mrs. Greenwood,” Florence gives me a small smile and a stiff hug.

“Come inside,” I motion to the house and walk up the steps together. Once inside Theodore comes into the main front room and smiles.

“Good to see you again,” he greets her.

I notice her smile widens when she sees him and she gives him a flirtatious look. I immediately want to call Frank to take her back to Texas. *Nice to know she’s the same old Florence.* “I’ll let you two catch up before Peter and Nellie get here,” Theodore says before slipping out of the room.

"Well, he just gets better looking every day, doesn't he?" Florence smirks as she sits down on the sofa.

"Florence, really?" I groan and cross my arms.

"What? I'm just giving you a compliment. I still can't believe he picked you. Who's Peter?" She raises her eyebrows.

"Peter *and Nellie* are our friends. They're coming over for games tonight," I tell her.

"Oh, so they're coming together?" she pouts. I start to tell her they're not together like that but figure I will spare Peter from my sister's claws and I nod.

"Mhm," I tell her.

"Oh. Well phooey. So, show me around!" Florence stands up and looks around in awe. I give her a tour and can't help but feel satisfaction when the jealousy shows on her face.

Now she is in my shadow.

I have to pry her from my closet as she gawks at the rows of dresses and hats. "The things I would do to a man if he bought me all of this," she shudders. I roll my eyes and want to tell her that not everything is picture perfect like she thinks.

I hear the doorbell and let out a sigh of relief that I won't have to be alone with my sister any longer. I find myself wondering why I was so excited to see her in the first place. *I have grown up a lot in these past few months and she no longer is the more experienced sister.*

I introduce Florence to Peter and Nellie. Florence's hand lingers a little longer than needed when she shakes Peter's hand. He glances at me and I roll my eyes back into my head.

A rare smile flashes across Peter's face as he cuts his eyes away from me.

Nellie and Florence chatter throughout the whole game of poker, making it hard to concentrate. They giggle at the inappropriate jokes they make and find a mutual love of fashion. After the game, Theodore puts on slow jazz music and we all sit in the room drinking.

"I hate to be rude, but I must slip out for a bit to make a few phone calls," Theodore gives a look to Peter who nods. *What kind of business are you taking care of, Theodore?*

I stare in annoyance at Nellie and Florence, who lean in to each other, laughing over their champagne glasses. They sit across the room on the two chairs by the windows. Peter and I sit on the sofa, both drinking whiskey. I started the evening with champagne, but after just an hour with my sister, I quickly switched my drink to something stronger.

"They seem like two versions of the same person," I analyze my sister and Nellie out loud. Peter looks over at me and back at them.

"I could see that."

"Does it bother you when she sleeps with other people?" I ask rather directly. His expression doesn't change and he shakes his head.

"No, I don't care for her like that."

I can't imagine feeling like that, and I frown as I take a drink. "You grew up with Theodore. You seem so quiet. And Theodore is so demanding of attention. Do you ever feel like a shadow?" I ask softly. I don't know why, but Peter has the type of presence that puts you at ease and makes you feel like you can be honest.

His warm hazel eyes look at me then back down at his water. He shifts his stocky body on the sofa and takes a drink. "I think there's two different types of people in the world. Those that are shadows and those that cast them," he says thoughtfully. I process his words as I look at my new friend and my sister, who whisper to each other, eyes wide at the gossip they're sharing. *Those two cast them.*

"So what do us shadows do? Just sit to the side while others bask in the glory and attention?" I wonder out loud.

"You act like being a shadow is a bad thing. Both are double edged swords. Everyone has their demons they fight," he mutters quietly.

"Theodore sure has a few," I look down at my leg where the bruises are barely visible now.

"I know he does." Peter's voice sounds sad and slightly angry.

"I don't know what to do when he gets in his moods," I admit in a hushed tone, so no one hears us.

"Just stay out of his way. Don't provoke him," he warns.

I nod and let out a sigh. "Don't blame yourself, do you hear me?" Peter reaches to touch my knee but stops and puts his hand in his pocket instead. I open my mouth to reply, but Theodore walks back in.

"Let's party!" he says loudly, raising the flask he started carrying around in his pocket high in the air. His body language is different and he seems to have found a new burst of energy. I wonder how he made a phone call that quickly. "To Florence, our saving grace at The Crystal!" Theodore announces. I turn and catch Florence's pleased smile as she clinks her drink to Nellie's.

I don't raise my glass, but I do drink the whole glass in one swift movement.

The next few days, I write to my mother and tell her all about the chickens and what we've been up to. I tell her about the tea and all the friends I'm making, when in reality, I have never felt more lonely. I only include one bill in each letter because the wad of cash in Theodore's drawer has started to shrink.

Twenty Seven

One afternoon I have to sit and entertain Mary Greenwood, who just happened to stop by thirty minutes before Theodore was going to be home. They were meeting to discuss business and she says she forgot the time. Her beady eyes watch my every move as she asks me question after question.

"Do you like The Crystal?" she questions.

"I do," I answer.

"What do you think about it?" Her eyebrow raises. I keep my face cool and calm and my answers short.

"Everything. It's a very nice establishment."

"Has anyone asked you about it?"

"About what?"

"Anything about The Crystal?" Her lips purse into a straight thin line, knowing that I am playing the game with her.

"Why would they ask me about The Crystal?"

Her eyes squint even more, but Theodore walks in and greets us. He tells her to come up to his office and greets me, but doesn't give me a kiss like he usually did.

One evening, Theodore doesn't come home, and I stay up all night trying to call The Crystal. I pace back and forth in the hall before I finally give up and toss and turn in bed.

I hear a loud commotion in the middle of the night and sit up in bed. The sun is barely rising outside when I throw my robe on and hurry down the hall. I reach the top of the steps when I see Theodore's arm around Peter and his bloody face. "Theodore! Oh my god!" I scream and run down, holding the banister so I don't fall.

When I reach him I grab his face in my hands and examine it. The top of his eye is cut and underneath it is a black bruise. "What happened?" I demand. I stare over at Peter, who gives me a regretful look.

"I had to take care of some business," Theodore grumbles, groaning when he speaks and holding his side.

"Help me get him in bed!" I tell Peter. We help him slowly make the way up the stairs and into our room. Theodore throws himself down on the bed, laying on his back and fumbling with his flask. He yanks the cap off and chugs the contents. "What kind of business does this to your face?!" I ask as I press a wet washcloth to his eye. He holds my hand to his face and closes his eyes.

"Peter? What the hell?" I turn to face him. He holds up his hands.

"Theodore didn't tell me about this meeting he had. He didn't take any backup with him, like an idiot," Peter tells me, directing the last comment to Theodore as he looks over my shoulder at him.

"I got the money they owed us!" Theodore groans and laughs. "Reach in my pocket, doll." I reach inside his jacket and pull out two giant stacks of money with rubber bands around them. Blood is splattered on the top bills.

I gasp and drop the money on the bed. "Damn it, Theodore. You could have been killed." Peter rubs the temples of his forehead. Theodore grins and looks devilishly handsome when he does.

"But I didn't. Now, leave me alone with my beautiful wife."

Peter gives me an apologetic look and leaves the room. I help Theodore undress and gasp when I see his bruised ribs and torso. I run my fingers over them and start to cry. "Hey," he grabs my chin and gives me a soft kiss. I try to push away when he deepens it.

"You're hurt, Theodore!" I protest.

"There's a good kind of hurt and a bad kind. Help me make it the good kind," he gives me a crooked smirk with his busted lip. I gently straddle him and lean down over him, kissing him softly. He rolls me over onto my back and puts his hand behind my head, grabbing a fistful of hair.

Our limbs become intertwined in a tangled mess of passion as he thrusts into me and I dig my nails into his back. I try to be careful around his bruises but he acts like they don't exist at all.

After, we lay wrapped around each other, breathing heavily, naked and exhausted. "I love you, doll."

"I love you more," I promise. We drift off to sleep together, my head on his chest and his hand on my head.

A few days later, Theodore drives us to The Crystal. His knuckles are bruised and cracked and his black eye is noticeable. We match our outfits together, both of us in all black. He barely speaks the entire drive and I wonder if I did something wrong. I reach over and touch the inside of his thigh. "You look handsome," I compliment. This brings a small crooked smile to his face and I find myself in awe of how good looking he is.

"Remember to not embarrass me," he says as we pull up.

"Why would you say that?" I frown, feeling hurt.

"I don't mean it like that, I'm sorry. I'm just saying there's a lot of important people here tonight, doll," Theodore says before he gets out of the car and opens my door. I don't reply as I take his hand and we walk into the building.

When we get down to the basement, I feel my stomach sink when I see my sister dancing on the stage. She looks beautiful. Her flapper outfit looks like it was made for her body. She notices me and kicks her leg even higher and gives a sultry smile to the audience. I glance at Theodore and he doesn't even look at the stage, to my relief. *Stop being so jealous and insecure. He chose you. He married you.*

We linger by the bar, thanking the guests for coming out and telling them to enjoy themselves. I sit with Theodore at one of the poker tables and to my surprise, I win a round.

Theodore tells me to keep playing and that he has a few things to do, but he'll be back soon.

A tall man with light hair takes his seat next to me not long after Theodore gets up. "I love your hair," the man tells me above the loud music.

"Oh, thank you." I hesitate and smile. I feel my cheeks warm as he scoots his chair closer to the table and turns to stare at me again. I keep my eyes on my cards even though I can feel him peer at me.

"May I get you a drink after this round?" he asks.

"I'm married," I reply. He smiles and takes a sip of his alcohol.

"So am I." He shrugs. My mouth hangs open and I shut it to not be rude. I want to throw my cards in his face. *Don't embarrass me.* Theodore's words ring in my mind and I take a deep breath.

Just stay calm and be polite. Don't make a scene.

I sit up straighter when the man drapes his arms over the back of my chair. The card dealer glances up from the game at the man and to his limb that is in a dangerous spot. I try to focus on the cards when it's my turn but I feel the man's hand touch my hair.

Twenty Eight

My heart thuds inside me as I try to scan the room for Theodore. I don't see him but I catch Florence speaking to one of the men standing at the bar. She trails her finger down his chest and is laughing at something he says.

"I've never seen hair like yours before," the man speaks close to my ear. I stiffen in my seat and wonder what to do. I don't want to stop in the middle of the game and encourage people to stare. I can't embarrass Theodore.

When he reaches over and touches my bare shoulder I pull away and clear my throat. "I seem to have forgotten something, I will catch the next game," I tell the card dealer. He gives me an understanding nod. I hurry away from the table and look for Theodore. I see him staring at me from the table he always has reserved for us.

I push past the sea of people and pause when I can see his glare. I sit down next to him and sit my glass on the table. He opens his mouth to say something but Florence appears and puts her hand on the table to get our attention.

"This is the best job, four men have given me money tonight!" She exclaims with a grin. I force a smile and try to appear normal.

"You're doing wonderful," Theodore tells her. I shoot Florence a dirty look and feel my body get hot with jealousy.

She flutters her eyes at him and prances off to dig her claws into another victim. I return my gaze back to Theodore, whose jaw is tight as he gets up and turns away from me. I watch as he strides off toward the bar and orders another drink. I notice the glances he gets from women as he passes them.

I head to the ladies' room and push open one of the stalls. To my shock, I see Ruby and Florence standing inside it. Florence looks up in surprise and I see the powder under her nose. "Get out!" she yells. I back up and quickly rush out of the restroom. I bump into Peter who was walking out of the men's room.

"I-I'm sorry. I just, I saw Florence and..." I stammer and look around. He grabs my arm softly and pulls me to the side. He unlocks a door and pushes me inside it.

I take a deep breath to steady my emotions and look around the room. A large brown desk with a lamp, telephone and a few notebooks sits in it. There's a few chairs that face the desk and then a long golden sofa.

"Is this your office?" I ask.

"No, Theodore's. Why are you so upset?" Peter shuts the door. The room immediately becomes quiet and you can barely hear the music and loud chatter from outside the room.

"I saw Florence, she was doing drugs," I whisper. Peter's face stays like it always does, showing very little emotion. "We have to tell Theodore!" I say.

"No, no you don't," Peter shakes his head.

"What if she brings some bad people in here? *Drug dealers*?" I ask as I purse my lips and scan the room.

"She won't."

"How can you be so sure?" I demand, frustrated at his casual response.

"Because it's *our* cocaine."

I freeze and stare at him. "How do you think Theodore pays for everything? It's not just from alcohol and horse races," Peter confesses.

"You're telling me he sells drugs?"

"Well, the people under him do. Listen, you have to keep this to yourself. We're having issues with a new sergeant with the law who's starting to sniff around. Not a word to anyone, alright? "

I push past him and yank the door open, slamming it closed behind me. I march down the hall, past Theodore and up the steps. I walk out of The Crystal and flag down Frank. He gets out of the car as Theodore rushes out the front door.

"Where are you going? What are you doing?" Theodore demands.

"Get away from me," I glare and slide in the back seat.

"Don't drive," he tells Frank. Frank stands on the sidewalk and doesn't get in the car.

"I know. I know about what you do!" I yell.

"Keep your voice down, Hazel."

"There you go again, always telling me what to do!" I shout. He sits in the seat next to me and slams the door closed. He motions for Frank to get in and drive.

Frank speeds off as Theodore pulls out his flask and takes a swig. "You lied. You have lied to me about everything!" I accuse. Theodore keeps a calm expression and ignores me as we drive out of the city.

"Talk to me!" I push his chest.

"We are going to talk when we get home," he says calmly.

"You sell drugs," I seethe quietly. His eyes dart over to Frank who turns on the radio and turns up the music. I scoff and return my glare back to my husband.

"I haven't lied to you about anything. You were just so desperate to escape Texas you didn't ask many questions!" He replies.

"You aren't who I thought I married."

His jaw is tight and he stares forward, not speaking a single word.

Frank drives so fast we arrive home quickly. He gets out of the car and goes to open our door, but Theodore jerks it shut. I feel panic start to fill my body when he turns to me and I can see his anger in the dark. Frank disappears around a bush.

"You're a drug dealer! Florence was doing cocaine in the bathroom!" I cry.

"What your sister does is none of my business," he states.

"Let me out of the car."

"Don't act like you're perfect and so much better than me," Theodore keeps his hand on the handle. I turn to open the door on my side and he grabs my wrist. "I saw you flirting with that man at the poker table. Right in front of everyone." He chastises.

"What?!" I exclaim, trying to pull my hand away from him, but his grip remains firm.

"Letting him touch your hair and pretending like you didn't notice."

"I wasn't flirting! He kept trying to make advances and I told him I'm married. I didn't want to make a scene," I blurt. His grip tightens on my wrist and he pushes my arm back into the seat.

"Theodore, you're hurting me," I whimper.

"Don't lie to me," his voice was calm.

"I'm not, please. Let me out," I whisper. He leans over me and pushes the door open. He lets go of my arm and shoves my body out of the car.

"There, go!" He yells as I fall out face first. My chin hits the gravel and I let out a sharp cry.

"Shit. Hazel!" Theodore panics and looks around for his flask before getting out of the car.

I drag the rest of my body out of the car and push myself up. I ignore his pleas to come back. I take off up the steps and run past Cora, who calls after me. I run past servants who give each other knowing glances. I lock myself in the bathroom and start to sob.

Is this my life? This isn't real. This isn't actually happening.

"Hazel!" I hear Cora's voice. I unlock the bathroom and barely open the door.

"What?" I try to sound like I'm not crying and I dry my face with the top of my dress.

"What happened? Why are you bleeding?" she asks.

"We got into a fight. It's nothing."

She pushes through and closes the door behind her. She has flour on her forehead and her round face frowns with concern. "Your lip is busted," she sighs and gets a washcloth and runs it under the sink.

I take it from her and hold it to my mouth, trying to keep in the tears as I stare back at her.

"I made him mad," I whisper.

"You shouldn't-" Cora is interrupted when the bathroom door flies open and Theodore stands there.

I feel my stomach turn and I take a step back when he walks in. "Thank you, Cora. You can go ahead and take the evening off," Theodore flashes his charming smile at her.

She pauses before leaving and turns to him. She gives him a look that shows her disappointment and walks out.

Theodore steps closer to me and I flinch when he reaches for my face. His face falls when I grimace and he drops his hand. "Doll..." he trails off, as his lip quivers and he looks broken.

"You did it again. You swore you wouldn't," I sound like a child when the words leave my mouth.

"I don't know what came over me. It won't happen again. I didn't mean to push you so hard. I swear," he reaches for me and I pull away.

"I don't believe you," I whisper.

"I love you," he croaks.

"You don't love me. You just love being loved," I sob and walk past him. I feel a part of me die inside, like he had put out a light that flickered inside my soul. He lets out a noise that sounds like something that would come from a hurt animal. I go down the hall and lock myself in one of the guest rooms.

I stay in the room until the next morning, even though Theodore knocks on the door for an hour before I fall asleep.

When I open the door the next morning Theodore looks up at me from the floor. "Did you sleep there?" I ask. He nods and pulls himself up.

His eyes are red and there's bags under them. Even when he has barely slept and has bruises all over his face, he's still the most handsome man I've ever seen. "I'm a terrible person, I hate who I am. The world would be better off without me." He grabs my hands and stares down at me.

I hate how bad it hurts when I hear the words. "Stop," I shake my head and put my hand on his chest.

"It's true, I'm so sorry. I don't blame you if you hate me." I look in his golden eyes and see the man I married. The one who brings me breakfast in bed, kisses every inch of my body, makes sure I have the chickens that make me happy.

I feel my heart break a little more and I feel myself being tugged in different directions, with very different emotions.

"I don't hate you," I finally say. His face is full of relief when he puts his hands on my hips.

"May I kiss you?" He gives me a broken smile. I nod and his lips gently touch mine, I pull back when it stings.

"My lip," I explain, reaching up and touching the cut.

"Oh," his voice is barely above a whisper.

Twenty Nine

The next few weeks go like they always do after we fight. Breakfast in bed. Hugs and promises. Sex so good I don't have to pretend my legs are shaking. Dinner in the garden or on the porch. Him calling me 'doll' after every sentence.

One evening we go for a horse ride and spend the rest of the night drinking. I drink until I feel like I'm floating and that life isn't what it is. When my head buzzes I feel like everything is right in the world.

In the middle of the night, I wake up to an empty bed. My body tingles and my head throbs as I walk the quiet halls in my nightgown. I notice Theodore's office door slightly ajar. I tiptoe closer, my palms starting to sweat as I become nervous. I quietly peek through the door and see Theodore speaking on the phone.

He's speaking loudly into it, looking frustrated as he runs his hand over his chin. "I got it, one kilo of blow. I told you it'll be to you by the end of the week. Now fuck off," He slams the phone down.

I watch as he leans down onto the table and puts a finger over one of his nostrils and snorts white powder with the other. He takes a swig from his flask that sits on his desk next to his gun.

"No," I whisper to myself as I step back and quietly retreat back to our room. I lay awake all night and close my eyes when he climbs in bed and pulls the sheets over himself. I pretend to be asleep when his hand reaches over and up my nightgown. I try to keep myself from stiffening. *Act like you're asleep, don't let him know you're awake. He'll stop.*

But his hands don't stop. His body climbs on top of me and I open my eyes with shock. "Theodore!" I push at his chest. He looks down at me and his pupils are so large I can barely see the honey color of his eyes.

"I want you," he mumbles in my ear.

"You're drunk and high!" I accuse.

"You're my wife, love me!" Theodore insists. His hand wraps around my neck and I become still. "I love you," he grunts in my ear and his hands push my legs apart.

In that moment I decide to become still and let whatever is going to happen, happen. I wonder if he can feel my heart beating out of my chest. I try to turn my head to look away but his hand is still wrapped around my neck and the other is now under my head, gripping my hair.

I close my eyes and think about home. I think about the tall hill with the tree that I used to write under. I imagine how the grass felt under my dress. I try to remember how it used to smell before it would rain.

The next morning we eat eggs in bed and he hands me a present. It's wrapped in light pink paper with a silver bow on top. "What's this?" I ask.

"Open it," he smiles. I pull out a small stuffed lion.

"Your favorite animal. I couldn't find a chicken," Theodore explains. I can't help but smile. *He's still good. Everyone has good and bad inside of them. I can help him get better.*

"Thank you," I lean over to kiss him on the cheek.

We hear the phone ring and shortly after there's a knock on the door and Edward speaks on the other side of the door. "Mrs. Greenwood's sister wants to know if she can come for dinner tonight. She is on the phone."

I groan, which causes Theodore to laugh. "I'll talk to her," I get up and pull on my robe.

"Hello?" I speak into the phone that sits at the end of the hall.

"How cool is this! Did you know our apartment has a telephone?" Florence's voice shrills in my ear.

"Imagine that," I say.

"You haven't invited me over. I've been waiting," Florence tsks.

"Sorry, I've just been busy. How is tonight?" I rub my forehead with my thumb and index finger.

"Perfect!"

I begin to tell her what time when I hear the phone click and the call ends. I stare down at the phone in annoyance. She still cuts me off before I can speak, even on the telephone.

That evening, Florence walks in the door wearing a dress I had never seen on her. It was short and flattered her small frame. "It's not quite as fancy as yours, but it's new." She smooths it out when I compliment her.

"I think it's great." I smile and sit across from her at the dinner table.

Cora brings out the roast chicken and vegetables. We start to eat in silence. "So, when are you going to have a baby?" Florence asks. Theodore chokes on his whiskey and my eyes dart up.

"What? Oh, are you already in that way?" She asks excitedly, looking between Theodore and I.

"No!" Theodore speaks before I can. I look over at him with a frown at how quickly he responds.

"We just got married, we don't have to rush to start a family," I tell her. I feel too embarrassed to tell her that Theodore doesn't want to make me a mother. I have started to feel hurt and jealous when babies or pregnancies are brought up in conversation. Especially at tea with all of the women, most of whom already have babies.

"Blah blah," she rolls her eyes.

"How do you like New York?" Theodore asks to change the subject.

"I love it! I will never go back to Texas. I love the city."

I find my thoughts drifting from the conversation as I think about what it would be like to start a family with Theodore. I don't approve of what he does for work, but it provides an amazing life for children. They'd never go to bed hungry. Maybe a baby would help us, help Theodore. Maybe he needed another reason to be better.

Cora brings out an apple pie and we tell her how amazing it smells. She smiles and gives me a look she has started to give me often, like she's checking on me. She has started to have lunch with me every day, offering little bits of advice when I ask for it.

After dessert, Florence says she needs to get back to her apartment to get sleep before work the next day. I watch as Frank drives off with her in the backseat and I turn to Theodore. He lights a cigar and the moon shines down on us.

"Why don't we have a baby?" I ask. Theodore sighs and takes a big puff of his cigar.

"I was afraid you'd bring that up. I just don't know if I want kids, Hazel. I told you that. You are enough for me."

"But maybe it would be good for us. I get lonely," I frown and rub my arm when a cold breeze blows.

"I'll try to be home more often. I have to work late a few times this week but maybe we can go on vacation soon. Just us two," he gives me a reassuring smile, his white teeth almost glowing in the dark.

"I don't want a vacation. I want a family."

"I am your family. Maybe later in life we'll discuss it."

I let out a sigh and nod. He puts his cigar out and walks inside. I feel frustrated as I look up at the stars. I hear music and I turn to see Theodore opening the windows in the front room. He comes back onto the porch and I smile as the music floats outside.

He takes my arms and wraps them around his neck. His hands hold my waist and we drift back and forth. I smile and lean my head on his shoulder as we dance. "I will be better, I promise. I want to be so much better."

"I know you do," I breathe. I mean it when I say it. I know he wants to be better. But I don't know if he can be. There's a darkness in Theodore that I don't understand. But like Peter said, most things are a double edged sword. Everyone has good and bad.

And in these moments where we sway to the music, I become blind to the bad and focus on the good. Because in the end, his cold shoulder will always feel warm to me.

When Theodore leans down and kisses me, I decide at that moment I will always choose him.

The next few days I try to spend more time with Theodore, but his work schedule is so busy I rarely see him. I start to stop by his work more often, which he seems to like. One day he even takes me right there on the couch in his office, with the door unlocked so anyone can walk in.

I sit in the empty basement room watching the dancers rehearse and practice a new dance. Florence struggles to keep up as she watches Ruby show her the routine. I try to be a better person but I can't help but smile inside when she looks frustrated and confused.

When they take a breath she walks over to the table and sits down with me. "It's harder than it looks," she pants.

"I don't doubt it. You know I would faceplant right off the stage," I say. We both laugh and I tell her about how I tripped down the aisle at our wedding. She gasps and her eyes widen.

"You did not!"

"I surely did," I giggle. She starts to giggle too and we look over at Theodore when he slams his hand on the bar counter.

"Tell him I said today, not tomorrow!" he shouts at the bartender. The bartender nods and scurries off. I turn back to Florence who is still looking over at the bar.

"He's a very passionate man," she comments.

"You have no idea," I mutter under my breath.

"Is he passionate in bed, too?"

I scoff at her and ignore her question. "I think you need to continue practicing unless you want to end up like me," I nod toward the stage. She rolls her big blue eyes and pouts her pink lips. She sulks off and climbs back onto the platform.

"And one, two and three!" Ruby counts, tapping her feet to keep a beat.

Thirty

At the end of June, I rip open a letter Margaret hands me. I don't even go into the bedroom, I read it right in the hall. It had been weeks since I had written them and never gotten a response.

'Dear Hazel,

I am sorry it has taken me so long to reply. Otis had a fever that lasted a long time. I used the money you sent for medicine. The doctor said he had diphtheria. He is doing much better now, but he won't be able to visit for a while. I am still uncomfortable with him leaving but he will not stop asking about you and the magic horse.

I will let you know as soon as he is well enough to travel. The money is almost gone and your father just keeps drinking. I am taking the eggs to town tomorrow to try to sell. I may sell a few chickens if things get much worse.

I hope you are well. Your sister has written one letter. She sounds happy.

With love,

Mother'

Otis had diphtheria? I try to swallow my spit that's now thick, and I rush back to our bedroom. I hesitate before taking out multiple bills next to Theodore's gun and putting them in an envelope. But I do it anyway, because I know how bad my mother needs it.

Over the next few weeks, Theodore and I start to grow farther apart. We argue more about pointless things. We only make love one time, and when we do, I feel like he's just doing it to get it over with. He works later each night that goes by. A few nights he doesn't come home at all.

We argue so angrily one night that I throw a stiff, round decorative pillow at him and his hand comes across my face. We both end the night crying and apologizIng, swearing it won't happen again. The next morning I sit in front of the vanity to get ready. I apply a red rouge to cover my split lip. I pause when I look at the tube in my hand, remembering my mother always applying it in the mirror of the car before we would go into town.

I am not like my mother. Theodore is not like John. This is different. It won't happen again.

I stare out the window on a warm Tuesday morning as Nellie sits and chats in the front room. "What do you think?" she asks. I turn and look at her in confusion.

"Sorry, about what?"

"About me going out with Timmy? You know, the guy I've been talking about for the past fifteen minutes." Nellie gives me an annoyed look and then frowns.

"What's up with you? What's wrong?" she asks.

"Sorry, nothing. I think you should go out with him. It sounds like y'all would be a great fit for each other."

"I'm not some dumb dora, tell me," Nellie insists. I laugh at her funny sayings and shrug my shoulders.

"Theodore and I are struggling. We fight so much and we were only intimate once this week."

"You're getting out of the honeymoon phase, as they call it. You need to fix that, fast." Nellie bites her lip with concern.

"But how?" I ask.

"Wear lingerie tonight to surprise him. They want to be greeted every night like they're the most spiffy things in the world," she rolls her eyes.

"And when he seems like he's in one of his dark moods that I know he gets, just act really happy. You know the way to a man's heart," she reminds me. I nod. *Grab the pillow. Act like your legs are trembling.*

"Ok, I'll try. I want things back to how they used to be. I know I haven't been as fun to be around as I used to," I figure.

"Maybe go away for the weekend. Spice things up," Nellie suggests.

So that's what we do. We pack our bags and head to the beach. Theodore rents a small house that sits right in front of the sand. When we arrive, I run to the water and let it wash up over my feet. “I haven’t ever seen the ocean,” I tell Theodore as he walks up next to me.

I reach for his hand and give it a squeeze. He smiles over at me and his toothpick twirls. “It’s even better than I imagined. It’s huge!” I look out at the water that crashes in front of us.

We both sit down in the sand with our feet in the water as the sun sets. Theodore had brought out a bottle of champagne so we drink as we watch the sun go down. “I have always loved your toothpicks,” I confess as I pick one up out of the sand. He grins and looks over at me.

“I thought you might,” He laughs.

“I remember the day we first met. I couldn’t stop thinking about the man who had a toothpick in his mouth.” I giggle as Theodore’s eyebrows raise and he gives a satisfied nod.

“I kept thinking about the girl who gave her ice cream cone away,” Theodore remembers.

I smile and feel butterflies in my stomach. “You did?”

He laughs and nods, “of course I did. I told you I had never met a girl like you before. I meant it.”

I scoot closer to him and he wraps his arm around my shoulders. “I think everything will be okay,” I whisper, reassuring myself as much as him. He leans back in the sand as the sky becomes dark.

My lips touch his as I lean over him. He pulls my dress over my head and kisses from my underwear back up to my lips. I giggle when his hands reach behind me and squeeze my butt. We spend the evening partially naked in the sand, rolling around and intertwining our bodies. It felt healing, under the moon in the wide open.

And that's how I got sand in places I didn't know you could get sand in.

We spend the first half of the next day in the large white bed. My head rests on the fluffy pillows as the wind blows through the open windows and makes the thin white curtain ripple. Birds chirp outside and I smile over at Theodore.

"I never want to leave here," I sigh. He smiles and runs his hand over my head, twirling one of my curls around his finger.

"We have to go back tomorrow, doll. As much as it pains me," he says.

"I know," I mope.

"I'll buy it. How about that? We can come back once a month, the drive isn't too far," he offers. I laugh and roll my eyes.

"I'm serious. Will it make you happy?"

I look around the small quaint room and out the window that overlooks the ocean. "Very," I answer.

"Then I'll write them a check they can't refuse. Anything for you." He leans over and plants a kiss on my forehead.

The weekend away passes too quickly. Everything about it was perfect. We don't argue, we sleep together twice a day and we laugh more than we had in weeks. On the drive home, we keep the windows down and let the wind blow across our faces.

The morning we get back, I help Cora make pancakes for breakfast. She tried to deny my help at first, but I reminded her that I was her boss as much as Theodore and that I insisted she took my help. She put her hands on her wide hips and finally stepped aside for me to enter the kitchen.

"Blueberries or chocolate chips?" she asks.

"Hmm, blueberries. I think Theodore prefers them," I decide, dumping the berries into the batter. I flip the pancakes as Cora whisks some eggs.

I turn when I hear someone walk in the kitchen and make sure to smile when I see Theodore. He's wearing one of my favorite gray tweed suits and a newsboy hat. "Good morning," I greet him and lean into his kiss when he pecks my cheek.

"Morning, can I help?" he asks with a smile.

"Theodore Greenwood! Never have you ever entered my kitchen and offered to help," Cora sounds shocked as she holds up the spatula, dripping egg down onto her dress. I smile when she doesn't seem to notice.

"Well, when my favorite person is in your kitchen, it makes it a little more tempting," Theodore leans over the counter across from me and watches as I flip a pancake.

"I see how it is," Cora says lightheartedly. I hand the spatula to Theodore and motion for him to come help.

His poor attempts at flipping the pancakes make me laugh so hard my eyes water. One flies off the side of the skillet, the other folds in half and one burns as he tries to scrape it off.

And so over the next few weeks, we wake up together and cook breakfast while Cora fusses over us about making her kitchen a mess. I greet him with a smile every night he comes home and I never turn down his advances in bed.

Each day I feel like I can breathe a little easier. Nellie and I go to lunch once a week at a different restaurant every time. Florence comes over once a week, and then I attend tea twice a month. I find myself so busy, I forget to write back home one week. I panic as I add extra bills to the envelope and apologize in the letter that I hastily send once I realize my mistake.

Thirty One

On a Wednesday morning, I invite Florence and Nellie over for lunch. Nellie arrives first, wearing a long flowy dress and a floppy wide hat with a ribbon tied around it.

"You look like you're ready for the beach!" I greet her. She smiles and walks into the front room where we always have our brunch.

"I guess I was dreaming about when you finally take me to your new beach house," she hints heavily.

"Theodore says it's all finalized this weekend, so hopefully soon," I promise.

As we sit down at the round table in front of the windows, the doorbell rings and I hear Florence's voice. Sometimes I forget how different we speak from people in New York until I hear my sister. "Good morning!" Florence waltzes in the room wearing a new blue dress.

She sits down at the table and looks at both of us. "How's dancing going?" I ask her.

"It's good. But I found a man I like, quite a bit," she smiles as she looks down at her hands.

"Oh, do tell! Who is he?" Nellie's eyes widen and she leans forward.

"His name is Robert. He's so handsome, a real looker. Knows his way in the sheets and has more money than you can shake a stick at," Florence says dreamily.

"Robert, what? What's his last name?" Nellie demands.

"Brown," Florence answers.

Nellie and I gasp at the same time. "What?" my sister asks.

"That's the famous golfer. His wife is our friend, we go to tea with her often. He's married!" I inform her, feeling sick to my stomach.

"I know that, but he's going to leave her. We're going to get married one day," Florence informs us. I scoff and look over to Nellie.

"Florence, every married man says he's going to leave his wife. And they're all lying!" She says as she shakes her head in disappointment.

"It's different," Florence snaps, looking embarrassed and like a child who's been caught doing something they shouldn't.

"It's not different. You have to stop seeing him, Florence. He's married to our friend!" I say in a loud whisper to keep the servant from hearing.

Florence lets out a shaky sigh and I know my sister well enough to know there's something else. "Tell me." I demand. She shakes her head and looks down at her lap.

"Don't make me tell Dorothy!" I threaten. Her eyes shoot up to me and she glares.

"Stop it!" her voice wavers. She glances between Nellie and I before leaning back in her seat.

"Fine, but you have to swear not to tell anyone. Not a single soul. No one knows yet, especially not Robert."

Nellie and I both nod and agree. "I'm pregnant," Florence whispers. Nellie and I gasp again at the same time.

"Oh, Florence..." I groan.

"It's fine. I'm going to fix it, just don't tell a soul. Robert is falling in love with me, I just need a little more time. He's going to divorce Dorothy."

I look at my sister with disgust and Nellie gives her a disapproving frown. "You swore you wouldn't tell anyone," Florence reminds us with panic.

"Fine," I mutter, feeling nauseous.

"I can't go to tea this weekend and look at Dorothy. I feel like I should tell her," I whisper to Nellie once we finish lunch and Florence leaves.

"Me neither, I know plenty of married men who are cheating. But they're not my friend's husband."

That evening I convince Theodore we need to go to the beach house to get away. He promises we will go the following week for a few days. I go to bed feeling like a horrible person for not immediately going over to Dorothy's house and telling her. *I promised Florence. And it's not like she won't find out soon anyway.*

On a Friday evening, I go to The Crystal with Nellie to drink and play a round of poker. She boasts and brags when she wins two rounds. "You have to be cheating!" I accuse.

"I would never," she feigns being hurt and puts a hand to her chest.

I get up to get us another round of drinks, swaying slightly from the alcohol when I bump into someone. I apologize and look up to see Robert Brown. My palms get sweaty as my eyes narrow a little bit as I look up at him. "Pardon me," he smiles.

"You really have her fooled," I say quietly.

"Pardon?" he asks, pretending to be confused.

"My sister, Florence." I nod my head towards the stage where she dances.

Robert looks around nervously and puts his hand up. "Look, I don't know what you think is going on. Sure, I've made some mistakes. But I only went out with her twice for drinks. I don't want any drama. I love my wife, I don't want anything to do with her anymore. Swear on my life," he glances over at the table where I see Dorothy sitting. My stomach sinks.

He smiles over at his wife and turns his back to me and walks away. I try to keep a neutral expression as I go back over to the bar and order another drink. Theodore walks out of his office and smiles at me. He walks over to me and taps the bar to get the bartender's attention. He quickly gets served a whiskey.

"What's wrong, doll?" He asks. I feel torn as I look up at Florence dancing and back to the table with Dorothy and Robert.

"I swore I wouldn't tell," I tell him quietly.

"Well, that doesn't count with your husband," he reassures me.

I chew on my lip and take a small sip of my drink. "Florence is pregnant," I whisper. He coughs on his drink and he looks pale.

"What?" he asks.

"Yes, you heard me correctly. And it seems to be a certain rich golfer's baby," I cut my eyes over to the table where the Browns sit.

"How far along is she?"

"I don't know, she hasn't said. I imagine not too far along."

Theodore takes a deep breath and throws his drink back. "I didn't think you'd be so upset," I say in surprise. Theodore pauses as he looks over at the stage where Florence dances and then back at me.

"She hasn't even been working here for three months and now I'm going to have to replace her. I can't have a pregnant dancer. She needs to be out before she shows and I don't know how fast I can replace her!"

I nod in understanding, I hadn't even thought of that. "Will she get rid of it? I know a woman who can do it. Can you convince her, you think?" Theodore asks.

"Theodore, that's illegal!" I gasp.

"Everything about our life is illegal, doll."

I shake my head and tell him I won't even ask her such a thing. He looks frustrated but before he can argue a man comes over and whispers in his ear. Theodore's face changes and he gives the man a nod.

"I'll be in my office for a little bit, you just try to enjoy yourself, alright?" He leans over and kisses my forehead before turning down the hall at the corner of the basement.

I tap my foot and look around the room. I stand up and order another drink before slipping down the hall and towards Theodore's office. I look around and wait for one of the women using the restroom to exit and leave. I press my ear against the door and try to make out the muffled conversation.

Only bits and pieces are audible but I catch enough. I hear Peter's voice mention something about the fuzz and a sergeant. Theodore starts to yell loud enough I can make out most of what he says. I strain my ear against the wooden door.

"Last thing we fucking need is this new asshole sticking his nose in our business. It's not enough having a few of the guys on our side that are under him. They can't do shit. Move the blow from the car in case they pull you over. Once he gets one whiff of something, the crack isn't our only worry. You understand?"

I struggle to make out Peter's response.

"You should have let me take him out before he was sergeant. He wouldn't have gotten this chance. Fucking told you," Theodore's voice raises again. I gasp and pull away from the door. I walk as quickly as possible up the stairs and out of The Crystal. My legs wobble and I feel like I could throw up as I tell Frank to take me home.

"What about Mr. Greenwood?"

"Just come back for him. He's busy and I feel sick. I need to go home!" I snap, getting in the car with my hands shaking. Frank hesitates but does as I say.

When we arrive home I scrub my face and climb in bed as fast as I can. I squeeze my eyes shut and try to fall asleep. *Theodore would kill someone? What else could 'taking someone out' mean?* I toss and turn in the bed until later that night I hear the door creak open.

My heart pounds as I hear Theodore go into the bathroom and come back out. The bed sinks as he sits on his side. "Are you awake, doll?" he whispers. I stay very still as he leans over and smooths my hair back. He rolls away and within a few minutes I hear his snores. I let out a shaky breath of relief.

I think about when I was little and I used to think there were monsters under my bed. Now I realize the monsters aren't under your bed at all, they're usually sleeping right next to you.

Thirty Two

The next morning, Theodore checks on me and asks if I was feeling any better. "Yes, I think I just had too much to drink last night," I lie.

"Well, I'm glad you're feeling well this morning. There's some things that have come up with work and I'll be gone out of town for a week. I hate to cancel our little trip, but you may have to go to the beach house without me. Maybe ask Nellie to go with you?" he suggests.

When I call Nellie and ask, she lets out a shrill shriek of excitement on the other end of the phone. "Oh God, I can feel the sand now. Yes, a thousand times, yes!"

I find slight relief during the week Theodore is gone. I feel like I can breathe easier, knowing I don't have to watch what I say or tiptoe around his moods. I know there will be no arguments. But when I lay in bed at night, it feels empty and cold. I find myself almost missing the fights because of the makeup sex, gifts and cuddles that always follow.

There's almost a comfort in the violence. A routine. I find comfort in knowing what to expect. *There must be something wrong with me.*

Friday evening Nellie picks me up and we drive to the beach house. I smile when I see the light blue house that sits in front of the beach. It almost looks out of place, the only house in sight with stretches of sand on either side of it. It looks tiny to me now, but I know it's larger than my old house in Texas. I have become accustomed to the mansions in New York.

Saturday morning Nellie and I sunbathe in swimsuits on the sand. I turn my head to look at her, holding my hand in front of my face to block the sun. "Nellie? Do you think Theodore is a good person?"

Her eyes widen and she blinks in surprise. "Wow. That is a deep question for a Saturday morning on the beach," she replies.

"I heard him and Peter talking in his office one day..." I trail off.

"Ah," she says, "look, you married a rich man. A handsome, rich man. You knew when you married him that he did some illegal things, did you not?"

I nod.

"Then don't upset yourself with the details. Try to ignore it and pretend he sells stocks or something," she shrugs.

"You didn't answer my question, though."

“Good people do bad things. And bad people do good things. I would say Theodore is the first kind,” Nellie reckons. I feel calmer after hearing her words and I nod in agreement.

When our weekend at the beach house ends, I look forward to seeing Theodore. I feel butterflies in my stomach as we pull in the round driveway. I grin and get out of the car and Theodore meets me at the front door.

He gives me a tight hug and tells me how much he missed me. “Did you get everything figured out? With your work?” I ask.

Did you kill the sergeant?

“Not quite, but let’s not talk about it,” he answers.

We spend the evening listening to jazz music and slow dancing in the main room. He has the fireplace going and the lights off as we sway back and forth. He takes my dress off and I pull his shirt off after we start to kiss.

We end up naked on the floor when a loud banging rattles the door. He groans in frustration and stops his thrusting and I cover my mouth to hold in my laughter. “What!” He yells.

“It’s the phone, sir,” Edward’s voice sounds uncomfortable as he shouts through the door.

“Tell them I’m busy!” Theodore retorts, thrusting his hips forward. I gasp and shake my head for him to stop. I turn red with embarrassment, horrified that Edward knows what we are doing.

“I would take the call if I was you, sir.”

Theodore pauses and moves off of me, pulling his pants up. He shoots me a remorseful look. “Go to bed, we’ll pick up where we left off after I take this," he says with a smirk as he buttons up his shirt. He pushes up the sleeves before sliding out the door.

Thirty Three

The next few months Theodore works late and becomes more anxious as each day passes. I notice his pupils are large more often than not, confirming my suspicion that he's started to use cocaine often. He starts to keep his flask in his pocket at all times. His moods are irrational, one moment he's happy and the next he's angry.

I continue to write to Mother and Otis. I send money with every letter. On a Thursday morning, I get a letter from Mother saying that Otis' health is almost back to normal, and that during the fall he should be able to visit Florence, or I can come back for him. She doesn't want him to ride the train alone.

One evening Florence comes over, and when I see her bump starting to form I gasp. "Florence! You can't possibly still be dancing," I touch my hand to her stomach. I feel the sting of jealousy when I feel her hard stomach protruding out slightly. *I'm married and she's not, yet she gets to have a baby.*

"Oh, did Theodore not tell you? I quit almost 6 weeks ago. I thought you knew. I have a job as a waitress now at the restaurant that's in the country club," she tells me as she sits down.

"Theodore doesn't tell me much of anything. Is that why you've been so busy and not returning my calls?" I ask.

She looks guilty as she picks at her fingernails. "The hours are a lot. It's different than at The Crystal. My feet hurt so bad at the end of each night," she complains.

I notice she hasn't worn the flower barrette Gregory had given her in a while and I wonder if it's because she and Robert had gotten serious.

"So?" I ask.

"So what?" she shifts uncomfortably on the sofa. It's not like Florence to seem so timid and unsure of herself.

"So when is Robert leaving Dorothy? I can't keep avoiding her much longer, she keeps calling."

"He isn't," Florence confesses. I shake my head and turn my body to her.

"You said he was. You said he was going to leave her and take care of you!".

"Well, I was wrong. He doesn't want anything to do with me or the baby."

"Florence, I'm so sorry. What are you going to do?" I ask.

"I don't know. Ruby's aunt lives near our apartment and may watch the baby if I can afford it. I don't know if I can pay my share of rent and a nanny." Her voice trembles and I awkwardly pat her leg.

I change the subject to something more lighthearted and offer her tea. We sit and talk for a few hours before Theodore walks through the front door. I can see him from the front room so I wave and smile. His eyes meet mine and then dart to Florence. His jaw tightens and he walks off down the hall.

He hadn't found someone else to replace her and I feel like he may blame me partially. She is my sister, after all.

Weeks pass and Theodore takes a Monday off to have a long weekend. We eat dinner Sunday night at the large dining table, because he insisted. I poke at the fish, which, to my relief, Cora had remembered to pick one without a face.

"I want to go to the beach house together, it's been months since you've been with me."

"I've been busy." Theodore holds his whiskey glass in his hand like he always does. I can tell by his eyes and body language he's high.

"I know you have been, I spend most days alone," I say cooly. He rolls his eyes and takes a bite of his salad.

"When were you going to tell me?" I ask. His hand freezes and his expression pales. He doesn't reply.

"You have a real problem, Theodore. You're high just as often as you're drunk. If you're not one, you're both!" I exclaim. The color in his face starts to return as he ignores me, taking another drink. I hate how calm and collected he is.

"What else do you hide from me?" I demand, feeling like I could explode.

"Don't raise your voice at me," he warns. I roll my eyes and throw my hands up in the air.

"Or what, Theodore? Are you going to hit me again?"

His hand grips his glass tighter and his knuckles turn white. I feel an adrenaline rush and a smile takes over my face.

"Don't talk to me like that. You need to respect me," Theodore growls.

"I know, I know what you want. Respect and attention. Everything is always about *Theodore*. Oh, everyone respects *Theodore."* I push myself back from the table and stand up, waving my arms around mockingly. It's like something inside me snaps and I lose control.

"You know what? I don't respect you. No one does! These people walking around your big ole house, waiting on you hand and foot? You know why they do that, dear? Take a guess! It's not respect. It's your *money*!"

Theodore's chair flies backward as he stands up and throws his drink on the ground next to my feet. "Oh, look at that. Just like my father did," I roll my eyes and grab my glass of water. I throw it down next to Theodore's feet and watch it shatter.

Before I can move out of his reach, his hand is on my throat and my back is flat on the table. My heart beats like a drum inside my chest and I stare into his eyes. I see a flash of his face when we were standing at the altar, his warm eyes staring into mine.

Till death do us part isn't a promise. It's a curse.

I hear a loud scream. "Stop!" Cora yells as she runs towards us. Theodore immediately lets go. Just as fast as it had started, it was over.

His face is full of sorrow and regret as he backs up and looks down at his hands. He starts to mutter apologies and his eyes dart around the room.

"Go for some fresh air!" Cora commands, pointing to the door. He sulks off and she turns to me. Her round face is full of concern as she grabs me and pulls me into her arms.

I stiffen at the hug at first and then start to sob. I lean into her shoulder as my tears wet her dress. "There, there. Let's get you in the bath, dear." I follow her upstairs, not caring who sees me crying as I pass them.

I strip down without shame and sink into the water she had turned on in the bath. She stands by the door, looking at me through the mirror. "You need to go back to Texas," she says quietly. I shake my head and sniff, unable to breathe through my stopped up nose.

"No, I can't. My father is ten times worse. And I love Theodore. I do," I stutter.

"This isn't love. Love doesn't hurt like this."

"He's everything to me, Cora."

She shakes her head and sighs. "I can't force you to make the right decision." She leaves the bathroom and I close my eyes.

When I get in bed I stare at the door, waiting for it to open. Feeling torn on whether I want it to stay closed or not. My eyes become heavy after watching the door past midnight and I fall asleep.

Thirty Four

The next morning I wake up alone. I pull on the green dress I wore when I met Theodore, not wanting to put on one of the fancy gowns that make me feel like someone else. I look at the tattered work dress that had been torn by a rooster that hangs at the back of the closet. *Who have I become?* I look around at the dresses and hats. I don't even recognize myself anymore. The way I speak is different. The way I laugh is different. I don't even walk the same.

I go downstairs to the kitchen where Cora already has breakfast made. "I would have helped, " I say softly.

"Theodore is waiting for you in the front room," Cora gives me a disappointed look and turns back to the dishes.

I gulp and turn on my heels. I walk into the front room with my stomach in knots. Theodore sits at the tiny table, a vase full of lilies sits in the middle of it. *Lilies won't fix everything,*

Theodore. Hey, sorry I tried to choke you the other night, here's some flowers.

I hesitantly take a seat across from him and stare at the pink vase. "I know I've said it before. But this time I mean it. I'm so sorry. I won't ever hurt you again," Theodore swears. I can't help the sarcastic laugh that escapes my mouth.

"I'm going to stop drinking as much. And no more blow, I promise. I'll keep sleeping in the guest room," he pleads.

I look at him, feeling drained and exhausted. "I don't want to keep doing this, Theodore. You build me up just to tear me down," I whisper.

His eyes become misty and I look away, it hurts too bad to see him cry. "I should just kill myself. I don't deserve you," Theodore mutters as he covers his face with his hands.

I am taken back by his comment and I feel even more nauseated. "Don't say that. Theodore, please."

"I'm a terrible person. I keep hurting the only person I love."

"Look at me."

He pulls his hands from his face and looks at me with his golden eyes red from crying. The scar on his eyebrow disappears with his furrowed expression. "Bad people do good things. And good people do bad things," I repeat what Nellie had told me. Theodore shakes his head.

"You're not a bad person. You just make bad choices. Be better. For me," my voice breaks.

"I will, I swear on my life. I love you, doll."

"I love you, too," I force myself to smile and he gets up to get the breakfast from the kitchen. He carries back the tray and sets it on the table.

"We can have breakfast every day in here if that makes you happy," he offers.

"That would be nice," I try to sound happy but it comes out monotone.

"And I wanted to give you this." He reaches inside his suit and pulls out a wad of money.

"What?" I ask, confused.

"For your family. I know you've been sending money back to them." He slides the money across the table.

I feel the color draining from my face and I glance at the money and back at him. "I'm not mad. You could have just asked me though, instead of taking it from the nightstand."

"I'm sorry," I stutter, my cheeks warming.

"Don't be. I know you care about Otis and I know your father would let them starve."

I slowly take the money and put it in the large pocket on the side of my dress. "My mother said he can come this fall," I give him a small smile.

"Good, we can take him to the zoo like you always wanted," he vows.

Things stay mostly good between us for the next few months. He does what he promises and stops the cocaine from what I can tell. He doesn't stop drinking, but he doesn't hit me. But he still seems stressed even when he finds a replacement for Florence.

Nellie and I start going to tea occasionally again. Dorothy seems naive about anything that happened between her husband and my sister. I barely can make it through one evening when one of the ladies announces her pregnancy. I feign happiness for her when really all I am is jealous.

Theodore and I eat breakfast every day in the front room. He keeps a fresh bouquet of lilies on the table at all times. On my birthday, I wake up with him bringing me breakfast in bed. After we eat, he sits cross legged on the bed and hands me a wrapped present.

"What is it?" I ask, shaking the box gently.

"I don't know why people ask that, like I would tell you right before you open it," Theodore laughs and nods for me to pull the ribbon. I lift the lid off the box and at first I squint my eyes in confusion.

I pick up one of the pieces of paper and read it. My mouth drops open and I look up at Theodore. He looks nervous and almost embarrassed.

"It's some of our memories. That's the ticket from the train ride," he explains. I pick up another piece of paper. A ticket to the theater in Dallas.

"You kept all of this?" I ask in disbelief. He nods and smiles.

A little jar of sand from the beach house, a replica of the green ribbon he had bought me and a few other tickets from things we had done sits in the box. "I love you," I say as tears fill my eyes and I lean forward to kiss him.

We spend the day at the horse races. He lets me make a bet on a horse that looked to be older than me.

"This hurts," he groans as he hands me the bills to bet with. I grin and clap when my horse ultimately loses.

"I have to use the restroom, I will be right back." I tell him as I get up from the seat and walk down one of the aisles.

On the way to the ladies room I see Robert Brown. My eyes narrow and he tries to pretend he didn't see me. He's standing in line for tickets when I march up to him.

"I hope you know what a terrible person you are," I say under my breath so no one can hear me.

"Look, I don't know what delusional thoughts Florence had, but I want nothing to do with any of it." He glances around to make sure no one is too close to us.

"Of course you don't. You just dump her with the baby and live in your mansion while she carries the shame," I seeth.

"I can tell you one thing, that baby is not mine. I told you, I went out with her for drinks a few times. Should I have done it? Probably not. But that bastard isn't mine," he scolds and puts his hands in his pockets.

My mind swims as I don't believe a thing he says, but my sister isn't a very truthful person either, so I don't know what to think. "Now, if you will excuse me," Robert says through gritted teeth.

I let him move past as I go to the ladies room. As I wash and dry my hands, I check my reflection in the mirror. I think about my sister as I go back to our seats. *She's slept with so many men she doesn't know who the father is.* I find it hard to feel bad for her the more I think about it.

On the drive home I fall asleep on Theodore's shoulder. He scoops me up and carries me into the house and tucks me in bed. "Thank you for today," I whisper.

"Happy Birthday, doll." He kisses my forehead and slips out of the room.

Thirty Five

Over the next month I hear Theodore yelling in his office and Peter comes over more frequently. I stop him in the hall one day as he's leaving Theodore's office. "What is going on?" I ask.

"Don't worry about it. We'll take care of it," Peter assures me. I reach for his arm and touch it to stop him from walking off.

He pauses and looks down at my hand. I pull it away and give him a pleading look. He glances back to Theodore's door. "There's been problems with the police. We think they're trying to launch an investigation," he says in a hushed voice.

"What does that mean?" I panic.

"It means to lay low. Don't speak to anyone. Even the ladies you think are friends. Don't trust anyone. Except me, Theodore, Mary and Nellie."

We both look at a maid carrying folded laundry as she passes us. "What will happen if they find out?" I whisper.

"They won't," he replies.

I try to argue, but Theodore walks out of his office and sees us. I see a flash of concern on his face before he smiles and approaches us. "Is there a secret meeting I don't know about?" He cocks an eyebrow.

"I was just asking if he and Nellie could come for game night soon. It's been too long," I smile.

"It has indeed," Peter agrees.

"Friday night!" Theodore commands as he pulls out a toothpick.

"We'll be there," Peter promises before he turns to leave.

A few weeks before Florence's due date we meet at a restaurant by her apartment. When I see her, I can't help but gawk at her stomach. Even with her baggy dress, it looks like she swallowed a watermelon.

"Stop staring at it," Florence hisses as we enter the diner.

"I'm sorry, but it's like half of your body at this point. It's hard to ignore!" I laugh. We slide into a booth and she groans when she sits down.

"I can't wait till this thing is out of me," she mutters.

"Are you excited?" I ask, looking down at the menu.

She avoids eye contact as she scans the dessert section. "I take that as a no," I mumble.

"Mother said I can come back home," Florence finally says.

"I'm kind of surprised," I admit.

"I told her I was fine here. I can't imagine raising a baby in that house," she shakes her head. We both order a slice of pie when the waitress comes to take our orders. She returns quickly with the slices and sets them in front of us with a cheery smile.

I try to think of how to approach the subject and clear my throat. "So, I saw Robert at the horse races a while ago." She glances up at me and frowns.

"I don't want to talk about him."

"He said the baby wasn't his."

She sets her fork down and pushes the plate of pie away from her. "I don't want to discuss this. I don't need you judging me!" she snaps.

"I'm not trying to-" I get cut off when she stands up out of the booth.

She puts a hand on her lower back and glares down at me. "If you wanted to invite me here just to make me feel bad, next time do it over the phone!"

She waddles off and I sit in the booth with a few customers turning and looking at me. I pull out the money and leave a generous tip for the waitress before getting out of the booth.

When I get home, I hear a loud crash from the hall. I peek around the corner and see Theodore's office slightly open. He hadn't planned on me being home for a few hours.

I tiptoe down the hall and look in the office with one eye. Theodore's raking his hand through his hair while pacing back and forth. He holds the telephone to his ear and shakes his head multiple times.

"No, no. You can't put it there. Put it in the speakeasy. Cut out the damn books and put it in them for all I care!" He yells into the phone. He pulls out his flask and takes a swig.

He slams the phone down and screams a slur of curse words. He turns and we lock eyes. "Shit," I whisper, turning and walking quickly down the hall. He slams the door shut and I hear it lock.

That night, I sit in the bath and he climbs in with me. "You can talk to me," I tell him.

"The less you know, the better." He hands me his razor. I smile and slowly run it over his jawline, watching the stubble disappear.

"You're drinking again," I analyze out loud, smelling the gin on his breath. He sighs and yanks the razor out of my hand.

"Damn it, Hazel. Cut me some slack!" He stands up out of the bath and wraps a towel around his waist. Water drips from his dark hair and runs down his face and muscular stomach.

I get out and follow him into the bedroom. I put lotion on my legs as I watch him dry off and pull on his pajama pants. "I don't want you to spiral out of control again," I say carefully. His jaw relaxes and he lets out a sigh.

"I know. I'm trying."

We get into bed and shut the lights off. Staring at the ceiling in the dark, thoughts fill my head. "Theodore?" I whisper.

"Hazel?" His voice whispers back. I smile.

"If you keep getting better, I think you'd make a really good dad."

Silence hangs in the air. "I want a baby," I whisper.

"I know you do," He finally says. My heart stings as I blink tears away. I toss and turn all night while listening to his snores.

A few days go by and I notice Theodore pulls out his flask more often when I'm not looking. His irritability starts to become higher and he seems more distant.

Thirty Six

One Sunday evening, Nellie and Peter come over for drinks and game night. I had tried to invite Florence, but she wouldn't ever answer the phone. I watch Theodore and Peter talk under their breath on the sofa while Nellie and I pick up the poker chips.

"I think Theodore may be using cocaine again," I whisper to her.

Her eyes scrutinize Theodore. "Why do you think that?" she asks.

"His behavior has started to get worse. Like it used to be," I explain.

"Listen, Peter told me the other day how they're having the police start to try to crack down on them. Theodore lost a lot of money on a drug deal because of it, now they have kilos of cocaine they can't do anything with. Money wrapped up in it, just sitting there, I'm sure that's why he's so stressed!" She whispers.

My eyes widen and I study her face. "Where are they keeping it? Not here?" I panic.

"No, I don't think so. I'm guessing The Crystal?" She shrugs. I watch as she lights a cigarette and takes a deep inhale.

The next day when Theodore is at work I linger in the hall. I try the door to his office but it's locked. *I know he's using it again. I just need proof.* I hide around the corner and watch as Cora unlocks and enters the office, walking back out shortly after with a tray of dirty dishes.

I walk around the corner and startle her as she reaches with one hand to lock it back. "Here, your hands are full. I'll lock it," I offer, reaching for the key. She gives me a doubtful look. I plead silently with my eyes. She looks down the hall and hesitates as she hands the key to me.

"Don't get caught," she whispers before carrying the tray down the hall.

I start to sweat and my hands shake as I push the door open. I close it quietly behind me before I walk over to the desk where a bottle of whiskey sits. I shift through the newspapers and crumbled notes that clutter the top of the desk. I don't see any residue of any powder so I start to open the drawers. Multiple guns sit in the top drawer.

I find stacks of papers, a ledger, a stamp. But no drugs. I scan the room and start to look behind a few of the books that line the shelves. I sit down in defeat on the sofa and try to think where else he could have hidden it. Something stabs me when I shift to get up and leave.

I pause and turn my body, sticking my hand down the back of the sofa and behind the cushion. As soon as my fingers touch it I freeze. *No. That's not what it is.* My stomach turns and my hands get icy cold. I take in a shaky breath as I pull it out.

Florence's shiny flower barrette stares back at me. I feel like I'm going to throw up as I drop it on the sofa and stand up.

"No, no." I whisper out loud. *Why would her barrette be stuck in the sofa? Why would she be in his office?*

Maybe Theodore found it at The Crystal and brought it home, thinking it was mine. But why wouldn't he ask me about it? And why would it be shoved in between the sofa?

Realization slowly hits me and I play the last few months back in my head. Florence trying to rush to get Robert to leave his wife for her. 'That baby is not mine. I can guarantee you that.' Robert's voice floats in my head.

I feel numb when I remember Theodore's drained face when I told him how Florence was pregnant. *He tried to get me to make her have an abortion.*

I grab the barrette and shakily walk out of the room, fumbling with the key as I lock the door. I cover my mouth and try to not throw up. My head spins and I feel like the walls are closing in on me as I run down the hall. My blood starts to boil and I feel anger replace the shock.

I find Frank as I hyperventilate and demand he take me to Florence's apartment. He pauses and notices the barrette in my hand. "Now!" I yell, yanking the door open and getting inside the car.

I stare at the barrette and swipe at the tears running down my face angrily. *Please. Please let this be some kind of mistake. There has to be some other reason.* I try to think of what I'll say to her. I think about somehow running her over with the car. *She should have stayed in Texas.* My heart sinks as I wonder if that's why Theodore wanted her to come work with him.

When we pull in front of her apartment, I tell Frank to wait by the front and I walk into the building. I look around and realize I have no idea what door number is hers. I get the attention of a man walking down the steps.

"Please, can you tell me what floor my sister is on? She has short blond hair and is pregnant, she's young," I plead through my tears. He looks worried and points to the stairs.

"I think she's on the second floor," he tells me.

I take off up the steps, tripping as I wipe the tears off my face. I clench the barrette in my hand until I think it may cut me. I round the corner when I see her stepping out through her apartment door. She closes it behind her and turns to me. Her expression falters when she sees me.

"Hazel! What's wrong?" She puts her hand on her round stomach.

I feel sick when I look at her belly. *That should be me. This is wrong.* She sees the barrette in my hand.

"You found it! I had been looking for it," she says and reaches for it. I squeeze it tighter and glare.

"Tell me why it was in Theodore's sofa in his office," I croak. For a second I think she's going to explain it to me. That this was all a misunderstanding.

But when her eyes widen and fill with tears, I know my answer. "Hazel, please. It's not what you're thinking. It was one time. It was a mistake and-" she panics.

"Is it his?" I cut her off, staring at her stomach. Her skin is pale as she looks around the hall at the people who pass by, trying to not appear nosey.

"Fucking tell me!" I yell. She flinches and nods, tears falling down her cheeks.

"How could you do this to me?" my voice cracks.

"I can explain, please. Come inside, not out here." Her eyes dart around with embarrassment.

"No, right here. I don't care if everyone knows what a heartless whore you are," I grind my teeth and try to keep my voice down. My blood rushes to my head and I feel my skin tingle with anger.

"When I first got here I got hooked on blow, real bad. I was so sad about Gregory. One night after I was done working I ran out. I panicked. You don't understand, I *had* to have it!" Florence's words spill out of her mouth. I shake my head, not understanding.

"I knew Theodore had some. He was always doing it at work, I saw it all the time. So I drove to your house. He was already drunk when I got there. Y'all had just had a big fight. We went to his office and got really high. It was a mistake. Hazel, it was one time, I promise."

My arms fall to my side and I stare at her, tears now streaming down my face uncontrollably. “You couldn’t stand me having something you couldn’t,” my voice comes out hoarse from crying.

“I didn’t mean for it to happen. Neither of us did. He was so angry, he wanted me to go back to Texas. He tried to get me to get rid of it, he loves you. He loves you so much. He doesn’t want me,” Florence pleads, taking a step closer to me.

I move away from her, distraught. “I’ll never forgive you. I don’t ever want to see you again!” I raise my voice and turn away from her.

“Please! Hazel, I am so sorry!” she sobs, calling after me. I run away from her and the sun hits my skin outside of the apartment.

People stop and stare as I wave Frank down and he drives up. I get in and slam the door. “Take me home,” I plead. He turns around and furrows his gray eyebrows.

“Is everything alright, Mrs. Greenwood?” he asks.

“No, it’s not. I just need to go home.”

He nods and drives me home, pressing his foot against the gas. I stare out the window with my head throbbing and close my eyes, trying to think what to do. My throat tightens when I think about Theodore’s hands on my sister. She carried his baby. I want to throw myself out of the car and end it right there.

When I get home I storm up the stairs with Cora following close behind me. She begs me to tell her what happened. Once in our room, I start tossing clothes into a suitcase.

"He slept with my sister," I finally confess, my voice barely above a whisper. Cora's face drops.

"Where are you going?" She asks.

"To the beach house. I can't sleep here. I don't know what I'm going to do," I frantically throw my journal and Otis' magic stone on top of my clothes.

"Let me come with you, you shouldn't be alone," Cora folds a few of my dresses for me and sets them in the second suitcase.

"No, no you stay here."

Once I hastily pack my bags, I grab the wad of cash from his nightstand. Cora and I carry the luggage down the stairs. "Put it all in the trunk," I tell Frank. He shoots a look over to Cora who nods her head. I take in a deep breath and think.

"Wait in the car. I'm going to talk with Theodore. Be ready to take me to the beach house," I finally decide.

"Are you sure you want-" Cora starts.

"Yes," I tell her. Frank gets in the car and sits in the driver's seat.

Thirty Seven

I wait in the front room with my third glass of whiskey when Theodore's car pulls up. My heart breaks when he walks in the door. I want to feel angry and I want to scream. I want to hurl the glass at his head.

But instead, I break down. As soon as I see his handsome face with his scarred eyebrow and strong jawline, I sob. "What's going on?" His face is full of worry as he takes a step towards me as I sit on the sofa. I throw the barrette at him and it falls at his feet.

"How could you!" I cry out. The color in his face drains and he becomes still. "You're a liar. A cheater and a liar!"

"Hazel..." his voice wavers and his face becomes twisted with regret.

"Why? Why her?" I demand.

"It was a mistake. God, it was such a mistake. I barely remember it. I was so high and drunk." He runs his hand over his face.

"She is pregnant with your baby," I whisper, my stomach clenching so badly it hurt.

"I'm sorry. I fucked up. I love you. I was in such a bad place, I wasn't myself. She can go back to Texas, I can fix this!" He reaches for my hands. I feel lifeless as his hands take mine and he pleads for me to look at him.

"I trusted you." A sob escapes my mouth.

"It was one time, it'll never happen again. I'll do anything you want. Just tell me what to do," he begs, tears starting to well up in his eyes.

"I hate you," I mutter. His face twists with distress.

"Please, please Hazel. I'll be better. I will do anything."

I stare at him and try not to let my emotions skew my judgment. I think about the birthday present he got me. I think about his body in the bath with mine. I look at the bouquet of lilies on the table.

"Tell me you don't love me. I know we can fix this." His breathing is shallow.

"I can love you but still hate you," I whisper. I see him breaking in front of me, and to my frustration, it hurts to see. I feel angry at myself.

How can I be so angry at someone who caused the most hurt I've ever felt, but still feel sympathy for them? It doesn't make sense. I pull away from him and walk around him. He follows me with tears streaming down his face.

“I’m leaving. I can’t do this,” I say. My heart pounds and my stomach turns as I walk down the front steps.

“Please! I love you,” Theodore begs behind me. I stop and face him.

“You’re not who I thought you were. This is beyond forgiveness.” I shake my head. It guts me when he moves to touch me and I turn my back to him. I get in the car and he runs after me. I lock the doors and he puts his hand on the window.

“Frank, don’t!” He commands, his voice breaking.

“Drive,” I tell Frank. He hesitates, looking torn on what to do. “If you don’t drive this car I am going to do it myself.” I threaten. He moves the car quickly out of the driveway. I can’t bear to look back and see Theodore standing there, broken. I close my eyes as tears stream down my face.

When we pull up in front of the blue beach house, I sob when I picture Theodore and I making love on the sand. I drag myself up the steps as Frank slowly sets the luggage inside.

“Mrs. Greenwood-” He starts, then stays silent, unable to find the words.

“Thank you, Frank,” I reach out and gently touch his shoulder. He gives me a sad smile and gets back in the car.

I sit on the beach until it’s dark and I can’t see in front of me as I walk back to the house. Once inside I stand in front of the bed and stare at it. *We used to eat breakfast in this bed.* I think about his body against Florence's. I wonder if he did the same things to her as he did to me.

My eyes are sore from crying and I lay down in the bed, ignoring the shrill ring of the phone as it rings for the tenth time. I know it's Theodore on the other end. I'm surprised he hasn't driven here already.

The next morning, I sit on the deck of the beach house and watch the seagulls fly in the sky. My head still throbs and my eyes are still sore. I try to tell myself that it will be okay. That I can go back to Texas and find a job there. I think about the wad of money that's in my bag. It'll keep me on my feet for a little bit.

I lay on the couch until the late evening when the phone rings three times in a row. I finally stand up and put the phone to my ear. "Stop callin me," I snap.

"Is this Mrs. Greenwood?" a female's voice I don't recognize asks.

"Yes," I answer cautiously.

"This is nurse Anne at the maternity ward, I'm calling about your sister, Florence McCoy."

"I don't want to talk to her, tell her I don't want to speak to her ever again." I say, feeling angry at my sister's tricks.

"Ma'am, you aren't understanding. Something has happened and the doctor wants you here as soon as you can."

"What do you mean? What happened?" I demand, panic filling my body.

"I can't discuss it over the phone, ma'am. The doctor will talk with you when you arrive," the nurse pauses and takes a deep breath, "I would hurry."

I slam the phone down and pull on the first dress I can find. I fumble for the keys to the car Theodore always leaves at the beach house. He always said that having a car with the top off was something you had to have when you were by the beach.

My hands shake as I drive the car down the road, it jerks as I turn the wheel. I try to remember what Theodore taught me about the stick shift. My hair whips in my face, stinging as the car flies down the streets.

My mind races as I speed. Did she have the baby? Did the baby not make it?

To my relief I remember where the hospital is outside of Manhattan and park in the first spot I see. I run through the doors and bump into three people. They yell and mutter at me, but I push through to the front desk. "My sister. I am here to see my sister. Florence McCoy," I pant, out of breath.

The woman behind the desk gives me a sympathetic look. She glances at one of the women working next to her and looks down at her paper. "Dr. Levy will be with you in just a moment, please have a seat."

I stand by the waiting area, my mind racing. I forget about Theodore sleeping with my sister when the Doctor approaches me. "Mrs. Greenwood?" he asks. I nod.

"Follow me please," he motions with his hand. I walk behind him as his long white coat sways with each step he takes.

He opens a door and I rush in to see my sister but there's just a table and a few chairs. I turn in confusion as he shuts the door behind him. "Why don't you sit down," he gestures to the chair. I shake my head.

"Your sister had her baby, a boy. He arrived early this morning," Dr. Levy pauses.

"Sadly, she had a hemorrhage after she delivered the baby. We did everything we could. But she bled too much," his voice is full of sadness and he talks slowly to let me process his words.

I feel nothing as I stare at his face. "I don't understand," I shake my head.

"Your sister passed away. You were her next of kin. She spoke of you before she passed."

I slowly sit down on the chair, unable to form words. "She left the baby in your custody. She didn't name the father," he explains. I gasp and shake my head.

"No. This can't be happening. She isn't dead!" There was some kind of mistake.

"I'm so sorry. We need a decision about the baby. He's in the nursery, if you want to see him. If you choose not to take him, he will be placed for adoption. There are plenty of wonderful Catholic couples ready to adopt," he assures me. My body shivers as I start to cry and let his words sink in.

"I want to see her," I whisper. He hesitates before bringing me to a cold room where she lays on a table.

You can feel the death in the air. You can even smell it. He pulls back the thin white blanket that lays over her and a sob lurches through my body.

"Oh my god," I reach out and touch her skin.

Once gold and warm, it's now pale and cold. Her lips are blue and her eyes stay shut. It seems like any moment her eyes should flutter open. But they don't. Her stomach still looks as if she had a baby inside her.

"Why?" I tremble, looking away from her body.

"She lost too much blood. It's very rare, but it happens. We tried everything we could. Her last words were to make sure you take the baby," the doctor shifts his feet awkwardly.

I swallow and try to not think about my last words to my sister. The things I had screamed at her. *But she slept with my husband.* I tearfully glance at her. *And now she's dead.*

I struggle with guilt and tell the doctor I want to see the baby. He takes me back to the room with the table and chairs. I tap my foot nervously as I wait. I imagine the world outside. People were just going about their day as usual, completely unaware of my sister's death. A nurse opens the door and walks in with a bundle in her arms.

Her face is solemn as she hands the baby swaddled in a blue blanket to me. I hesitate before reaching out and taking him. When I look down, a tear slides off my nose and onto his tiny forehead. His hair is dark like Theodore's but eyes blue like Florence's. His lips are small and pursed.

"Hi, there," I whisper to him.

"Take as much time as you need, but we do need a decision by the end of the night." The nurse gives me a sad smile and turns to walk off.

"I don't need any time. He's not going with anyone else," I respond. She looks relieved and tells me someone will be in with paperwork soon.

I stare down at my nephew when the door shuts and I pull out his hand. His tiny fingers wrap around my thumb and I smile through my sobs.

"I'm so sorry. I'm so sorry you were born into this," I tell him.

A man with a set of papers enters the room after a few minutes and guides me on where to sign and what to read. I sign them all quickly with no hesitation.

"And he needs a name," the man picks up his pen. A name.

"I-I don't know," I stammer. He waits a few minutes for me to decide. "Henry. After my father," I finally say.

"Middle name?"

"Theodore," I finally answer.

A nurse brings in a basket with cloth diapers, a bottle, formula and an outfit. She explains how to mix the bottle and warm it up. She stresses the importance of sanitizing them after each use. I nod, trying to take in what she says, but my head is cloudy and I feel overwhelmed.

"Here's some pamphlets," she hands me the papers.

"That's it? I just...leave?" I look down at Henry. She gives me a regretful nod. I stand up, my legs wobbly and my hands cold.

She carries the basket to my car and I look down at Henry. "What do I do with him when I drive?" I ask.

"Just lay him next to you. Don't take any sharp turns and you'll be fine."

I drive slowly as I make my way back to the beach house. I think about going home to Theodore, but I can't bear the thought of looking at him. I glance down at Henry, who starts to fuss a little.

My mind is filled with memories of Florence and the things we did together. My body lurches with sobs as I press the gas pedal harder. She used to wrap her arms around me every night that I cried myself to sleep. And now she's gone.

When I pull in front of the beach house, I carefully carry Henry in and pick up the telephone. I don't remember anyone's phone number except our house. I close my eyes and try to picture dialing Nellie's number but can't.

To my relief Margaret answers the phone. "Margaret, it's Hazel. I need to speak to Cora, now." I wait a few minutes before Cora answers.

"Hazel, dear?" her worried voice reaches my ear. I let out a relieved sigh at her voice.

"Florence died. Florence had the baby and is dead. I have him. I'm at the beach house. I don't know what to do," I choke. The phone is silent. "Cora?" I rasp.

"Yes, yes dear. I'm sorry. I don't know what to say."

"I need you to help me. I can't do this alone," I beg.

"Of course," she quickly answers.

"Can you have Frank bring you to the beach house? I can't come home."

"Yes, I'll leave now."

An hour later Cora is boiling the bottle and showing me how to mix the formula. She brought two bags of groceries with her and a small suitcase. "I can't believe she's gone," I say as I struggle to pin the diaper around Henry's wiggling body.

"Cora, I said some horrible things to her. The last time I saw her I hated her. I wanted her to die," I whisper.

"You had every right to be angry, child. You didn't truly want her to die. Not in your heart," Cora takes Henry and wraps him up in the blanket.

"Go to sleep. I'll take care of him tonight." She shoos me off and I collapse into the bed. I give in to the exhaustion and fall asleep.

Thirty Eight

The next morning, I wake up to Henry's loud cries. I sit up in bed and everything comes back to me. I want to close my eyes again and fall asleep so I don't have to remember anything.

I want to talk to Florence. I just want to talk to her one more time.

I pull on a dress and make my way into the small living room. Cora is burping Henry, his fragile body leaning over her shoulder. Her hand firmly pats his back as she sings a song to him under her breath.

I can't do this. I don't know anything about babies. I'm not prepared.

"Margaret called Nellie this morning. She's coming by today with everything that Florence had in the apartment for him." Cora tells me when she sees me.

He should be with Florence, not me.

I take Henry from her and look down at him as I bounce him in my arms softly. "I should tell Theodore. It's his baby," I whisper. My heart squeezes as I think about having to tell him that Henry was born. His baby. *His child that wasn't made with me.*

"I can forgive him. I can't do this alone," I think out loud as I pace with Henry in my arms.

"Maybe you should take a few days and think about it," Cora warns.

"You know how this world is. You know how they treat divorced women. I'll never be able to remarry. And I can't raise a baby alone. Where will I go?" my voice shakes.

"I hate myself for it, but I still love him. It was one mistake. Surely one mistake shouldn't ruin a whole marriage."

Cora looks like she wants to say something, but she stays silent. I take in a shaky breath and call the house. No one answers. I call three more times. I frown as Nellie walks in the door.

Her eyes fall to Henry and her eyes go misty. "Sweets, oh I am so sorry!" she puts her arms around me. "I don't understand how Theodore could do such a thing," she shakes her head. I hand Henry to Cora.

"I can't get a hold of him, I need to talk to him. He doesn't know." I rub my forehead.

"Did you try calling Peter?" Nellie suggests.

"I don't know his phone number," I sigh.

"I do, here." Nellie turns the dial and hands me the phone.

"Peter?" I ask when I hear someone pick up the other end.

"Hazel," Peter says.

"Is Theodore there? No one is answering at home."

"He sent everyone home. He wouldn't let anyone in the house."

"But why is he ignoring me?"

There's a pause. "I don't think he's there," Peter's voice sounds tight.

"Is he with you?" I let out an exasperated sigh.

"No."

The Crystal. "I'm going to go to The Crystal. I bet he's there," I say.

"No!" Peter shouts. I jump and look over at Nellie who gives me a confused look.

"What do you mean, no?" I question.

"Just stay where you are, Hazel. Promise me."

"What's wrong?" I demand. My stomach turns as I wait for his response.

"Just stay there."

"I need to see him," I say before I slam down the phone. I get my shoes and sit on the couch to put them on. "I need y'all to stay here and take care of Henry. I'll be back," I tell Nellie and Cora.

"Let me come with you," Nellie offers.

"I need to see him alone," I give her a small smile and walk to the door.

"Be safe," Cora warns.

I get in the car and drive to The Crystal with a heavy foot. I keep myself from crying so I can see the road in front of me, focusing on my breathing as I prepare myself to see Theodore.

As I pull up, I see Theodore's white and gold Model T parked in front of the building. I enter through the front door and it's eerily quiet. I look around for the bartender but don't see him. I walk down the dark hall to where the basement door is and knock.

I wait for a minute before trying to handle and push it open. The speakeasy is silent, with few lights on. I walk down the hall and see Theodore's office. The door is cracked open and light jazz music drifts out of it. My nerves make me stop and take a deep breath before I look through the door.

Theodore is leaning over his desk, snorting cocaine and his gun sits next to him. "Theodore?" I ask. His head jerks up and I am startled by his rugged appearance.

His eyes are bloodshot and it looks like he hasn't slept in two days. He wears a tucked in white button up shirt with the sleeves rolled up.

"Hazel!" he stands up and hastily walks over to me. I flinch when he grabs both of my shoulders.

"You need to leave." He demands. I scoff, feeling hurt and betrayed. Just two days ago he was practically begging on his knees for me to stay.

"Florence is dead."

His hands drop and he stares at me in shock. His pupils are large and I can see the cocaine under his nose. "What?" he mutters.

"She gave birth. To your son. She lost too much blood," I choke on the words as they leave my mouth.

"And the baby?" His voice is quiet and his eyes are dark.

"He's healthy. She left him to me. I took him so he didn't get put up for adoption. His name is Henry Theodore."

Theodore stills and he looks mournful. "I'm so sorry, Hazel. For everything," his voice sounds raw.

"I want to make us work. I don't want to raise your son alone." I reach for him. His eyes are filled with pain as I hold his hand.

"I'm poisonous. I can't change, I keep trying. I'm broken and I'll only destroy you and him. I've already done so much damage," Theodore says as he pulls away from me and goes back to his desk. He shakes his head as he sits down and drinks out of his flask.

I furrow my eyebrows and walk to his desk, putting my hands on it. "Don't talk like that. You don't get to do this. You said we can make it work. You have to, for your son." I insist, leaning in closer. How could he say that?

"You don't understand. I'm doing this for you," his voice breaks and he starts to cry.

"Doing what? Refusing to be with me?"

I turn when I hear rushing footsteps and Peter barges in the room. His eyes are wide with panic when he sees me.

"I told you to not come!" he pants, holding onto the door frame. I look between them in confusion.

"Come back with me, Theodore. Come to the beach house. Meet your son!" I plead.

“Please, try to understand. I love you. I have loved you since the moment I saw you in that seamstress’ store. I fucked up, but I always loved you. Let yourself be happy. Be with who makes you happy.” Theodore’s face clenches with anguish as he speaks. Panic fills my body at his tone.

“Then come back with me. I need you, I can’t do this without you.” I start to cry and Peter tries to take my arm. I yank away from him and spin towards Theodore.

“I kept saying I’d change. I tried, god I fucking tried. I can’t. I will keep hurting you,” he groans.

“Nothing will hurt me more than this!”

“The beach house is in your name. I never put my name on it. It’s yours, and so is the car that’s there. No one can take it. There’s money that’s clean in a bank account that Peter will give you access to. None of it is tied to me.” Theodore rattles off quickly.

The phone on Theodore’s desk rings and he glances at it then back to Peter. Peter grabs my arm, holding firm this time. “Get her out safe,” Theodore instructs. He pours another drink and that’s when I look around the room for the first time since entering it.

My mouth hangs open at the stacks of money and cocaine that lines the room. Blocks of the white drug so high it would reach my chin.

“What’s going on?” I try to pull away from Peter, who looks like he wants to cry.

“Take care of Henry, tell him how much I love him.” Theodore stands up and walks over to me quickly. He grabs behind my neck like he always does and firmly presses his lips to mine. I can taste his tears as he pulls away and looks in my eyes.

He waves his hand for Peter to take me out of the room. I look back in confusion as Theodore sits back at the desk and gives me a sad smile. He puts a toothpick in his mouth and gives me a small wink.

I start to thrash and pull back from Peter. "Stop! I want to stay! Theodore, please. Theodore, I forgive you!" I scream, my voice hoarse. Peter mutters an apology under his breath before he picks me up and throws me over his shoulder

"I love you, doll!" Theodore calls out as Peter leaves the room and runs down the hall. My head slams against his back as I scream and sob in confusion. The sun blinds me as we go outside The Crystal and a car pulls up, screeching to a stop.

Thirty Nine

“I want my husband! Peter, let me go,” I beg as he shoves me in the backseat. I hear sirens in the distance and I feel bile rise in my throat. “He needs to get out! What’s going on?” I yell as Peter gets in the seat next to me and slams the door shut.

“Drive! Fucking drive!” Peter screams at the man in the front seat. I jump at his tone, never having heard him even raise his voice before. The car takes off and I try to pull away from Peter. He keeps his arm around my shoulder as I turn my head to look behind us as a police car passes us.

“Turn around, Hazel.” Peter’s voice is filled with desperation as I turn.

I look at The Crystal and let out a scream when a loud explosion fills my ears. The building goes up in flames and I reach for the car door, prepared to open it even while we’re moving.

“Let me out! Oh my god. Theodore! Theodore is in there!” I shout, clawing at Peter’s arms that wrap around me and hold me tightly. “Stop!” I shriek as tears fall down my face and my body shakes as I sob.

Peter presses his face into my hair and I feel him start to cry. “I’m sorry,” he mumbles against the side of my head. I can’t speak. I try to open my mouth but the words don’t come out, just a deep guttural cry.

I sob against Peter as we pull in front of the beach house. “I want to go home!” I stutter through the tears.

“You can’t. The police are already there by now, they’re searching all of it.”

I look at him in confusion and dismay. “We need to go back. What if Theodore got out?” I demand.

“He didn’t, Hazel.” Peter’s eyes are filled with tears.

“You don’t know for sure!”

“I do. Hazel, he did all of it on purpose. He blew up The Crystal. He planned it.”

My stomach turns and I shake my head. “I don’t understand! I don’t understand!” I wail, pushing against Peter’s chest and trying to get out of the car. He holds me against him and doesn’t let go.

“Listen to me!” He shouts. I freeze and stay seated when he lets go of me and pulls back. His hazel eyes stare deep into mine and I can see his pain, almost as deep as mine.

“For months we’ve had the fuzz on our trail. We were tipped off that they launched an investigation on Theodore. They knew about The Crystal. They knew about all the stuff he did, but they could nail him for the drugs. He knew that the chances of us coming out of this clean would be slim. When you found out about Florence, I guess he checked out. He called me and told me his plan. I tried to talk him out of it. I did, but there was no changing his mind," Peter explains.

"He has enough money in a bank account that's not linked to him to take care of you for the rest of your life. He never put the beach house in his name, I guess he always was thinking one step ahead. They're going to take the house and probably everything in it. He wanted to protect us. He put everything that could connect me to any of it in his office. Every kilo of coke. All of it. He didn't tell me right out he was going to stay in it when he blew it up" Peter's voice is barely above a whisper when he speaks the last sentence.

"We could have figured it out," I cry.

"I tried. I swear on my life I tried to convince him. He said if I tried to stop him, he would kill himself. I thought he'd end up leaving before he set it all on fire." Peter's tone is gruff from crying.

I blink and sit still. Unable to move. "He's gone. He and my sister are gone."

He helps me out of the car and all but carries me into the house. Cora's face falls and she takes Henry out of the room when Peter breaks the news. Nellie falls onto the floor and sobs. She punches Peter in the chest and accuses him of letting it happen.

I stand stiffly by the door, watching it all. My brain shut down and I don't show any emotion. I feel like every tear I could cry is gone. Everything I can say has already been spoken. Every emotion already felt.

I take Henry from Cora and climb in bed with him. I lay on my side and curl my body around him. I pull him into me. Holding on to the one thing I have left of the two people I had loved and hated the most.

Forty

Five months pass and I sit on the beach watching Otis splash through the water and shriek as my mother chases him. A notebook and pencil sit next to me. I had forgotten what it felt like to scribble your thoughts and feelings on paper. I had missed it. I feel older now, the last few months completely changing and shaping me.

I smile faintly as Henry claps his hands. He sits next to me on the blanket, leaning to the side as he tries to balance himself. He still hasn't mastered sitting up fully by himself. His dark hair is thick like his father's and he has his mother's eyes and lips.

"Ma" he babbles.

"Yes, Mama!" I grin and pick him up.

"He's getting big," Peter's voice comes from behind me. I turn in surprise and smile as he walks towards me. His hands are in his pocket and he kicks the sand as he strides.

“I didn’t know you were coming by,” I stand up and put Henry on my hip.

“I just wanted to see how you were doing,” he says as he pokes Henry in the stomach and smiles.

“I’m doing good, I think. Some days are better than others,” I say, glancing to the beach where my mother is watching us. “Do you want to come inside?” I gesture to the house. He nods and follows me up the porch steps.

He sits inside at the kitchen table that has a vase of lilies sitting in the middle. Theodore had paid someone to deliver them weekly until I decide I want them to stop.

It’s been five months, but I can’t bear the thought of not seeing them every day. It’s like a piece of him is still with me.

I pull out some cookies Cora had made yesterday. I hired her to come work three days a week. Not that I needed it now that my mother and Otis had moved in, but I had gotten used to her presence.

I sit Henry down on the floor with a toy and sit across from Peter. “Nellie didn’t want to come with you?” I ask.

“I didn’t ask her,” he clears his throat.

“Oh,” I hesitate, waiting for him to explain.

He crosses his arms and looks at me thoughtfully. “Before Theodore died, he knew I would take care of you,” he says. I nod.

“You have, you check in on us all the time. You fix the sink when it’s broken. You hold me when I lose control and cry for hours.”

"I want to keep taking care of you," he says slowly. I look up at him and realize what he's trying to say. Henry starts to cry and reaches his arms up.

Before I can get him, Peter reaches down and pulls him up. He shakes the rattle in front of him and looks up at me.

I swallow and glance at the white lilies, feeling torn. *I still love Theodore.* The trinkets of our life that sit on a shelf in the kitchen stare back at me. A photograph of us on our wedding day, with Theodore's crooked grin and my shy smile looking back at me. The stuffed lion sits next to it.

'Let yourself be happy. Be with who makes you happy.' Theodore's words run through my head. I look back at Peter, who is bouncing Henry on his knee, breaking off pieces of the cookie for him.

I realize the few moments in the last five months that I have felt like I could go on another day is when Peter was around.

Otis bounds in the door and sees the plate of cookies. "Cookies!" he shrieks, running up and grabbing the biggest one. I smile and ruffle his hair.

"Guess what!" I gasp. He looks up at me, eyes wide and his mouth stuffed with the cookie.

"I think there's more treasure buried in the sand. I saw pirates sail off this morning," I whisper.

"I'll find it!" he promises before taking off back outside.

We sit in silence for a moment before I give him a smile. "Look at us, the two shadows," he remarks. I smile at the memory of the conversation we had what felt like years ago.

I smile because I know there is love between the two of us, love between the shadows.

That evening, I sit in the dark while Peter stands with his feet in the water holding Henry. The moonlight dances off the water. My lips turn up in a small smile as I watch Henry's cheeks round with laughter.

The sound floats in the air and reminds me of Theodore. His laugh was always my favorite sound, but now I think I found a new one.

I look up at the stars and picture Theodore smiling down on me, with a toothpick twirling between his lips.

"I'm not sure if you were a good person who did bad things, or a bad person who did good things. But I loved you either way, even if I didn't want to. Our love may just be a blip in the universe, but you will always be my infinity," I whisper up to him.

Made in the USA
Middletown, DE
05 November 2023